**Other must-have reads from
#1 *New York Times* bestselling author
Stephanie Laurens**

**And coming soon from
Alison DeLaine**

STEPHANIE LAURENS

and
ALISON DeLAINE

the Trouble

with Virtue

HARLEQUIN® HQN™

ISBN-13: 978-0-373-77818-8

THE TROUBLE WITH VIRTUE

Copyright © 2013 by Harlequin Books S.A.

The publisher acknowledges the copyright holders
of the individual works as follows:

A COMFORTABLE WIFE
Copyright © 1996 by Stephanie Laurens

A LADY BY DAY
Copyright © 2013 by Alison Atwater

Recycling programs
for this product may
not exist in your area.

Printed in U.S.A.

www.Harlequin.com

CONTENTS

A COMFORTABLE WIFE

Dear Reader,

In writing *An Unwilling Conquest,* the third book in the Lester trilogy, one character, Philip, Lord Ruthven, positively begged to be made a victim of love. His attitude as displayed in *An Unwilling Conquest* could not go unanswered—and that's how *A Comfortable Wife* came about. Miss Antonia Mannering was the young lady who had Philip most determinedly in her sights. As a husband. The possibility of love never entered her head—she was far too levelheaded, and she knew Philip too well. She was looking for a husband, and by now he should be looking for a wife—to her, their aims were compatible. All should have been terribly comfortable, except...

What happens when love gets stirred into their equation is told in *A Comfortable Wife.* I hope you enjoy seeing Philip succumb to a passion that becomes more precious than anything else in his life.

Stephanie Laurens

CHAPTER ONE

"THIRTY-FOUR, MY DEAR HUGO, is a decidedly sobering age."

"Heh?" Startled from somnolence, Hugo Satterly opened one cautious eye and studied the long-limbed figure gracefully lounging on the opposite carriage seat. "Why's that?"

Philip Augustus Marlowe, seventh Baron Ruthven, did not deign to answer—not directly. Instead, his gaze on the summer scenery slipping past the carriage window, he remarked, "I would never have thought to see Jack and Harry Lester competing over who would provide the first of the next generation of Lesters."

Hugo straightened. "Tricky prediction, that. Jack suggested laying odds but Lucinda heard of it." Hugo grimaced. "That was the end of it, of course. Said she wasn't about to have us all watching her and Sophie, counting the days. Pity."

A fleeting smile touched Philip's lips. "An uncommonly sensible woman, Lucinda." After a moment he added, more to himself than to his friend, "And Jack was lucky with his Sophie, too."

They were returning from a week's house party at Lester Hall; the festivities had been presided over by Sophie, Mrs Jack Lester, ably seconded by Lucinda, now Harry Lester's bride. Both recent additions to the Lester family tree were discreetly but definitely *enceintes,* and radiant with it. The unabashed happiness that had filled the rambling old house had infected everyone.

But the week had drawn to its inevitable close; Philip was conscious that, despite the calm and orderly ambiance of his ancestral home, there would be no such warmth, no promise for the future, awaiting him there. The idea that he had invited Hugo, a friend of many years, confirmed bachelor and infrequent rake, to join him solely as a distraction, to turn his thoughts from the depressing path he saw opening before him, floated through his mind. He tried to ignore it.

He shifted in his seat, listening to the regular pounding of his carriage horses' hooves, firmly fixing his attention on the ripening fields—only to have Hugo ruthlessly haul his problem into the light.

"Well—I suppose you'll be next." Hugo settled his shoulders against the squabs and gazed at the fields with unruffled calm. "Dare say that's what's making you glum."

Narrowing his eyes, Philip fixed them on Hugo's innocent visage. "Surrendering to the bonds of matrimony, walking *knowingly* into parson's mousetrap, is hardly a pleasant thought."

"Don't think of it at all myself."

Philip's expression turned decidedly sour. A gentleman of independent means and nought but distant family, Hugo had no need to wed. Philip's case was very different.

"Don't see why you need make such a mountain of it, though." Hugo glanced across the carriage. "Imagine your stepmother'll be only too happy to line up the young ladies—all you need do is look 'em over and make your selection."

"Being no less female than the rest of them, I'm certain Henrietta would be only too glad to assist. However," Philip continued, his tone tending steely, "should she be mistaken in one of her candidates, 'tis *I*, not she, who will pay the price. For life. No, I thank you. If mistakes capable of wrecking my life are to be made, I'd rather make them myself."

Hugo shrugged. "If that's the case, you'll have to make your own list. Go through the debs, check their backgrounds, make sure they can actually speak and not just giggle and that they won't simper over the breakfast cups." He wrinkled his nose. "Dull work."

"Depressing work." Philip shifted his gaze once more to the scenery.

"Pity there aren't more like Sophie or Lucinda about."

"Indeed." Philip delivered the word tersely; to his relief, Hugo took the hint and shut up, settling back to doze.

The carriage rattled on.

Reluctantly, Philip allowed his likely future to take shape in his mind, envisioning his life with one of society's belles by his side. His visions were unappealing. Disgusted, he banished them and determinedly set his mind to formulating a list of all the qualities he would insist on in his wife.

Loyalty, reasonable wit, beauty to an acceptable degree—all these were easy to define. But there was a nebulous something he knew Jack and Harry Lester had found which he could find no words to describe.

That vital ingredient was yet proving elusive when

the carriage turned through tall gateposts and rumbled down the drive to Ruthven Manor. Tucked neatly into a dip of the Sussex Downs, the manor was an elegant Georgian residence built on the remains of earlier halls. The sun, still high, sent gilded fingers to caress the pale stone; stray sunbeams, striking through the surrounding trees, glinted on long, plain windows and highlighted the creepers softening the austere lines.

His home. The thought resonated in Philip's head as he descended from the carriage, the gravel of the forecourt crunching beneath his boots. With a glance behind to confirm that Hugo had awoken and was, in fact, alighting, he led the way up the steps.

As he approached, the front doors were set wide; Fenton, butler at the Manor since Philip had been in short-coats, waited beside them, straight as a poker but smiling.

"Welcome home, my lord." Deftly, Fenton relieved his master of his hat and gloves.

"Thank you, Fenton." Philip gestured as Hugo strolled in. "Mr Satterly will be staying for a few days." Unencumbered by ancestral acres, Hugo was a frequent visitor to the Manor.

Fenton bowed, then reached for Hugo's hat. "I'll have your usual room made ready, sir."

Hugo smiled in easy acquiescence.

Completing a brief scan of his hall, Philip turned back to Fenton. "And how is her ladyship?"

On the floor above, poised at the top of the grand staircase, her head cocked to listen, Antonia Mannering decided that his voice was deeper than she remembered it. His question, however, was quite obviously her cue.

Drawing in a deep breath, she closed her eyes in

fleeting supplication, then opened them and started down. In a hurry. Not so precipitously as to be labelled hoydenish but rapidly enough to appear unconscious of the arrivals presently in the hall. She cleared the landing and started down the last flight, her eyes on the treads, one hand lightly skimming the balustrade. "Fenton, her ladyship wishes Trant to be sent up as soon as may be." Only then did she allow herself to glance up.

"Oh!" Her exclamation was perfectly gauged, containing just the right combination of surprise and fluster; she had practised for hours. Antonia slowed, then halted, her gaze transfixed. As it transpired, she needed no guile to make her eyes widen, her lips part in surprise.

The scene before her was not as she had pictured it—not exactly. Philip was there, of course, turning from Fenton to view her, his strongly arched brows lifting, his eyes, grey, as she knew, reflecting nothing more than polite surprise.

Swiftly, she scanned his features: the wide brow, heavy-lidded eyes and strongly patrician nose, the finely drawn lips above a firm and resolute chin. There was nothing in his expression, mildly distant, to cause her heart to beat wildly. Nevertheless, her pulse started to gallop; her breathing slowly seized. Panic of a wholly unprecedented nature fluttered to life within her.

His gaze dropped from her face; snatching in a breath, Antonia grabbed a dizzying moment to take in his broad-shouldered frame. Freed by a smooth shrug, a many-caped greatcoat slid into Fenton's waiting arms; the coat thus revealed was an unremarkable grey but so distinguished by line and form that not even she could doubt its origins. Brown hair waved in elegant disorder;

his cravat was a collage of precise folds secured by a winking gold pin. Buckskin breeches clung to his long legs, outlining the powerful muscles of his thighs before disappearing into highly polished Hessians.

Dragging in a second breath, Antonia hauled her gaze back to his face. In the same instant, his eyes lifted and met hers.

He held her gaze, a frown in his eyes. His gaze shifted, focused on her hair, then dropped to her face. His frown dissolved into undisguised amazement.

"Antonia?"

Philip heard astonishment echo in his voice. Mentally cursing, he struggled to recapture his habitually indolent air, a task not aided by the fleeting smile Antonia Mannering cast him before gathering her skirts and descending the last stairs.

He stood anchored to the tiles as she glided towards him. His mind reeled, juggling memories, trying to reconcile them with the slender goddess crossing his hall, calm serenity in her heart-shaped face, a gown of sprig muslin cloaking a figure he unhesitatingly classed as exemplary.

The last time he had seen her she'd been only sixteen, thin and coltish but even then graceful. Now she moved like a sylph, as if her feet barely touched solid earth. He remembered her as a breath of fresh air, bringing ready laughter, open smiles and an unquenchable if imperious friendliness every summer she had visited. Her lips now bore an easy smile, yet the expression in her eyes as she neared was guarded.

As he watched, the curve of her lips deepened and she held out her hand.

"Indeed, my lord. It is some years since last we met.

Pray excuse me." With an airy wave, Antonia indicated her descent from above. "I hadn't realized you'd arrived." Smiling serenely, she met his eyes. "Welcome home."

Feeling as if Harry Lester had scored a direct hit to his jaw, Philip reached out and took her fingers in his. They quivered; instinctively, he tightened his grip. His gaze dropped to her lips, drawn irresistibly to the delectable curves; he forced his eyes upwards, only to become lost in a haze of gold and green. Dragging himself free, he lifted his gaze to her lustrous golden curls.

"You've cut your hair." His tone reflected his dazed state as clearly as it did his disappointment.

Antonia blinked. One hand still trapped in his, she hesitantly put the other to the curls bouncing above one ear. "No. It's all still there…just…twisted up."

Philip's lips formed a silent "Oh".

The odd look Antonia threw him, and Hugo's urgent cough, hauled him back to earth with a thump. Thrusting aside the impulse to pull a few pins and reassure himself that her golden mane was indeed as he recalled, he drew in a definite breath and released her. "Allow me to present Mr Satterly, a close friend. Hugo—Miss Mannering. My stepmother's niece."

Hugo's suave greeting and Antonia's unaffected reply gave Philip time to repair his defences. When Antonia turned back, he smiled urbanely. "I take it you finally succumbed to Henrietta's pleas?"

Her expression open, Antonia met his gaze. "Our year of mourning was behind us. The time seemed ripe to visit."

Resisting an unexpected urge to grin delightedly, Philip contented himself with, "My humble house is honoured—it's a pleasure to see you within its walls again. I hope you've planned an extended stay—having you by will greatly ease Henrietta's mind."

A subtle smile curved Antonia's lips. "Indeed? But there are many factors which might influence how long we remain." She held Philip's gaze for an instant longer, then turned to smile at Hugo. "But I'm keeping you standing. My aunt is presently resting." Antonia glanced at Philip. "Do you wish to take tea in the drawing-room?"

Beyond her, Philip glimpsed Hugo's appalled expression. "Ah...perhaps not." He smiled lazily down at Antonia. "I fear Hugo is in need of more robust refreshment."

Brows rising, Antonia met his gaze. Then her lips curved; an irrepressible dimple appeared at the corner of her mouth. "Ale in the library?"

Philip's lips twitched. His eyes on hers, he inclined his head. "Your wits, dear Antonia, have obviously not dulled with age."

One delicate brow arched but her eyes continued to smile. "I fear not, my lord." She nodded to Fenton. "Ale in the library for his lordship and Mr Satterly, Fenton."

"Yes, miss." Fenton bowed and moved away.

Returning her gaze to Philip's face, Antonia smiled calmly. "I'll let Aunt Henrietta know you've arrived. She's just woken from her nap—I'm sure she'll be delighted to receive you in half an hour or so. And now, if you'll excuse me...?"

Philip inclined his head.

Hugo bowed elegantly. "Look forward to seeing you at dinner, Miss Mannering."

Philip shot him a sharp glance; Hugo was too busy returning Antonia's smile to notice.

Forsaking Hugo, Philip fleetingly met Antonia's eyes before she turned away. He watched her cross the hall, then climb the stairs, her hips gently swaying.

Hugo cleared his throat. "What happened to that ale?"

Philip started. With a quick frown, he gestured towards the library.

BY THE TIME she reached her bedchamber door, Antonia had succeeded in regaining her breath. She had not imagined her little charade would require such an effort. Her stomach was still tied in knots; her heart had yet to find its customary rhythm. Nervousness was not a reaction to which she was normally susceptible.

A frown knitting her brows, she opened the door. The windows were set wide; the curtains billowed in a gentle breeze. The scents of summer filled the airy chamber—green grass and roses with a hint of lavender from the borders in the Italian garden. Shutting the door, Antonia crossed the room. Placing both palms on the window sill, she leaned forward, breathing deeply.

"Well, I declare! That's your best new muslin."

Whirling, Antonia discovered her maid, Nell, standing before the open wardrobe. Thin and angular, her grey hair pulled tight in an unbecoming bun, Nell was busy replacing chemises and petticoats in their appointed places. Task complete, she turned, hands going to her hips as she surveyed Antonia. "I thought you was keeping that for a special occasion?"

A secretive smile tugged at Antonia's lips; shrugging, she turned back to the view. "I decided to wear it today."

"Indeed?" Nell's eyes narrowed. She picked up a pile of kerchiefs and started to sort them. "Was that the master who arrived just now?"

"Yes. Ruthven." Antonia leaned against the window frame. "He's brought a friend—a Mr Satterly."

"Just the one?"

Nell's tone had turned suspicious. Antonia smiled. "Yes. They'll be at dinner. I'll have to decide what to wear."

Nell snorted. "Shouldn't take you long. If you're to sit down with gentlemen from London, it's either the pink taffeta or the jonquil silk."

"The jonquil silk, then. And I'll want you to do my hair."

"Naturally." Nell closed the wardrobe doors. "I'd best give a hand downstairs but I'll be back to pretty you up."

"Hmm." Antonia leaned her head against the window frame.

Nell swallowed her snort and headed for the door. Hand on the knob, she paused, eyeing the slim figure by the window with open affection. Antonia did not move; Nell's eyes narrowed, then her features relaxed. "Should I warn Master Geoffrey to come to the table prepared to be civil?"

The question jerked Antonia from her reverie. "Heavens, yes! I forgot about Geoffrey."

"That's a first," Nell muttered.

Frowning at the bedpost, Antonia didn't hear. "Be sure to warn him *not* to come to table with his nose in a book."

"Aye. I'll make the matter plain." With a grim nod, Nell departed.

As the door clicked shut, Antonia turned back to the garden, letting her senses slide into the sylvan beauty. She loved Ruthven Manor. Coming back had felt like coming home; at some instinctive level she had always belonged, not at Mannering Park, but here—amid the gentle rolls of the Downs, surrounded by trees so old they stood like massive sentinels all around the house. Those feelings and her affection for Henrietta had both influenced her decision.

Given Geoffrey was soon to enter the world, it was time for her to do the same. At twenty-four, her prospects were few; prosaic consideration had brought her here.

Philip, Lord Ruthven, had yet to take a wife.

Antonia grimaced, her unprecedented nervousness very fresh in her mind. But there was no place in her scheme for faintheartedness; this afternoon, she'd taken the first step. Playing out her part was now inevitable— aside from anything else, she would never forgive herself if she didn't at least *try.* If Philip didn't see her in that light, so be it.

Recalling her promise to warn her aunt of his arrival, she shook herself. Glancing in the mirror, she fluffed her curls, her fingers stilling as she recalled Philip's fixation. Her lips quirked. Almost as if he'd been bowled over—in the circumstances, a definitely heartening thought.

Holding tight to that prop to her confidence, she headed for her aunt's rooms.

Downstairs in the library, duly fortified by a tan-kard of superlative ale, Hugo turned his thoughts to satisfying his curiosity. "Mannering, Mannering," he mused, then cocked a brow at Philip. "Can't quite place the family."

Jerked from contemplation of the most beguiling lips he'd ever seen, Philip set aside his empty tankard. "Yorkshire."

"Ah—that explains it." Hugo nodded sagely. "The wilds to the north."

"It's not as bad as that." Philip settled back. "Mannering Park, so I understand, is an estate of some significance."

"So what's the darling of it doing here?"

"She's Henrietta's niece—her father was Henrietta's only brother. He and Lady Mannering used to visit every summer." Philip felt the years roll back, saw again a young girl with long thick plaits astride his father's favourite hunter. "They'd leave Antonia here while they went the rounds through summer. She was always about." Laughing, chattering but, somehow, never irritating. He was ten years her senior, but that had never stopped her—he'd never been able to retreat behind any superior social facade, not with Antonia. He'd watched her change from a delightfully precocious brat to an engagingly quick-witted young girl; he had yet to come to terms with her most recent transformation.

"Their visits stopped when her father died." Philip paused, calculating. "Eight years ago now. I understand Lady Mannering declared she was too weary to face the social round thereafter. Henrietta was—is—very fond of Antonia. She issued a standing invitation but apparently Lady Mannering could never spare her daughter."

Hugo raised his brows. "So at long last Miss Mannering's escaped the maternal clutches?"

Philip shook his head. "Lady Mannering died about a year ago. Henrietta renewed her entreaties with a vengeance but, if I recall Henrietta's ramblings aright, Antonia was adamant on remaining at Mannering Park to care for her brother—he's much younger than she." Philip frowned. "I can't remember how old he'd be now—I can't even remember his name."

"Whatever, it looks like she's changed her mind."

"Knowing Antonia, that's unlikely. Not unless she's altered dramatically." After a moment, Philip added, "Perhaps her brother's gone up to Oxford?"

Studying his friend's distant expression, Hugo sighed. "I hate to be obvious but there's a mystery here, in case you haven't noticed."

Philip glanced at him. "Mystery?"

"You've seen the lady!" Hugo sat up, gesticulating freely. "There she is—beautiful as be damned. Not a giddy girl, nor yet too long in the tooth but the sort to stop a charge of *chasseurs* in their tracks. *And,* to all appearances, she's unwed." Sinking back in his chair, Hugo shook his head. "Doesn't make sense. If she's as well-born and well-connected as you say, she'd have been snapped up years ago." As an afterthought, he asked, "They do have gentlemen up north, don't they?"

Philip's brows slowly rose. "I'm sure they do—and they can't all be blind." A long moment passed while they both considered a situation that, in their experience, constituted a conundrum. "A mystery indeed," Philip eventually mused. "Given the facts you've so eloquently expounded, I can only conclude that you and I, dear Hugo, might be the first to catch sight of Miss Mannering in many a long year."

Hugo's eyes slowly widened. "You're not suggesting her mama kept her locked up?"

"Not locked up, but possibly very close. Mannering Park *is* isolated and, I gather, Lady Mannering became something of a recluse." Uncrossing his legs, Philip stood, his expression unreadable. Settling his sleeves, he glanced at Hugo. "I rather think I should pay my anticipated visit to Henrietta. As to Miss Mannering's state, I strongly suspect we'll discover that to be a direct consequence of her mother's malaise."

HENRIETTA, LADY RUTHVEN, put it rather more forcefully.

"A damned shame, if you ask me. No!" She held up one hand, pink chins quivering with indignation. "I know one is not supposed to speak ill of the dead but Araminta Mannering's neglect of poor Antonia was nothing short of *wicked!*"

They were in Henrietta's sitting-room, a cosy apartment made bright with flowers and floral embroideries. Henrietta occupied her favourite armchair beside the hearth; Philip stood before her, one arm negligently extended along the mantelpiece. At the back of the room, Henrietta's dresser, Trant, sat stitching industriously, head bent, ears flapping.

Lifting eyes of faded blue presently lit by her ire to Philip's face, Henrietta went on, "Indeed, if it hadn't been for the good offices of the other local ladies, that poor child would have grown to womanhood with not the first *inkling* of the social graces." Her expression mulish, she fluffed up her shawls. "And as for contracting a suitable alliance—it pains me to say it but I'm *quite sure* that that was the furthest thought from Araminta's mind!"

With her frown as near as it ever came to forbidding, she looked like an irate owl. Philip set himself to soothe her. "I met Antonia as we came in. She seemed wholly confident, quite in her customary mould."

"Of course!" Henrietta threw him a scornful glance. "The girl's no namby-pamby chit full of die-away airs! Araminta left the running of that huge old house entirely on Antonia's shoulders. Naturally she knows how to greet visitors and act the hostess—she's been doing it for years. Not only that, she had to manage the estate and take complete care of Geoffrey, too. It's a wonder she hasn't become bowed down beneath the weight of all the accumulated responsibilities."

Philip raised one brow. "Her shoulders—indeed, her carriage—seem to have held up admirably under the strain."

"Humph!" Henrietta shot him a glance, then settled deeper into her armchair. "Be that as it may, it's not right! The poor child should have been brought out years ago." She fell silent, idly toying with a fringe, then she looked up at Philip. "I don't know if you were aware of it but we offered to sponsor her—take her to London and introduce her to the *ton*. Puff her off with all the trimmings. Your father insisted—you know Horace always had a soft spot for Antonia."

Philip nodded, aware that was the truth. Even when, as a scrawny twelve-year-old, Antonia had blithely put a saddle on his father's favourite hunter and taken the ferocious beast on a long amble about the lanes, his sire, stunned as they all had been, had praised her bottom rather than spanked it. His sire had never disguised the admiration he felt for Antonia's particular brand of straightforward confidence, an admiration Philip was well aware he shared.

"We argued and even pleaded, but Araminta wouldn't hear of it." Henrietta's gaze grew cold. "It was perfectly plain she considered Antonia's place was to act as her nursemaid and chatelaine; she was determined the girl would have no chance at any other role."

Philip said nothing, his expression remote.

"Anyway," Henrietta said, her tone that of one who would brook no denial, "I'm determined, now that she has come to me, to see Antonia right." Lifting her head, she fixed Philip with a challenging stare. "I intend taking her to London for the Little Season."

For one instant Philip felt shaken, but by what force he couldn't comprehend. Holding fast to his customary imperturbability, he raised his brows. "Indeed?"

Henrietta nodded, the action an eloquent testimony to the strength of her resolution.

A pause ensued, which Philip, somewhat diffidently, broke. "Might I enquire as to whether you have any…" he gestured languidly "…further scheme in mind?"

A beatific smile lit Henrietta's lined face. "I intend on finding her a husband, of course."

For an instant, Philip remained perfectly still, his expression utterly impassive. Then his lids fell, veiling his eyes. "Of course." Gracefully, he bowed; when he straightened, his expression was as bland as his tone. "Hugo Satterly's downstairs—I should return to him. If you'll excuse me?"

Only when the door had closed behind him and she had listened to his footsteps retreat along the corridor did Henrietta allow herself a gleeful cackle. "Not a bad start, if I do say so myself."

Trant came forward to plump the cushions at her back and straighten her myriad shawls. "Seems like they've already met."

"Indeed—nothing could be more fortunate!" Henrietta beamed. "So like dear Antonia to remember to summon you to make sure I didn't oversleep. I detect fate's blessing in Philip arriving at just that moment."

"Maybe so, but he didn't seem all that taken. You don't want to get your hopes too high." Trant had been with her mistress ever since her marriage to the late Lord Ruthven. She had seen young ladies aspiring to the role of her mistress's successor come and go with sufficient frequency to entertain serious reservations as to the present Lord Ruthven's susceptibility. "I don't want you getting moped if it don't come off."

"Nonsense, Trant!" Henrietta turned to view her henchwoman. "If there's one thing I've learned after sixteen years of observing Philip, it's that one should never place any reliance on how he reacts. His nerves, I'm persuaded, have become so deadened by fashionable disinterest that even should he suffer a…a *coup de coeur,* he would merely raise a brow and make some mildly polite comment. No impassioned speeches or wild declarations from Philip, of that you may be sure. Nevertheless, I'm determined, Trant."

"So I see."

"*Determined* to see that languidly uninterested stepson of mine legshackled to Antonia Mannering." Henrietta thumped her chair arm for emphasis, then swivelled to look at Trant who had retreated to the window seat. "You have to admit she's everything he needs."

Without raising her eyes from her stitchery, Trant nodded. "She's that and more—you'll get no argument from me on that score. We've watched her grow and know her background—good bones, good breeding and all the graces you could want."

"Precisely." Henrietta's eyes gleamed. "She's just what Philip needs. All we have to do is ensure he realizes it. Shouldn't be too difficult—he's not at all dull-witted."

"That's what worries me, if you want to know." Trant snipped a thread and reached into her basket. "Despite that sleepy air of his, he's wide awake enough on most suits. If he gets wind of your plans, he might just slip his leash. Not so much a case of not liking the girl as of not liking the persuading, if you take my meaning."

Henrietta grimaced. "I do indeed. I haven't forgotten what happened when I invited Miss Locksby and her family for a week and promised them Philip would be here—remember?" She shuddered. "He took one look, not at Miss Locksby but at her mother, then recalled a prior engagement at Belvoir. *Such* a coil—I spent the entire week trying to make amends." Henrietta sighed. "The worst of it was that after that week I couldn't help but feel grateful he wouldn't marry Miss Locksby— I could never have borne Mrs Locksby as a relative."

A sound suspiciously like a smothered snort came from Trant.

"Yes, well." Henrietta fluffed her shawls. "You may be sure that I understand that we must go carefully in this—and not just because of Ruthven. I warn you, Trant, if Antonia gets any inkling of my active interest, she's likely to… to…well, at the very least, she's likely to become uncooperative."

Trant nodded. "Aye. She likes running in harness no more'n he."

"Exactly. But whether they like it or not, I see this as my duty, Trant. As I've said before, I don't believe it's my place to criticize Ruthven, but in this particular area I feel he's allowing his natural indolence to lead him to neglect his obligations to his name and to the family. He must marry and set up his nursery—he's thirty-four years gone and has shown no signs whatever of succumbing to Cupid's darts."

"Mind you," Henrietta declared, warming to her theme, "I freely admit that susceptibility on his part would be the most desirable avenue to pursue, but we cannot base our plans on improbabilities. No! We must do what we can to, very tactfully, promote a match between them. Antonia is now *my* responsibility, whatever she may think. And as for Ruthven—" Henrietta paused to lay a hand on her ample bosom "—I consider it my sacred duty to his sainted father to see him comfortably established."

CHAPTER TWO

AT PRECISELY SIX O'CLOCK, Philip stood before the mirror above the mantelpiece in the drawing-room, idly checking his cravat. It was the household's habit to gather there during the half-hour preceding dinner; Henrietta, however, rarely made it down much in advance of Fenton's appearance.

Focusing on his reflection, Philip grimaced. Dropping his hands, he surveyed the room. When no distraction offered, he fell to pacing.

The latch clicked. Philip halted, straightening, conscious of a surge of expectation—which remained unfulfilled. A boy—or was it a young man?—came diffidently into the room. He stopped when he saw him.

"Er…who are you?"

"I believe that's my line." Philip took in the wide hazel eyes and the thick thatch of wavy blonde hair. "Antonia's brother?"

The youth blushed. "You must be Ruthven." He blushed even more when Philip inclined his head. "I'm sorry—that is, yes, I'm Geoffrey Mannering. I'm staying here, you know." The boy stuck out his hand, then, in a paroxysm of uncertainty, very nearly pulled it back.

Philip solved the problem by grasping it firmly. "I didn't know," he said, releasing Geoffrey's hand. "But had I considered the matter, I should, undoubtedly, have guessed." Studying the boy's open face, he raised a brow. "I presume your sister felt she needed to keep you under her wing?"

Geoffrey grimaced. "Exactly." His eyes met Philip's, and he promptly blushed again. "Not that she's not probably right, of course. I dare say it would have been dev—" he caught himself up "—*deuced* slow staying at Mannering by myself."

Rapidly revising his estimates of Geoffrey's age downwards and his intelligence upwards, Philip inclined his head. The boy had the same ivory skin Antonia possessed, likewise untouched by the sun—strange in one of his years. "Are you down for the summer?"

Geoffrey flushed yet again, but this time with gratification. "I haven't actually gone up yet. Next term."

"You've gained entrance?"

Geoffrey nodded proudly. "Yes. Quite a stir it was, actually. I'm only just sixteen, you see."

Philip's lips curved. "No more than I would expect of a Mannering." He had years of experience of Antonia's swift wits on which to base that judgement.

Engaged in an entirely unaffected scrutiny of Philip's coat, Geoffrey nodded absentmindedly. "Dare say you don't remember me, but I *was* here, years ago, when the parents used to leave Antonia and me with Henrietta. But I was mostly in the nursery—and when I wasn't I was with Henrietta. She used to be very...well, *motherly,* you know."

He draped an arm along the mantelpiece, and Philip's smile wry. "I do, as it happens. You've no idea how grateful I was, first to Antonia, then to you, for giving Henrietta an outlet for her maternal enthusiasms. I'm extremely fond of her, but I seriously doubt our relationship would be quite so cordial had she been forced to exercise her talents on me in lieu of other, more suitable targets."

Geoffrey regarded Philip measuringly. "But you must have been quite…that is, almost an adult when Henrietta married your father."

"Not quite a greybeard—only eighteen. And if you think you've outgrown Henrietta's mothering just because you've reached sixteen, I suggest you think again."

"I already know that!" With a disgusted grimace, Geoffrey turned aside, picking up a figurine and turning it in his hands. "Sometimes," he said, his voice low, "I think I'll always be a child in their eyes."

Philip flicked a fleck of lint from his sleeve. "I shouldn't let it bother you." His tone was even, man to man. "You've only so many weeks to go before they'll be forced to cut the apron strings."

Geoffrey's expressive features contorted. "That's just it—I can't believe they actually will. They've never let me go before." His brow clouded. "Mama wouldn't hear of me going to school—I've had all my learning from tutors."

The door opened, cutting short their *tête à tête*. Philip straightened as Antonia came into the room. Geoffrey noted the movement. Replacing the figurine, he unobtrusively followed suit.

"Good evening, Antonia." Philip watched as she approached, a picture in soft yellow silk, the sheening fabric draping her curves, clinging, then hanging free, concealing then revealing in tantalizing glimpses. Her guinea-gold curls rioted in prolific confusion about her neat head; her expression was open, her hazel gaze, as always, direct.

"My lord." Graciously, Antonia inclined her head, her eyes going to her brother. "Geoffrey." Her serene smile faded slightly. "I see you two have met." Inwardly, Antonia prayed Geoffrey hadn't developed one of his instant dislikes—something he was distressingly prone to do when confronted with gentlemen.

Philip returned her smile. "We've been discussing Geoffrey's impending adventure in joining the academic establishment."

"Adventure?" Antonia blinked, her gaze shifting to Geoffrey, then back to Philip.

"Adventure indeed," Philip assured her. "Or so it was when I went up. I doubt it's changed. High drama, high jinks, life in all its varied forms. All the experience necessary to set a young gentleman's feet on the road to worldly confidence."

Antonia's eyes widened. "Worldly confidence?"

"*Savoir faire,* the ability to be at home in any company, the knowledge with which to face the world." Philip gestured broadly; his grey eyes quizzed her. "How else do you imagine gentlemen such as I learned to be as we are, my dear?"

The words were on the tip of Antonia's tongue—she only just managed to swallow them. "I dare say," she replied, in as repressive a tone as she could. The teasing light in Philip's eyes was doing the most uncomfortable things to her stomach. A swift glance at Geoffrey confirmed that her precocious brother was not ignorant of the purport of their host's sallies. Tilting her chin, she caught Philip's eye. "I'm sure Geoffrey will find the *academic* pursuits all absorbing."

Whether Philip would have capped her comment she was destined never to know; the door opened again, this time admitting Henrietta, closely followed by Hugo.

As she turned to her aunt, Antonia surprised a fleeting look of chagrin on Philip's face. It was there and then gone so rapidly she was not, in truth, entirely certain she had interpreted his expression correctly. Before she could ponder the point, Fenton entered to make his announcement.

"My honour, I believe?"

Antonia turned to find Philip's arm before her. Glancing across, she saw Henrietta being supported by Mr Satterly, the pair already deep in conversation. With a regally acquiescent glance, Antonia placed her hand on Philip's sleeve. "If you will, my lord."

Philip sighed. "Ah, what it is to be master in one's own house."

Antonia's lips twitched but she made no reply. Together, they led the way to the dining-room. They were five, leaving Philip at the head of the table and Henrietta at the foot with Hugo Satterly on one side and Geoffrey on the other. With a subtle smile, Philip delivered Antonia to the chair next to Geoffrey, the one closest to his own.

The conversation was at first general, with Hugo relating a succession of *on dits*. Having heard them all before, Philip bided his time until Henrietta, eager for gossip, predictably buttonholed Hugo, demanding further details. Equally eager to learn of the world he had yet to join, Geoffrey drank in Hugo's entertaining replies.

With a faint smile, Philip shifted in his chair, bringing Antonia directly under his gaze. "I understand, from what Henrietta let fall, that you've lived the past eight years very quietly."

Antonia met his gaze directly, her expression serious and, he thought, a touch sombre. She shrugged lightly. "Mama was unwell. There was little time for frivolities. Naturally, once I was of an age, the ladies about invited me to join their parties." She looked away as Fenton removed her soup plate. "To the Assemblies at Harrogate."

"Harrogate." Philip kept his expression impassive. She might as well have been buried alive. He waited until Fenton laid the next course before venturing, "But your mother must have entertained to some degree?"

Sampling a morsel of turbot cloaked in rich sweetbread sauce, Antonia shook her head. "Not after Papa's death. We received, of course, but more often than not, when the ladies arrived, Mama was too ill to come down."

"I see."

The quiet comment drew a quick glance from Antonia. "You must not imagine I've been pining away, dreaming of a gay life." Reaching for a dish of morels, she offered them to Philip. "I had more than enough to occupy myself, what with running the household and the estate. Mama was never well enough to tend to such matters. And there was Geoffrey, of course. Mama was always in a fret that he was sickly, which, of course, he never was. But she was sure he had inherited her constitution. Nothing would convince her otherwise."

Philip looked past Antonia; Geoffrey was wholly immersed in the conversation at the other end of the table. "Speaking of Geoffrey, how did you manage to find tutors to keep up with him? He must have been quite a handful."

Instantly, he realised he'd discovered the key to Antonia's confidence. Her eyes fairly glowed. "He certainly was. Why, by the time he was nine, he had outstripped the curate."

There followed an animated catalogue of Geoffrey's successes, liberally sprinkled with tales of misdeeds, catastrophes and simple country pleasures. In between the highlights of Geoffrey's life, Philip heard enough to gauge what manner of existence had been Antonia's lot. What encouragement was needed to keep her revelations flowing, he artfully supplied. As her history unfolded, he realised the unnamed curate was featuring remarkably often.

Laying aside his fork, he reached for his wineglass. "This curate of yours seems to have taken his duties very seriously."

Antonia's smile was fond. "Indeed. Mr Smothingham was always a great support. He really is a true knight—a most chivalrous soul." With a small sigh, she gave her attention to the gooseberry fool Fenton had placed before her.

Leaving Philip to wonder how he could possibly feel so aggressive towards a probably perfectly innocent curate whom he had never met. He cleared his throat. "Henrietta mentioned she was thinking of going up to town for the Little Season."

"Indeed." Savouring the tartness of the gooseberry treat, Antonia slanted him a glance. "She's invited me to accompany her. I hope you don't disapprove?"

"Disapprove?" Philip forced his eyes wide. "Not at all." Picking up his spoon, he attacked the frothy concoction before him. "In fact, I'll be relieved to know she'll have your company."

Antonia smiled and gave her attention to her dessert.

Philip rejected his, reaching instead for his wine-glass. He took a long sip, his gaze on Antonia. "Am I to understand you're looking forward to taking the *ton* by storm?"

She met his gaze with another of her disconcertingly direct looks. "I don't know." Her brows rose; her lips curved lightly. "Do you think I would find it diverting?"

Beyond his will, Philip's gaze was drawn to her lips, to the rich fullness of the ripe curves. He watched as the tip of her tongue traced their contours, leaving them sheening. His expression rigidly impassive, Philip drew in a deep breath. Slowly, he lifted his eyes and met Antonia's steady gaze. "As to that, my dear, I would not dare hazard a guess."

He had only questioned her intentions in London to assure himself she was a willing partner in Henrietta's schemes. His motives, Philip assured himself, were entirely altruistic. Henrietta could be a battleship when she was so moved. Unless he had misread the signs, when it came to Antonia's future, Henrietta was definitely moved.

"I'm not in the mood for billiards." Tossing back the last of his port, he stood and settled his coat. "Let's join the ladies, shall we?"

Geoffrey, for the first time elevated to the rank of gentleman to the extent of remaining to pass the port, saw nothing odd in the suggestion.

Hugo was not so innocent. He turned a face of amazed incomprehension on Philip.

Philip ignored it, leading the way to the drawing-room without further comment.

If Henrietta was surprised by his unheralded break with long-established habit, she gave no sign. Seated on the *chaise,* she looked up from her needlework to smile benignly. "Wonderful—just what we need. Geoffrey, do go and sing a duet with Antonia."

Henrietta waved towards the pianoforte, which stood before the long windows, presently open to the terrace. Antonia sat at the instrument, her fingers on the keys. A gentle, elusive air hung faint in the evening breeze.

With an obedient nod, Geoffrey headed for his sister. Antonia smiled a welcome, breaking off her playing to reach for the pile of music sheets resting on the piano's edge. With his customary lazy grace, Philip strolled in Geoffrey's wake. Left standing by the *chaise,* Hugo studied the small procession, then shrugged and brought up the rear.

"Let's try this, shall we?" Antonia placed a sheet on the stand.

Geoffrey scanned the lines, then nodded.

Philip took up a position by the side of the grand piano from where he could watch Antonia's face. As her fingers ranged the keys and the first chords of an old ballad filled the room, she looked up and met his gaze. A slight smile touched her lips; for an instant, their gazes held. Then she looked down and the music swept on.

She and Geoffrey sang in unison, Geoffrey's pure tenor weaving in and about her fuller tones. For one stanza, she sang alone; Philip briefly closed his eyes, listening not to the song, but to the music of her voice. It was not the light voice of the girl he remembered but richer, a warm contralto with an undercurrent of huskiness.

As Geoffrey's voice blended once more with hers, Philip opened his eyes. He saw Antonia glance encouragingly up at Geoffrey, then they launched into the last verse. As the final chords died, he, Henrietta and Hugo burst into spontaneous applause.

Almost squirming, Geoffrey blushed and disclaimed. Her expression one of affectionate exasperation, Antonia turned and deliberately met Philip's gaze. Lips curving, she arched a delicate brow. "Are you game, my lord?"

Philip detected at least two meanings in her challenge; he was uncertain if there was a third. Languidly, he inclined his head and straightened, responding to the more obvious of her prompts. Coming around the piano, he dropped a hand on Geoffrey's shoulder. "After that masterful effort, I fear my poor talents will be a disappointment to you all, but if you can find a *simple* ballad, I'll endeavour to do my poor best." He took up his stance behind Antonia's shoulder; Hugo took his place by the side of the piano.

With an approving smile, Antonia obliged with a rolling country ballad; Philip's strong baritone managed the changing cadences with ease. Unexpectedly caught up in the simple entertainment, Hugo consented to favour them with a rollicking shanty with a repeating refrain; Antonia made the performance even more humourous by consistently lengthening the long note at the end of the second last line of the reprieve. The shanty had a full twenty verses. First Geoffrey, then Philip, joined in, assisting Hugo through the increasingly jocular song. By the end of it, they were all laughing, very much out of breath.

A smile wreathing her face, Henrietta applauded vigorously, then summoned them to take tea.

Laughter lighting her eyes, Antonia swivelled on the stool to find Philip beside her. Deliberately, she looked up and met his eyes. Despite his easy expression, the grey orbs were veiled. Calmly, she raised a brow, then watched as the chiselled line of his lips lengthened into a definite smile.

He held out his hand. "Tea, my dear?"

"Indeed, my lord." Tilting her chin, Antonia laid her fingers in his palm and felt his hand close about them. A peculiar shiver shot up her arm, then slithered slowly down her spine. Ignoring it, she rose. Side by side, they crossed the room to where Henrietta was dispensing the tea.

With studied calm, Antonia accepted her cup but made no move to quit her aunt's side. A host of unfamiliar sensations flickered along her nerves; her heart was thudding distractingly. Such unexpected susceptibility was not, to her mind, a helpful development. She had never before been so afflicted—she hoped the effect would fade quickly.

To her relief, Henrietta kept up a steady spate of inconsequentialities, abetted by Hugo Satterly. Geoffrey, having gulped his tea, wandered back to the piano. Sipping slowly, Antonia concentrated on settling her nerves.

From behind his languid mask, Philip watched her.

"Actually, Ruthven—" Henrietta turned from Hugo "—I had meant to consult you as soon as you appeared about holding some entertainment for the neighbours. We haven't done anything in years. Now Antonia's here to help me, I really feel I should grasp the nettle with both hands."

Philip raised a brow. "Indeed?" None who heard those two syllables could doubt his reluctance.

Henrietta nodded imperiously. "It's one's duty, after all. I had been thinking of a grand ball—musicians, dancing, all the trimmings."

"Oh?" Philip's tone grew steadily more distant. He exchanged a glance with Hugo.

"Yes." Henrietta frowned, then grimaced. "But Antonia pointed out that, after all this time, we should really do something for our tenants as well."

Philip glanced at Antonia; she was sipping her tea, her eyes demurely cast down. He swallowed a disbelieving "humph."

"All things considered—and I really do not feel I can let this opportunity slide, Ruthven—I do believe dear Antonia's suggestion is the best." Folding her hands in her lap, Henrietta nodded decisively.

"And what," Philip asked, his tone deliberately even, "*is* dear Antonia's suggestion?"

"Why, a *fête-champêtre*—didn't I say?" Henrietta regarded him wide-eyed. "A positively *inspired* idea, as I'm sure even you will allow. We can set everything up on the lawns. Battledore and shuttlecock, races, bobbing for apples, archery, a play for the children—you know how these things go. We can have the food and ale set up on trestles for the tenants and entertain our neighbours on the terrace, overlooking all the fun."

Henrietta gestured grandly. "A whole afternoon in which everyone can enjoy themselves. I rather think we should hold it in the next week or so, before the weather turns, but naturally you'd have to be present. Shall we say next Saturday—a week from now?"

Philip held her enquiring gaze, his expression as informative as a blank wall. A garden party was infinitely preferable to a local ball—but at what price? A vision of hordes of farmers and their wives tramping across his lawns swam through his mind; in his imagination he could hear the high-pitched shrieks of multitudes of children and the screams as some, inevitably, fell in the lake. But worse than all that, he could clearly see the bevy of simpering, silly, local young misses to whom he would, perforce, have to be civil.

"Naturally, I'll assist in any way I can."

Antonia's soft words cut across Philip's thoughts. He glanced her way, then, one brow slowly rising, turned back to Henrietta. "I admit to reservations that acting as hostess at such a large and varied gathering will overly tire you."

Henrietta's grin was triumphant. "No need to worry over me. Antonia can stand in my stead for the most part—I'm looking forward to sitting on the terrace with the other dowagers, keeping an eye on it all from a suitable elevation."

"I can imagine," Philip returned drily. He shifted his gaze to Antonia. "Yet your 'most part' is not precisely a light load."

Antonia's chin came up; she shot him a distinctly haughty glance. "I think you'll discover, my lord, that I'm more than up to snuff. I've managed such gatherings at Mannering for years—I anticipate no great difficulty in overseeing my aunt's entertainment."

Philip ensured his expression held just enough scepticism to make her eyes flash. "I see."

"Good." Henrietta thumped the floor with her cane. "So it's Saturday. We'll send out the invitations tomorrow."

Philip blinked. Hugo, he noticed, looked vaguely stunned. Henrietta, of course, was beaming happily up at him. Drawing in a deep breath, he hesitated, then inclined his head. "Very well."

As he straightened, he deliberately caught Antonia's eye. Her expression was innocent but her eyes, tapestries of green and gold, were infinitely harder to read. She raised her brows slightly, then reached for his empty cup.

Eyes narrowing, Philip surrendered it. "I intend to hold you to your offer."

She treated him to a sunny, utterly confident smile, then moved away to straighten the tea trolley.

Suppressing a snort, Philip turned to find Hugo beside him.

"Think I'll go join Geoffrey." Hugo wriggled his shoulders. "In case you haven't noticed, there's an aura about here that's addling wits."

THE DEW WAS still on the grass when Antonia headed for the stables the next morning. Early-morning rides had been a long-ago treat; Philip's return had resurrected pleasant memories.

Entering the long stable, she paused, allowing her eyes to adjust to the dimmer light. Rising on her toes, she looked along the glossy backs, trying to ascertain whether the chestnut gelding the headgroom, Martin, had told her was Philip's favourite, was still in his box.

"Still an intrepid horsewoman, I see."

Antonia smothered her gasp and swung about. The

velvet skirts of her habit swirled, brushing Philip's boots. He was so close, she had to tilt her head up to meet his eyes, one hand on her riding hat to keep it in place.

"I didn't hear you." The words were breathless; inwardly, Antonia cursed.

"I noticed. You seemed absorbed in some search." Philip's eyes held hers. "What were you looking for?"

For an instant, Antonia's mind went blank; prodded by sheer irritation, she replied, "I was looking for Martin." She turned to survey the empty stable, then slanted a glance at Philip. "I wanted him to saddle a horse for me."

Philip's jaw firmed. He hesitated, then asked, "Which of my nags have you been using?"

"I haven't been out yet." Picking up her skirts, Antonia strolled down the aisle, knowledgeably gauging the tall hunters and hacks.

Philip followed. "Take your pick," he said, knowing very well she would.

"Thank you." Antonia stopped before a stall housing a long-tailed roan, a raking, raw-boned stallion Philip privately considered had a chip on his shoulder—he was perennially in a bad mood. "This one, I think."

With any other woman, Philip's veto would have been automatic. Instead, he simply snorted and strode on to the tack-room. Returning with a sidesaddle, bridle and reins, he found Antonia crooning sweet nothings to the giant horse. The stallion appeared as docile as the most matronly mare.

Swallowing another "humph," Philip swung the stall door wide. Quickly and efficiently, he saddled the stallion, glancing now and then at Antonia, standing at the horse's head communing with the beast. He knew perfectly well she could have saddled the horse herself; she was the one woman in all the millions he would trust to do so.

But it would have been churlish to suggest she wrestle with the saddle, not when she made such a delightful picture, her habit of topaz-coloured velvet a deeper gold than her hair, the tightly fitting bodice outlining the womanly curves of her breasts, nipping in to emphasize her small waist before flaring over her hips. As if sensing his regard, she looked up; Philip jabbed an elbow into the roan's side and cinched the girth. "Wait while I saddle Pegasus."

Antonia nodded. "I'll walk him in the yard."

Philip watched as she led the stallion out, then returned to the tack-room. He was on his way back, his arms full of his own tack, when ringing footsteps sounded on the cobbles of the yard. Frowning, Philip set his saddle on the stall door. Hugo, he knew, would still be sound asleep. So who...?

"Hello! Sorry I'm a bit late." Geoffrey waved and headed for the tack-room. As he passed, he flung Philip a grin. "I guessed you'd ride early. I won't keep you." With that, he disappeared into the tack-room.

Philip smothered a groan and dropped his head against his horse's glossy flank. When he straightened and turned, he found himself eye to eye with Pegasus. "At least you can't laugh," he muttered savagely.

By the time he emerged from the stable, Antonia had discovered the mounting block and was perched atop the roan, a slim slender figure incomprehensibly controlling the great beast as she walked him around the yard.

Gritting his teeth, Philip swung up to the saddle;

in less than a minute, Geoffrey joined them, leading a grey hunter.

"All right?" he asked, looking first to Philip and then to Antonia.

Philip nodded. "Fine. Let's get going."

They did—the brisk ride, flying as fast as the breeze, did much to restore his temper. He led the way but was unsurprised to see the roan's head keeping station on his right. Geoffrey followed on his heels. It had been years—at least eight—since Philip had enjoyed that sort of ride: fast, unrestrained, with company that could handle the going as well as he. One glance as they cleared a fence was enough to reassure him that Antonia had not lost her skill; Geoffrey was almost as good as she.

In perfect amity with their mounts, they fled before the wind, finally drawing rein on an open hillock miles from the Manor. Philip wheeled, dragging in a deep breath. His eyes met Antonia's; their smiles were mirror images. Exhilaration coursed through his veins; he watched as she tipped her head up and laughed at the sky.

"That was *so good!*" she said, smiling still as her eyes lowered and again met his.

They milled, catching their breaths, letting their mounts settle. Philip scanned the surrounding fields, using the moment to refresh his memory. Antonia, he noticed, was doing the same.

"That copse," she said, pointing to a small wood to their left, "had only just been planted last time I rode this way."

The trees, birches for the most part, were at least twenty feet tall, reaching their fingers to the sky. The undergrowth at their bases, home to badgers or fox, was densely intertwined.

"This brute's still fresh." Geoffrey wheeled the grey tightly. "There looks to be some ruins over that way." He nodded to the east. "Think I'll just shake the fidgets with a quick gallop." He glanced at Philip and lifted a brow.

Philip nodded. "We'll go back by way of the ford. You can join us on the other side."

Geoffrey located the stream and the ford, nodded agreement and left.

Antonia watched him cross the fields, an affectionate smile on her lips. Then she sighed and turned to Philip, her eyes holding an expression he could not immediately place. "I can't tell you how relieved I am to see he hasn't lost the knack."

Leading the way off the knoll, Philip raised his brows. "Of riding neck or nothing? Why should he?"

Keeping pace beside him, Antonia's lips twisted; she gave a light shrug. "Eight years is a long time."

Philip blinked. A long moment passed before he asked, "Haven't you—and Geoffrey—been riding regularly?"

Antonia looked up, surprised. "I thought you knew." When Philip threw her a blank look, she explained, "Papa died in a hunting accident. Virtually immediately Mama sold his stable. She only kept two carriage horses—she said that's all we'd need."

Philip kept his eyes fixed ahead; his face felt like stone. His tone was carefully even when he asked, "So, essentially since you were last here, you've been unable to ride?"

Simply voicing the idea made him blackly furious.

She had always found immense joy in riding, delighting in her special affinity with the equine species. What sort of parent would deny her that? His opinion of the late Lady Mannering, never high, spiralled downwards.

Her attention on the roan, Antonia shook her head. "For me, it didn't really matter, but for Geoffrey—well, you know how important such skills are to young gentlemen."

Philip forced himself to let her answer pass unchallenged; he had no wish to reopen old wounds. As they gained the flat, he tried for a lighter note. "Geoffrey has, after all, had excellent teachers. Your father and yourself."

He was rewarded with a swift smile.

"Many would say that I'm hardly a good example, riding as I do."

"Only because they're jealous."

She laughed at that, a warm, husky, rippling sound Philip was certain he'd never heard before. His eyes locked on her lips, on the column of her white throat; his gelding pranced.

Instinctively, he tightened his reins. "Come, let's ride. Or Geoffrey will tire of waiting."

They rode side by side, fast but not furiously, chestnut and roan flowing effortlessly over the turf. Geoffrey joined them at the ford; they wheeled and rode on, ultimately clattering into the stableyard a short hour after they had left it.

The two men swung down from their saddles; Philip tossed his reins to Geoffrey, who led both grey and chestnut away.

Before Antonia had well caught her breath, she lost it again. Philip's hands closed, strong and sure, about her waist. He lifted her, as if she weighed no more than a child, lowering her slowly until her feet touched the ground.

Antonia felt a blush tinge her cheeks; it was all she could do to meet his gaze fleetingly. "Thank you, my lord." Her heart was galloping faster than any horse.

Philip looked down at her. "The pleasure, my dear, is entirely mine." He hesitated, then released her. "But do you think you could possibly stop 'my lording' me?" His tone, slightly acid, softened. "You used to call me Philip."

Still breathless, but at least now free of his paralysing touch, Antonia wrestled her wits into order. Frowning, she looked up and met his grey gaze. "That was before you came into the title." Considering, she tilted her head. "Now that you have, I'll have to call you Ruthven—like everyone else."

His eyes, cloudy grey, held hers; for an instant, she thought he would argue. Then the ends of his long lips twisted, in grimace or self-deprecation she couldn't say. His lids fell; he inclined his head in apparent acquiescence.

"Breakfast awaits." With a graceful flourish, Philip offered her his arm. "Shall we? Before Geoffrey devours all the herrings."

CHAPTER THREE

"AH—I WONDERED WHO was attacking my rose bushes."

Startled in the act of lopping off a developing rose-hip with a buccaneer-like swipe, Antonia jumped. Half turning, she glanced reprovingly at Philip as he descended the steps to the walk. "Your rose bushes, my lord, are running to seed. Not at all the thing." With a decisive click, she removed another deadhead.

She had spent the morning inscribing invitations for the *fête-champêtre*. In the silence of the afternoon, with Henrietta napping, she had taken to the gardens. After their ride that morning, she hadn't expected to see Philip before dinner.

Smiling lazily, Philip strolled towards her. "Henrietta mentioned you were easing her burden by taking things in hand around the house. Am I to take it you intend to personally deal with anything you discover running to seed around here?"

Poised to pluck a half-opened rose, the delicate bloom cradled in her hand, Antonia froze. Philip had halted a bare foot away; she could feel his gently teasing gaze on her half-averted face. Catching her breath, surreptitiously, she hoped, she looked up and met his eyes. "As to my personal interest, I rather suspect it depends on the subject. However," she said, turning back and carefully snipping the rose, "as far as the garden is concerned, I intend speaking with your head gardener immediately." She laid the bloom in the basket on her arm, then looked up. "I take it you don't disapprove of my…" she gestured gracefully "…impertinence?"

Philip's smile deepened. "My dear Antonia, if acting as chatelaine can be termed impertinent, you may be as impertinent as you please. Indeed," he continued, one brow rising, his gaze sweeping her face, "I find it distinctly reassuring to see you thus employed."

For an instant, Antonia met his gaze, then, with the slightest inclination of her head, turned and glided along the path. Reassuring? Because, as she hoped, he saw such actions as evidence of her wifely skills? Or because she might, conceivably, make his unfettered existence more comfortable?

"The design of your gardens is unusual," she said, glancing back to find him strolling in her wake like a predator on her trail. "I've studied both contemporary and classical landscapes—yours seems a combination of both."

Philip nodded. "The fact that the lake and stream are so distant from the house rendered the usual water features ineligible. Capability Brown saw it as a challenge." His eyes met Antonia's. "One he couldn't resist."

"Indeed?" Inwardly cursing the breathlessness that seemed to afflict her whenever he was near, Antonia halted beside a clump of cleomes. "To my mind, he's succeeded in moulding the raw ingredients into a veritable triumph. The vistas are quite enchanting." Setting aside her basket, she bent over the clump of soft white flowers, selecting and snipping two stems for her collection.

Beside her, Philip stood transfixed, his gaze on an

unexpected but thoroughly enchanting vista. Antonia shifted, then straightened; Philip quickly lifted his gaze to the neat row of conifers bordering the sunken garden. "Yes," was all he could think of to say.

Antonia threw him a swift, slightly suspicious look; he promptly smiled charmingly down at her. "Have you been through the peony walk?"

"Not for a few days."

"Come, walk with me there—it's always a pleasant route."

Antonia hesitated, then acquiesced. Together, they climbed the steps from the sunken garden, then turned into the narrow hedged walk where peonies of every description filled beds on either side of the flags. Although past their best, the plants were still blooming, displaying splashes of white and all shades of maroon against glossy green leaves. The path had been laid like a stream, gently twisting; here and there, small specimen trees grew, no longer in blossom but adding interest with their foliage.

They strolled in companionable silence, stopping intermittently to admire the extravagant displays. Antonia paused to examine the blooms carried on one long stem; Philip watched the subtle play of her thoughts rippling through her expression.

She was, on the one hand, so very familiar—on the other, so startlingly different.

He had almost grown accustomed to the change in her voice, to the husky undertone he found so alluring. Her eyes, a complex medley of greens and golds, had not altered but her gaze, although still direct, seemed more deeply assured. As for the rest of her, that had certainly changed. There was poise, now, where before had been youthful hedonism; elegant grace had replaced a young girl's haste.

His gaze caressed her hair, glinting golden in the sunlight; he was prepared to accept that it was still as long and thick as he recalled. The curves that filled her muslin gown were, however, an entirely new development—a thoroughly distracting development.

Her head used to barely reach his shoulder, yet when she turned, Philip found his lips level with her forehead.

Bare inches away.

His gaze dropped and met hers, wide and, he realised, somewhat startled. Her scent wafted about him, rose, honeysuckle and some essence he could not name.

Her gaze trapped in his, Antonia caught her breath, only to find she could not release it. Unable to move, unable to speak, unable to tear her eyes from the darkening grey of his, she stood before him, feeling like a canary staring at a cat.

Smoothly, Philip stepped back. "It's nearly time for luncheon. Perhaps we should return?" His lids veiled his eyes; languidly, he waved to a cross-path that would lead them back to the house.

Slowly exhaling, Antonia glanced up at the sky. Her heart was racing. "Indeed." In search of a topic—any topic—she asked, "What was it that brought you to the garden?"

Philip's gaze ranged ahead, his expression bland as he considered and rejected the truth. In the distance, he saw Geoffrey returning from the stables. "I wanted to ask if Geoffrey had had any experience of driving. After what you told me of your last years, I imagine he's lacked male guidance. Would you like me to teach him?"

Looking down, he caught the peculiar expression that flitted, very briefly, across Antonia's features.

"Oh, yes," she said, throwing him a grateful glance. "If you would, you would earn his undying gratitude. And mine."

"I'll take him out then."

Antonia nodded, her eyes downcast. Side by side, they walked towards the house. Puzzling over her strange look, Philip shot her a shrewd glance, then slowly smiled. Schooling his features to an expression of deep consideration, he said, "Actually, I have to confess I've no experience of teaching striplings. Perhaps, as you are, unquestionably, a superior horsewoman and in loco parentis, as it were, I should practise my tutoring skills on you?"

Antonia's head came up; she fixed him with a clear, very direct glance. "You'll teach me to drive?"

Philip managed to keep the smile from his face. "If you would care for it."

"I didn't think—" Antonia frowned. "That is, I'd understood that it was no longer particularly fashionable for ladies of the *ton* to drive themselves."

"Only in certain circumstances and only—pray God—when they can actually manage the reins." Halting at the bottom of the terrace steps, Philip turned to face her. "It's entirely acceptable for a lady to drive a gig or a phaeton in the country."

Antonia raised a brow. "And in town?"

Both Philip's brows rose. "My dear Antonia, if you imagine I'll let you tool my horses in the Park, you're misguided, my child."

Antonia's eyes flashed; she lifted her chin. "What carriage do you drive in London?"

"A high-perch phaeton. Forget it," Philip tersely advised. "I'll permit you to drive my curricle, but only here."

Brows rising haughtily, Antonia started up the steps. "But when we get to London—"

"Who knows?" Philip mused. "You might turn out to be ham-fisted."

"Ham—!" Antonia rounded on him—or tried to, only to feel his fingers close about her elbow. Effortlessly, he propelled her over the threshold into the morning-room where Henrietta sat tatting.

"One step at a time, my dear." His words were a murmur in her ear. "Let's see how well you can handle the reins before you reach for the whip."

THAT COMMENT, OF COURSE, ensured she was on her mettle when, the following afternoon, Philip lifted her to the box-seat of his curricle. Determined that nothing—not even he—would distract her from her lesson, Antonia thrust her ridiculous sensitivity to the back of her mind and carefully gathered the reins.

"Not like that." Philip climbed up beside her, settling on the seat alongside. Deftly plucking the reins from her fingers, he demonstrated the correct hold, then laid the leather ribbons in her palms, tracing their prescribed path through her fingers with his. Despite her gloves, Antonia had to lock her jaw against the sensation of his touch. She frowned.

Philip noticed. He sat back, resting one arm along the back of the seat. "Today, we'll go no faster than a sedate trot. Not having second thoughts, are you?"

Antonia shot him a haughty look. "Of course not. What now?"

"Give 'em the office."

Antonia clicked the reins; the horses, a pair of perfectly matched greys, lunged.

Her shriek lodged in her throat. Philip's arm locked about her; his other hand descended over hers as she grappled with the reins. The curricle rattled down the drive, not yet fast but with the greys lengthening their stride. The next seconds passed in total confusion—by the time she had the horses under control and pacing, restless but aware of her authority at the other end of the ribbons, Antonia was more rattled than she had ever been in her life before.

She shot Philip a fiery glance but could not—dared not—take exception to the steely arm anchoring her safely to his side. And despite the urge to tell him just what she thought of his tactics, she felt ridiculously grateful that he had not, in fact, taken control, but had let her wrestle with his thoroughbreds, entrusting their soft mouths to her skill, untutored though he knew that to be.

It took several, pulse-pounding minutes before she had herself sufficiently in hand to turn her head and meet his improbably bland gaze with one of equal impassivity. "And now?"

She saw his lips twitch.

"Just follow the drive. We'll stay in the lanes until you feel more confident."

Antonia put her nose in the air and gave her attention to his horses. She had, as she had earlier informed him, some experience of driving a gig. Managing a dull-witted carriage horse was not in the same league as guiding a pair of high-couraged thoroughbreds. At first, the task took all her concentration; Philip spoke only when necessary, giving instructions in clear and precise terms. Only when she was convinced she had mastered the "feel," the response of the horses to her commands, did she permit herself to relax enough to take stock.

Only then did the full import of her situation strike her.

Philip's arm had loosened yet still lay protectively about her. Although still watchful, he sat back beside her, his gaze idly scanning the fields. They were in a lane, bordered by hedges, meandering along a rolling ridge. Glimpses of distant woods beyond emerald fields, of orchards and of willows lining streams, beckoned; Antonia saw none of them, too distracted by the sensation of the solid masculine thigh pressed alongside hers.

She drew in a deep breath and felt her breasts swell, impossibly sensitive against her fine chemise. If she'd been wearing stays, she would have been sure they were laced too tight. That left only one reason for her giddiness—the same ridiculous sensitivity that had assailed her from the first, from the moment she had met Philip in the hall. She had put it down to simple nervousness—if not that, then merely a dim shadow of the infatuation she had felt for years.

An infatuation she had convinced herself would fade when confronted with reality.

Instead, reality had taken her infatuation and turned it into—what?

A shiver threatened—Antonia struggled to suppress it.

She didn't, in fact, succeed.

Through the arm about her, Philip felt the telltale reaction. Lazily, he studied her, his gaze shrewd and penetrating. Her attention was locked on his leader's ears. "I've been thinking—about Geoffrey."

"Oh?"

"I was wondering if, considering his age, it might not be advisable to temporarily delay his departure for Oxford. He hasn't seen much of the world—a few weeks in London might be for the best. It would certainly put him on a more even footing with his peers."

Her gaze on the road, Antonia frowned. After neatly if absentmindedly taking the next corner, she replied, "For myself, I agree." She grimaced and glanced fleetingly at Philip. "But I'm not sure he will—he's very attached to his books. And how can we argue, if the time wasted will put him behind?"

Philip's lips curved. "Don't worry your head about convincing him—you may leave that to me."

Antonia shot him a glance, clearly not sure whether to encourage him or not.

Philip pretended not to notice. "As for his studies, his academic performance is, I'm sure, sufficiently strong for him to catch up a few weeks without difficulty. Where's he going?"

"Trinity."

"I know the Master." Philip smiled to himself. "If you like, I'll write and ask permission to keep him down until the end of the Little Season."

Antonia slowed the greys in order to turn and study him. "You know the Master?"

Philip lifted a haughty brow. "Your family is not the only one with a connection to the college."

Antonia's eyes narrowed. "You went there?"

Philip nodded, his expression impassive as he watched her struggle with her uncertainty.

In the end, convinced there was no subtle way in which to frame her question, Antonia drew in a deep breath and asked, "And what, do you think, will be the Master's response to such a request—from you?"

Philip met her gaze with bland incomprehension. "My dear Antonia, whatever do you mean?"

She shot him a fulminating glance, then turned back to the horses. "I mean—as you very well know—that such a request from one whose reputation is such as yours can be construed in a number of ways, not all of which the Master is likely to approve."

Philip's deep rumbling laughter had her setting her teeth.

"Oh, well done!" he eventually said. "I couldn't have put it better myself."

Antonia glared at him, then clicked the reins, setting the horses to a definite trot.

Philip straightened his lips. "Rest assured that my standing with the Master is sufficient that such a request will be interpreted in the most favourable light."

The glance Antonia threw him held enough lingering suspicion to make him narrow his eyes. "I do not, dear Antonia, have any reputation for corrupting the innocent."

She had, he noted, sufficient grace to blush.

"Very well." Antonia nodded but kept her gaze locked on the leader. "I'll mention the matter to Geoffrey."

"No—leave that to me. He'll be more receptive to the idea if I suggest it."

Antonia knew her brother well enough not to argue. Head high, she turned the horses for home, deter-

minedly disregarding the inward flutter Philip had
managed to evoke.

After studying her profile, Philip said no more until
she pulled the horses up before the front steps. Descending, he strolled leisurely around to come up beside her,
meeting her watchful, slightly wary gaze with open appreciation. "A commendable first outing. To my mind,
you're still holding them a little tight in the curves but
that judgement will come with practice."

Before she could reply, he twitched the reins from her
hands and tossed them to the groom who had come running from the stables. While the movement had her distracted, he closed his hands about her waist, well aware
of the tension that gripped her as he lifted her down.

"You'll be pleased to know," he glibly stated, holding her before him and gazing down into suddenly wide
eyes, "that I'm completely satisfied that your peculiar
ability to communicate with the equine species oper-
ates even when you're not perched upon their backs."

Antonia continued to stare at him blankly. Reluctantly, Philip released her.

"You—" Antonia blinked wildly. It was an effort to
summon not only her voice but the indignation she felt
sure she should feel. Breathless, she continued, "Do you
mean to say that today was a…a *test?*"

Philip smiled condescendingly. "My dear Antonia, I
know of your talents—it seemed rational to test them.
Now I know they're sound, there seems little doubt
you'll prove a star pupil."

Antonia blinked again—and wished there was some
phrase in his speech to which she could take exception.
In the end, she drew herself up and fixed him with a direct and openly challenging stare. "I assume, my lord,

that when we go out tomorrow, you'll permit me to get above a trot?"

The subtle smile that played about his lips did quite peculiar things to her nerves. "I wouldn't suggest you reach for the whip just yet, my dear."

"WELL! THAT SEEMED a most successful outing." Henrietta turned from the window high above the drive, having watched her stepson and niece until they'd disappeared into the hall below.

"That's as may be." Trant continued to fold linens, laying them neatly on the bed. "But I'd reserve judgement if I was you. Early days yet to read anything into things like simple drives in the countryside."

"Phooh!" Henrietta waved the objection aside. "Ruthven rarely drives ladies—let alone lets them drive *him*. Of *course* it means something."

Trant merely sniffed.

"It means," Henrietta went on, "that our plan has real promise. We must ensure they spend as much time in each other's company as possible—with as little distraction as we can manage."

"You're planning on encouraging them to be alone?" Trant voiced her query with a suitably hesitant air.

Henrietta snorted. "Antonia is twenty-four, after all—hardly a green girl. And whatever Ruthven's reputation, he has never, to my certain knowledge, been accused of seducing innocents."

Trant shrugged, unwilling to risk further comment.

Henrietta frowned, then shifted her shawls. "I'm convinced, in this case, that strict adherence to society's dictates is not necessary. Aside from anything else, Ruthven will not—would not—seduce any lady residing under his own roof under my protection. We must put our minds to making sure they spend at least some part of every day together. I'm a great believer in propinquity, Trant—if Ruthven is to see what a gem Antonia is, we'll need to keep her before him long enough for him to do so."

THREE DAYS LATER, Antonia climbed the stairs and entered her bedchamber. She had spent all morning going over the plans for the *fête,* to be held, as Henrietta had decreed, two days hence; it was now midafternoon, and Henrietta was napping. As usual, the garden was her destination but she had fallen into the habit of checking her appearance whenever she ventured forth. Crossing to the dressing-table, she smiled absentmindedly at Nell, seated by the window, a pile of darning beside her. "Don't strain your eyes. I'm sure some of the younger maids could lend a hand with that."

"Aye—no doubt. But I've little confidence in their stitches—I'd rather see to it myself."

Picking up her brush, Antonia carefully burnished the curls falling in artful disorder from the knot on the top of her head.

Nell threw her a swift glance. "Seems you've been seeing a lot of his lordship lately."

Antonia's hand stilled, then she shrugged. "I wouldn't say a lot. We ride in the mornings, of course. Geoffrey, too." She did not think it necessary to mention that for at least half the time she spent on horseback, she and Philip were alone; Geoffrey, encouraged to try the paces of his mount, was rarely within hailing distance. "Other than that, and the three occasions he's let me drive his curricle, Ruthven only seeks me out if he has some matter to discuss."

"That so?" Nell remarked.

"Indeed." Antonia tried to keep the irritation from her voice. Although Philip often sought her company during the day, spending half an hour or more by her side, he invariably had some reason for doing so. She sank the brush into one curl. "He's a busy man, after all—a serious landowner. He spends hours with his agent and bailiff. Like any sensible gentleman, he puts effort into ensuring his estate runs smoothly."

"Strange—it's not what I'd have thought." Nell shook out a chemise. "He seems so...well, lazy."

Antonia shook her head. "He's not lazy at all—that's just an image, a fashionable affectation. Ruthven's never been truly lazy in his life—not over anything that matters."

Nell shrugged. "Ah, well—you know him better than most."

Antonia swallowed a "humph" and continued to tend her curls.

Five minutes later, she was descending the steps from the terrace when she heard her name called. Looking about, she saw Geoffrey striding up from the stables. One glance at his face was enough to tell her her brother was in alt.

"A great day, Sis! I had them trotting sweetly from the first. Who knows—next time our teacher might let me take out his greys."

Antonia grinned, sharing his delight. "Bravo—but I wouldn't get your hopes too high." While Ruthven had entrusted his greys to her, he had started Geoffrey with a pair of match chestnuts, by any standards a well-bred pair but not in the same league with his peerless Irish greys. "In fact," Antonia said, linking her arm in Geoffrey's, "I'd rather you didn't suggest it—he's really been very generous in helping you take the reins."

"I wasn't about to," Geoffrey replied, fondly condescending. "That was just talk." Obediently, he fell in beside her as she strolled the gravel path. "Ruthven's been far more encouraging than I'd ever looked to see. He's a great gun—one of the best!"

Antonia heard the fervour in his tone; glancing up, she saw it reflected in his face.

Unconscious of her scrutiny, Geoffrey went on, "I assume you know he's suggested I should accompany you to London? I wasn't too sure at first—but he explained how it would set yours and Henrietta's minds at ease—if you could see me in society a bit, build your confidence in me, that sort of thing."

"Oh?" When Geoffrey glanced her way, Antonia hurriedly changed her tone. "I mean—yes, that's right." After a moment, she added, "Ruthven's very good at thinking of such things."

"He said that's one of the traits that distinguishes a man from a boy—that a man thinks of his actions in the wider context, not just in terms of himself."

Despite her inclination, Antonia felt a surge of gratitude towards Philip; his subtle mentoring would help to fill the large gap their father's death had left in Geoffrey's life. Any lingering reservations she had regarding Geoffrey's visit to London evaporated. "I think you would be very wise to take Ruthven's hints to heart. I'm certain you can have every confidence in his experience."

"Oh, I have!" Geoffrey strode along beside her,

then recalled he should match his steps to hers. "You know—when you decided to come here, I thought I'd be—well, the odd man out. I didn't think Philip would still be friendly, like he was to you all those years ago. But it's just the same, isn't it? He might be a swell and a gentleman about town and all that, but he still treats us as friends."

"Indeed." Antonia hid a glum grimace. "We're very fortunate to have his regard."

Grinning, Geoffrey disengaged. "Think I'll take a fowling piece out for the rest of the afternoon."

Antonia nodded absentmindedly. Alone, she let her feet follow the gravel walks, her mind treading other paths. Geoffrey, unfortunately, was right. While Philip could be counted on to tease and twit her, in all their hours together, whether strolling the gardens or driving his greys, she had never detected anything in his manner to suggest he saw her other than as a friend. An old friend, admittedly—one on whom he need not stand on terms—but nothing more than an agreeable companion.

It was not what she wanted.

Looking back, analysing all their interactions, the only change the years had wrought was what she termed her "ridiculous sensitivity"—the leaping, fluttering feeling that afflicted her whenever he was close, the tension that immobilized her limbs, the distraction that did the same to her wits, the vice that made breathing so difficult every time he touched her, every time he lifted her down and held her between his strong hands, every time he took her hand in his to help her up a step or over some obstacle.

As for the times his fingers had inadvertently brushed the back of her hand—they were undoubtedly the worst. But all that came from her, not him. It was simply her reaction to his presence, a reaction that was becoming harder and harder to hide.

Halting, she looked around and discovered she'd reached the Italian garden. Neat hedges of lavender bordered a long, raised rectangular pool on which white water lillies floated. Gravelled walks surrounded the pool, themselves flanked by cypress and box, neatly clipped. It was a formal, quite austere setting—one which matched her mood. Frowning, Antonia strolled beside the pool, trailing her fingers in the dark water.

Her "ridiculous sensitivity" was the least of her problems. Philip still saw her as a young girl and the *fête* was looming; soon after, they would leave for London. If she wanted to succeed in her aim, she would have to *do* something. Something to readjust his vision of her—to make him see her as a woman, a lady—as a potential wife. And whatever she was going to do, she would have to do it soon!

"Well, my lady of the lake—are my goldfish nibbling your fingers?"

Antonia whirled and saw the object of her thoughts strolling towards her. He was wearing a flowing ivory shirt, topped with a shooting jacket, a scarf loosely knotted about his tanned throat. His long thighs were clad in buckskin breeches, his feet in highly polished top-boots. One brow rising in gentle raillery, his hair tousled by the breeze, he looked every inch the well-heeled landowner—and a great deal more dangerous than the average country gentleman.

Calmly, Antonia lifted her wet fingers and studied them. "Not noticeably, my lord. I suspect your fish are too well fed to be tempted."

Philip halted directly before her; Antonia nearly jumped when his fingers slid about her wrist. Lifting her hand, he examined her damp fingers. "Fish, I understand, are not particularly intelligent."

His heavy lids lifted; his gaze, sky grey with clouds gathering, met hers.

Antonia's heart lurched, her stomach knotted; familiarity didn't make the sensations any easier to bear. His fingers felt strong and steely, his grip on her wrist warm and firm. Her diaphragm seized; she waited, breathless, trapped by his gaze.

Philip hesitated, then the ends of his lips lifted lightly. Glancing down, he reached into a pocket and drew out a white handkerchief. And proceeded to wipe each finger dry.

Her heart pounding, Antonia tried to speak. She had to clear her throat before she could. "Ah—did you wish to speak to me about something?"

Philip's smile deepened. She always asked. On principle, he never prepared an answer; inventing one on the spot kept him on his toes. "I wanted to ask if there was anything you needed for the *fête*. Do you have all you require?"

Antonia managed to nod. His stroking of her fingers, even with his touch muted by the fine lawn handkerchief, was sending skittering sensations up her arm. "Everything's under control," she eventually managed.

"Really?"

There was just enough amused scepticism in Philip's tone to make her stiffen. She lifted her fingers from his slackened grasp and met his gaze. "Indeed. Your staff have thrown themselves into the spirit of the thing—

and I must thank you for the services of your steward and bailiff. They've been most helpful."

"I hope they have." With a gesture, Philip invited her to walk beside him. "I'm sure the entertainments will be a credit to you all."

Haughtily, Antonia inclined her head and fell into step beside him. Slowly, they paced beside the narrow pool.

Philip glanced at her face. "What brings you here? You seem…pensive."

Antonia drew in a deep breath and held it. "I was thinking," she said, tossing back her curls, "of what it would be like when we're in London."

"London?"

"Hmm." Looking ahead, she airily explained, "As you know, I've not much experience of society. I understand poetry is much in vogue. I've heard it's common practice for *ton*nish gentlemen to use poetry, or at least, poetic phrases, to compliment ladies." She slanted an innocent look upwards. "Is that so?"

Philip's mind raced. "In some circles." He glanced down; Antonia's expression was open, enquiring. "In fact, in certain company it's de rigueur for the ladies to answer in similar vein."

"It is?" Antonia's surprise was unfeigned.

"Indeed." Smoothly, Philip captured her hand and placed it on his sleeve. "Perhaps, as you'll shortly be joining the throng, we ought to sharpen your rhymes?"

"Ah—" Her hand trapped beneath his warm palm, Antonia struggled to think. His suggestion was a considerable extrapolation of her plan.

"Here." Philip stopped by a wrought-iron seat placed to look over the pool. "Let's sit and try our wits."

Not at all certain just what she had started, Antonia subsided. Philip sat beside her, half turning, resting one arm along the back of the seat. "Now—where to start?" His gaze roamed her face. "Perhaps we should stick to mere phrases—considering your inexperience?"

Antonia shifted to face him. "That would undoubtedly be wise."

Only years of experience allowed Philip to keep the smile from his lips. "And perhaps I'd better start the ball rolling. How about—'Your hair shines like Caesar's gold, for which battalions gave their lives'?"

Wide-eyed, Antonia stared at him.

"Your turn," Philip prompted.

"Ah…" Antonia bludgeoned her wits then lifted her gaze to his hair. She dragged in a breath. "'Your hair glows like chestnuts, burnished by the sun'?"

"Bravo!" Philip smiled. "But that was purely a visual description—I think I win that round."

"It's a competition?"

Philip's eyes gleamed. "Let's consider it one. My turn. 'Your brow is white as a snow martin's breast, smooth as his flight through the sky.'"

On her mettle, Antonia narrowed her eyes, studying the wide sweep of his brow. Then she smiled. "'Your brow is as noble a Leo's ever was, your might not less than his.'"

Philip's smile deepened. "'Emerald your eyes, set in gold, precious jewels their value untold.'"

"'Grey clouds and steel, mists and fog, stormy seas and lightning, mix in the depths of your gaze.'"

Brows rising, Philip inclined his head. "I'd forgotten what a quick learner you are. But onward! Let's see…" Slowly, he raised his hand and gently, very gently, brushed her cheek with the back of one finger. "'Your cheeks glow soft, ivory silk over rose.'" His voice had deepened.

For a long instant, Antonia sat as one stunned, wide-eyed, barely breathing. The only thought in her head was that her stratagem was working. The effects of his touch slowly dissipated; her wits filtered back. She swallowed, then frowned and met his gaze. "It should have been my turn to lead. So—'Firm of chin and fair of face, your movements marked by languid grace.'"

Philip laughed. "Mercy! How can I hope to counter that?"

Antonia's smug glance turned superior.

Philip studied her face. "All right. But—" Glancing down, he saw her hands, lightly clasped in her lap. "Ah, yes." Shifting, he reached out and circled her wrist once more, gently tugging one hand free. Under his fingers, he felt her pulse leap.

She didn't resist as he lifted her hand, turning it as though examining her slim fingers. Fleetingly, he let his gaze meet hers. Then, still holding her captive, he trailed the fingers of his other hand against her sensitive palm.

The swift intake of her breath sounded sharp to Antonia's ears. Philip's eyes flicked up to hers; a smile unlike any she'd yet seen slowly curved his lips. His fingers shifted, so that his fingertips supported hers.

"'Delicate bones, sensitive skin, awaiting a lover's caress.'"

His voice was deep and low, the cadence striking chords deep within her. Antonia watched, trapped by his gaze, by his touch, as he slowly lifted her hand and, one by one, touched his lips to her fingertips.

The quivers that ran through her shook her to her core.

"Ah…" Desperation flayed her wits to action. "I've just remembered." Her voice was a hoarse whisper. She coughed and cleared her throat. "A message I promised to deliver for my aunt—I shouldn't have forgotten—I should go straight away." Retreat, disorderly or otherwise, seemed imperative yet, despite all, she couldn't bring herself to tug her hand free.

Philip's eyes held hers, steady, unyielding, an expression in the grey that she did not recognize. "A message?"

For one long moment, he studied her eyes, then the planes of his face relaxed. "About the *fête?*"

Numb, Antonia nodded.

Philip's lips quirked; ruthlessly, he stilled them. "One you have to deliver immediately?"

"Yes." Abruptly, Antonia stood; she felt immeasurably grateful when Philip, more languidly, rose too. He still hadn't let go of her hand. In an agony of near panic, she waited.

"Come—I'll escort you back."

With that, Philip tucked her hand into the crook of his elbow and turned her to the house. All but quivering, Antonia had perforce to acquiesce; to her relief, he strolled in companionable silence, making no reference by word or deed to their game by the pool.

He halted by the steps to the terrace and lifted her hand from his sleeve, holding it and her gaze for an instant before releasing her. "I'll see you at dinner." With a gentle smile and a nod, he strode away.

Antonia watched him go. Slowly, a warm flush of triumph permeated her being, driving out the skittering panic of moments before.

She had achieved her object. However, Philip now viewed her, it was not as a young friend of the family.

"GOOD NIGHT, THEN." With a nod and a smile, Geoffrey left the billiard-room to his host and Hugo, having unexpectedly taken revenge on Hugo for an earlier defeat.

"Quick learner," Hugo muttered in defense of his skills.

"Mannerings are," Philip replied, chalking a cue. The rest of the household had retired, Antonia somewhat breathlessly assuring him that she intended getting an early start on the preparations for the *fête*. A smile in his eyes, Philip waited while Hugo racked the balls, then he broke.

"Actually," Hugo said, as he watched Philip move about the table, "I've been trying to catch you for a quiet word all day."

"Oh?" Philip glanced up from his shot. "What about?"

Hugo waited until he had pocketed the ball before answering. "I've decided to return to town tomorrow."

Philip straightened, his question in his eyes.

Hugo grimaced and pulled at his ear. "This *fête*, y'know. All very well for you in the circumstances— you'll have Miss Mannering to hide behind. But who's to shield me?" Palms raised in appeal, Hugo shuddered. "All these earnest young misses—your stepmama's been listing their best features. Having succeeded with you, I rather think she's considering fixing her sights on me. Which definitely won't do."

Philip stilled. "Succeeded?"

"Well," Hugo said, "it was pretty obvious from the start. Particularly the way her ladyship always clung to yours truly. I was almost in danger of thinking myself a wit until the penny dropped. Perfectly understandable, of course—what with Miss Mannering being an old family friend and you being thirty-four and the last in line and so on."

Slowly, Philip leaned over the table and lined up his next shot. "Indeed."

"Mind," Hugo added. "If I couldn't *see* your reasoning—Miss Mannering being well in the way of being a peach—I wouldn't have thought you'd stand it—being hunted in your own house."

Sighting along his cue, Philip smelt again the teasing scent of lavender, heard the scrunch of gravel beneath slippered feet, saw again Antonia's airily innocent expression as she ingenuously led him along the garden path.

His shot went awry. Expression impassive, he straightened and stepped back.

Hugo studied the table. "Odd of you to miss that."

"Indeed." Philip's gaze was unfocused. "I was distracted."

CHAPTER FOUR

THE NEXT MORNING, Antonia awoke with the larks. By nine o'clock, she had already spoken with the cook and Mrs Hobbs, the housekeeper, and seen the head-gardener, old Mr Potts, about flowers for the morrow. She was turning away from a conference with Fenton on which of the indoor tables should be used on the terrace when Philip strode into the hall.

He saw Antonia and immediately changed course, his heels ringing on the black and white tiles. He halted directly before her.

"You didn't come riding."

Staring up into storm-clouded eyes, Antonia felt her own widen. "I did mention that there was a great deal to do."

His jaw firming, Philip cast a jaundiced eye over the figures scurrying about his hall. "Ah, yes." His quirt struck the white top of one boot. "The *fête*."

"Indeed. We're going to be terribly busy all day."

He swung back to Antonia, his gaze intent. "*All* day?"

Antonia lifted her chin. "All day," she reiterated. "And all tomorrow, too, until the festivities begin. And then we'll be even more busy."

Beneath his breath, Philip swore.

Antonia stiffened. Her expression aloof, she waved

to the dining-room. "I believe you'll find breakfast still available—if you hurry."

The look Philip cast her could only be called black. Without a word, he swung on his heel and headed for the dining-room.

A frown in her eyes, Antonia watched him go— then realized what seemed so strange. He was striding. Briskly.

"Excuse me, miss, but should I put this chair with those for the terrace?"

"Ah…" Antonia swung around to see a footman struggling with a wing-chair. "Oh, yes. The dowagers will need all of those that we can find. They'll want to doze in the sun."

As she laboured through the morning, Antonia kept her mind firmly fixed on her aim. The *fête* had to be a success—a complete, unqualified tour de force. It was a perfect opportunity to demonstrate to Philip that she was, at least at a county level, fully qualified to be his bride.

Summoning two maids, she led them to the Italian garden and pointed out the lavender. "You need to cut not just the flower but the stem as well—as long as you can. We'll need them to freshen the withdrawing-rooms."

Watching the maids as they set to work, Antonia found her gaze drawn to the seat at the end of the pool. The look in Philip's eyes as he'd kissed her fingers returned, crystal clear, to her mind. A smile tugged at her lips. Despite her panic, she had made definite progress there. Unbidden, the memory of his odd behaviour in the hall rose to taunt her. A frown chased the smile from her eyes.

"This right, miss?"

Jerked back to reality, Antonia examined the spike held up for her approval. "Perfect." The little maid glowed. "Be sure to collect two handfuls each—take them up to Mrs Hobbs as soon as you're done." Ruthlessly banishing Philip from her mind, Antonia stalked back to the house, determined more than ever to focus on the job at hand.

HE WOULD HAVE taken refuge in the library or the billiard-room but she had commandeered those as well. In a mood close to perilous, Philip abandoned his search for peace and quiet to wander through the throngs of his servitors, all furiously engaged in executing Antonia's commands.

He wondered if he should tell her her assertiveness was showing. He knew it of old—her tendency to take charge, to organise, to get things done. His lawns looked like chaos run mad, but even he could see, beneath the hectic bustle, that it was effective, organised activity. Pausing to watch two of his farm labourers struggle to erect a stall, he mused on Antonia's very real talent for getting people to work for her, often for no more direct reward than her smile and a brief word of approbation. Even now, he could see her at the far end of the lawn, where a narrow arm of the distant lake lipped a reed-fringed shore, exhorting the undergardeners to get all the punts cleaned and launched.

"Watch it there, Joe! Easy now, lad—just let me see if we've got this thing straight."

Refocusing on the action more immediately before him, Philip saw the younger of the two labourers trying to balance the front beam of the stall while simultaneously holding one of the side walls erect. The older man, a hammer and wooden strut in his hands, had backed, trying to gauge if the beam and wall were at the right angle. Joe, however, had no hope of keeping both pieces still.

Philip hesitated, then stepped forward and clapped the older man on the shoulder. "Give Joe a hand, McGill—I'll direct you."

McGill touched his cap. "If you would, m'lord, we'll get on a dashed sight faster."

Joe simply looked grateful.

Before they were done, Philip had his coat off and was helping to hammer in nails. That was how Antonia found him when she did her rounds, checking on progress.

She couldn't keep the surprise from her face.

Philip looked up—and read her expression. It didn't improve his mood. Nor did the instant urge he felt to call her to him—or go to her. Instead, he held her gaze, his own, he knew, dark and moody. Half of him wanted to speak to her, the other half wasn't at all sure it was a good idea—not yet. He hadn't yet decided how he felt about anything—about her, about what he inwardly labelled her machinations. Looking away, he grimly hammered in another nail. He hadn't felt this uncertain in years; pounding metal into wood was a comforting occupation.

Released from his mesmerising stare, Antonia couldn't resist a swift survey of his shoulders and back, muscles flexing beneath his fine shirt as he worked, his hands, long-fingered but strong, gripped about nail and handle. When she moved on, her mouth was dry, her heartbeat not entirely even. Oblivious of the activity about her, she reviewed their recent meetings. He was usually so even-tempered, too indolent to be moved to any excess of emotion—his aggravated mood was a mystery.

She glanced back—he had paused, shoulders propped against the side of the stall. He was watching her, his gaze brooding and intent.

"Miss—do you want the doilies put out now or tomorrow?"

"Ah…" Whirling, Antonia blinked at the young maid. "Tomorrow. Leave them in the morning-room until then."

The maid bobbed and scurried away. Drawing in a deep breath, Antonia followed more gracefully in her wake.

Philip watched her go, hips gently swaying as she climbed the slope, then pushed away from the wall and reached for another handful of nails.

An hour later, lunch was served—huge plates of sandwiches and mugs of ale laid out on the trestles already up and waiting. Exhorted by Antonia, no one stood on ceremony; as he helped himself to a sandwich stuffed full of ham, Philip noticed Geoffrey's fair head among the crowd. The boy waved and pushed through to him.

"Antonia's put me in charge of the Punch and Judy. Fenton's helping me—one of the footmen is going to do Punch but I think I'll have to do Judy. None of the maids will stop giggling long enough to say the lines."

Philip uttered a short laugh. Geoffrey's eyes were alight.

"We've got the booth up, but the stage is going to take some work."

Philip clapped him on the shoulder. "If you can keep the children out of the lake, I'll be forever in your debt."

Geoffrey grinned. "I might take you up on that once we get to London."

"Just as long as it's not my greys you're after."

Geoffrey laughed and shook his head. Still grinning, he moved away.

Sipping his ale, Philip saw his steward and bailiff, both ostensibly lending a hand. Normally, both men considered themselves above such activities; Philip wondered whether it was his presence that had changed their minds—or Antonia's confident imperiousness.

His eye ranging the throng, he saw one of the maids—Emma was the name that came to mind—artfully jog Joe's elbow. Joe was a likely lad, well grown and easy-mannered, barely twenty. As he watched Emma apologise profusely, smiling ingenuously up at Joe, Philip felt cynicism raise its mocking head. Joe smiled down at her, truly ingenuous. The little scene was played out in predictable vein; Philip moodily wondered if it might not be his duty to warn Joe that, despite the common assumption that man was the hunter, there were times when he might prove to be the prey.

As he himself had found.

He could see it now—now that Hugo had ripped the scales from his eyes. Henrietta's behaviour should have triggered his innate alarms—instead, as he'd admitted, he'd been distracted. Not by the usual flirtatious encouragements—they wouldn't have worked. But Antonia had not sought to attract him in the usual way—she'd used other wiles—more sophisticated wiles—wiles more likely to succeed with an experienced and recalcitrant gentleman rake who had seen it all before.

She'd used their old friendship.

With a grimace, Philip set aside his empty tankard and hefted the hammer he'd been using. He was still not sure how he felt—how he should feel. He had thought Antonia was different from the rest. Instead, she'd simply been using different tactics.

His expression still grim, he headed back to help McGill and Joe put up the rest of the refreshment stalls. They were banging the supports into place on the last of the stalls when a sound to his left had him turning his head. Antonia stood three feet away.

She met his gaze, then, with a slight smile, gestured to the tray she had placed on the counter of the next stall. "Ale—I thought it might be more acceptable than tea."

Philip glanced about and saw the womenfolk bearing trays and mugs to the men. Most of the small workforce had completed their tasks; the refreshment was welcomed by one and all.

Looking back, Philip met Antonia's calmly questioning gaze, then turned and, with one heavy blow, drove his last nail home. Laying the hammer aside, he called Joe's and McGill's attention to the ale. Antonia stepped back, hands clasped before her. Turning, Philip picked up a mug—and took the two strides necessary to trap her between the stall and himself.

Scanning his lawns, he took a long draught of ale. "Is there much more to do?"

Distracted from watching his lean throat work as he downed the ale, Antonia blinked and quickly looked about. "No—I think most of what we can do we've done." She reviewed her mental lists. "The only thing remaining is for the barrels to be brought out. We decided to leave them under tarpaulins for the night."

Still not looking at her, Philip nodded. "Good. That leaves us time to talk before dinner."

"Talk?" Antonia stared at him. "What about?"

Philip turned his head and met her gaze. "I'll tell you when we meet."

Antonia studied his eyes, what she could see of them before he looked away. "If it's about the *fête*—?"

"It's not."

The finality in his tone declared he was not about to explain. Inwardly, Antonia frowned; outwardly, she inclined her head gracefully. "In that case, I'll just—"

Her words were cut off by shouts and yells and a muffled rumbling. Antonia turned—as did everyone else—to see an ale barrel come rolling down the lawn.

"Stop it!" someone yelled.

"Heavens!" Antonia picked up her skirts and hurried forward.

For one stunned instant, Philip watched her rush towards the barrel. Then, with a comprehensive oath, he flung aside his tankard and went after her.

She slowed as she drew in line with the oncoming barrel, deaf to the cries of warning. Close on her heels, Philip wrapped one arm about her waist and swung her out of harm's way, pulling her hard against him.

"Wha—!"

Her strangled exclamation was music to his ears.

"Philip!" Antonia eventually got out, all in a breathless rush. "Put me *down!* The barrel—!"

"Weighs at least three times as much as you and would have flattened you into the ground." Philip heard it rumble past them.

His terse words came from directly behind Antonia's right ear. Horrified, she waggled her toes but couldn't touch the grass. He had scooped her up, holding her with her back against his chest, one large hand splayed across her middle, easily supporting her weight. He made no move to obey her injunction. She considered struggling—and blushed. The realisation of her predicament sent shock waves to merge with the odd heat spiralling through her.

Men had rushed from all around to slow the rolling barrel. Antonia watched as they brought it under control, then turned it and rolled it towards the stall which would serve the ale.

Only then did Philip consent to set her feet back on solid earth.

Antonia immediately drew in a deep breath. She drew in another before she turned around.

Philip got in first. "You would never have stopped it."

Antonia put her nose in the air. "I hadn't intended to try—I would merely have slowed it until the men reached it—then they could have managed it as they did."

Philip narrowed his eyes. "After it had rolled right over you."

Antonia eyed his set chin, then lifted her eyes to his. Her jaw slowly set. "In that case," she said, determinedly gracious although she spoke through clenched teeth. "I suspect I must thank you, my lord."

"Indeed. You can thank me by coming for a ride."

"A ride?"

Philip caught her hand. Lifting his head, he scanned the scene. "Everything's finished here, isn't it?"

Casting about for relief, Antonia found none. "Perhaps the Punch and Judy—"

"Geoffrey's got that in hand. I don't think it would be wise for you to undermine his authority."

Antonia's jaw dropped. "I *wouldn't*—" she began hotly.

"Good. Let's go." Philip started for the booth where he'd left his coat, towing her along, not caring who saw. His jaw set, he swiped up his coat but didn't stop, tugging Antonia up so he could trap her hand in the crook of his elbow.

Stunned, Antonia blinked free of the masculine web that held her. Her eyes narrowed. "I believe you've forgotten one point, my lord."

Philip glanced frowningly down at her. "What?"

Antonia smiled sweetly. "I can't ride in this dress."

She shut her ears against his muttered curse. He abruptly changed direction; in seconds, they were through the side door and into the hall.

Philip halted at the foot of the stairs. "You've got five minutes," he said, releasing her. "I'll wait here."

Antonia sent him a furiously disbelieving look. And watched his eyes slowly narrow.

With an exaggerated sniff, she tossed her head and headed up the stairs.

It took longer than five minutes to scramble into her habit but Philip was still waiting, pacing at the foot of the stairs, when she came down. He looked up, nodded, then waved her on.

Her chin defiantly high, Antonia sailed ahead.

The grooms had their horses ready; Philip must have sent word. He gripped her waist and tossed her up, then swung up to his chestnut's back. He wheeled; Antonia fell in beside him. As usual, they rode before the wind, streaking across his fields.

Philip had decided where to stage their talk. Somewhere they would be assured of being private. Hardly in line with accepted precepts, but he was beyond such considerations. He led her deep into the Manor woods to a cool glade where a stream widened into a pool.

He swung down and tethered Pegasus to a low-hanging branch. A jay shrilled. Sunshine dappled the grass, growing thick and lush by the water's edge. Enclosed by old oaks, the glade was still and silent—entirely theirs.

Antonia frowned as Philip lifted her down; the catch in her breath, the need to still her heart, no longer even registered. Her hand in his, he strode away from the horses, towards the pool. He was moving far too fast for her liking.

"What is it?" she asked, hurrying to keep up with his long strides. She glanced up at his face. "Is something amiss?"

Abruptly, Philip halted. Jaw clenched, he swung to face her. "As to that, I'm not sure."

His eyes, Antonia saw, were patterns of roiling grey. Throughout the day, his abrupt movements, his clipped accents, had undermined her confidence—now he was talking in riddles. Taking advantage of his slackened grasp, she pulled her hand from his. Standing her ground, she lifted her chin. "There's something bothering you—that much is plain."

"There is indeed," he replied, his hands rising to his hips, his eyes boring into hers.

When she simply continued to stare at him, waiting, open challenge in her gaze, Philip muttered a curse.

Tense as a bowstring, he glanced away, then abruptly turned back. Capturing her gaze, he caught her hand; he lifted it, deftly turned it and placed a kiss on her wrist, on the pulse point exposed by her glove.

And felt her reaction, the quick shiver she tried to suppress, stiffening against it. Her eyes widened but not with amazement. The rise and fall of the lace ruffle at her breast increased.

Philip's eyes narrowed. "Tell me, Antonia. Am I seducing you—or are you seducing me?"

For an instant, Antonia was sure the world had spun. She blinked. "Seducing…?" Stunned, she stared at him.

"Seducing." Ruthlessly, Philip held her gaze. "As in capitalising on the age-old attraction that sometimes flares between a man and a woman."

Antonia strangled the impulse to repeat the word attraction—she could hardly deny its existence. She could feel it shimmering between them. Dazed, she blinked again. What was he suggesting? "I…?"

"Don't know what I'm talking about?" Philip supplied, catching her chin in one hand.

The cynicism in his tone stung. Antonia's eyes flashed. "I wouldn't know how to *begin* seducing you!"

"Know?" Philip pretended to consider the point while the tension that had held him all day wound tight. "I don't suppose you would actually need to know how—you could do it by instinct alone." Looking down at her, at her wide green-gold eyes, her softly curved lips, he felt the tumult inside him swell. The urge to surrender to it waxed strong—he who never permitted himself to be driven, compelled, coerced, frustrated, aggravated or obsessed.

"Whatever," he said, his voice deepening, darkening. "You've succeeded." If he took what was offered, would he know peace again? On the thought, he bent his head and set his lips to hers.

And felt, as he had known he would, her instantaneous response. It rose to his touch, to his caress, easily overriding her equally instinctive stiffening. Her unfettered reaction was balm to his bruised ego—at least she was, at this level, as helpless as he. Her lips softened; at his subtle urging, hesitant, beguiling, they parted under his.

Antonia felt the whirlpool rise and snatch her up, so strong she could only ride its tide. Her wits scattered, her senses stretched, heightened by excitement, eager, clamouring for experience. She felt his arms slide around her; as her limbs softened, they tightened and locked, crushing her to him.

Wanting more of his caress, she tilted her head and felt his lips firm. Driven, she pressed closer. The magic of his kiss had her firmly in thrall; tentatively, she returned it, revelling in the shocking intimacy, marvelling at the sensations crowding her mind. The seductive hardness of the muscles surrounding her, the tempting heat of his large body—all were new discoveries; the slow crescendo building within her, the swelling tempo of her heart, were fascinating, novel perceptions.

His strength surrounded her, his kiss intoxicated her. The feel of him, the taste of him, overwhelmed and excited her. Dragging her hands from where they had been trapped against his chest, she wound them about his neck, returning his kiss with an ardent fervour she hadn't known she possessed.

Philip groaned and crushed her even more tightly to him, her breasts firm and swollen against his chest.

He let one hand roam over her hips, urging her against him, moulding her to him.

The whirlpool had caught him, too.

He was too experienced to let it pull them down. Nevertheless, dragging them both free of its turbulent power took all the strength he possessed. When he finally managed to raise his head, soothing her hungry lips with a gentle brush of his, they were both breathing raggedly.

Tense, his muscles locked tight, he waited for common sense to return and save them. Very slowly, Antonia's lids rose. Mesmerised, he watched as her eyes were revealed, the gold flecks blazing, the green more deeply jewel-like than he had ever seen. Then darkness swam in, dulling the brilliance. Her breath caught; she caught her lower lip between her teeth, her eyes widening with what could only be alarm.

She stiffened in his arms.

Philip felt the panic grip her. "Don't," he said in the instant before she started struggling.

To his relief, she stilled, a frightened bird locked in the cage of his arms, tense and quivering.

Holding her gaze, Philip dragged in a deep breath, his chest swelling, making him unwillingly aware of the softness pressed against it—and took a firm grip on the reins. "I'm not about to ravish you."

She was an innocent; he had frightened her.

The expression in her wide, shadowed eyes was not one he could read but he thought he detected a hint of scepticism. Exasperation drove him to say, "Oh, I'm thinking about it." Pressed to him as she was from shoulders to knees, she could hardly miss the evidence of his desire. "But I'm not about to do it—all right?"

His jaw ached, as did the rest of him; experience was not enough to hide his frustration. He concentrated on keeping still—he had no intention of moving until the dangerous moment had passed, until the compulsion driving them both had faded.

Antonia had no breath with which to answer. Her heart was still thudding in her ears. For a long moment, she simply held his gaze, wondering dazedly how much he could see. Had he noticed how unrestrained her ardour had been—how wantonly she had kissed him? Was the aching need still pulsing within her visible in her eyes?

She could only pray it wasn't.

Stunned, staggered, shocked beyond measure, she felt heat rise to her cheeks. When he raised one brow, she recalled his question and forced herself to nod. Then blushed even more.

"We've got to go back." Once more in control, Philip forced his arms from her and caught her hand.

"Back?" Before she could say more, Antonia found herself towed unceremoniously back to her horse. Recollections returning, her mind was awhirl. "But—"

With a muted snarl, Philip rounded on her, trapping her with her back against her horse. He towered over her, muscles locked, jaw clenched, his eyes a steely-grey. "Antonia—do you *want* to be ravished here and now?"

She actively considered the question—then caught herself and blushed furiously. She felt like sinking. The effort it took to make herself shake her head was even more damning.

"Then we go back," Philip said through clenched teeth. "Immediately." He grasped her waist and tossed her up to her saddle, then pulled her reins free and threw them up to her. In seconds, he had Pegasus free and was mounting.

Without further words, he led the way back to the Manor.

As the miles sped past, Antonia's memory cleared; by the time they reached the Manor, her cheeks were flushed, her eyes glittering.

They pulled up in the stableyard, but no one came running. Philip glanced about, then remembered he had given the stablehands permission to visit the local inn in compensation for their sterling efforts in organising another of Antonia's entertainments—pony rides for the younger children, with a series of low jumps in the nearest paddock for the older children to attempt. Smothering an oath, he dismounted. "We'll have to take care of the horses ourselves."

Her lips compressed, Antonia kicked free of her stirrups, slid down from her perch—and rounded on him.

"After accusing me of attempting to seduce you, you *expect* me to—?" Words failed her; her eyes blazed. With a smothered scream, she flung her reins at his head, swung on her heel and marched out of the yard.

CHAPTER FIVE

SEDUCING HIM? As if that was possible.

Smothering a snort, Antonia dragged her brush through her thick wavy hair. Sunshine streamed in through her bedchamber window; the morning breeze came with it, bringing the crisp tang of grass and dew-washed greenery. The day of the *fête* had dawned bright and clear; unable to sleep, she had risen and donned her sprig muslin, then sat down to tend her curls.

And consider how best to deal with her host.

She might have tried to make him notice her, she might have tried to make him see her as a potential wife. But to accuse her of *seducing* him?

"Hah!" Frowning direfully at the mirror, she gritted her teeth and ruthlessly dealt with a tangle. She was *not* such a scheming female!

The very notion that a lady such as she, of severely restricted experience, *could* seduce a gentleman of his vast and, she had no doubt, *varied background,* was ludicrous. None of the seducing that had been done to date could be laid at *her* door.

She knew very well who had been seducing whom.

Those moments in the woods had opened her eyes; until then she had been too distracted by her reactions, too caught up with suppressing them, to focus on what drew them forth. Now she knew.

The Lord only knew what she was going to do about it.

The hand holding her brush stilled; Antonia studied the face that looked back at her from her mirror, the trim figure displayed therein. It had never occurred to her that Philip, with all the accommodating ladies of the *ton* from whom to choose, would fix any real part of his interest on her.

She had thought to be his wife but had envisaged he would feel nothing beyond mere affection for her—that and the lingering warmth of long-standing friendship. That was what she had expected, what she had steeled herself to accept—the position of a conventional wife.

His actions in the woods suggested she had miscalculated.

He wanted her—*desired* her. A delicious thrill ran through her. For an instant, she savoured it, then, frowning again, resumed her brushing. A serious problem had surfaced with his ardour—namely, hers. Or, more specifically, how, given a gentleman's expectations of his wife, she was supposed to keep her feelings hidden or, at the very least, acceptably disguised.

The door opened; Nell walked in, stopping in amazement at the sight of her.

"Great heavens! And here I'd thought to wake you."

Antonia brushed more vigorously. "There's still a lot to do—I don't wish to be rushed at the last."

Nell snorted and came to take the brush. "Seemingly you're not the only one. I just saw his lordship downstairs. Thought he must be going riding, but then I noticed he wasn't in top boots. Very natty, he looked, I must say."

"Indeed." Clasping her hands in her lap, Antonia infused the word with the utmost disinterest. Philip had tried to speak with her last night, first in the drawing-room before dinner, when Geoffrey's enthusiasm had saved her, then later, when she was pouring the tea. She had affected deafness to his low-voiced "Antonia?" and handed him a brimming cup.

She was not about to forgive him, to let him close again, not until the panicky feelings inside subsided, not until she was again confident of carrying off their interaction with the assurance expected of a prospective wife.

"Dare say you'll have your hands full today, acting as hostess in her ladyship's stead." Nell deftly wound the golden mass of Antonia's hair into a tight bun, teasing tendrils free to wreathe about her ears and nape. "She told Trant she intends going no further than the terrace."

Antonia shifted on the stool. "She's getting too old to stand up to the crowds—I'm only glad I can help her in this way."

"Aye—and his lordship, too. Can't think that he'd appreciate having to face it all by himself."

Antonia glanced searchingly at Nell but there was no evidence of intent in her maid's homely features. "Naturally I'll be on hand to aid his lordship in any way I can."

A role she could hardly escape, having worked so diligently to earn it. Being at odds with Philip on today of all days was going to be simply impossible. They would have to make their peace before the guests arrived.

As soon as Nell pronounced her fit to face the day, Antonia headed downstairs. As she descended the last flight, her nemesis strolled into the hall. Looking up, he stopped at the foot of the stairs—and waited. Antonia paused, meeting his gaze. In the hall above, a door opened then slowly closed. Drawing in a steadying breath, Antonia continued her descent, her expression determinedly aloof.

Philip turned to face her, effectively blocking her way. As Nell had intimated, he was precise to a pin in a grey morning coat, his cravat tied in a simple but elegant knot. A subdued waistcoat, form-fitting breeches and glossy Hessians completed the outfit—perfect for a wealthy gentleman about to greet his neighbours. His movements, Antonia noted, were once again lazy; his habitual air of languid indolence hung like a cloak about him. She stopped on the last step, her eyes level with his. "Good morning, my lord." She kept her tone coolly polite.

Only his eyes, his grey gaze sharply intent as it met hers, gave evidence of yesterday's turmoil.

"Good morning, Antonia." Holding her gaze, Philip raised a brow. "Pax?"

Antonia narrowed her eyes. "You accused me of seducing you."

"A momentary aberration." Philip kept his eyes on hers. "I know you didn't." He had managed that all by himself.

She was, after all, an innocent; regardless of any scheme she and Henrietta had concocted, what had flared between them was more his doing than hers.

Antonia hesitated, studying his bland countenance.

Despite his determination to remain distant, Philip felt his lips twist. He reached for her hand. "Antonia—"

The sound of a heavy footstep had them both looking up.

"Henrietta." Lips tightening, Philip caught Antonia's

gaze. "I need you as my hostess, Antonia." His fingers tightened about hers. "I want you by my side."

It took a moment for Antonia to subdue her response to his touch, his plea. Stiffly, she inclined her head; behind her, she could hear Henrietta on the landing. "You may count on me, my lord." She kept her voice low. "I won't let you down."

Philip held her gaze. "And *I* won't let *you* down." For an instant, he held still, then, eyes glinting, swiftly raised her fingers to his lips. "I'll even promise not to bite."

As THE DAY PROGRESSED, Antonia found herself grateful for the reassurance. Henrietta had elected to greet her visitors at the bottom of the terrace steps; Fenton was stationed at the front of the house, directing all arrivals around the corner to the south lawn.

After settling Henrietta by the balustrade, Antonia, her eye on Mrs Mimms, approaching like a galleon under full sail, two anaemic daughters in tow, murmured, "I'll just go the rounds and check—"

"Nonsense, my dear." Closing her crabbed fingers about Antonia's wrist, Henrietta smiled up at her. "Your place is beside me."

Antonia frowned. "There's no need—"

"What say you, Ruthven?" Henrietta glanced at Philip, standing behind her, his gaze fixed on Mrs Mimms. "Don't you think Antonia should stand by us?"

"Indubitably," Philip stated. He shifted his gaze to Antonia, subtle challenge in his eyes. "How else, my dear, will we cope with Mrs Mimms—let alone the rest of them?"

She had, of course, to acquiesce; the result was predictable. Introduced by a beaming Henrietta as "My very dear niece—dare say you remember her—spent many summers here with us all. Don't know how we could have managed this without her," she found herself transfixed by Mrs Mimms' basilisk stare.

"Indeed? Helping out?" Mrs Mimms cast a knowledgeable eye over the tables and booths scattered over the lawns and terrace. Her lips thinned as her gaze fell on Philip, already greeting the next guests. "I see."

Those two bare words effectively summarized Mrs Mimms's reading of the situation. Determined not to let it, or anything else, rattle her, Antonia smiled serenely. "I do hope you enjoy yourself." With a gentle nod, she allowed her gaze to shift to Horatia and Honoria Mimms, both of whom had yet to drag their attention from Philip. Their protuberant eyes were fixed on his face in cloying adoration. "And your daughters, too, of course."

Mrs Mimms glanced sharply at her offspring. "Come along, girls!" She frowned intimidatingly. "Stop dilly-dallying!" With a swirl of her skirts, she led the way up the terrace steps.

Mrs Mimms was not alone among the local ladies in having seen in the Manor's invitation a chance to press their daughters' claims. That much was made clear as the guests flooded in. Antonia found herself the object of quite a few disconcerted stares. Many recalled her from her earlier visits; while most greeted her warmly, the matrons with unmarried daughters in tow were distinctly more reserved.

Lady Archibald was characteristically forthright in her surprise. "Damnation! Thought you'd disappeared. Or at least were safely wed!"

Antonia struggled to hide her grin. It was impossible to take offence; her ladyship, while hardly the soul of tact, possessed an indefatigably kind heart. She watched as her ladyship, frowning, looked down on the mousy young lady hugging her shadow, her gaze, like all the other young ladies' gazes, seemed to be fixed on Philip. Lady Archibald humphed. "Come along, Emily. No point in making sheep's eyes in *that* direction."

Antonia made a point of shaking hands with Emily to soften that trenchant remark. But the girl appeared not to have heeded it, continuing to cast shy but glowing glances at Philip.

After directing her ladyship and Emily to the terrace, Antonia turned to greet the next guest, in doing so, she met Philip's eye.

She had never before seen such an expression of aggravated exasperation on his face. It was a fight to keep her lips in the prescribed gentle smile; her jaw ached for a full five minutes. Thereafter, she studiously avoided his gaze whenever smitten young ladies stood before them.

The novelty of the event had ensured a large turnout. All their neighbours had accepted, rolling up the drive in chaises and carriages, many open so the occupants could bask in the bright sunshine. Philip's tenants came in carts or on foot, lifting their caps or dropping shy curtsies as they passed the reception line on their way to join the congregation on the lawn.

Amongst the last to arrive was the party from the Grange, some miles beyond the village. Sir Miles and Lady Castleton were new to the district since Antonia's last visit; she studied them as they approached, her ladyship strolling in the lead, an aloof expression on her lovely face, a slim, dark-haired young lady in her wake.

"My dear Ruthven!" With a dramatic gesture, Lady Castleton presented her hand. A statuesque brunette, fashionably pale, she was elegantly gowned in figured muslin, her face set in lines of studied boredom. "What a novel—quite *exhausting*—idea!" A cloud of heady perfume engulfed the reception party. Her ladyship's gaze shifted to Henrietta. "I don't know how you could bear to handle all this, my dear. You must be positively prostrated. So naughty of Ruthven to expect it of you."

"Nonsense, Selina!" Henrietta frowned and straightened her shoulders. "If you must know, having a major gathering was *my* idea—Ruthven was merely good enough to humour me."

"Indeed," Philip drawled, releasing her ladyship's hand after the most perfunctory shake. He turned to Sir Miles. "I can confirm that it was not my will that gave rise to today's entertainment."

Sir Miles, bluffly genial, was a stark contrast to his wife. Chuckling, he pumped Philip's hand. "No need to tell me that! Not a man here doesn't know what it's like."

"As you say." Philip's smile remained easy as he nodded to the girl who stood between Sir Miles and his wife. "Miss Castleton."

"Good afternoon, my lord." Boldly, Miss Castleton presented her hand with the same dramatic flair as her mother. She accompanied it with an openly inviting, distinctly brazen look. Not as tall as Antonia, she was possessed of a full figure, more revealed than concealed by her fine muslin gown.

Philip glanced at her hand as if mildly surprised to find it hanging before him. He clasped it but fleetingly, his gaze, blank, shifting to Lady Castleton, then Antonia as he half turned.

"Haven't introduced you to my niece." Henrietta gestured to Antonia, adroitly deflecting attention from Miss Castleton, who promptly pouted. "Miss Mannering."

With a calm smile, Antonia held out her hand.

Lady Castleton's sharp, black-eyed gaze travelled over her; an arrested expression flitted over her pale face. "Ah," she said, smiling but not with her eyes. Briefly touching Antonia's fingers, she looked down at Henrietta. "It's reassuring to see that you've found someone to act as companion at last."

"Companion?" Henrietta blinked; Antonia noted her aunt's straight back but could not fault her guileless expression as she exclaimed, "Oh—I keep forgetting you're *newcomers!*" Henrietta smiled, all confiding condescension. "No, no—Antonia's often visited here. Been her second home for years. Now her mama's passed on, she's naturally come to stay with me." Turning, Henrietta squeezed Antonia's arm. "But you're right in part—it's a great relief to have someone capable of organising all this sort of thing—exhausting at my age but, as you must know, *quite* one's duty."

Antonia took her cue, smiling fondly at Henrietta. "Indeed, but I assure you, aunt, I haven't found it exhausting at all." Glancing up, still smiling, she met Lady Castleton's hard gaze. "I'm quite used to organising such affairs—all part of a young lady's education, as my mama was wont to say."

Lady Castleton's eyes narrowed. "Indeed?"

"Be that as it may," Philip said, deftly coming between Antonia and Henrietta, "I believe it's time we adjourned to the terrace." Capturing Antonia's hand, he tucked it into one elbow, then held his other arm rigid as Henrietta leaned heavily upon it. "Sir Miles?"

"Indeed, m'lord." Before Lady Castleton could reclaim the initiative, Sir Miles drew her arm through his, then offered his other arm to his daughter. "Couldn't agree more. Let's go, what?"

Without a backward glance, Sir Miles ushered his ladies up the steps.

Philip waited until they were out of earshot, then glanced pointedly down at the ladies on his arms. "Might I suggest, my dears, that we get this exhausting, exceedingly well-organised event underway?"

They saw Henrietta settled in her seat at one end of the long table, then Philip escorted Antonia to her chosen position halfway down the board. "I never thought to say it, but thank heaven for Ladies Archibald and Hammond."

As she sat, Antonia glanced at the head of the table where the two ladies in question, imposing matrons both, flanked Philip's empty chair. Settling her skirts, she cast a questioning glance up at him.

Philip bent close. "They take precedence over Lady Castleton." With a glint of a smile and a lifted brow, he straightened and moved away.

Antonia disguised her grin as a cheery smile; she hunted for Lady Castleton and found her seated on the opposite side, some places away, her exquisite features marred by an expression of disaffected boredom. Her ladyship's disdain, however, was not evinced by others; as the food, laboured over by Mrs Hobbs, Cook and a small battalion of helpers, appeared on the crisp damask cloth, genial conversation rose on all sides. As

Fenton and his minions filled goblets and glasses, the festive atmosphere grew.

Philip proposed a toast to the company, then bade them enjoy the day. When he sat, the feast began.

From the corner of her eye, Antonia kept watch over the steady stream of maids carrying platters to the lower tables. To her mind, Philip's tenants were, in this instance, as important if not more so than his neighbours. Neighbours would be invited on other occasions; this was one of the few when tenants partook of their landlord's largesse. Trestles groaned as trays loaded with mouth-watering pastries, succulent savouries and roasted meats, together with breads, cheeses and pitchers of ale, were placed upon them. The company seemed in fine fettle; she could detect nothing but unfettered gaiety around the tables on the lawn.

She had wondered whether the noise from the lower tables would prove overwhelming. As she returned her attention to the conversations about her, she dismissed the thought; those on the terrace were more than capable of holding their own.

The long meal passed without incident, bar an altercation which arose at the table set aside for the tenants' children, which their fathers promptly quashed. When the fruit platters were all but empty, the boards were drawn; the dowagers and others ill-inclined to the games, contests and feats of skill slated to fill the afternoon, settled in their chairs on the terrace to enjoy a comfortable cose and possibly a nap in the warm sunshine.

The more robust of the guests adjourned to the lawns.

Straightening from having a last word with Henrietta, Antonia found Philip by her side.

When she looked her surprise, he raised a brow. "You didn't seriously imagine I'd brave the dangers of the lawns without you to protect me?"

"Protect…?" Antonia temporarily lost her track when he drew her close, trapping her hand in the crook of his elbow. He was very large—and very hard. She was not yet accustomed to his nearness. "What am I supposed to protect you against?" She managed what she felt was a creditably sceptical look.

Her nemesis merely smiled. "Piranhas."

"Piranhas?" Antonia cudgelled her brains as, with an elegant nod for the dowagers, Philip led her down the steps. "I thought they were fish," she said once they gained the lawns.

"Precisely. Social but carnivorous and definitely cold-blooded."

"On your lawns?"

"Indeed. Here comes a young one, now."

Antonia looked up to see Miss Castleton bearing down upon them, arm linked with Honoria Mimms.

"Ah—Miss Mannering, is it not?" Miss Castleton came to a halt directly before them. "Poor Honoria seems to have ripped her flounce."

Looking thoroughly puzzled, Honoria was twisting about, trying to see her trailing flounce. "I don't know how it happened," she said. "I felt it rip but when I turned around there was nothing for it to catch on. Luckily, Calliope was standing close by and told me how bad it was."

"Perhaps, if you would be so good, Miss Mannering," Calliope Castleton glibly broke in, "you might take poor Honoria up to the house and help her to pin up her lace?"

Honoria blushed beet-red. "Oh, I *couldn't*—! I mean, you have all your other guests…"

"Exactly," Philip calmly interjected. "As you've been such a good friend to Miss Mimms, Miss Castleton, I know you won't mind helping her to the terrace and asking one of the maids for assistance." He bestowed a smile of calculated charm on Honoria Mimms. "I'm afraid, my dear, that I have great need of Miss Mannering's talents at present."

Miss Mimms was dazzled. "*Naturally,* my lord." Her eyes were wide and shining. "I wouldn't *dream* of…of *discommoding* you."

"Thank you, my dear." Philip took her hand and bowed over it, his grateful smile enough to turn any young girl's head. "I am in your debt."

Honoria Mimms looked as if she would burst. Her round face alight, she grabbed Miss Castleton's arm. "Come on, Calliope—I'm sure we can take care of this ourselves."

Beaming, Miss Mimms towed Miss Castleton towards the terrace. The sound of Miss Castleton's protests died behind them.

Antonia opened her eyes wide. "Miss Castleton didn't seem all that taken with your suggestion, my lord."

"I dare say. Miss Castleton, as you will have noticed, is somewhat enamoured of her own path."

Antonia's eyes lit; her lips quirked.

Philip noticed. "Now what is there in that to make you laugh?" Mentally replaying the conversation, he could see nothing to account for the laughter he sensed welling within her. He lifted one brow interrogatively. "Well?"

Antonia's smile broke. "I was considering, my lord," she said, shifting her gaze to the crowds before them, "whether your last comment might not be an example of the pot calling the kettle black?"

She glanced up at him; he trapped her gaze, both brows rising. For a long moment, he held her mesmerised; Antonia felt a shiver start deep inside, spreading through her until it quivered just beneath her skin.

Only when awareness blossomed in her eyes did Philip glance away. "You, my dear, are hardly one to talk." After a moment, he added, his tone less dark, "I suspect that we should mingle. When are the archery contests scheduled to start?"

The hours passed swiftly, filled with conversations. They strolled the lawns, stopping every few feet to chat with their guests. Antonia was of the firm opinion that Philip should spend at least five minutes with each of his tenants; it transpired he was of similar mind; she was not called on to steer him their way. A fact for which she gave due thanks.

Her control of the *fête* and its associated events might be absolute; it did not extend to him.

To her surprise, he held by her side, even waiting patiently while she exchanged recipes with one of his farmers' wives. Despite the years, the majority of his tenants were still known to her; they were keen to renew their acquaintance as well as catch up with their landlord. After every encounter, Philip drew her close before moving on.

Exactly as if she did indeed provide the protection he claimed.

While most of the mamas had read the signs aright and consequently made no effort to put their darlings in his way, their darlings proved less perceptive. Miss Abercrombie and Miss Harris, greatly daring, accosted them as they strolled.

"Such a frightfully warm day, don't you think, my lord?" Miss Abercrombie's gaze was certainly sultry. She fanned herself with her hand, the action drawing attention to the ample charms revealed by her deeply scooped neckline.

"Quite positively *enervating,* I think." Miss Harris, not to be outdone, fluttered her lashes and cast Philip a languishing look.

Antonia felt him stiffen; his expression was shuttered, remote.

"Before you find yourselves prostrated, ladies, might I suggest you repair to the drawing-room?" Philip's tone alone lowered the temperature ten degrees. "I believe there are cold drinks laid out there." With a distant nod, he changed tack, steering Antonia away from the budding courtesans.

After one glance at the rigid set of his lips, Antonia amused herself looking over the stalls. She could have told all the young misses that gushing declarations and fluttering lashes were definitely the wrong way to approach their host. He disliked all show of emotion, preferring the correct, properly restrained modes of interaction. He was a conventional man—she strongly suspected most gentlemen were.

They paused to allow Philip to discuss crop rotation with one of his tenant farmers. Covertly studying him, Antonia smiled wryly. His languid indolence was very much to the fore, at least in his projected image.

The girls watching could not hear his brisk words on ploughing and the optimum depth of furrows. As handsome as any, with that subtle aura of restrained power which derived, she suspected, from that affected indolence, while strolling the lawns with smoothly elegant stride, every movement polished and assured, he was a natural target for the sighing, die-away looks of the massed host of young girls.

Quelling an unhelpful shiver, Antonia looked around. Horatia Mimms and two of the girls from the vicarage stood in a knot nearby, giggling and whispering. Feeling immeasurably older, she let her gaze pass over them.

Concluding his discussion, Philip placed his hand over hers and turned towards the archery butts. "Looks like the contests are well underway." He glanced down at her. "I'm not at all sure you shouldn't be the one to present the ribbon to the winner."

Antonia shook her head. "*You* are their master—to the youngsters you're an idol. Of course they want you to award the prize."

She shifted as she spoke, swinging slightly forward to glance into his eyes. Unfortunately, that placed her in Horatia Mimms's path. In a balletic manoeuvre, Horatia flew forward, her trajectory calculated to land her, gracefully tripping, in Philip's arms. Instead, she cannoned into Antonia's back.

With a stifled cry, Antonia catapulted forward, coming up hard against Philip's chest. His arms closed around her, steel bands crushing her to him as he lifted her free of the wild tangle that was Horatia, now sprawled on the grass.

"Are you all right?" Easing his hold, Philip looked down at her.

Antonia nodded, struggling to find her voice. "Just

a bump—" She couldn't help a wince as she tried to pull back.

Philip steadied her, his hands firming on her back, gently kneading. His gaze shifted to the scene before them, where a winded Horatia was being helped to her feet by her two supporters from the vicarage.

Philip's eyes blazed. "That was the most *inconsiderate* piece of witless behaviour it has ever been my misfortune to witness!"

Helpless in his arms, unable to stop her senses luxuriating in the feel of his warm hands massaging her back, her forehead resting, for one weak moment, against his chest, Antonia stifled a hysterical giggle. From his tone, from the tension holding him, she knew his temper was on a very short leash. Luckily, they were halfway between the stalls and the crowds watching the archery; there were few witnesses to the scene.

"I cannot believe your parents—" Philip's gaze coldly swept all three girls "—will find your antics at all acceptable." His icy words cut like a lash. "I intend to make plain to them—"

Antonia pushed hard against his chest, forcing him to loosen his hold. As she struggled free of his arms, she wasn't at all surprised to glimpse three white faces, stricken with alarm. "I'm perfectly all right." One glance at Philip was enough to confirm he wasn't mollified by her assurance. His face remained stony, his expression chilling. Antonia felt like grimacing at him; she contented herself with narrowing her eyes warningly before facing the girls. "Miss Mimms—I hope you sustained no injury?"

White as a sheet, Horatia Mimms blinked, then dazedly looked down. A long grass stain marred the pink of her muslin skirts. "My best dress!" she moaned. "It's ruined!"

Philip snorted. "You may consider yourself—"

Antonia stepped back—onto his foot. Philip broke off and frowned down at her.

"Perhaps, Miss Carmichael, Miss Jayne, you could accompany Miss Mimms into the house and see if the stain will shift?"

The vicar's daughters nodded, quickly taking Horatia's arms. But Horatia unexpectedly stood her ground, her cheeks slowly turning an unfortunate shade of red. She looked helplessly at Antonia. "I'm most extremely sorry, Miss Mannering. I didn't mean to—" She broke off and bit her lip, her gaze dropping to the ground.

Antonia took pity on her. "An unfortunate occurrence—we'll say no more about it."

The relief that flooded all three faces was almost comical. With quick bobs, the three took themselves off, moving out of Philip's orbit as fast as they could.

"An unfortunate occurrence, my foot!" Philip glowered after them. "The little wretches—"

"Were only behaving as young girls often do." Antonia slanted him a glance. "Particularly when presented with such provocation as is present here today."

Philip's eyes narrowed. "I do not appreciate being the butt of their silly fancies."

Antonia smiled. "Never mind." She patted his arm soothingly. "Come and present the archery prizes—from the whoops, I think the contests must be over."

Philip sent her a darkling glance but allowed her to steer him to the area by the lake where the archery contest had been held.

He might not appreciate the adoration of young girls,

but he clearly had no difficulty coping with the same emotion in youthful cubs. Antonia watched as they danced about him while he gave an impromptu speech congratulating the winners of the three competitions. With the prizes awarded, he returned to her side.

They adjourned to the terrace for tea. Despite numerous invitations to do otherwise, Philip held trenchantly to her side. Then it was time to cross to where the junior equestrians had been kept busy for most of the afternoon.

They regained the lawns, only to discover Lady Castleton in their path. Her daughter walked beside her on the arm of Mr Gerald Moresby, a younger son of Moresby Hall.

"There you are, Ruthven." Lady Castleton placed one manicured hand firmly on Philip's sleeve. "You've been positively hiding yourself away amongst the farmers, sir—quite ignoring those who would, one might imagine, have far greater claim to your attention."

One glance convinced Antonia that her ladyship saw nothing outrageous in her statement. Philip, she noticed, looked bored.

Oblivious, Lady Castleton rolled on. "So you've driven us to make our wishes plain, my lord. Calliope has conceived a great wish to view your rose garden but unfortunately Gerald cannot abide the flowers—they make him sneeze."

"Quite right." Gerald Moresby grinned. "Can't abide the smell, y'know."

"So," Lady Castleton concluded, "as Miss Mannering is apparently acting as hostess in her aunt's stead, I suggest she takes Mr Moresby on an amble about the lake while you, my lord, can lend me your arm and escort myself and Calliope through your rose garden."

Gerald rubbed his hands together, his gaze on Antonia. "Capital idea, what?"

Antonia did not think so. Eight years ago, Gerald had been a most untrustworthy character. Judging by the expression in his pale blue eyes and the way his weak mouth shifted, he had not improved with the years.

Sensing sudden tension beside her, she glanced up to find Philip's gaze fixed on Gerald's face, his lips curved in a smile that was not entirely pleasant.

"I'm afraid, dear lady," Philip smoothly said, shifting his gaze from Gerald Moresby's lecherous countenance, thereby denying a sudden urge to rearrange it, "that as Miss Mannering and I are sharing the honours in entertaining my tenants, our time is not our own. I'm sure you understand the situation," he sauvely continued, "being yourself the chatelaine of an estate."

He was well aware of Lady Castleton's background; it did not encompass any great experience of "lady of the manor" duties.

Which was why, stumped by his comment, unable to contradict it, her ladyship resorted to a cold-eyed stare.

"I knew you'd understand." Philip inclined his head, his hand trapping Antonia's where it rested on his sleeve. "But I'm afraid you'll have to excuse us— the junior equestrians await." He included Lady Castleton and her daughter in his benedictory smile; it didn't stretch as far as Gerald Moresby.

As they passed out of earshot, Antonia drew a deep breath. "How positively…" She paused, hunting for words.

"Brilliant?" Philip suggested. "Glib? Artful?"

"I was thinking of ruthless." She cast him a reproving glance.

The look he bent upon her was less readable. "You *wanted* to wander by the lake with Gerald Moresby?"

"Of course not." Antonia quelled a shudder. "He's a positive toad."

Philip humphed. "Well, Miss Castleton's a piranha, so they're well matched—and we're well rid of them."

Antonia had no wish to argue.

They arrived at the edge of the roped-off area in time to watch the final rounds of the low jumps. Johnny Smidgins, the headgroom's son, won by a whisker. His sister, little Emily, a tiny tot barely big enough to hold the reins, guided a fat pony through the course to take the girls' prize.

Everybody made much of them both. Ruthven gravely shook Johnny's hand and presented him with a blue ribbon. Antonia couldn't resist picking up little Emily and giving her a quick kiss before pinning her blue rosette to her dress. Sheer pride struck the little girl dumb; Philip patted her curls and left well alone.

After that, only the last event remained—the Punch and Judy show. Virtually everyone, even some of the dowagers, crowded before the stage erected in front of the green wall of the shrubbery.

The children sat on the grass, their elders standing behind them. Among the last to join the throng, just as the makeshift curtain arose to whoops, claps and expectant shrieks, Antonia and Philip found themselves at the very back of the crowd. Philip could see; despite ducking and peering, Antonia could not.

"Here." Philip drew her aside to where a low retaining wall held back a section of lawn. "Stand on this."

Gathering her skirts, Antonia took his proffered hand and let him help her up. The stone was not high but narrow on top.

"Put your hand on my shoulder."

She had to to keep her balance. He stood beside her, and they both turned to watch the stage.

Geoffrey's script was hilarious, the puppets inspired. Some of the props, including such diverse items as the cook's favourite ladle and a moth-eaten tiger's head from the billiard-room, were both novel and inventively used. By the time the curtain finally dropped—literally—Antonia was leaning heavily on Philip's shoulder, her other hand pressed to the stitch in her side.

"Oh, my!" she said, blinking away tears of laughter. "I never knew my brother had such a solid grasp of *double entendres*."

Philip threw her a cynical look. "I suspect there's a few things you don't know about your brother."

Antonia raised a brow. She straightened, about to lift her hand from his shoulder. And sucked in a breath as her bruised back protested.

Instantly, Philip's arm came around her.

"You *are* hurt."

The words, forced out, sounded almost like an accusation. Leaning into the support of his arm, Antonia looked at him in surprise. Courtesy of the stone wall, their eyes were level; when his lids lifted and his gaze met hers, she had a clear view of the stormy depths, the emotions clouding his grey eyes.

Their gazes locked; for an instant, his sharpened, became clearer, then he blinked and the expression was gone. Her heart thudding, Antonia dropped her gaze and let him lift her gently down. She stretched and shifted, trying to ease the spot between her shoulder blades where Horatia Mimms's elbow had connected. She wished he would massage it again.

He remained rigid beside her, his hands fisted by his sides. Antonia glanced up through her lashes; his face was unreadable. "It's only a bit stiff," she said, in response to the tension in the air.

"That witless female—!"

"Philip—I'm perfectly all right." Antonia nodded at the people streaming across the lawns. "Come—we must bid your guests farewell."

They did, standing by the drive and waving each carriage, each family of tenants, goodbye. Needless to say, Horatia Mimms was treated to an unnerving stare; Antonia held herself ready throughout the Mimms's effusive leave-taking to quell, by force if necessary, any outburst on Philip's part.

But all passed smoothly; even the Castletons eventually left.

When all had departed, Antonia returned to the lawns to supervise the clearing. Philip strolled beside her, watching the late-afternoon sun strike gold gleams from her hair.

"I'm really very impressed with Geoffrey," he eventually said. "He took on the responsibility of staging the Punch and Judy and saw it through."

Antonia smiled. "And very well, too. The children were enthralled."

"Mmm. As far as I know, none fell in the lake, either—for which he has my heartfelt thanks." Philip glanced down at her. "But I think some part of his glory is owed to you." They had almost reached the nearest shore of the lake. Brows rising in question, Antonia stopped on a small rise; meeting her gaze, Philip halted beside her. "You must have had a hard time bringing him up, essentially alone."

Antonia shrugged and looked away across the lake. "I never regretted having the care of him. In its way, it's been very rewarding."

"Perhaps—but there are many who would say it was not your responsibility—not while your mother still lived."

Antonia's lips twisted. "True, but after my father died, I'm not entirely certain my mother did live, you see."

There was a pause, then Philip answered, "No. I don't."

Antonia glanced at him, then turned and headed back towards the house. Philip kept pace beside her. They were halfway to the terrace before she spoke again. "My mother was devoted to my father. Totally caught up with him and his life. When that ended unexpectedly, she was lost. Her interest in me and Geoffrey sprang from the fact we were his children—when he died, she lost interest in us."

Philip's jaw set. "Hardly a motherly sort."

"You mustn't misjudge her—she was never intentionally negligent. But she didn't see things in the light you might expect—nothing was important after my father had gone."

Together, they climbed the rising lawns towards the terrace. As they neared the house, Antonia paused and looked up, putting up a hand to shade her eyes so she could admire the elegant facade. "It took a long time for me to understand—to realise what it was to love so completely—to love like that. So that nothing else mattered anymore."

For long moments, they stood silently side by side, then Antonia lowered her hand. She glanced briefly at Philip then accepted his proffered arm.

On the terrace, they turned, surveying the lawns, neat again but marked by the tramp of many feet.

Philip's lips twisted. "Remind me not to repeat this exercise any time soon."

He turned—and read the expression in Antonia's eyes. "*Not* that it wasn't a roaring success," he hastened to reassure her. "However, I doubt my temper will bear the strain of a repeat performance too soon."

The obvious riposte flashed through Antonia's mind so forcefully it was all she could do to keep the words from her lips.

Philip read them in her eyes, in the shifting shades of green and gold. The planes of his face hardened. "Indeed," he said, his tone dry. "When I marry, the problem will disappear."

Antonia stiffened but did not look away. Their gazes locked; for a moment, all was still.

Then Philip reached for her hand. He raised it; with cool deliberation, he brushed a lingering kiss across her fingertips, savouring the response that rippled through her, the response she could not hide.

Defiantly, her eyes still on his, Antonia lifted her chin.

Philip held her challenging gaze, one brow slowly rising. "A successful day—in all respects."

With languid grace, he gestured towards the morning-room windows. Together, they went inside.

"AH, ME!" GEOFFREY yawned hugely. "I'm done in. Wrung out like a rag. I think I'll go up."

Setting the billiard cues back in their rack, Philip nodded. "I'd rather you did—before you pass out and I have to haul you up."

Geoffrey grinned. "I wouldn't want to put you to the trouble. G'night, then." With a nod, he went out, closing the door behind him.

Philip shut the cue case; turning, his wandering gaze fell on the tantalus set against the opposite wall. Strolling across, he poured himself a large brandy. Cradling the glass, he opened the long windows and went out, thrusting his free hand into his pocket as he slowly paced the terrace.

All was still and silent—his home, his estate, rested under the blanket of night. Stars glimmered through a light cloud; stillness stretched, comforting and familiar, about him. Everyone had retired to recoup after the hectic day. He felt as wrung out as Geoffrey but too restless to seek his bed.

The emotions the day had stirred still whirled and clashed within him, too novel to be easily dismissed, too strong to simply ignore. Protectiveness, jealousy, concern—he was hardly a stranger to such feelings but never before had he felt them so acutely nor in so focused a fashion.

Superimposed over all was a frustrated irritation, a dislike of being compelled even though the compulsion sprang from within him.

In its way, it was all new to him.

He took a long sip of his brandy and stared into the night.

It was impossible to pretend that he didn't understand. He knew, unequivocally, that if it had been any other woman, he would have found some excuse, some fashionable reason, for being elsewhere, far distant, entirely out of reach.

Instead, he was still here.

Philip drained his glass and felt the fumes wreathe through his head. Presumably this was part of being thirty-four.

CHAPTER SIX

Two days later, Philip stood at the library windows, looking out over the sun-washed gardens. The business that had kept him inside on such a glorious day was concluded; behind him, Banks, his steward, shuffled his papers.

"I'll take the offer in to Mrs Mortingdale's man then, m'lord, though heaven knows if she'll accept it." Banks's tone turned peevish. "Smidgins has been doing his best to persuade her to it but she just can't seem to come at putting her signature to the deed."

Philip's gaze roamed the gardens; he wondered where Antonia was hiding today. "She'll sign in the end—she just needs time to decide." At Banks's snort, he swung about. "Patience, Banks. Lower Farm isn't going anywhere—and all but surrounded by my land as it is, there'll be precious few others willing to make an offer, let alone one to match mine."

"Aye—I know," Banks grumbled. "If you want the truth it's that that sticks. It's nothing but senseless female shilly-shallying that's holding us up."

Philip's brows rose. "Shilly-shallying, unfortunately, is what one must endure when dealing with females."

With a disapproving grunt, Banks took himself off.

After a long, assessing glance at his gardens, Philip followed him out.

She wasn't in the rose garden, and the formal garden was empty. Deserted, the peony walk slumbered beneath the afternoon sun. The shrubbery was cool and inviting but disappointingly uninhabited. Eyes narrowed, Philip paused in the shadow of a hedge and considered the known characteristics of his quarry. Then, with a grunt to rival Banks's, he strode towards the house.

He ran her to earth in the still-room.

Antonia looked up, blinking in surprise as he strolled into the dimly lit room. "Hello." Hands stilling, she hesitated, her gaze shifting to the shelves of bottles and jars ranged along the walls. "Were you after something?"

"As it happens, I was." Philip leaned against the bench at which she was working. "You."

Antonia's eyes widened. She looked down at the herbs she was snipping. "I—"

"I missed you this morning." Philip lifted a brow as her head came up; he trapped her gaze with his. "Can it be you've grown tired of riding?"

"No—of course not." Antonia blinked, then looked down. "I was merely worn out by the *fête*."

"Not still stiff after your collision with Miss Mimms?"

"Indeed not. That was barely a bruise." Gathering up her chopped herbs, she dumped them into a bowl. "It's entirely gone now."

"I'm glad to hear it. I finished with Banks earlier than I'd expected—I wondered if you were wishful of chancing your skill with my greys?"

Brushing her hands on her apron, Antonia considered the prospect. It was definitely enticing. And she'd have to take the first step some time—chancing her skill in an entirely new arena.

"If you can hold them in style," Philip mused, "perhaps I could demonstrate the basics of handling a whip?" Brows lifting, he met her gaze.

Antonia did not miss the subtle challenge in his eyes. Just how much he truly saw she did not know, but the only way of testing her developing defences was to risk some time in his company. "Very well." She nodded briskly, then stretched on tiptoe to peer through the high windows.

Philip straightened. "It's a beautiful day—you'll just need your hat." Capturing her hand, he drew her to the door. "I'll have the horses put to while you fetch it."

Before she could blink, Antonia found herself by the stairs. Released, she threw a speaking look at her would-be instructor before, determinedly regal, she went up to find her hat.

Ten minutes later, they were bowling down the gravelled sweep, the greys pacing in prime style. The drive, through leafy lanes to the nearby village of Fernhurst, was uneventful; despite her stretched nerves, Antonia could detect not the slightest hint of intent in the figure lounging gracefully by her side. He appeared at ease with the world, without a thought beyond the lazy warmth of the bright sunshine and the anticipation of an excellent dinner.

Quelling an unhelpful spurt of disappointment, she lifted her chin. "As I've taken you this far without landing you in a ditch, perhaps you'd consent to instruct me on handling the whip?"

"Ah, yes." Philip straightened. "Put the reins in your left hand, then take the whip in your right. You need to loop the lash through your fingers." After she had fumbled for a minute, he held out a hand. "Here—let me show you."

The rest of the drive passed with the horses pacing steadily, equally oblivious to Philip's expert and intentionally undistracting wielding of the lash and her less-than-successful attempts to direct them with a flick to their ears.

Indeed, by the time they reached the Manor drive, she would have given a considerable sum just to be able to flick their ears. Philip's stylish expertise with the long whip, sending the lash reaching out to just tickle a leaf then twitching it back so it hissed up the handle, back to his waiting fingers, was not at all easy to emulate.

She was frowning when he lifted her down.

"Never mind—like many skills, it's one that comes with practice."

Antonia looked up—and wondered where he'd left his mask. His eyes had taken on the darker hue she had first recognized in the glade; his hands were firm about her waist, long fingers flexing gently. Cambric was thicker than muslin but even combined with her chemise, the fabric was insufficient to protect her from the heat of his touch.

He held her before him, his gaze on hers; she felt intensely vulnerable, deliciously so. Her wits were drifting, her breath slowly seizing.

His gaze sharpened, the grey darkening even more.

For one pounding heartbeat, Antonia was convinced he was going to kiss her—there, in the middle of his forecourt. Then the planes of his face, until then hard and angular, shifted. His lips curved lightly, gently mocking. He reached for her hand, his fingers twining with hers. His eyes still on hers, he raised her hand and pressed a kiss to her knuckles.

Philip's smile was wry. "Another accomplishment requiring practice, I fear."

The sound of hurrying footsteps heralded the arrival of a stable lad, apologetic and breathless. Philip benignly waved aside the lad's stuttered excuses; as the carriage was removed, he settled Antonia's hand on his sleeve. She glanced up, suspicion and uncertainty warring in her eyes.

One brow rising in unconscious arrogance, Philip turned her towards the house. "We've made definite progress, my dear, don't you think?"

"*THAT*'S BETTER!" PERCHED at her window high above the forecourt, Henrietta heaved a sigh and turned back into the room. "I tell you, Trant, I was beginning to get seriously worried."

"I know." Trant's gaze was sharp as she scanned her mistress's features.

"After the *fête*—*well!*—you have to admit no prospect *could* have looked brighter. Ruthven was so pointedly attentive, so *insistent* on remaining by Antonia's side, no matter the lures thrown at his head."

Trant sniffed. "I never heard it said he had bad taste. Seemed to me those 'lures' would more rightly send him in the opposite direction. Miss Antonia, no doubt, seemed a veritable haven."

Henrietta humphed. "To you and me, Trant, Miss Castleton and her ilk may appear quite impossibly ill-bred, *but,* while I have nothing but the highest regard for Ruthven's intelligence, there's no question that gentlemen see such matters in a different light. All too prone to overlook substance in favour of the obvious—and you have to admit Miss Castleton had a great deal of the obvious on view. I must say I was greatly relieved that Ruthven appeared unimpressed."

Busy mending, Trant couldn't suppress a snort. "Unimpressed? More properly a case of being distracted."

"Distracted?" Henrietta stared at her maid. "Whatever do you mean?"

Trant stabbed her needle into her work. "Miss Antonia's not precisely unendowed, even if she isn't one as flaunts her wares. Looked to me like the master's eye was already fixed." Trant glanced up from beneath her heavy brows, watching to see how her mistress reacted to that suggestion.

Henrietta's considering expression slowly dissolved into one of smug content. "Well," she said, reaching for her cane. "They're together again, no doubt of that, and if Philip's inclination is engaged, so much the better. I've been worrying that something had gone amiss— Antonia's been on edge, positively skulking about the house." Her eyes narrowed. "I dare say that might be nerves on her part—and Philip, of course, is simply taking things at his usual pace."

Snorting, Henrietta stood, a martial light in her eyes. "Time to shake the reins. I believe, Trant, that it's high time we planned our removal to London."

PARTING FROM PHILIP in the hall, Antonia sought her chamber. Nell was elsewhere; Antonia sent her hat skimming to land on the bed, then crossed to the window. Leaning on the wide sill, she breathed in the warm scented air.

She'd survived.

More importantly, despite the unnerving sensation that, within the landscape of their relationship, she had yet to gain a proper footing, that she might stumble at any step and was not certain he would catch her if she did, there seemed little doubt that she and Philip were intent on walking the same path.

Thankfully, he plainly understood her need for time—time to develop her defences, to develop a proper, wifely demeanour, to learn how not to embarrass him and herself with any excess of emotion. How else could she interpret his words? Sinking onto the window-seat, Antonia propped an elbow on the sill and rested her chin in her palm.

A cloud drifted over the sun; sudden coolness touched her. An echo dark with warning, her mother's voice replayed in her head. *"If you're wise, my girl, you won't look for love. Believe me, it's not worth the pain."*

Subduing a shiver, Antonia grimaced. Her mother had uttered those words on her deathbed, a conclusion drawn from experience, from a badly broken if selfish heart. In pursuing her present course, was she risking all her mother had lost?

Being Philip's wife was what she wanted to be, had always wanted to be; she had not come to Ruthven Manor seeking love.

But what if love found her?

Ten minutes' wary pondering brought no answer.

With a disgruntled grimace, Antonia banished her uncertainty—and focused her mind on her immediate goal.

Before they went to London, she was determined to be sufficiently accustomed to Philip's attentions to have the confidence to appear with him in public. The accumulated wisdom on which she had to rely—the few strictures her mother had deigned to bestow plus the snippets of advice gleaned from the Yorkshire ladies—was scant and very likely provincial; she would, however, learn quickly. Philip himself was an excellent model, coolly sophisticated, always in control. Parading through the *ton* on his arm would, she felt sure, be the ultimate test.

Once she had conquered her reactions and demonstrated her ability to be the charming, polished, coolly serene lady he required as his wife, then he would ask for her hand.

The road before her was straight—as Philip had intimated, it was simply a matter of learning to handle the reins.

Lips lifting, confidence welling, she rose and crossed to the bellpull.

SHE SLEPT IN the next morning; she was almost running when she rushed into the stableyard, her skirts over one arm, her crop clutched in one hand, the other holding on to her hat. Only to see Philip leading out both Pegasus and her mount, the tall roan, Raker. Both horses were saddled. Halting precipitously, Antonia stared. Philip saw her and raised a brow; lowering her hand from her hat, Antonia lifted her chin and calmly walked to Raker's side.

Philip came to lift her up; she turned towards him, raising her hands to his shoulders as she felt his slide, then firm, about her waist. Wide-eyed, she met his gaze—and saw his brows lift, a quizzical expression in his eyes.

She opened her mouth—and realized how he would answer her question. She clamped her lips shut, debating the wisdom of a glare.

Philip's lips twitched. "I saw no reason why you wouldn't." With that, he lifted her to her saddle.

Antonia made a production of arranging her skirts. By the time she was ready, Geoffrey had joined them; with a nod, Philip led the way out.

A three-mile gallop was precisely what she needed to shake her wits into place. Riding never failed to soothe her; atop a fine horse, she could fly over the fields, beyond the touch of time, beyond the present. It was an escape she had sorely missed over the past eight years; she knew very well no man alive bar Philip would permit her to ride in such a way.

She glanced at him, to her left a half-length in advance, his body flowing easily with the big gelding's stride. Man and horse were both strong; combined they presented a picture of harnessed power.

Quelling a shiver, Antonia looked ahead.

They pulled up on a knoll overlooking green meadows; they had not previously ridden this way. A stone cottage sat in the midst of a small garden, a narrow lane leading to its gate.

"Who lives there?" Antonia leaned forward to pat Raker's sleek neck. "This is still your land, isn't it?"

Philip nodded. "But that patch—" with his crop, he transcribed the boundaries of what Antonia estimated was a twenty-acre block "—belongs to a recently bereaved widow, a Mrs Mortingdale."

Wheeling slowly, Antonia checked her bearings. "Wouldn't it be sensible for you to purchase it— incorporate it with your holdings? She couldn't be getting much return on such a small piece."

"Yes and no in that order. I've made her an offer but she's yet to come to terms with selling up. I've told

Banks to increase the offer slightly and let it stand. She has family elsewhere; she'll come around in time."

Geoffrey was eager to investigate a nearby ridge; Philip nodded and he left with a whoop.

Antonia clicked her reins and set Raker to ford the narrow stream by which they'd paused. "You seem very busy of late." He had spent most of the past two days with Banks. "Surely the estate doesn't normally take so much of your time?"

"No." Slanting her a glance, Philip brought Pegasus alongside. "But it seemed a propitious time to get the books to order."

Antonia frowned. "I would have thought after harvest would be more useful. That's when I did the tallies at Mannering."

Philip's lips quirked; he forced them straight. "Indeed? I rather think, however, that the exigencies I presently face are somewhat different to those you encountered at Mannering."

Puzzled, Antonia glanced at him. "I'm sure they are—I didn't mean to criticise."

Philip's answering glance was distinctly wry. "For which forbearance, my dear, I am truly grateful."

Antonia straightened. "You're talking in riddles."

"Not intentionally." Meeting her sceptical gaze, Philip raised a languid brow. "What do you think of Henrietta's plans for London?"

Antonia hesitated, then shrugged and obediently turned her mind to her aunt's projections. "Leaving in a week seems wise. I would certainly appreciate a little time to accustom myself to the pace before the balls begin—and there's Geoffrey, too." Her brow clouded.

"Once the parties start, I doubt I'll have much time to spend with him."

Philip's gaze was on Geoffrey, heading back at a gallop. "Once he finds his way about, I doubt you'll need worry your head over him. I can't see him as a slow-top." Glancing at Antonia, he saw the concern in her eyes. "Of course, given he'll be under my roof, I will, naturally, be keeping an eye on him."

Antonia shot him a surprised look as Geoffrey thundered up. "Oh?"

"Indeed." Wheeling to head home, Philip met her gaze. "The least I can do. In the circumstances."

Antonia blinked. With a brisk nod for Geoffrey, Philip tapped his heels to Pegasus's sides; the chestnut surged. Raker followed. By the time they regained the stables, Antonia had thought better of enquiring as to precisely what circumstances he referred—she wasn't, she decided, ready to deal with his likely answer.

London and the *ton*—her proving ground—was, after all, still before her.

PHILIP DECIDED TO precede his stepmother and her guests to town, ostensibly to ensure Ruthven House was ready to receive them, in reality to take a quick look-in at his clubs and test the waters of the *ton* before permitting Antonia or Geoffrey to take a dip in society's sea. Departing one day before them would be enough; leaving early and driving his curricle, he would reach Grosvenor Square by midday, giving him two full days in which to gauge the tide before they arrived on the scene.

He did not, however, intend to leave the Manor before settling one significant point with his stepmother's niece. Time and place were crucial to his cause; he waited until the night before he was to leave, until tea had been taken and the cups stacked on the tray.

Antonia set the tray on the trolley then, turning, headed for the bellpull. Standing before the fireplace, Philip reached out as she passed him, capturing her hand before she reached her objective. Ignoring her surprised look, he spoke to Geoffrey, yawning by the *chaise*. "I left that book you wanted on the desk in the library."

Geoffrey's eyes brightened. "Oh, good! I'll take it up to bed."

He was already turning to the door. Philip raised a resigned brow—and raised his voice. "Perhaps, when you cross the hall, you could send Fenton in?"

Without turning, Geoffrey waved. "I will." He paused in the doorway to beam a belated smile at them all. "Good night."

As the door clicked shut, Philip glanced briefly at Antonia, then shifted his gaze to Henrietta, comfortably ensconced on the *chaise*. "I had thought to show your niece the beauties of the sunset. I believe I've heard you extoll its splendours when viewed from the terrace at this time of year?"

Transfixed by a gaze far too sharp for her comfort, Henrietta shifted. "Ah—yes." When Philip's gaze remained pointedly upon her, she shook her wits into order. "Yes, indeed! The effect can be quite…" she gestured airily "…breathtaking."

Philip smiled. Approvingly. Any doubt in Henrietta's mind that he had divined her secret purpose was firmly laid to rest.

"I believe you intend retiring early?"

Caution and curiosity warred in Henrietta's breast.

Caution won. "Indeed," she said. Affecting a die-away air, she reclined against the cushions and waved list-lessly. "If you'll ring for Trant, I think I'll go up im-mediately."

"An excellent notion." Philip crossed to the bellpull and tugged it twice. "You wouldn't want to overdo things."

Henrietta did not risk a reply. With a mildly affec-tionate smile, she waved dismissal to them both.

Intrigued, Antonia bobbed a respectful curtsy. Philip bowed with his customary grace, then, taking Antonia's arm, turned her towards the long windows which stood open to the terrace. "Come—give me your opinion."

Guided irresistibly through the gently billowing cur-tains, Antonia dutifully lifted her eyes to the western sky. "On the sunset?"

"Among other things."

Philip's tone, clipped and dry, had her shifting her gaze to his face.

Looking down into her wide eyes, he saw specula-tion leap into being, only to be replaced by a certain wariness. He halted by the balustrade, his gaze locked on hers. "I believe, my dear, that it's time for a little plain speaking."

Antonia felt giddy. Searching his eyes, she asked, "On what subject?"

"On the subject of the future. Specifically, ours." In an endeavour to disguise the tension that had, some-what unexpectedly, gripped him, Philip sat on the stone balustrade. Meeting Antonia's gaze levelly, he raised an impatient brow. "It can hardly come as a surprise to you that I hope you will consent to be my wife?"

"No." The word was out before she had considered

it; Antonia blushed furiously and tried to erase the admission with a wave. "That is…"

The look on Philip's face halted her.

"*Plain* speaking I believe I said?"

Antonia lifted her chin. "I had *hoped*—"

"You and Henrietta *planned*."

"Henrietta?" Utterly bemused, Antonia stared at him. "What has Henrietta to do with it?" She blinked. "What plans?"

Faced with her patent bewilderment, Philip had to accept his error. "Never mind."

Antonia stiffened; her eyes flared. "But I *do* mind! You thought—"

"I *didn't* think!" Philip made the admission through clenched teeth, belatedly realizing the truth. Antonia, wilful, stubborn Antonia, was no more likely to be a party to Henrietta's machinations than he. "I *assumed*— incorrectly, I admit. However, that subject is now entirely beside the point—I no longer particularly care how we reached our present pass." Much to his amazement, that statement, too, held the undeniable ring of truth. "What concerns me now—what we need to discuss—is what comes next."

Forcing himself to remain seated, Philip caught Antonia's glittering gaze and held it. "We both know what we want—don't we?"

Antonia studied his expression, grey eyes clear, filled with undisguised, unmistakable purpose. Holding his gaze, she drew in a slow breath, then nodded.

"Good—at least we agree on that much." Philip linked his fingers, laying them on one thigh, the better to resist a distracting urge to catch hold of her. "My affairs are currently in order. The matter of settlements can be decided at any time."

Antonia's eyes widened. "Your discussions with Banks..."

"Indeed." Philip couldn't resist a superior glance.

Antonia sniffed. "If we're speaking of planning—"

"Which thankfully we aren't." Ignoring her haughty glance, Philip continued, "Henrietta is your nearest adult relative. I don't see much point in asking her permission to pay my addresses—she's going to be unbearably smug as it is. As for Geoffrey, I doubt he'll object."

"Given he's halfway to idolising you," Antonia retorted. "I sincerely doubt it, too."

Philip's brows rose. "Do you mind?"

Antonia met his gaze; inherently truthful, she shook her head. A species of dizzying panic was gathering momentum inside her. Consternation threatened. This was all happening much too soon.

"Which leaves only your inclination in question." His tone deepening, Philip held out his hand. "So—will you, dear Antonia, agree to be my wife?"

The world was definitely spinning. Her heart raced— Antonia could feel it beating wildly in her throat. Disregarding the fact, her gaze trapped in the grey of his, she laid her hand in Philip's palm. "Yes, of course. Eventually."

Philip's fingers closed about hers, then convulsively tightened. His features, about to relax into lines of arrogant satisfaction, froze; his expression wavered between shock and incredulity. "Eventually?"

Antonia gestured vaguely. "Afterwards."

"Afterwards *when?*"

She frowned. "After we return from London was what I had imagined."

"Well, imagine again." Abruptly, Philip stood. "If you *imagined* I'd consent to letting you swan through London's ballrooms without the protection of a betrothal, free as a bird, attracting God-knows-what attention, you are, my dear, fair and far out. We'll announce our betrothal tomorrow—I'll place a notice in the *Gazette* when I reach town."

"Tomorrow?" Antonia stared at him. "But that's impossible!"

"Impossible?" Philip towered over her, his expression growing more intimidating by the second.

Lifting her chin, Antonia met his gaze squarely. "Impossible," she reiterated—and watched his eyes darken, felt his fingers tighten about hers. "I thought you understood," she said, as the familiar vice tightened about her chest. Frowning, she dropped her gaze to his cravat. "You *do* understand—of course you do." Raising her head, she looked directly into his eyes. "So why can't you see it?"

For one long instant, Philip closed his eyes. Then, opening them, he drew in a deep, steadying breath and forced himself to release her hand. "I fear, my dear, that despite your conviction, I must claim temporary mental obfuscation. I have no idea what it is that I'm supposed to be able to see, much less why or how it, whatever it might be, comes to render my proposal ineligible."

Antonia blinked at him. "I didn't say your proposal was ineligible—just that it's impossible to announce our betrothal before we return from London."

Philip frowned at her; the tension locking his muscles slowly dissipated. "Let's see if I've got this straight.

You agree to marry me as long as we don't announce our betrothal until *after* we return from London." He held Antonia's gaze. "Is that right?"

Antonia coloured. "If…I mean…" hands clasped before her, she lifted her chin "…presuming you still want me as your wife."

"*That,* thank heavens, is not in question." Eyeing her uptilted face, Philip had to fight the urge to take advantage of it. He fell to pacing, two steps away, then two steps back. "Kindly get it fixed in your head that I wish to marry you—if I had my way, immediately. Society and the laws, however, require a certain interval between proposal and execution. I had therefore planned…" he paused to throw Antonia a narrow-eyed glance "…in light of our apparent similarity of purpose, to announce our betrothal immediately so that we may be married on our return from town. Now you inform me that that's not possible!"

Antonia stood her ground. "It may be theoretically possible, but it's a great deal too soon."

"Too *soon?*"

Shutting her ears to his disbelief, Antonia nodded. "Too soon for me. You must see that, Philip. You know what…that is…" She frowned, searching for words to delicately allude to the effect he had on her. "You know how I react—I don't yet know how to go on in *ton*nish society. I need to learn the knack—and I can't do that if we're betrothed."

"Why not?" Philip frowned back. He kept pacing. "What difference does it make if we're betrothed, married or merely acquaintances?"

Antonia lifted her chin. "As you very well know, if we were married or betrothed, people—certainly all the ladies—would expect me to know how things were done, how to behave in all circumstances. They would expect the lady you had chosen as your bride to be accomplished in such matters."

Seeking his face, she fixed her eyes on his. "As you also know, I don't have any experience of society at large—nothing more than a limited exposure to selected entertainments in Yorkshire. That's hardly sufficient basis on which to, as you phrased it, swan through the *ton*. I'd fall at the first hurdle." Her lips twisted wryly. "You know I would. In that particular arena, I've no experience in the saddle, and even less confidence in my ability to clear the hedges."

Philip slowed, then stopped. His frown had deepened.

Calmly, Antonia held his gaze. "You told me I needed to practice my skills before I tried handling the whip. The same is true here—I need to learn how to go on, how to behave as your wife, *before* we marry."

Philip grimaced then glanced away. To his mind, she needed no instruction in how to behave socially; her innate breeding, her natural directness, her honest openness, would stand her in good stead. Her performance on the day of the *fête* had been exemplary, but she clearly did not see that success as equivalent to facing the *ton,* a point he could hardly argue.

An uncertain, less-than-confident Antonia was a being he had little experience of, yet he felt a pressing need to reassure her, to accede to her plans. He scowled at his lawns. "Everyone will know that having hailed from Yorkshire, you might be feeling your way."

"Exactly." Antonia nodded. "And should our betrothal have been announced, they'll be watching like hawks, taking note of any and all mistakes I make. If I am merely your stepmother's niece being introduced to the *ton,* beyond natural curiosity no great attention will focus on me. I'll be able to study how ladies go on without giving rise to any adverse comment."

Philip remained silent; sensing victory, Antonia pressed her point. "You know that's true. In the eyes of the *ton,* a deficient upbringing is no excuse for gauche behaviour."

"You couldn't be gauche if you tried."

Antonia smiled. "Unintentionally, perhaps." She sobered, studying his profile, the rigid line of his shoulders. Straightening her own, metaphorically girding her loins, she drew in a deep breath. "I comprehend...that is, I imagine your expectations of your wife are that she will manage your households, act as your hostess both here and in town, and... and..." Dragging in another breath, she rattled on, "In short, that she will fulfill all the usual functions and roles ascribed by society."

"I would want your friendship, Antonia." That and a great deal more. Philip kept his gaze on the gardens, unwilling to let her glimpse the emotions visible in his eyes.

Heartened by his statement, Antonia replied, "I, too, would hope our friendship would continue." She waited; when he said no more, she prompted, "I do want to marry you, Philip, but you do see, don't you, why we can't be betrothed until after our return?"

Philip turned, his jaw set, his gaze sharp and penetrating. For a long moment, he studied her eyes, and the conviction therein. She was asking for four, possibly five weeks of grace. Curtly, he nodded. "Very well— no—*announcement* of our betrothal. There is, however, no reason whatever why we cannot be betrothed, but keep the fact a secret."

Antonia met his gaze with one of her very direct looks. "Henrietta."

Philip swore beneath his breath. Hands rising to his hips, he swung away, facing the lawns again. Henrietta! His fond stepmama would never be able to keep the news to herself. And a legal betrothal was impossible without her knowledge.

It was an effort not to grind his teeth. He drew in a very deep breath, then slowly let it out. "Antonia, I am not about to let you waltz through the ballrooms of London without some agreement." He turned on the words, shifting to stand directly before her, trapping her with his gaze. "I will agree—*grudgingly,* make no mistake—not to press you for a formal betrothal, secret or otherwise, until we return to the Manor—which we will do immediately once you've gained sufficient experience of the *ton.*"

Holding hard to his reins, acutely conscious of the debilitating effects of frustration, Philip reached for her hands. Lifting them, he held them, palm to palm, between his and looked down into her eyes. "Antonia, I want you as my wife. If we cannot be betrothed formally, then I ask that we be betrothed privately—an agreement between the two of us."

Briefly, Philip glanced up at the sickle moon, riding high in the softly tinted sky, then looked down to recapture Antonia's green-gold gaze. "I ask that we plight our troth witnessed only by the moon—to consider ourselves promised, you to me and me to you, from now until we return to the Manor, after which we will wed as soon as custom permits."

He felt her fingers flutter between his, sensed the catch in her breath. For a long moment, he held her gaze, then, slowly, he separated her hands and carried one to his lips. "Do you agree, Antonia?" He brushed a kiss across her knuckles, then lifted her other hand, his eyes all the while on hers. "To be mine?"

His words were so deep, so velvety dark, Antonia barely heard them. She sensed them deep inside her, and felt a compulsion she couldn't deny. His lips grazed her fingers, and she shivered. "Yes." She had always been his.

His eyes still held her trapped; slowly, he drew her hands up and out. When he let them go, they fell to his shoulders; his shifted to her waist, spanning it, then firming as he drew her close.

Antonia felt a quake ripple through her. "Philip?"

The question was the merest whisper. Philip heard and understood. "All troths must be sealed with a kiss, sweetheart."

Her heart blocking her throat, Antonia felt her bodice brush his coat. She watched his head lower; her lids fell.

His lips found hers; warm and persuasive, their pressure soothed and reassured. Antonia relaxed, then stiffened as he gathered her into his arms, locking her in his embrace. Yet his hold remained gentle; his hands stroked her back.

Again she relaxed, again the kiss took hold, sweeping her into some magical realm of mystery, of sensation. His lips firmed; hesitantly, she parted hers, a flicker of nervousness distracting her momentarily, called forth by recollections of their encounter in the woods. But this time there was only warmth and pleasure, enticing, beckoning caresses that made her hungry—for what she didn't know. No unbridled passions arose to confront her, to elicit the wanton craving she was convinced she had to hide.

Reassured, she drifted deeper, giving herself up to gentle pleasure.

It took all of Philip's skill to keep the kiss, if not light, then at least non-conflagrationary. He was acutely aware of her untutored responses, of the way her body slowly softened in his arms, accepting his embrace in the same way her lips accepted his kiss. As in all things, she was deliciously direct, unambiguously open, totally innocent of intrigue. For one of his ilk, the novelty was as heady as summer wine.

He forced himself to draw back, to gradually bring the kiss to an end, despite the ravenous hunger eating him. He was familiar with that demon; while it might make his life hell, he was its master.

When he eventually lifted his head, it was to the pleasure of watching Antonia's eyes, heavy-lidded, slowly open. She blinked at him, then made an obvious effort to compose herself.

"Ah…" Gently, Antonia tried to draw back, only to feel his arms firm.

"Not yet." Prodded by his demon, Philip lowered his head and stole another kiss, then another, before she could catch her breath.

"Philip!" Antonia barely got the word out; this time she insisted on pulling back.

Reluctantly, Philip dropped his arms but kept hold of one of her hands. "You're mine, Antonia." Possessiveness surged; he shackled it, unaware of the deep resonance of his voice, of the dark glitter in his gaze, of the way his fingers tightened about hers. Raising her hand, he pressed a kiss to her fingertips, then turned her hand and pressed a warm kiss to her palm. "Never forget it."

Antonia shivered as he released her hand.

Holding her with no more than his gaze, Philip lowered his head one last time, barely touching his lips to hers. "Sleep well, my dear. I'll see you next in London."

She drew back, wide-eyed and, he thought, wondering. Then she inclined her head and slowly turned away. He let her go, watching as she retreated into his house, to spend the night under his roof, as she would from now on.

The smile on his lips slowly fading, Philip turned back to the lawns. After a moment, he grimaced feelingly, then descended the steps; hands in his pockets, he strode into the cool night.

CHAPTER SEVEN

"THERE'S A MESSAGE arrived for you, m'lord. Up from the Manor."

Seated in a wing-chair in his library, Philip waved Carring, his major-domo, forward. After spending an afternoon about town, calling in at his club and spending an hour at Manton's, he had retreated to his library secure in the knowledge that few of his peers had yet quit their summer hunting grounds. The continuing fine weather gave little incentive for returning to town before the round of balls and parties that made up the Little Season. Which meant Antonia would have a relatively quiet few weeks in which to gain her balance.

The silver salver Carring presented held a note addressed in Banks's finicky script. Frowning, Philip picked it up and unfolded it. He read Banks's few lines, then swore. "The damned woman's finally made up her mind!"

"Is that good news or bad news, m'lord?" Carring held himself correctly by his master's side, his lugubrious tone absolving his query of any hint of impertinence.

Philip considered the point, eyeing Banks's missive with distaste. "Both," he eventually replied. "It means that at long last we'll be able to close the sale of Lower Farm. Unfortunately, Mrs Mortingdale wants to see me

in person over the matter of certain unspecified assur-
ances." Exasperated, he sighed. "I'll have to go back."
He glanced at the clock. "Not tonight. Tell Hamwell
to have the greys ready at first light—wake me before then."

If he took the Brighton road, he could reach the
Manor by midday; if luck was with him, he might be
free of the vacillating widow in time to make the trip
back that evening.

"Very good, m'lord." Carring, ponderously round
and suited all in black, unhurriedly headed for the door.
There, he turned, his hand on the knob. "Am I to take
it, my lord, that her ladyship and her visitors will still
be arriving tomorrow?"

"They will." Philip's tones were clipped. "Make sure
all is ready."

Carring's brows rose fractionally as he turned away.
"Naturally, m'lord."

CONTRARY TO HIS plans, it was early afternoon two days
hence before Philip returned to Grosvenor Square.

Carring helped him out of his greatcoat. "I take it the
business of Lower Farm was successfully completed,
m'lord?"

"Finally." Resettling his coat, Philip turned to the
hall mirror to check his cravat. "Her ladyship and the
Mannerings arrived yesterday?"

"Indeed, m'lord. I comprehend their journey passed
without incident."

"No highwaymen—not even a scheming landlord to
chouse us over the reckoning."

Turning, Philip beheld Antonia, a vision in soft turquoise muslin floating down the stairs. A stray sunbeam

lancing through the fanlight struck golden gleams from her hair. "I should hope not," he said, moving forward to meet her. Taking her hand, he raised it to his lips, brushing a kiss across her fingers. "I presume my coachman and grooms took good care of you?"

Antonia raised a brow. "Of all of us. But what of you? Did the widow eventually weaken?"

"She finally came to her senses." Tucking her hand in his arm, Philip turned her down the corridor. "However, nothing would do for it but that she had to see me in person so that I could give her an assurance—word of a gentleman—that I would keep her farm labourers on."

As he opened the door to the back parlour and handed her through, Antonia mused, "Actually, that seems rather wise—and kind of her, too."

Philip hesitated, then reluctantly nodded. "But I would have kept them on anyway. As it was, her summons meant I wasn't here to greet you. It appears I'm fated to return to my house to find you gracing my hall."

He shut the door behind them. Antonia slanted him a questioning glance as he came to stand beside her. "Do you find that so disturbing?"

Philip looked down into her green-gold eyes. "Disturbing?" For all his experience, he felt his senses slide. Taking firm hold of his wits, he clasped his hands behind his back. "On the contrary." His lips curved in a deliberately provocative smile. "That's precisely the result I'm aiming for. In this particular case, however, I had looked forward to welcoming you on your first evening in London."

Antonia smiled back. "We would hardly have been scintillating company." Calmly, she strolled to the *chaise* before the windows. "Henrietta retired immediately. Geoffrey and I had an early dinner and followed her upstairs." With a swish of her skirts, she settled on the flowered chintz.

"And this morning?" Gracefully, Philip sat beside her, neither overly close nor yet greatly distant. "I have difficulty believing you slept until noon."

"No, indeed." Antonia's smile grew gently teasing. "Geoffrey and I did discuss riding in the Park—he was sure you wouldn't mind if we raided your stable. But I convinced him to wait for your return."

Philip's expression blanked as he imagined what might have been.

Antonia shifted to face him. "What is it?"

Philip grimaced. "There's something I should explain—to you both." He focused on Antonia's face. "About riding in town."

Antonia frowned. "I had thought it was acceptable to ride in the Park."

"It is. It's the definition of the term 'riding' wherein the *ton* and the Mannerings differ."

"Oh?" Antonia looked her question.

Philip pulled a face. "For ladies, the prescribed activity known as 'riding in the Park' involves a slow walk for much of the time, with at the most a short canter. Galloping, at least as you know it, is not just frowned upon—for you, it's utterly out of the question."

Antonia sat back, her expression a study of disgust and dismay. "Good heavens!"

One of her curls fell in a golden coil over one ear; Philip put out a hand and wound the curl about one finger, then, letting it slowly slip free, he gently brushed his finger against her cheek.

Her eyes flicked to his; Philip felt the familiar tension tighten. He let it hold for one discreet moment, then smoothly retrieved his hand.

"Ah…I don't think I'd actually want to ride if I had to restrain myself to a walk or a canter." Forcing in a breath, Antonia shook her head. "I don't think I could."

"An unquestionably wise decision." Philip shifted slightly. "But we'll only be in town for four weeks or so—you'll be able to ride to your heart's content once we return to the Manor."

"Well, then." Antonia gestured resignedly. "I'll just have to consider it a sacrifice made in pursuit of a greater goal."

Lips lifting, Philip inclined his head. When he looked up, his smile had faded. "Unfortunately, that's not all."

Antonia transfixed him with one of her direct looks. "What?"

"Driving in the Park." His eyes on hers, Philip grimaced. "I know I mentioned I might consent to let you drive yourself but I had, at that time, imagined myself on the box beside you."

Antonia frowned. "So?"

"So, my dear, given we are *not* about to announce our betrothal, the sight of *you* driving *me* behind my greys in the Park would lead to instant and quite rabid speculation—something I take it you are keen to avoid."

"Oh." The single syllable accurately conveyed Antonia's feelings.

"Despite such restrictions," Philip continued, his tone deliberately light, "London is generally considered a haven of entertainment." Catching Antonia's eye, he lifted a brow. "What have you planned for this afternoon?"

Shaking aside her disappointment, a childish response, she told herself, Antonia straightened. "Henrietta thought a visit to the modistes in Bruton Street to decide which to choose." Colouring slightly, she met Philip's gaze. "I'm afraid my wardrobe is hardly up to town standards."

"Having only just escaped from Yorkshire?" Reaching out, Philip took her hand. "I fear I'm not surprised."

Reassured by his touch rather than his cynical tone, Antonia continued, "Then we thought to stroll Bond Street to look in on the milliners, followed perhaps by a quick turn through the Park."

Idly playing with her fingers, noting the contrast between her slim digits and his much larger hands, Philip considered, then nodded. He glanced up at the clock on the mantelshelf. "Henrietta should be stirring from her nap. Why don't you go and tell her I've arrived?" Turning his head, he met Antonia's slightly surprised gaze. And smiled. "Give me ten minutes to change and I'll accompany you." Rising, he drew her to her feet, then lifted her hand to his lips. "On your first outing in town."

Twenty minutes later, as she settled into a corner of the Ruthven town carriage, Henrietta and her shawls beside her, Philip directly opposite, Antonia was still in the grip of what she told herself was quite uncalled-for gratification. Despite her trenchant lecturing, her happiness swelled. She had never imagined Philip would join them.

The carriage rattled over the cobbles and rounded a corner. Swaying with the movement, Antonia met Philip's eye; she smiled, then let her gaze drift to the window. She had started allowing herself to think of him as her husband; she was, after all, going to be his wife.

That thought, unfortunately, focused her mind on the anxiety nagging quietly in the back of her mind. Philip's proposal had made success in London even more imperative; the *ton* was her last hurdle—she could not, must not, falter here.

Luckily, the drive to Bruton Street was too short for her to dwell too deeply on her prospects; the carriage pulled up outside a plain wooden door. Philip jumped down, then turned to assist her to the pavement.

As she straightened the skirts of her simple gown, Antonia's gaze fell on the creation displayed in the window beside the door, a breathtakingly simple robe of blue silk crêpe. It was, to her eyes, the epitome of stylish elegance, combining simplicity of line with the richness of expensive fabric. An all-but-overwhelming desire to have such a gown rose within her.

"*Not* in blue," came Philip's voice in her ear.

Antonia jumped, then shot him a frown, which he met with a raised brow and an all-too-knowing smile. Offering her his arm, he gestured to the door through which the footman was assisting Henrietta. "Come and meet Madame Lafarge."

Guided up a narrow stair and into a salon draped in silk, Antonia felt her eyes widen. Small knots of ladies, young and old, were scattered about the apartment, grouped on chairs, each with an attendant hovering, offering samples of cloths. Murmured discussions, intent and purposeful, hummed in the air.

Philip was not the only gentleman present; others were freely giving their opinions on colours and styles. Quite a few turned to look at her; one groped for his quizzing glass, half raising it to his eye before apparently thinking better of it. An assistant hurried up;

Philip spoke quietly and she scurried away, disappearing through a curtained doorway.

Five seconds later, the curtain was thrown back; a small, black-clad figure glided into the room, pausing for a dramatic instant before heading towards them.

"My lord. My lady." The woman, black-eyed and black-haired, spoke with a pronounced accent. She bowed, then, straightening, lifted her hands palms up as she said, "My poor talents are entirely at your disposal."

"Madame." Philip inclined his head. He introduced Henrietta, then stood back and let her take charge. Turning his head, he caught Antonia's eye.

Confused, she lifted a brow at him but was distracted by Henrietta's introduction.

Nodding in acknowledgement of Antonia's greeting, Madame Lafarge walked slowly around her, then gestured down the room. "Walk for me, *mademoiselle*—to the windows and back, if you please."

Antonia glanced at Philip; he smiled reassuringly. She strolled down the long room, drawing covert glances from the modiste's other patrons with miffed looks from some of the younger ladies. By the time she returned to Philip's side, Henrietta and Madame had their heads together, whispering avidly.

"Excellent." Nodding, Henrietta straightened. "We'll return for a private session tomorrow at ten."

"*Bien.* I will have all ready. Until tomorrow, my lady. My lord. *Mademoiselle.*" Madame Lafarge bowed deeply, then gestured to an underling to see them to the door.

Gaining the pavement in advance of Henrietta, slowly descending the steep flight on the arm of her footman, Antonia let her gaze travel the short street, taking in the numerous signs indicating the establishments of modistes and the odd tailor. Turning to Philip, standing patiently by her side, she raised a determined brow. "Why here?"

Philip raised a brow back. "Because she's the best—at least for style and, in my humble opinion, for that indefinable something that gives rise to true elegance."

Glancing again at the blue gown in the window, Antonia nodded. "But it was you who had the entrée—not Henrietta."

When, turning, she fixed an openly enquiring gaze upon him, Philip wished her understanding was not quite so acute. He considered a white lie, but she had already noted his hesitation.

Again her brow rose, her expression half playful, half distant. "Or is that one of those matters into which young ladies should not enquire too closely?"

It was; for the first time in his lengthy career, the fact made Philip uncomfortable. Inwardly frowning, he kept his expression impassive. "Suffice to say that I have had call to make use of Madame's expertise in the past."

"For which," Henrietta said, puffing slightly as she came up with them, "we are both duly grateful." She fixed Philip with an approving stare. "Wondered why you had John Coachman stop here." Turning to Antonia, she explained, "*Horrendously* difficult to interest personally, Madame. But if you can catch her eye, then your wardrobe, you may be assured, will be enough to set the tabbies on their tails." Straightening, Henrietta waved to her coachman, "You may wait for us at the end of Bond Street, John." Then she gestured her footman forward. "Come, Jem, give me your arm. We can stroll from here."

Philip offered Antonia his arm. She hesitated only fractionally before placing her hand on his sleeve. Head high, a distant smile on her lips, she strolled by his side as they followed Henrietta into Bond Street.

Her joy in his company, in his introducing her to Madame Lafarge, had been quite effectively depressed.

Their foray up and down the fashionable thoroughfare was punctuated by frequent halts before the windows of milliners and glovers, haberdasherers and bootmakers.

"No sense in deciding on anything until we've consulted with Lafarge tomorrow," Henrietta opined. "Elsewise, we'll end with the wrong colour or style."

Dragging her gaze from a quite hideous chip bonnet sprouting a border of fake daisies, Antonia nodded absentmindedly. One of their last halts was before the windows of Aspreys, the jewellers. Necklaces and rings, baubles of every conceivable hue, glittered and winked behind the glass.

Her gaze locked on the display, Henrietta pursed her lips. "If memory serves, your mama was never one for jewellery."

Antonia, still wrestling with unwelcome realization, shook her head. "She always said she didn't need much. But I have her pearls."

"Hmm." Henrietta squinted at a necklace and drop earrings set on a velvet bed towards the back of the display. "Those topazes would suit you."

"Where?" Blinking, Antonia summoned enough interest to follow her aunt's gaze.

"Not topazes."

Philip spoke from behind them; it was the first utterance he had made since they'd gained Bond Street. Both Antonia and Henrietta turned in surprise.

Endeavouring to retain his habitually impassive mien, Philip reached past them to point to the items arrayed on a bed of black silk in pride of place in the centre of the window. "Those."

"Those" were emeralds. Eyeing the exquisite green gems, set, not in the usual heavily ornate settings, but with an almost Grecian restraint in simple gold, Antonia felt her eyes grow round. Just like the gown in Lafarge's window, the delicate necklace with pendant attached, matching earrings and matching bracelets exerted a charm all their own. She would love to have them—but that was impossible. Even she could tell they were worth the proverbial king's ransom. They were, she suspected, the sorts of gifts a gentleman might give to his mistress, especially were she one of those beings referred to in hushed whispers as "high-flyers"—the sort who might qualify for peignoirs from Madame Lafarge. She stifled a sigh. "They're certainly beautiful." Determinedly, she turned away. "There's John."

The carriage was waiting just up from the corner. His face expressionless, Philip stepped back. Without comment, he gave Antonia his arm across the street then handed his stepmother, then her niece into the carriage.

Henrietta leaned forward. "I'd thought to go for a quick turn about the Park—just to let Antonia get a feel for the place. Will you join us?"

Philip hesitated. He shot a glance at Antonia; the shadows of the carriage hid her eyes. She made no move to encourage him. Gracefully, he stepped back. "I think not." Feeling his jaw tighten, he forced his face to impassivity. "I believe I'll look in on my clubs."

He executed a neat bow, then shut the door and gave John Coachman the office.

PHILIP ROSE LATE the next day, having spent the evening idly gaming with Hugo Satterly, whom he had opportunely sighted late in the afternoon napping behind a newsheet in White's. After a leisurely dinner, they had moved on to Brooks and settled in for the evening, a sequence of events so common they had not even bothered to discuss their intent.

Determined to cling to such comfortable routines, he descended his stairs at noon, carefully pulling on his gloves. As he set foot in his hall, the library door opened, and Geoffrey looked out.

"Ah—there you are." Grinning engagingly, Geoffrey came forward.

Instantly suspicious, Philip raised one brow. "Yes?"

Geoffrey's grin turned ingenuous. "I wondered if you recalled your promise that you'd help me in town if I kept all of the children out of the lake during the *fête?*"

"Ah, yes," Philip mused. "As I recall, no one got wet."

"Exactly." All but bouncing on his toes, Geoffrey nodded. "I wondered if you'd consider sponsoring me at Manton's—in return for my sterling efforts?"

His smile was infectious; briefly, Philip returned it. Manton's was, in fact, one of the safer venues for one of Geoffrey's years. "I'll have to speak with Manton himself—he doesn't normally encourage youngsters."

Geoffrey's face fell. "Oh."

"Don't get your hopes too high," Philip advised, turning to accept his cane from Carring who had silently approached. "But he may make an exception."

Turning to Geoffrey, he raised his brows. "Provided, that is, that you can handle a pistol?"

"Of course I can! What sort of countryman can't?"

"As to that, I can't say." Extracting a card from his case, Philip handed it to Geoffrey. "If you get caught anywhere, use that. If not, meet me outside Manton's at two."

"Capital!" Eyes glowing, Geoffrey scanned the card, then put it in his pocket. "I'll be there." With a nod, he turned to go, then turned back. "Oh, I say—Antonia mentioned about the riding."

"Ah, yes." Philip waved away the hat Carring offered.

"Would it be a problem if I took one of your horses out in the mornings? I was speaking with your grooms. They seemed to think it was all right—that is, permissible—for me to ride early, say about nine."

"Indeed." Philip nodded. "And yes, before you ask, you can gallop down the tan—as long as you remain on the track. The keepers don't appreciate having their lawns cut to pieces."

"Oh, good!" Geoffrey's face glowed. "Antonia explained how she can't gallop but I thought that might just be one of those feminine things."

"Precisely," Philip replied. With a wave, he headed for the door.

ONE OF THOSE *feminine things*.

The words returned to haunt Philip as he idly strolled the clipped lawns bordering the carriageway in the Park, his gaze scanning the landaus and barouches wending their way along the fashionable avenue. He had dined well with friends at a select eatery in Jermyn Street, then met Geoffrey at Manton's.

After prevailing on the proprietor to overlook Geoffrey's age, an argument greatly assisted by his protégé's undeniable skill with a pistol, he had left Geoffrey happily culping wafers and repaired to Gentleman Jackson's Boxing Salon. Declining an invitation to don a pair of gloves and spar with the great man himself, an acquaintance of many years, he had strolled the rooms, catching up with cronies and identifying the notables already in town. What gossip there was he had gleaned, then, with no pressing engagement, he had let his feet wander where they would.

They had brought him here. He wasn't sure whether he approved or not.

On the thought, he spied the Ruthven barouche, rolling slowly around the circuit. He raised his arm; his coachman saw him and drew the carriage into the verge. He strolled up as John was explaining his actions.

"Oh, it's you." Turning, Henrietta fixed him with one of her more intimidatory stares. "Perfect. You can take Antonia for a stroll on the lawns."

Philip's answering glance held a definite hint of steel. "Precisely my intention, ma'am."

Henrietta fluffed her shawls and sank back against the cushions. "I'll wait here."

His lips compressed, Philip opened the door and held out his hand commandingly—before pulling himself up. His gaze flew to Antonia's face; the blank look in her eyes struck him like a blow. He drew in a quick breath. "That is, if you would like to take the air, my dear?" Where on earth had his years of experience gone? He had never acted so insensitively in his life.

Bundling an uncharacteristic spurt of temper and a less well-defined hurt aside, Antonia forced herself to nod. Outwardly serene, she placed her fingers in his. She did not meet his gaze as he assisted her out of the carriage, even though she could feel it on her face.

Settling her hand on his sleeve, Philip drew in a deep breath. And set himself to regain the ground he'd lost.

About them, the lawns were merely dotted with other couples, not crowded as they would be in a few weeks' time. "The company, I'm afraid, is somewhat thin at the moment." Glancing down at Antonia's face, he smiled. "As soon as the weather turns, the *ton* will flood back and then the entertainments will start with a vengeance."

Determined to hold her own, Antonia lifted her chin. "I've heard that there's no place on earth to rival London for all manner of diversions."

"Quite true." Philip succeeded in catching her eye. "Are you looking forward to being diverted?"

Shifting her gaze forward, Antonia raised her brows. "I suppose I am. Henrietta seems quite caught up with it all. She was certainly in her element at Lafarge's this morning."

"Ah, yes. How did your session with Madame go?"

Antonia shrugged lightly. "I have to admit I'm very impressed by her designs. She's sending the first of the gowns tomorrow." Glancing down at her cambric skirts, she pulled a face. "Not a moment too soon, I suspect." Her gaze rose to take in the stylish toilettes of two ladies strolling by.

"After tomorrow, my dear, you'll take the shine out of all the London belles."

Despite her determination to remain aloof, Antonia's

lips twitched. She shot Philip a glance—which he was waiting to catch.

He laid a hand on his heart. "Nothing more than the truth, I swear."

She had to laugh; to her surprise, it cleared the air, allowing her to respond more easily.

"The smaller, less formal parties will be starting soon, I imagine."

"Indeed," she replied evenly. "Henrietta already has a small stack of invitations."

"And then will come the crushes as the major hostesses return to the fray."

"Hmm." She hid a frown.

Philip glanced down at her. "I thought you were looking forward to experiencing the *ton* in all its glory?"

Fleetingly, Antonia met his gaze. "I certainly expect my time here to be an experience—an undertaking necessary to extend my understanding of society and its ways. As for enjoyment—" She shrugged. "I don't know enough to anticipate it."

Philip studied her face, open and honest as always; his expression softened. "Strange to tell, there's more to London than *ton* parties."

Antonia looked up, brows lifting.

"There's the theatre and opera, of course—but you know of them. Then there's Astley's and Vauxhall across the river, both worth a visit if it's simple pleasures you seek." Looking down, Philip met her gaze. "And I own to surprise that neither you nor Geoffrey has yet developed a yearning to see the museum."

Without waiting for her comment, he continued, blithely extolling the virtues of the capital, detailing sights and possible excursions, gently twitting her on her ignorance until, with a laugh, she conceded, "Very well—I will own that I might, indeed, enjoy my stay in London. I hadn't realized there was so much we—" Abruptly, Antonia caught herself up. She drew in a steadying breath. "So much to see," she amended.

Trying but failing to trap her gaze, Philip inwardly frowned. "Having been interred in the wilds of Yorkshire as you have, that's hardly surprising. We must make an effort to take in some of the sights at least, before the season gets into full swing."

Antonia glanced up and met his gaze. "That would be very...pleasant."

Philip smiled. "We'll have to see what we can squeeze in."

They had reached the barouche; opening the door, he handed her in. "Until later," he said, his eyes on hers.

Antonia nodded, regally assured. Henrietta humphed and tapped John Coachman on the shoulder. Philip watched the carriage draw away; a frown slowly formed in his eyes. An odd constraint seemed to have sprung up between them—he couldn't for the life of him see why.

AT SIX O'CLOCK that evening, Antonia started up the stairs. The dinner gong had just sounded; it was time to change her gown. Nearing the landing, she heard footsteps above. Looking up, she met Philip's gaze. She stopped on the landing, watching as he descended.

He was wearing a stylish coat of Bath superfine over ivory inexpressibles; an intricately tied cravat, tasselled Hessians and a waistcoat of amber silk completed the outfit. His hair looked freshly brushed, waving gently about his head. In one hand, he carried a pair of gloves, flicking them gently against one thigh.

His lips curving, he stopped directly before her.

"I had wondered, my dear, if you are free tomorrow afternoon, whether you might care to drive to Richmond? We could take tea at the Star and Garter and return in good time for dinner."

The poor light on the stairs hid the flash of happiness that lit Antonia's eyes. It also hid the faint blush that succeeded it. "I…" Lifting her chin, she clasped her hands before her. "I wouldn't wish to disrupt your normal routine, my lord—I'm sure there are other claims on your time."

"None that can't wait." Philip hid his frown. "Are you free?"

She met his gaze but he could read nothing in her eyes. "I can't recall any other engagement."

Philip tightened his grip on his gloves. "In that case, I'll meet you in the hall at…shall we say half past one?"

Gracious but determinedly distant, Antonia inclined her head. "I'll look forward to the outing, my lord."

What, Philip wondered, had happened to his name? "Antonia—"

"Will you be dining with us this evening?" It took all Antonia's courage to ask the question; she waited, breath bated, for the answer, dismally aware she was only making a rod for her own back.

Philip hesitated, then forced himself to shake his head. "I'm dining with friends." He was, at Limmer's. As if from a distance, he heard himself say, "I often do." The shadows hid her eyes, too well for him to be sure of her expression. Few men of his age, married or not, dined frequently at their own board; it was a fact of fashionable life, not a situation of his own choosing.

"Indeed?" Determinedly bright, Antonia flashed him

a brittle smile. "I'd better go up or I'll be late. I wish you a good night, my lord." With another fleeting smile and a nod, she went past him and on up the stairs. She was, she sternly lectured herself, being foolish beyond permission. To feel rejection when none was intended, to feel downhearted just because he was behaving as he usually did. This was, after all, what she had come to London to learn—how she would fit into his life.

She reached the upper gallery and all but ran to her room.

Philip listened to her footsteps fade. Slowly, he resumed his descent. By the time he reached the hall, the planes of his face had hardened. She had said not a word out of place, said nothing to make him suspect she was wishful of his company. Not once had she made the mistake of trying to make him feel guilty; she had made no demands of him whatever.

Why, then, did he feel so dissatisfied? So certain something was, if not precisely wrong, then very definitely not right?

CHAPTER EIGHT

AT HALF PAST ONE the following afternoon, Philip stood in his hall and watched Antonia descend the stairs. She was wearing a new carriage dress delivered that morning from Madame Lafarge's workshop, a creation in leaf-green twill that emphasized her slender shape and set off the gold of her hair. The bodice and skirt were edged with forest-green ribbon, the same shade as the parasol Philip held furled in one hand.

It, too, had come from Madame Lafarge, expressly chosen on his instructions and delivered by one of Madame's lackeys at precisely one o'clock.

The parasol held behind his back, Philip strolled forward, taking Antonia's hand to help her down the last steps. "You look positively enchanting."

Buoyed by the confidence stemming from her first London gown, Antonia returned his smile. When Philip's gaze dropped, shrewdly judging, she obligingly twirled, her skirts flaring about her. "Madame's skill is beyond question."

"True." Philip recaptured her hand. "But as I am sure she would tell you, perfection can only be attained when one works with the very best of raw materials."

His eyes met Antonia's; her heart skittered alarmingly. She lowered her gaze and bobbed a curtsy. "I fear you flatter me, my lord."

A frown fleetingly crossed Philip's face. "Philip." He held up the parasol, then presented it with a flourish.

Antonia put out a hand to the carved wooden handle, her expression a study in surprise. "For me?" Taking it, she held the parasol as if it were glass. Mesmerised, she stared, then threw Philip a wavering smile. "Thank you." Her voice was husky. "I'm sorry—you must think me a fool." Blinking rapidly, she looked down. "It's been a long time since anyone gave me anything like this—for no real reason."

Philip's mask slipped. It took effort to wrestle it back into place, to hide his reaction to her words. "I would gladly give you more, Antonia—but until we make our relationship public, I'm reduced to such trumpery to win your smiles."

She gave a shaky laugh, then held the parasol against her gown. "It's a perfect match."

"Indeed." Philip smiled. "Obviously an inspired choice."

Antonia's expression immediately turned suspicious. Philip laughed. Taking her arm, he guided her to the door.

Once in his curricle, bowling along behind his greys, the awkwardness Antonia found herself all too often a prey to evaporated. Unfurling the parasol, she deployed it to protect her complexion, then hit upon the notion of asking Philip's advice on how to most elegantly dispose it. His suggestions were half serious, half teasing. She enjoyed the drive, and his company, relaxing enough to let her pleasure show.

The outing passed off without a hitch; Philip returned well content.

THEREAFTER, HE MADE a point of spending some part of every day by Antonia's side, trying with all the skill at his command to ease the reticence he sensed behind her smiles. He escorted both Mannerings to Astley's Amphitheatre, spending most of the performance in pleasant contemplation of the emotions flickering across Antonia's face. The following afternoon, he yielded to their entreaties and took them on a tour of St Paul's and the city, surprising himself with how much he remembered of the history of the town.

Throughout, Antonia appeared serenely content, yet her underlying hesitancy disturbed him. Aside from anything else, she frequently reverted to addressing him as "my lord," something, he had noticed, she only did when trying to keep him at a distance.

Then came the first of the informal parties.

Philip had already changed for the evening but had yet to quit the house. He was in the library, idly flicking through the stack of invitations on his desk when he heard voices in the hall. Lifting his head, he identified Geoffrey's voice raised in a bantering tone; Antonia answered with a laugh, gayer than any he'd heard in a long while.

Intrigued, he strolled to the door.

The sight that met his eyes as he paused in the doorway locked the breath in his chest. Antonia stood in the centre of his hall, her hair burnished guinea-gold by the chandelier above. Bright curls clustered in artful disarray on the top of her head; a few gilded wisps wreathed about her delicate ears and nape, drawing attention to her slender neck. Her shoulders, warmly tinted ivory, were quite bare, entirely revealed by a stunningly elegant gown of the palest green. Lafarge's hand was easily discerned in the long, flattering lines, in the smooth sweeps of the skirt, in the subtle way the bodice emphasized the contours beneath. Tiny puffed sleeves were set well off the shoulders, so small they in no way distracted from the long, graceful curves of Antonia's arms.

Her face was uptilted; as he watched, she laughed, responding to Geoffrey, out of sight up the stairs. Deep inside, Philip felt something tighten, harden, clarifying and coalescing into one, crystal-clear emotion. Antonia's cheeks were delicately flushed, her eyes alight; her lips, rose tinted, parted as she smiled, raising her hands, not yet covered by the regulation long gloves, palms upwards.

"I assure you I am very definitely your sister—if you come down here I'll demonstrate that my unique technique for boxing your ears is very much intact."

Geoffrey answered; Philip didn't register his words. Compelled, he moved slowly forward, out of the shadows that had thus far hidden him.

Antonia heard him; she turned and her eyes met his. His gaze held her as she held his attention, absolutely, completely.

He sensed the swift intake of her breath, saw her eyes widen then darken. Her arms slowly drifted together, as if to fold about her, responding to some age-old instinct to protect her body from his gaze. Moving with slow deliberation, Philip reached for her hands, taking them in his to hold them wide. Then, slowly, he raised one to his lips.

He felt his chest swell against the vice clamped so powerfully about it. "You are beauty personified, Antonia."

His voice was deep, darkly enticing; Antonia felt it reverberate through her, felt its seductive quality sink to her marrow. Still moving like one in a dream, he raised one of her arms high; obediently, she twirled, compelled to turn her head to keep her eyes on his. The normally shimmering grey was dark with storm clouds, harbingers of passion. She couldn't tear her gaze from them, from the promise in their depths.

He moved with her; for a moment, it was as if they were dancing, twirling about each other, gazes locked. Then he stopped; her silk skirts shushed softly about her legs, then settled as she halted, facing him.

An age seemed to pass as, eyes locked, they stood, tensed, quivering, as if balanced on the edge of some invisible precipice. Antonia couldn't breathe, dared not blink.

Geoffrey's clattering footsteps as he came down the stairs broke the spell.

"Don't think you *can* reach my ears anymore." Grinning widely, he strode towards them.

Smoothly, Philip released Antonia's hand; turning, he noted Geoffrey's dark coat and neat but simple cravat. "From your sartorial elegance, I take it you're to make one of the party tonight?"

Geoffrey pulled a face. "Aunt Henrietta thought that seeing I was here, I might as well broaden my horizons."

"It's just an informal gathering of family and friends at the Mountfords in Brook Street." Still breathless, Antonia struggled to keep her tone even. "Nothing too elaborate. According to Henrietta it'll be mostly genteel conversation with some country dances to help the less experienced ladies get accustomed to *ton*nish ways."

Philip had heard of such mild affairs. "I believe it's

the regulation way one commences one's first season."
He glanced at Antonia; excitement glowed in her eyes.
"Tell me, do you dine in Brook Street or here?"

"Here." Antonia gestured. "I was just on my way to
the drawing-room."

"And I was following, intending to get in a little practice." Frowning, Geoffrey shook his head. "Cotillions
and quadrilles are all the same to me."

"Nonsense." Antonia linked her arm through his. "If
you think to slide out of standing up with such comments you'll have to think again." Glancing at Philip,
she smiled. Politely. "But you were on your way out—
we're holding you up."

"No," Philip lied. "I'm dining in tonight."

"Oh?" Antonia blinked in surprise.

"Indeed. Why don't you make a start putting your
brother through his paces? I'll join you in a moment
and adjudicate."

The smile Antonia flashed him was as bright as the
sun. Inventively grumbling, Geoffrey allowed her to
drag him away.

Amused, Philip watched. When the drawing-room
door shut behind them, he turned towards the library.
Only then did he see his major-domo standing in the
shadows of the stairs. Philip's expression blanked. "Carring." He wondered how much Carring had seen. "Just
the one I want."

In the library, Philip crossed to his desk. He scrawled
a note to Hugo, informing him that he had been unexpectedly detained but would join him later. Sealing the
missive, he directed it then handed it to Carring. "Have
that delivered to Brooks."

"Immediately, m'lord. And shall I instruct Cook you've changed your mind?"

Ten full seconds of silence ensued. "Yes. And I expect you should also instruct a footman to lay an extra place at table." Philip eyed his henchman straitly. "Was there anything else?"

"No, indeed, m'lord." Carring's expression was smugly benign. "As far as I can tell, all's well with the world." On that cryptic utterance, he departed, Philip's note in hand.

Philip wasted no more than a moment glowering at Carring's black back before rising and heading for the drawing-room.

When, fifteen minutes later, Henrietta entered the drawing-room, she discovered her stepson dancing a cotillion with her niece. Geoffrey was perched on a nearby chair, grinning delightedly.

THE GATHERING AT the Mountfords' was much as Antonia had imagined it.

"So glad to see you again, my dear." Lady Mountford greeted Henrietta fondly; she acknowledged Antonia's curtsy and Geoffrey's bow with a matronly nod. "You'll find there's no need to stand on ceremony tonight. My girls are about—you've already met, but introduce yourselves and chat as you please. Getting to know your peers is what the night's for—the musicians won't arrive until later." Her ladyship waved them into a spacious salon already well-filled with young ladies and, in the main, equally young gentlemen.

"You can help me over there." With her cane, Henrietta indicated a large grouping of comfortable chairs at one end of the salon. "Plenty of old friends there for me to catch up with while you two learn the ropes."

Geoffrey assisted her to a chair in the middle of the group. Antonia helped settle her shawls, then, when Henrietta waved them away, turned back into the room.

"Well!" she murmured, anticipation in her voice. "Where to start?"

"Where indeed?" Geoffrey had already scanned the room. "Here—take my arm." Antonia threw him a surprised look. He grimaced. "It'll make me less conspicuous."

Smiling affectionately, Antonia did as he asked. "You don't look conspicuous at all." With his Mannering height and Mannering build, set off by his relatively restrained attire, Geoffrey looked, if anything, a few years older than some of the young sprigs currently gracing her ladyship's floor. Some, indeed, decked out in the height of fashion, looked far younger than they doubtless wished.

"Hmm." Geoffrey's gaze was fixed on a gentleman to their left. "Just look at that silly bounder over there. His collar's so high he can't turn his head."

Antonia raised her brows. "You being such an expert on fashion?"

"Not me," Geoffrey answered, busy scanning the crowd for further spectacles. "But Philip said no true gentleman would be caught dead sporting such extreme affectations—restrained elegance is the hallmark of the out-and-outers."

"The out-and-outers?"

Geoffrey glanced at her. "Top o' the trees. The Corinthians. You know."

Antonia hid a grin. "No—but I suspect I can imagine. Am I to take it you aspire to such heady heights?"

Geoffrey considered, then shrugged. "I can't say I'd mind being top o' the trees some day, but I've decided to concentrate on getting a working notion of this *ton* business for now—I'll be going up in a few weeks after all."

Antonia nodded. "A wise idea, I'm sure."

"Philip thought so, too." Geoffrey was looking over the room. "What's say we do as we were bid and go introduce ourselves to some fellow sufferers?"

"Just as long as you refrain from informing them of their status." When he looked expectantly down at her, Antonia raised a brow. "I'm on your arm, remember? You're supposed to lead."

"Oh, good!" Geoffrey grinned and lifted his head. "That means I get to choose."

Predictably, he chose the group gathered about the prettiest girl in the room. Luckily, this included Cecily Mountford who, mindful of her mama's strictures, promptly introduced them to the three ladies and four gentlemen loosely grouped before the fireplace. None was more than twenty. Geoffrey was immediately included as one of the group; Antonia, her age declared not only by her innate poise but also by the elegant lines of Lafarge's creation, stood on its outskirts, metaphorically if not literally. Not that any attempted to exclude her—indeed, they treated her so deferentially she felt quite ancient. The young gentlemen blushed, stuttered and bowed while the young ladies leaned forward to shake hands, casting glances of muted envy at her gown.

It rapidly became apparent that their hostess's injunction to set formal restraint aside had been enthusiastically embraced; with the customary facility of youth, the company quickly got down to brass tacks.

The beauty, a sweet-faced young miss in a pale blue gown with dark ringlets bobbing on her shoulders, proved to be a Miss Catriona Dalling, an orphan from east Yorkshire who was in town under the aegis of her aunt, the Countess of Ticehurst.

"She's a dragon," Miss Dalling informed the company, her big blue eyes huge, her distinctly squared little chin jutting aggressively. "No! I tell a lie—she's worse than that, she's a *gorgon!*"

"Is she truly insisting on marrying you to the highest bidder?" Cecily Mountford was no more bashful than her guests.

Lovely lips set in a line, Miss Dalling nodded. "What's more, she's set her heart on poor Ambrose here." Dramatically, she put a hand on the bright green embossed silk sleeve of the young gentleman on her right and squeezed meaningfully. "So now we're *both* being persecuted!"

Ambrose, who gloried in the title of the Marquess of Hammersley, was a pale, obviously nervous young gentleman, short and slightly stocky; he blushed and muttered and tried to smooth the creases Miss Dalling's strong little fingers had left in his sleeve.

Geoffrey frowned. "Can't you both just say no?"

The comment earned him a host of pitying looks.

"You don't understand," Miss Dalling said. "My aunt is set on me marrying Ambrose because he's a *marquess,* and we haven't had one of those in the family before and a marquess is better than an earl, so she sees it as advancing the family's cause. And *Ambrose's* mama is pushing the match because of my inheritance, because his estates are not bringing in enough to dower all his sisters. *And,*" she added, with a darkling look, "because I'm so young she thinks I'll be easy to manage."

Antonia couldn't help but wonder if the Marquess's mama was blind.

"It's all arranged for consequence and money," Miss Dalling continued with undisguised contempt. "But it won't do! I've decided to marry for love or not at all!"

Her dramatic declaration drew approving nods from all around, particularly from the Marquess. Antonia inwardly frowned, wondering if they were all really so young, so untutored in society's ways—or if they were merely headstrong, trying their wings in vocal but not active rebellion.

Miss Dalling's championship of the gentle passion provoked argument on all sides, most, Antonia noted, thoroughly supportive of the heiress's position while openly condemning her aunt's.

Her spirits clearly unimpaired by the browbeating she had assured the company she had endured *en route* to Brook Street, Catriona Dalling flashed her an engagingly confiding smile. "I understand you're in town for the first time, as indeed we all are, but you have doubtless more experience than we in searching for your one and only love. I do hope you'll forgive me for speaking so plainly and rattling on so, but I dare say you can see things have reached a pretty pass. Ambrose and I will have to make a stand, don't you think?"

Arguments raged about them, revolving about how to spike Lady Ticehurst's ambitions; Geoffrey, Antonia could hear, was urging the participants to check with their men of affairs. Looking into Miss Dalling's unquestionably innocent eyes, she felt the weight of her years.

"While I would certainly not condone your being coerced into marriage, Miss Dalling, the fact remains that most marriages within our class are arranged, at one level or another. Some, perhaps, are underpinned by affection or long-standing acquaintance, but others are promoted on the basis of what I admit sound cold-blooded reasons. However, in the absence of either party's affections being fixed elsewhere, don't you think there's the possibility that your aunt's suggestion might, in the end, bear fruit?" In making the suggestion, Antonia's gaze touched the Marquess; she felt an immediate pang of uncertainty.

"There is that, of course." Miss Dalling nodded sagely. "But you see, I *have* found my only true love, so the argument does not hold."

"You have?" Antonia could not help eyeing her in concern. The heiress looked barely older than Geoffrey. "Forgive my impertinence, Miss Dalling, but are you sure?"

"Oh, yes. Absolutely sure." Catriona Dalling's decisive nod set her ringlets bouncing. "Henry and I have known each other since we were children and we're quite sure we want to marry. We had thought to wait for a few years—until Henry has proved himself in running his father's farms, you see—but Aunt Ticehurst stepped in."

"I see." The heiress's straightforwardness rang truer than any impassioned declarations. Antonia frowned. "Have you explained your attachment to your aunt?"

"My aunt does not believe in love, Miss Mannering." The militant gleam was back in Catriona Dalling's eye. "She might be more amenable were Henry a marquess too, only unfortunately he's simply a squire's son, so she's not disposed to acquiescence."

"I had not realized," Antonia admitted, "that your situation was quite so…awkward. To be urged to turn your back on love, given the connection is not ineligible and your attachment has proved constant, must be distressing."

Catriona gave another of her decisive nods. "It would be, if I had the slightest intention of giving in to the pressure. As it is, I'm determined to stand firm. Not only would marrying Ambrose ruin my life and Henry's, it would undeniably ruin Ambrose's as well."

Viewing the determined cast of Miss Dalling's fair features, and seeing the Marquess, weak-chinned and timid, in earnest conversation with Geoffrey beyond, Antonia could only concur.

"One way or another, I'm determined to win out. It's not as though love matches are all that rare these days." Catriona gestured grandly. "Even in days gone by, such affairs were known. My very own aunt—not Ticehurst, of course, but my other aunt, her sister, now Lady Copely—she defied the family and married Sir Edmund, a gentleman of sufficient but not extravagant means. They've lived very happily for years and years—their household is one of the most comfortable I know. If I could have as much by marrying for love, I would be entirely satisfied." She paused only for breath. "And only last year, my cousin Amelia—my Aunt Copely's eldest daughter—she married her sweetheart, Mr Gerard Moggs." She broke off to point out a young couple across the room. "They're over there—you can see for yourself how happy they are."

Antonia looked, effectively distracted from Miss

Dalling's concerns. This was, after all, what she had come to London to see—married ladies consorting in public with their spouses.

What she saw was a young gentleman of twenty-five or -six, standing by a *chaise* on which a pretty young lady was seated, angled around and looking up to meet her husband's gaze. Mr Moggs made some comment; his wife laughed up at him. She laid a hand on his sleeve, squeezing lightly, affectionately. Mr Moggs responded with an openly adoring look. Reaching out, he touched a finger to his wife's cheek, then bent and whispered in her ear before straightening and, with a nod, leaving her.

Antonia noted he went no further than the refreshment table, returning with two glasses.

"Miss Mannering, is it not?"

With a start, Antonia turned to find a gentleman of much her own age bowing before her. He was neatly if fashionably dressed, having avoided the excesses to which the younger generation had fallen prey.

"Mr Hemming, my dear Miss Mannering." As he straightened, Antonia looked into mild brown eyes set under wavy brown hair. "I hope you'll excuse my impertinence, but Lady Mountford tipped me the wink that the musicians are about to start up. Can I prevail on you to honour me with the first cotillion?"

The invitation was accompanied by an engaging smile; Antonia responded spontaneously, graciously extending her hand. "Indeed, Mr Hemming. I would be pleased to stand up with you."

She was well-versed in the cotillion, more adept, as it transpired, than Mr Hemming. Despite his pleasant disposition, he was forced to give his attention to the figures, leaving Antonia free to pursue her principal purpose. As she twirled and swirled, it was easy to examine those not dancing for couples who might be husband and wife. Other than the Moggs, she found no likely candidates. As for the Moggs, they, she felt certain, were hardly representative specimens.

It would, she felt sure, be unwise to use their behaviour as a guide to how she might behave with Philip. For a start, Philip was a good deal older than Mr Moggs. As, hand held high, she pirouetted, Antonia scanned the room. Indeed, she couldn't imagine Philip at such a gathering—there were no gentlemen like him present.

The age difference was telling in another way. She could not, by any fanciful stretch of her imagination, imagine Philip casting adoring glances at her, in public or otherwise. Likewise, she was quite certain any affectionate squeezes would result in a frown and a reprimand for damaging his suiting.

Gentlemen, her mother and all Yorkshire ladies had assured her, were made uncomfortable by any public show of fondness; ladies must never, so she had been taught, wear their hearts on their sleeves. While Miss Dalling and her family, one branch at least, as well as the youth of the *ton,* might freely acknowledge the softer emotions, Antonia could not believe that gentlemen of Philip's age and temperament had been won over.

The dance ended and she sank into the prescribed curtsy. Mr Hemming, beaming, raised her. "An excellent measure, Miss Mannering." Gallantly, he offered her his arm. "I take it you'll be attending the coming balls and parties?"

"I expect we'll attend our fair share." Antonia accepted his arm; he very correctly escorted her back towards the fireplace.

"Have you seen Lord Elgin's marbles? Quite worth a visit, in my humble estimation."

Antonia was about to reply when they were joined by an acquaintance of Mr Hemming's, a Mr Carruthers. Introduced, Mr Carruthers bowed extravagantly. Within minutes, two others had joined them, Sir Frederick Smallwood and a Mr Riley. Before Antonia could blink, she found herself at the centre of a small circle of gentlemen. They chatted amiably, pleasantly; she danced the quadrille with Sir Frederick and the last cotillion with Mr Carruthers. Mr Riley begged to be remembered when next they met.

Then the party started to break up. Geoffrey appeared by her elbow with the information that Henrietta was ready to depart; Antonia excused herself to her cavaliers and politely withdrew.

Once she had settled Henrietta in the carriage, draping extra shawls about her shoulders, Antonia sat back and pondered all she had seen. "Aunt," she eventually asked, as the carriage rocked into motion, "is it common for married gentlemen to accompany their wives to such entertainments?"

Henrietta snorted. "Noticed the Moggs, did you? Hardly surprising—they attracted quite a bit of interest, that pair of lovebirds." Her tone suggested the matrons had not been impressed. "But to answer your question—no, it's not general practice, but not only is Gerard Moggs quite openly besotted with his wife, she's also in an interesting condition, so I expect we'll have to excuse him."

Antonia nodded; she now had the Moggs in their proper perspective.

"Quite a fine line, actually—just how much husbandly attention is allowable." Henrietta spoke into the darkness, her voice only just audible over the rattle of the carriage wheels. "Not, of course, that the question arises in many cases—gentlemen being what they are. Only too glad to keep to their clubs and their dinners. Most put in an appearance at the best balls and parties, enough to nod to their wives in passing, but the consensus has always been that, in town at least, husbands and wives follow essentially separate social calendars." She fluffed her shawls. "That, of course, limits the opportunities for the sort of exhibition you witnessed tonight."

Any doubts as to her aunt's opinion of the Moggs' behaviour was laid to rest. Antonia shifted in her seat. "I had thought gentlemen often escorted ladies to the various entertainments?"

"Indeed." Henrietta yawned. "But, in the main, such escort duties fall to the unmarried males, the confirmed bachelors or the yet-to-be-snared. Only occasionally would a married lady expect her husband to act as her escort, and then only if he was wishful of attending the same function."

The shadows hid Antonia's frown. Her enjoyment of the outings Philip had organised, the laughter they had shared, the undeniable pleasure she found in his company—would all that change once they were wed? Be relegated to history, never to be experienced again? What, she wondered, was the point of being married— of having a firm friendship with one's husband—if being married prohibited him from spending time in your company?

The carriage swayed around a corner then rumbled on into Grosvenor Square; Geoffrey shifted in his corner. As they drew up outside Ruthven House, he jumped down, smothering a yawn. Between them, Antonia and he helped Henrietta up the steps; Carring stood at the top, holding the door wide.

Behind him, in the glow of the hall chandelier, Antonia spied Philip. He strolled forward as Carring shut the door. "A pleasant evening?"

The question was addressed to her but Geoffrey answered it.

"Dull work," he said, around another yawn. "Nothing of any substance except for the heiress's dragon of an aunt. She really did look like a gorgon."

"Indeed?" Philip raised an amused brow.

"Absolutely," Geoffrey assured him. "But I'm for bed."

"In that case," Henrietta said, poking him in the ribs, "you can give me your arm up the stairs." She glanced over her shoulder. "Send Trant up at once, please, Carring."

Carring bowed deeply. "Immediately, m'lady."

Antonia stood by Philip's side, watching until her brother and her aunt gained the upper landing.

"Come into the library." Philip's words and his hand at her elbow had her turning in that direction. "Was there much dancing?"

He had gone out after they had left, stifling a ludicrous wish that he could join them, instead meeting Hugo and a small coterie of friends at Brooks. Together, they'd gone on to Boodles, then to a select establishment in Pall Mall, but he'd been too restless to settle to the play. In the end, he'd cried off and returned home to idly pace the library floor.

"Two cotillions and a quadrille." Antonia yielded to his persuasion. They entered the library; Philip shut the door behind them.

"And you danced them all?"

"Indeed."

Philip stopped by one of the wing chairs flanking the fireplace, filled with a cheery blaze. Antonia sat, her skirts sighing about her. Philip paused, studying her. "Would you like a nightcap?"

Antonia looked up, her expression arrested, then smiled and shook her head.

Philip was not deceived. "What?"

Her smile reminded him forcefully of the irrepressible girl she had been. "Actually," she said, her eyes dancing, "I would dearly love a glass of warm milk but I cannot imagine how Carring would react to such a request."

"Can you not?" Philip's brows slowly rose. Turning, he crossed to the bellpull.

"Philip!" Antonia sat up.

Philip waved her back. "No—I have a score to settle—hush!" He returned to take the chair opposite hers.

Carring entered, ponderously solemn. "You rang, m'lord?"

"Indeed." Philip's expression was utterly bland. "Miss Mannering would like a nightcap, Carring. A glass of warm milk."

Carring's eyes flickered, then he bowed. "Will that be for two, m'lord?"

It took Philip a moment to master his tone. "No— you may pour me a brandy when you return."

"Very good, m'lord." Bowing, Carring withdrew.

As soon as the door closed, Antonia succumbed. "The thought of you drinking warm milk," she eventually got out, hugging her aching ribs.

Despite himself, Philip's lips curved upwards. "One day, I keep telling myself, I'll have the last word."

He was not destined to succeed that night. Carring reappeared bearing a glass of perfectly warmed milk on a silver tray. He deposited it on the table by Antonia's side with the same care he would have taken had it been aged port, then crossed to the cabinet and poured Philip's brandy, leaving the large glass by his master's elbow.

"Thank you, Carring. You may lock up."

"M'lord." With his usual deep obeisance, the major-domo withdrew.

Reaching for the brandy glass, Philip discovered it was half-full. A subtle hint, he supposed, of Carring's estimation of his state. Taking a sip, he smiled at Antonia. "With whom did you dance?"

Cradling her glass in her hand, she settled back in the chair. "Most of those present were more Geoffrey's age than mine but there were a few older gentlemen present—Mr Riley, Mr Hemming, Sir Frederick Smallwood and a Mr Carruthers."

"Indeed?" Philip did not recognize the names, which gave him some idea of their station. He fixed her with a mildly enquiring gaze. "And did you, like Geoffrey, find it dull work?"

Antonia smiled. "While it certainly did not rival Astley's, it was not totally without interest."

"Oh?"

It was more to the light in his eyes and his tone that

she responded, relating her observations on all she had seen as she slowly sipped her milk.

Philip watched the firelight strike gleams from her hair; the play of the fire-glow over her pale face, over her lips, sheened by the milk, held him in thrall. The cadence of her voice rose and fell; he sipped his brandy and listened as she painted a picture he had seen many times—through her eyes, it held an innocence, a sparkling freshness he had long grown too jaded to see.

She concluded with a thumbnail sketch of the major protagonists in what promised to be one of the season's more entertaining imbroglios.

"Indeed," Antonia said, setting aside her empty glass. "The situation of Miss Dalling and the Marquess does seem to be of some urgency—but how much of that derives from Miss Dalling's undeniable sense of the dramatic I could not say. Whatever, I'm certain Miss Dalling will prevail, gorgon aunt or no." She looked across at Philip, smiling, inviting him to share her amusement.

To her surprise, his face remained expressionless. Abruptly, he stood, setting his glass on the table beside him. "Come. It's time you went upstairs."

There was a note in his voice she could not place. Bemused, Antonia gave him her hands and let him draw her to her feet. Only then, as she stood directly before him, feeling the warmth of the fire strike through her thin gown did he meet her gaze. In the flickering firelight, his eyes were dark, slate-grey and stormy. Antonia felt her breath catch; she hesitated, then, calmly, her lips gently curving, she inclined her head. "Good night, Philip."

She was not going to retreat in disorder this time, nor take refuge in distance.

Stiffly, Philip returned her nod. He tensed to step back, to let her go—his fingers twined with hers and held tight. He hesitated, his gaze on her face, then slowly, gently, he drew her towards him until her bodice brushed his coat. His fingers slid from hers; he lifted both hands to frame her face.

Antonia held his gaze, her breath tangled in her chest, her heart pulsing in her throat. She saw his lids lower, his head angle over hers, then slowly descend. Her hand rose to his shoulder as she stretched upwards, her lips slightly parted.

He kissed her, not forcefully but confidently, as one sure of his welcome. His lips firmed, his tongue teased and tantalised, tracing the ripe curves of her lips. She parted them fully, inviting him to taste; he did, sampling her softness, laying claim to all she offered with a possessive, consummate skill.

The fire burned; the flames leapt. For long minutes, a gentle magic held sway.

Then, very slowly, very deliberately, Philip drew back. His lips bare inches from Antonia's, he waited until her lids fluttered opened. He studied her eyes, burnished gold in emerald-green. When they focused, he straightened. Holding tight to his reins, he released her.

"Good night, Antonia." His smile held a wry quality he doubted she'd understand. "Sweet dreams."

She blinked; her eyes searched his, neither frightened nor puzzled, but with an intensity he could not place. Then her lips curved. "Good night."

The soft whisper reached him as she turned away. He watched her go, saw her glance back, once, at the door, then slip through it, shutting it softly behind her.

Drawing in a deep breath, Philip turned towards

the fire. Bracing one arm against the mantelpiece, he gazed into the flames. Wonderingly, he ran the tip of his tongue over his lips—and fought to quell a shudder.

He had never imagined milk could taste erotic.

CHAPTER NINE

AT NOON THE next day, Philip returned to his home after breakfasting with friends at a coffee house in Jermyn Street. His expression unruffled, his disposition one of calm expectation, he entered the cool dimness of his hall.

Carring rolled forward to relieve him of his great-coat and cane.

Philip resettled his sleeves. "Is Miss Mannering about?"

"Indeed, m'lord." Carring fixed his gaze on the wall beyond Philip's right shoulder. "Miss Mannering is presently in the ballroom receiving instruction from the dancing master. *Maestro* Vincente."

Philip studied his major-domo's eloquently blank expression. "The ballroom?"

Carring inclined his head.

The ballroom lay beyond the drawing-room. The familiar chords of a waltz reached Philip's ears as he neared the door. Like all his doors, it opened noiselessly; crossing the threshold, he swiftly scanned the room.

The curtains had been drawn back along one side; sunlight spilled in wide beams across the floor. Geoffrey sat at the piano at the far end, industriously providing the music, frowning as he squinted at the music sheets. In the centre of the polished parquetry, Antonia, distinctly stiff, revolved awkwardly in the arms of a middle-aged man Philip unhesitatingly classed as an ageing roué.

Maestro Vincente showed little evidence of Italian blood. Short and rotund, he sported a florid, suspiciously English complexion. He was wearing a brown tie-wig and a bottle-green coat of similarly ancient vintage; his spindle shanks were clad in knitted hose. Most damning of all, Maestro Vincente possessed a distinctly lecherous eye.

Philip strode forward, letting his boot-heels ring on the boards. The music abruptly halted. Antonia looked up; Philip saw the relief in her eyes. His jaw hardened. "I fear there has been a misunderstanding."

Maestro Vincente's eyes started. He hurriedly released Antonia. "A misunderstanding?" His high-pitched voice rendered the exclamation a squeak. "No, no. I was hired, dear sir, I assure you."

Halting by Antonia's side, Philip looked down on the hapless maestro. "In that case, I regret to inform you that your services are no longer required." Without looking at the door, he raised his voice. "Carring?"

"M'lord?"

"Maestro Vincente is leaving."

"Indeed, m'lord."

"But…really! I must insist…!" Hands outspread, Maestro Vincente appealed to Philip.

Philip ignored him; gripping Antonia's elbow, he guided her down the room.

"If you'll just come this way, *sir?*" Carring's heavy tones left no room for argument. As always, he had the final word, efficiently ushering the deflated maestro out of the room.

The door shut; Antonia stared at Philip. "Why did you do that?"

Halting by the piano, Philip raised a supercilious brow. "He was hardly a proper person to instruct you in anything."

"Precisely what I said," Geoffrey interjected.

Antonia ignored her brother. She fixed Philip with an exasperated look. "Be that as it may, how, pray tell, am I now supposed to learn to waltz? In case it's escaped your notice, these days, every young lady *must* be able to waltz. The *ton* will expect it of—" Abruptly, she broke off. She glanced at Geoffrey, then continued, "Of me."

Philip nodded. "Indeed. So, having dismissed your appointed instructor, it would seem only fair that I take his place."

Antonia's eyes widened. "But—"

Exuberant chords drowned out her protest. Before she could marshal her wits, they were effectively scattered as Philip drew her into his arms.

"I assure you I'm every bit as competent as Maestro Vincente."

Antonia threw him a speaking look.

Philip met it with an improbably humble expression. "I've been waltzing around the *ton*'s ballrooms for… let me see." He frowned, then raised his brows. "More years than I can recall."

Antonia humphed and straightened her spine. As usual, she felt breathless; as he effortlessly steered her into the first gliding steps, a definite giddiness took hold. She wasn't at all sure this was a good idea but the challenge in his grey eyes made demurring unthinkable.

Tilting her chin, she tried to concentrate on where he was headed.

"Relax." Philip looked down at her. "Stop thinking and you'll follow my lead easily enough." When she looked her uncertainty, he raised one brow. "I'll even forgive you should you scuff my Hessians."

Antonia widened her eyes at him. "Given you've just high-handedly dismissed my dancing master, who came with quite remarkable recommendations I'll have you know, then I should think you must accept whatever consequences follow." As she capped the haughty comment with a toss of her curls, Antonia was struck by the oddity of the situation. Philip's intervention had been an impulsive, spur-of-the-moment reaction, unquestionably out of character. She cast a glance up at him—he was frowning.

He caught her eye. "Who recommended Maestro Vincente?"

Antonia grimaced. "Lady Castleton and Miss Castleton. They were full of his praises, so Henrietta said."

Philip's expression turned cynical. "The Castleton ladies appear to have a definite predilection for toads. Sir Miles has my sympathy."

Antonia wrinkled her nose. "I did wonder how they had stood him." She shuddered expressively. "He was decidedly slimy."

Philip's smile was fleeting, quickly superseded by a frown. He glanced at Geoffrey, busy with the keys, then captured Antonia's eye. "Kindly understand you have no cause whatever, henceforth, to have any dealings with toads, fish or any other amphibian or reptilian species." He held her gaze steadily. "Do I make myself clear?"

Antonia stared at him. "But what if—?"

"There are no circumstances I can imagine that would make acquaintance nor even contact with such persons necessary." His gaze fixed on her face, Philip steered them through a turn. "Henceforth, should you be approached by any such persons, I would take it kindly if you referred them to me." He paused, his imagination playing with the possibilities. "No—let me rephrase that." His jaw hardened; again he trapped Antonia's gaze. "Should any such approach you, I will *expect* you to refer them to me."

"Indeed?"

"Indeed. In fact," Philip continued, spurred on by memories of her wilful confidence, "if you do *not* call any such incidents to my notice, I will not be held accountable for my reactions."

"Philip—he was only a dancing master."

He frowned at her, noting the affectionate laughter lurking in her eyes. The sight soothed the aggressive compulsion gripping him. "It's not the dancing master I'm worried about," he acidly informed her. "Incidentally, you're waltzing quite creditably."

Antonia's eyes flew wide; she nearly missed her step but Philip's arm tightened, holding her steady. "So I am," she said, distinctly breathless. She lowered her gaze to his shoulder. Distracted by his conversation, she had not been directing her limbs at all. Of their own volition, they had followed his assured lead; as the music flowed, they continued to do so. Freed, her mind opened to the sensations of the dance, to the subtle play of her skirts about her legs, to the hardness of his thighs as they brushed hers through the turns.

The seductive swirl of the music was mirrored in

their movements; the smooth swoop and sway was a sensual delight. Philip's hand at her waist was firm, his touch confident as he guided her where he willed. Tentatively, she shifted the fingers of her right hand and felt his clasp tighten possessively.

Quelling a shiver of pure awareness, Antonia had a fleeting, distinctly scarifying vision of waltzing like this, held captive in Philip's arms, under the long noses of the *ton*. How on earth would she manage with every nerve-ending afire? Appalled, she banished the vision—she did not need to deal with that potential calamity today. Today, she was here, waltzing with Philip, with none—not even Geoffrey, too busy at the piano— to watch. Today, she could enjoy herself.

Unexpectedly, she felt a sense of warmth and triumph steal through her. A soft smile curved her lips. Raising her head, she let her gaze touch Philip's. "I have to admit that your…technique is a great improvement over Maestro Vincente's."

Philip humphed.

"That aside," she smoothly continued, "I had meant to thank you for your gift—the reticule." Today's gift— the latest in a long line. Ever since he had given her the parasol, no day had passed without some small token appearing in her room—a pair of gloves to match the parasol, a big bunch of satin ribbon in the same shade, a fashionable new bonnet, a pair of exquisite half-boots. This morning, a small beaded reticule she had admired in a Bond Street window had found its way to her dresser. "It goes perfectly with my new gold silk— I'll carry it tonight to the Quartermains."

Philip studied her smile, pleased yet exasperated, too. "Mere trumpery, as I said, but if it finds favour in your eyes, then I'll rest content." For now. He was irritatingly aware that, could he behave as he wished, he would shower her with jewels, furs and all manner of expensive tokens of an affection he was prepared to admit was very real. But while she wished their liaison to remain unacknowledged, trumpery was all he could afford. He was finding the restriction unexpectedly irksome.

The piece they had been waltzing to drew to its conclusion. "That's it!" Geoffrey declared. "All very well for you," he said, as both Antonia and Philip glanced his way. "But my fingers are cramping."

Philip grinned. Reluctantly releasing Antonia, he caught her hand, drawing her with him as he strolled towards the pianoforte. "What time did you start? Half past eleven?"

Flexing his fingers, Geoffrey nodded.

"Very well—we'll meet again tomorrow at the same time."

Geoffrey nodded again; it was Antonia who protested. "Tomorrow?"

Turning, Philip raised her hand and placed a quick, proprietorial kiss on her knuckles. "Indeed." He raised a brow at her. "You can hardly imagine you're an expert already?"

"No-oo." Looking up into his eyes, Antonia hesitated. Here in his ballroom, they'd be essentially alone; she was increasingly confident of behaving appropriately while they were private. And practice was surely needed to strengthen her defences against the evening when she would waltz with him in public, in a crowded ballroom under the glare of the chandeliers. Drawing in a deep breath, she nodded. "No doubt you're right."

The look Philip sent her made her arch her brows haughtily.

Antonia lifted her chin. "Until tomorrow at eleven-thirty, my lord."

LATER THAT AFTERNOON, Antonia with Geoffrey in tow again crossed the path of Catriona Dalling and the Marquess of Hammersley.

Together with Henrietta, they had taken advantage of the bright autumnal sunshine and driven forth in the Ruthven barouche to see and be seen in the Park. Tempted by the clemency of the weather, they had left Henrietta in the barouche, chatting to Lady Osbalde-stone, and descended to join the numerous couples fashionably strolling the lawns. They were halfway down the Serpentine Walk when they came upon Miss Dalling and the Marquess.

Heads together, voices lowered, the pair broke off what appeared to be frantic plotting to greet Antonia and Geoffrey. Shaking hands, Miss Dalling declared, "Fate has clearly sent you to us, for we stand greatly in need of support."

"Oh?" Geoffrey's eyes lit.

"Why do you need support, Miss Dalling?" Antonia felt rather more reticent over leaping to Miss Dalling's conclusions.

"Please call me Catriona," Miss Dalling said, smiling radiantly. "I truly believe we were meant to be friends."

Antonia could not help responding with a smile. "Very well—and you must call me Antonia. But why do you need aid?"

"My mama." Ambrose, who had already exchanged

names with Geoffrey, looked dejected. "She's arrived in town, deadly keen to see the knot tied."

"More than *keen*," Catriona decried. "Positively insistent! What with Aunt Ticehurst on one side and the Marchioness on the other, we're being *hounded* into marriage! We were just deciding what to do when you came up."

"Nothing too drastic, I hope. You would not wish to bring any scandal down upon your head."

"Indeed not." Catriona shook her head so vigorously her dark ringlets danced. "Any breath of scandal would avail us nought, for they would simply use that to force our hands. No—whatever we do must be done in such a way that there's no possibility Aunt Ticehurst and Ambrose's mama can use it against us."

"So what do you plan to do?" Geoffrey asked.

Catriona's brow clouded. "I don't know." For an instant, her lips quivered, then she blinked and lifted her chin. "That's why I've decided to send for Henry."

"Henry?"

"Henry Fortescue, my intended." Catriona's lips firmed. "*He'll* know what to do."

"A capital idea, I think." Ambrose looked hopefully at Geoffrey.

"But there's one problem." Catriona frowned. "I cannot write a letter to Henry for Aunt Ticehurst keeps a very close watch on me. We're not even out of her sight here—she's in her brougham, watching from the carriageway. I was just telling Ambrose he'll have to write for me."

"Ah…" Ambrose shifted his weight from one foot to the other. "No one more eager than I to be free of this coil." He looked pleadingly at Catriona. "But you can see, can't you, that it's not really the thing? Me writing to your intended telling him to come and see you?"

Catriona's expression turned mulish. "I don't see—"

"By Jove, yes!" Geoffrey looked horror-struck. "Dashed awkward."

"Precisely." Ambrose nodded rapidly. "Won't do—the poor fellow won't know what's afoot."

Antonia managed to keep her lips straight. "Indeed, Catriona, I do feel that any note would be better coming from you."

Catriona sighed. "But *that*'s the problem—how can we manage it?"

No one had an answer. At Antonia's suggestion, they strolled the path, all racking their brains for a solution.

"The museum!" Geoffrey halted; the others swung to face him. Eyes alight, he grinned at them. "I read somewhere that they have desks at the museum for scholars—you bring paper and pen and they provide the desk and inkwell for a small fee."

Catriona beamed. "We can go there tomorrow—" She broke off; her smile faded. "No, we can't. Aunt Ticehurst would insist on coming too."

Geoffrey glanced at Antonia. "Perhaps…?"

Antonia read his look and inwardly sighed. Shifting her gaze to the scenery, she considered. "Not tomorrow—that would appear too precipitous. But perhaps we could arrange to make a party to visit the museum the day after tomorrow? I understand Lord Elgin's marbles are a sight not to be missed."

She looked at Catriona in time to be dazzled by the transformation her words had wrought. Smiling, Catriona was the most radiantly beautiful girl.

"Oh, Miss Mannering—I mean, Antonia!" Catriona

caught Antonia's hand and clasped it warmly. "I will be your dearest friend for life! That's a brilliant suggestion."

Geoffrey humphed.

"If we present the thing right," Ambrose mused. "They'll be sure to approve." He turned to Catriona. "If we make it sound like I invited you and then asked Miss Mannering and Geoffrey to make up the party, it will allay their suspicions."

"Indeed, yes! Nothing could be better." Buoyed with purpose, Catriona flashed both Antonia and Geoffrey another stunning smile. "As I said, fate clearly intended us to meet. Nothing could have been more *fortuitous!*"

TWO DAYS LATER, Philip strolled across Grosvenor Square, basking in the afternoon sunshine. Swinging his cane as he walked, he noted that the leaves still clinging to the trees were golden and brown. They had completely changed colour since his return to London, their altered hue a record of the passage of time. To his mind, somewhat unexpectedly, that time had been well spent.

Their first days, admittedly, had been a trifle strained, but once Antonia had found her feet, their interactions had run smoothly. The Little Season would commence tomorrow evening; the round of balls and parties would fill the coming weeks. Given Antonia would be introduced as Henrietta's niece, no one would remark on his presence by her side. No eyebrows would be raised when he waltzed with her. A subtle smile curved his lips. Even more to his liking was what would happen every night when they returned to Ruthven House. He had been at pains to establish their nightly routine. At the end of every day, they would repair to his library, comfortable and at ease, she to drink her milk and favour him with her observations, he to sip his brandy and watch the firelight gild her face.

As he climbed the steep steps to his door, Philip realised he was smiling unrestrainedly. Abruptly sobering, he schooled his features to their usual impassive mien. Carring opened the door, bowing deeply before relieving him of his gloves and cane.

Philip glanced at the hall mirror, then frowned and straightened one fold of his cravat. Satisfied, he opened his lips.

"I believe Miss Mannering and Master Geoffrey have gone to the museum, m'lord."

Philip shut his lips. Turning, he shot Carring a narrow-eyed glance, then headed for the library.

The museum? Philip wandered about the library, ultimately halting before his desk to idly flip through his mail. He glanced at the stack of invitations piled on the desk but felt no burning desire to examine them. What to do with the afternoon? He could go to Manton's and hunt up some congenial company. Grimacing, he remained where he was. Long minutes passed as he stared unseeing out of the window, fingers tapping on the polished mahogany. Then his jaw firmed. Turning on his heel, he headed back into the hall.

Carring was waiting by the front door, Philip's gloves and cane held ready in his hands.

Philip cast him a withering look, accepted both gloves and cane, then strode out.

He reached the museum to find it unexpectedly crowded; it took him some time to locate his stepmother's niece. It was Geoffrey he found first, deep in examination of a group of artifacts purported to be Stone Age relics. Geoffrey's absorption was so intense Philip had to clap him on the shoulder to get his attention.

Blinking, Geoffrey focused on Philip's face, then smiled absentmindedly. "Didn't expect to see you here. Antonia's over there." He pointed to the next room, a large alcove beyond one of the display cases, then promptly returned to the relics.

Exasperation growing, Philip left him to them and pushed through into the next room.

Only to discover his stepmother's niece surrounded by no fewer than five gentlemen.

Antonia looked up to see Philip bearing down upon her. She smiled warmly. "Good day, my lord."

"Good afternoon, my dear."

As his fingers closed tightly about hers, Antonia registered the change from languid indolence to clipped abruptness. Rapidly whipping her wits to order, she turned a suddenly wary gaze on her companions. "Ah—I believe I have mentioned Sir Frederick Smallwood, my lord."

Philip nodded stiffly in reply to Sir Frederick's bow. "Smallwood."

Disregarding the menace underlying his tone, Antonia doggedly introduced every last one of her court. "Mr Carruthers was about to favour us with the tale of the discovery of the stone implements displayed over there." Antonia smiled encouragingly at Mr Carruthers.

A student of antiquities, Mr Carruthers promptly launched into his dissertation. As his tale unfolded, encompassing numerous tangents, all described in glowing detail, Antonia felt Philip shift impatiently. When Mr Dashwood asked a question, which led to a lively discussion involving all the other gentlemen, Philip leaned closer and whispered in her ear, "You can't be so bored you consider *this* amusement?"

Antonia threw him a warning glance. "It's an improvement over staring at the relics."

"The trick is to keep strolling." Philip caught her hand and placed it on his sleeve. "That way, you don't end up collecting so much extraneous baggage."

His hand closed over hers, his intention plain; Antonia held firm. "No!" she hissed. "I can't leave here—I'm waiting for someone."

Philip's eyes locked on hers. The arrested look in them made Antonia's heart skip a beat. "Oh?" he said. One brown brow slowly arched. "Who?"

Antonia cast a distracted glance at her companions; their discussion was slowly winding down. "I'll explain it all later—but we have to stay here." With that, she gave her attention to Sir Frederick.

"Tell me, my dear Miss Mannering." Sir Frederick smiled engagingly. "What do you say to the age of these gold cups?" He gestured to a large display in the centre of the room. "Are we really to believe such workmanship dates from before Christ?"

Philip raised his eyes to the ceiling. Resisting the urge to simply haul Antonia away, he clenched his jaw and endured fifteen minutes of the most utterly inane discussions. Having very little to do with younger gentlemen, he had never before suffered any similar experience. By the time Antonia abruptly straightened, he was ready to admit that young ladies of the *ton* might have a cross to bear he had not hitherto appreciated.

Scanning the room, his gaze passed over a stunningly pretty girl strolling forward on the arm of a pasty-faced youth. Failing to discover any likely candidate for Antonia's attention, he was rescanning their surroundings when Antonia broke off her conversation. "Ah—here's Miss Dalling."

Miss Dalling and her companion were well-known to the other gentlemen; introduced, Philip exchanged greetings. He did not need Antonia's swift glance to realize it was Miss Dalling and the Marquess for whom she'd been waiting. Her reasons, however, remained a mystery.

Miss Dalling turned wide lavender-blue eyes upon the assembled company. "All these old things are quite fascinating, are they not?"

While Catriona chattered animatedly, Antonia, somewhat distractedly, considered her court. When she had planned this excursion, she had imagined strolling quietly about the displays on Geoffrey's arm while Catriona with Ambrose in attendance composed her missive. But no sooner had she set foot in the museum than gentlemen had appeared as if sprouting from the woodwork, all intent on passing the time by her side. Luckily, Mr Broadside and Sir Eric Malley had had previous engagements which had forced them to leave; that still left her with five unexpected cavaliers to dismiss.

She had not the first idea how to accomplish the deed.

"Perhaps," she said, smiling meaningfully at Catriona, "we should stroll about the rooms?"

"Oh, yes! I expect I should take particular note of some of the displays." Eyes twinkling, Catriona took Ambrose's arm. Antonia surmised the summons to Henry Fortescue had been successfully inscribed and handed into Ambrose's care.

Her hand on Philip's sleeve, Antonia smiled upon her court. "Gentlemen, I thank you for your company. Perchance we'll meet tonight?"

"Yes, indeed—but no need to break up the party." Sir Frederick gestured expansively.

"No—indeed no," came from Mr Dashwood. "Haven't actually *looked* at anything in the museum for years—only too pleased to take a squint around."

"I'll come too—just in case you need some information on the artifacts." Mr Carruthers nodded benignly.

Antonia's answering smile was weak. When they strolled from the room, all five gentlemen ambled in their wake. As they wended their way between the display cases, she bit her lip—then slanted a glance up at Philip. He met it with an expression she was coming to know well—pure cynicism combined with insufferable male superiority. He arched a distinctly supercilious brow at her. Antonia narrowed her eyes at him, then, head high, shifted her gaze forward.

Philip hid his smile. He saw Geoffrey and shot him a glance sharp enough to bring him to heel. When they reached the centre of the main room, he halted and pulled out his watch. Consulting it, he grimaced. "I'm afraid, my dear, that we've run out of time. If you want your surprise, we'll have to leave now."

Antonia stared at him, her lips forming a silent "Oh."

"Surprise?" Geoffrey asked.

"The surprise I promised you all," Philip glibly replied. "Remember?"

Geoffrey met his gaze. "Oh! That surprise."

"Indeed." Smoothly turning to Antonia's trailing court, Philip raised a languid brow. "I'm afraid, gentlemen, that you'll have to excuse us."

"Oh—yes. Naturally!"

"Until next time, Miss Mannering. Miss Dalling."

To Antonia's inward disgust, amid a host of similar phrases, her five encumbrances obediently took themselves off. As the last bowed and withdrew, she glanced up at Philip, only to see his jaw firm.

"I suggest we get moving immediately." Before any of them could question his intent, he had them all outside, Catriona and Ambrose included. A hackney was waiting at the kerb; Philip hailed it and bundled Catriona, Ambrose and Geoffrey aboard. Shutting the door on them, he slapped the side. "Gunters."

The jarvey nodded and clicked his reins. The old coach lumbered away.

Left standing on the pavement, distinctly bemused, Antonia stared at Philip. "What about us?"

Exasperated, he looked down at her. "Do we have to follow?"

Antonia stiffened. "Yes!"

Philip narrowed his eyes at her, but she refused to retreat. Heaving a long-suffering sigh, he called up another hackney.

"Now," he said, the instant the hackney's door shut upon them. "You can explain what Miss Dalling and the Marquess are about."

Antonia was perfectly willing to do so; by the time the hackney drew up outside Gunters, Philip was considering retreating himself. Unfortunately, the sight that met his eyes as he glanced out of the hackney window rendered that course of action impossible.

"Good God!" he said, sitting forward and reaching for the handle. "The silly clunches are standing outside."

Predictably, Catriona Dalling had started to attract

an audience. Gritting his teeth, Philip handed Antonia down, then deftly extricated Miss Dalling and, feeling very like a sheepdog with his sheep, ushered his little group into the shop.

It was hardly a venue at which he was well known. Nevertheless, the waitress took one look at him and immediately found a discreet booth big enough to accommodate the whole party. By the time he sank onto the bench beside Antonia, Philip found he was actually looking forward to an ice.

The waitress took their orders; the ices arrived before they had well caught their breaths. Catriona, Ambrose and Geoffrey attacked theirs in style; Philip and Antonia were rather more circumspect.

Catriona finished first and patted her lips with her napkin. "Ambrose will post my letter tomorrow," she informed the table at large. "I know Henry will come posthaste to the rescue—just like the true knight he is." She clasped her napkin to her bosom and affected a romantically distant gaze. Then she sighed. "He'll know exactly what to do for the best. Everything will be right as a trivet once he arrives."

When she and Ambrose fell to discussing their respective guardians' likely plans, Philip caught Antonia's eye. "I can only hope," he murmured, "that Mr Fortescue is up to handling Miss Dalling's dramatic flights. Don't ever think I'm not grateful for your lack of histrionic tendencies."

Antonia blinked, then smiled and looked down at her ice. As she took another mouthful, her smile grew. She had wondered if Philip would prove at all susceptible to Catriona's undeniable beauty. Apparently not.

His comment, indeed, suggested quite otherwise; she couldn't help feeling pleased.

Watching her, Philip narrowed his eyes, astute enough to guess what lay behind her smug smile. He attacked his ice, inwardly humphing at the implied slight to his taste. To any with experience, certainly any of his ilk, Miss Dalling's mere prettiness could not hold a candle to Antonia's mature beauty. The heiress might be a handful in her own way but she was very definitely not the same sort of handful his bride-to-be obviously was. He glanced at Antonia, then, all but automatically, scanned the room.

Four gentlemen rapidly averted their eyes. Philip's expression hardened. At the museum, all five gentlemen had had Antonia in their sights, a fact that had not escaped him.

Shifting in his seat, Philip let his gaze rest on her face.

She felt it; turning, she briefly studied his eyes, then lifted a brow. "I think perhaps it's time we left. We have Lady Griswald's musical soirée this evening."

As they left the shop, Philip found himself wondering who would be at Lady Griswald's tonight. Antonia shook his arm.

"Catriona and Ambrose are leaving."

Philip duly took his leave of the pair, who intended visiting Hatchard's before returning to Ticehurst House. With Antonia on his arm and Geoffrey ambling behind, Philip headed in the opposite direction. Absorbed with thoroughly unwelcome considerations, he stared, unseeing, straight ahead.

Antonia cast a puzzled glance up at him. She opened

her lips to comment on his brown study, simultaneously following his gaze. Her words froze on her lips.

Ten yards ahead stood two ladies, both exquisitely gowned and coiffed. Both were ogling Philip shamelessly.

She might have been raised in Yorkshire but Antonia knew immediately exactly what sort of ladies the two were. She stiffened; her eyes flashed. She was about to bestow a chillingly haughty glance when she caught herself up—and glanced at Philip.

In the same instant, Philip refocused and saw the two Cyprians. Absentminded still, he idly took stock of their wares, then felt Antonia's gaze. He glanced down at her, just in time to see her lids veil her eyes. She stiffened and pointedly looked away, every line infused with haughty condemnation.

Philip opened his mouth—eyes narrowing, he bit back his words. He had, he reminded himself, no need to excuse himself over something she should not, by rights, even have noticed. He halted. "We'll take a cab."

He hailed a passing hackney. The three of them climbed in; Antonia sat beside him, cloaked in chilly dignity. Philip stared out of the window, his lips a thin line. He had had to put up with her being ogled all afternoon, let alone what might happen tonight. She had no right to take umbrage just because two ladybirds had cast their eyes his way.

By the time the hackney turned into Grosvenor Square, he had, somewhat grudgingly, calmed. Her sensitivity might irritate but her intelligence was, to him, one of her attractions. It was, he supposed, unreasonable to expect her to be ignorant on specific topics—such as his past history or potential inclinations.

The hackney pulled up; he let Geoffrey jump down, then descended leisurely and helped Antonia to the pavement, affecting indifference when she refused to meet his eyes. He tossed a half-crown to the jarvey then, studiously urbane, escorted her in, pausing in the hall to hand his cane to Carring.

"So," he said, coming up with her as she removed her bonnet. "You're bound for Lady Griswald's tonight?"

Still avoiding his gaze, Antonia nodded. "A musical soirée, as I said. Hordes of innocently reticent young ladies pressed to entertain the company with their musical talents." Looking down, she unbuttoned her gloves. "Not, I believe, your cup of tea."

Her words stung; ruthlessly, Philip clamped down on his reaction, shocked by its strength. His polite mask firmly in place, he waited patiently beside her—and let the silence stretch.

Eventually, she glanced up at him, haughty wariness in her eyes.

Trapping her gaze, he smiled—charmingly. "I hope you enjoy yourself, my dear."

Briefly, her eyes scanned his, then, stiffly, she inclined her head. "I hope your evening is equally enjoyable, my lord."

With that she glided away; regally erect, she climbed the stairs.

Philip watched her ascend, then turned to his library, his smile converting to a wry grimace. He was too old a hand to try to melt her ice; he'd wait for the thaw.

CHAPTER TEN

THREE NIGHTS LATER, the atmosphere was still sub-zero.

Following Henrietta and Geoffrey up Lady Caldecott's stairs, Antonia on his arm, Philip cast a jaundiced glance over the crowd about them. Their first two evenings of the Little Season had been spent at mere parties, relatively quiet affairs at which the guests had concentrated on catching up with the summer's developments rather than actively embarking on any new intrigues. Lady Caldecott's Grand Ball marked the end of such simple entertainments.

They had yet to gain the ballroom door, but at least three of his peers had already taken due note of Antonia, serenely beautiful if somewhat tense by his side. Even at a distance, he could detect the gleam in their eyes. He didn't need to look to know she presented a stunning spectacle, garbed in another of Lafarge's creations, a shimmering sheath of pale gold silk trimmed at neckline and hem with delicate lace edged with tiny pearls. Despite his intentions, his eyes were drawn to where her mother's pearls lay about her throat, their priceless sheen matched by her ivory skin.

She glanced up, cool distance in her gaze. "It's dreadfully crowded. I hope Henrietta will manage."

Philip's gaze flicked forward to where Henrietta doggedly stumped upwards, leaning heavily on Geoffrey's arm. "I think you'll discover she's made of stern stuff. She won't wilt in this climate."

Antonia hoped he was right. The crowd was dense, the press of bodies up the stairs disconcerting. It was her first experience of this degree of enthusiasm. "Is this what they term a 'crush'?" Glancing up, she surprised an arrogant, almost aggressive look on Philip's face. It disappeared as he looked down at her.

"Indeed." Philip shackled the urge to draw her closer. "The epitome of every hostess's ambitions. That said, I suspect Lady Caldecott has overstepped her mark. Her ballroom, I hesitate to inform you, is not this," he gestured at the crowd surging about them, "large."

The accuracy of his prediction was confirmed when, fifteen cramped minutes later, they passed down the receiving line and gained the ballroom.

Henrietta, too short to see beyond the shoulders surrounding them, jabbed Geoffrey in the arm. "There should be a group of three or four *chaises* somewhere about. Where?"

Geoffrey lifted his head.

"To the left," Philip said.

"Good! That's where my set will gather. You—" Henrietta poked Geoffrey again "—can escort me there and then you may take yourself off. As for you two—" she cast a glance at Philip and Antonia "—you'll have to take care of yourselves." Henrietta smiled, decidedly smug. "In this crush, we'll never find each other—you can fetch me when it's time to leave."

Philip's brows rose but he made no demur. He bowed gracefully. "As you wish, ma'am."

Antonia bobbed a curtsy. Henrietta shuffled into the crowd and was immediately lost to sight. As Philip resettled her hand on his sleeve, Antonia looked about, taking stock of her first Grand Ball. Silks and satins, ribbons and lace, paraded before her. A hundred voices were raised in avid chatter; perfumes drifted and mingled into a heady haze, wafting as bejeweled ladies nodded and curtsied. Elegant gentlemen in superbly cut evening coats inclined their heads; comforted by the hardness of Philip's arm beneath her hand, Antonia smiled coolly back.

"Before we go any further," Philip said, interrupting her reconnaissance, "I would be greatly obliged if you would write my name in your card against the first waltz." A number of gentlemen were headed their way.

Antonia looked up at him. "The first waltz?"

Philip nodded. "Your first waltz." There had been only cotillions, quadrilles and country dances over the past two nights; he was determined her first waltz in the capital would be his.

Reading as much in his eyes, Antonia resigned herself to the inevitable. Lips compressed, she opened the small card Lady Caldecott had handed her. The first waltz was the third dance; under Philip's watchful eye, she duly inscribed his name in the space beside it—then showed him the card.

He actually read it before nodding. Antonia set her teeth. She would have caught his eye and glared—she was distracted by Hugo Satterly who appeared through the ranks before them.

"A great pleasure to welcome you to town, Miss Mannering." Hugo bowed with ready grace, his pleasant smile creasing his face.

He was but the first to express that sentiment. To Antonia's surprise, they were rapidly surrounded by a

select group of elegant gentlemen, none of whom bore
any relation to her relatively innocuous, easy-to-manage
cavaliers of the past weeks. These gentlemen were all
contemporaries of Philip's, many his friends, smoothly
claiming his offices in making the introductions. At
first, she wondered if it was he rather than she with
whom they had stopped to chat. They were, however,
assiduous in claiming the blank spaces in her dance
card; long before the first cotillion, her card was grati-
fyingly full.

Surrounded by broad shoulders, she waited for the
musicians to start up, not entirely sure if she was relieved or otherwise when her circle of gentlemen plainly
set themselves to entertain her. Philip, however, large
and relatively silent by her side, gave her no hint he saw
anything remarkable in their attentions; lifting her chin,
Antonia smiled graciously on her would-be cavaliers.

A lull in the conversation brought Hugo Satterley's
voice to her ears; he was standing beyond Philip—a
quick glance confirmed it was to Philip he spoke.

"Meant to thank you for coming out that night—
dashed awkward, but it saved my hide."

Philip's eyes narrowed. "If I'd known it was simply
a matter of making a fourth at whist I wouldn't have
set foot beyond my door. From your note, I'd imagined
some life-threatening situation."

Hugo opened his eyes wide. "If you think engaging oneself to entertain the Bishop of Worcester and
then finding oneself one short for the table isn't life-
threatening, you know nothing of the Bishop. Can't tell
you how grateful I was to be saved from excommuni-
cation."

Philip's snort was drowned by the summoning of the violins.

"Ah!" Eyes brightening, Hugo turned to Antonia. "My dance, I believe, Miss Mannering?"

Antonia smiled and gave him her hand. Hugo deftly cleared a path onto the dance floor; while they waited for the rest of the company to find places in the sets, Antonia turned to him. "I overheard your comment on the Bishop of Worcester. Was it recently you entertained His Grace?"

"Just the other night." Hugo grimaced. "Deuced awkward, but I had to do it—he's m'godfather, you know. He'd received a summons from his sister, Lady Griswald, to some musical affair. Old man's tone deaf—virtually ordered me to rescue him."

Antonia's eyes widened. "I see." She managed a weak smile. She'd returned from Lady Griswald's to find Philip absent; that night had been the first on which she'd declined her nightcap.

"At last!" Hugo held out his hand as the music for the cotillion began.

Antonia had danced countless cotillions in recent weeks; habit, she was certain, was all that kept her twirling in the right direction. A horrible suspicion had taken root in her mind; as it grew, a sinking sensation swelled inside her. She was relieved when, at the cotillion's end, Hugo returned her to Philip's side. Unfortunately, a gavotte with Lord Dewhurst followed virtually immediately. Raising her from her final curtsy, his lordship guided her around the room. After passing some time in idle, on her part disjointed, conversation, they finally came up with Philip; her heart sank when she saw the steely look in his eyes.

Reclaiming Antonia's hand, Philip settled it on his sleeve then caught Lord Dewhurst's eye. "I believe, Dewhurst, that our hostess is searching for you."

"Heh?" Jerked from contemplation of Antonia's smile, Lord Dewhurst focused on Philip's face. His expression turned to one of dismay. "Don't say that. Dash it all—this is what comes of letting on I'm on the lookout for a wife." Openly chagrined, he confided to Antonia, "If her ladyship's after me, it'll mean she's got some protégée that she wants me to look over. I'll have to take refuge in the cardroom."

His features impassive, Philip scanned the crowds. "If her ladyship's on the prowl, I wouldn't waste any time."

Lord Dewhurst sighed and bowed over Antonia's hand. "Dashed shame. But no doubt we'll meet at the next ball, Miss Mannering." With a hopeful smile, he straightened. "I'll look forward to furthering our acquaintance."

Antonia smiled with what grace she could muster; his lordship turned away, his eyes on her to the last. Lord Marbury stepped in, keen to engage her attention.

Philip gritted his teeth.

Tonight, strolling the rooms, his favoured method for disposing of unwanted encumbrances, was out of the question; Lady Caldecott had outdone herself with a vengeance. There was barely room to stand; the dance floor would be impossibly crowded.

Not that the idea of waltzing with Antonia at excusably close quarters was bothering him. Quite the opposite. But the crowding left him with few options to thin out her court.

He was contemplating a few novel possibilities when

the musicians returned and set bow to string. Sternly suppressing a surge of anticipation, he turned to Antonia. "The first waltz. My dance, I believe, my dear."

"Indeed, my lord." Straightening her spine, Antonia inwardly cursed the fluster that threatened. Her smile overbright, she gave Philip her hand. "I rely on you to lead me through this maze."

With the merest inclination of his head, he led her to where couples were jostling for space on the floor. Tense as she was, the overcrowding claimed all of Antonia's attention; it was only when they were precessing freely, albeit in distinctly circumscribed circles, that she relaxed enough to think. Only to have her senses rush in—a most peculiar panic gripped her.

Philip was holding her very close, a fact necessitated by the proximity of the surrounding couples. As realization sank in, Antonia felt her breath catch, felt the familiar vice close about her chest. Held against him, the shift and sway of their bodies as they revolved through the dance was a dizzying distraction, a potent inducement to set her wits free and let her senses slide into a world of sensation. Her gaze wide, unseeing, she stiffened, struggling to shackle her wits, to keep her face, her posture, free of any hint of the drugging effect of the dance, of her awareness of Philip.

She felt him glance down at her. She looked up, only to discover his lips mere inches away; her gaze, beyond her control, focused on them. They twisted wryly.

"Relax. You're stiff as a poker."

The comment, spoken in a tone that was clearly private, only made her stiffen further. Forcing her gaze upwards, she met his gaze. She watched a frown gather in his eyes. "I—"

She had no idea how to explain, how to describe the panic mushrooming within her. This was the first waltz of the Little Season, her first public waltz with him— and any second she was going to stumble.

Instinctively, Philip gathered her closer, his hand at her waist reassuringly caressing her spine as he guided her into a turn.

Like a brand, the heat of his hand seared Antonia, exciting skin not accustomed to his touch. At the same moment, his thigh parted hers in the turn, hard muscle impressing itself against her softer flesh.

Her breath caught on a stifled gasp; her feet missed a step.

Philip caught her to him, preventing her stumble. Frowning, very aware of her distress, he deftly stepped clear of the circle of dancers rounding the end of the room. Smoothly releasing Antonia, he took her hand and ushered her before him towards the doors standing open to the terrace, his shoulders effectively screening her from any interested stares. Pale, she cast a wide-eyed glance up at him; he met it with a superficial smile. "This crowd is impossible—a little fresh air will clear your head."

Antonia hoped it would. She felt dreadful; her head had started to throb. She felt immeasurably grateful when Philip propelled her irresistibly out of the door.

The cool night air hit her like a slap; she stopped dead. "Wait! We can't—"

"There's nothing the least improper in our being out here." Philip's accents, warningly clipped, came from directly behind her. "We are, after all, hardly private."

Glancing about, Antonia discovered he was right. The terrace was a wide, stone-flagged extension of the

ballroom floor; other couples like them had sought refuge on its uncluttered expanse. There were sufficient
others present, strolling and chatting in groups, to nul-
lify any question of impropriety. None, however, was
close enough to overhear their conversation.

"Now." Capturing Antonia's attention by the simple
expedient of putting one finger under her chin and turning her face to him, Philip raised a commanding brow.
"What's wrong?"

Antonia met his gaze, then lifted her chin free of his
finger. Her stomach had knotted tight. "I…simply had
trouble with the waltz."

Philip couldn't help himself. "Strange. I was under
the impression you considered yourself something of an
expert—certainly in no need of further lessons." The
morning after Lady Griswald's musical soirée, she had
failed to appear in the ballroom. Geoffrey, too, had not
shown; when questioned in suitably nonchalant vein,
Geoffrey had let fall that his sister had somewhat wasp-
ishly informed him that she had learned quite enough.

Antonia risked a glance from beneath her lashes,
then, tilting her chin, fixed her gaze on the gardens.
"I did not feel it right to take so much of your time.
You've been very generous—I did not wish you to feel
duty-bound."

Philip managed not to growl. "I never saw teaching
you to waltz as a duty." A pleasant distraction, yes—one
he had missed. "And it's quite obvious you need further
lessons." The startled glance she threw him was some
small consolation. "We'll start again tomorrow. But
aside from all that, I'm a great deal more than seven,
you know."

Startled by the change in his tone, Antonia glanced

up; Philip trapped her gaze. "I've taught you well enough and you learn like a sponge—it wasn't the steps of the waltz that brought you undone." His gaze sharpened. "What was it? Has anyone done anything to upset you?"

His second question and the tension behind it convinced Antonia prevarication would not be wise. She hesitated, then drew in a strengthening breath and, her gaze unfocused, admitted, "I find I have great difficulty keeping a proper distance."

Philip frowned. "The distance between us was perfectly proper. I'm far too old a hand to step over the line during the first waltz of the season."

Antonia threw him an exasperated look. "*That*'s not what I meant."

Philip looked down at her. "Then what *did* you mean?"

Antonia glared. "You know perfectly well what I mean. And it's not at all helpful to tease me about it." Her voice caught; swinging around, she quickly crossed to the balustrade.

Eyes narrowing, Philip watched her, then followed at a more leisurely pace. When he stopped beside her, she was staring into the darkness, her hands clasped tightly before her. "I vaguely recall having this conversation before. While I'm naturally flattered that you persist in thinking me omniscient, I must confess that what you apparently find obvious is very frequently far from obvious to me."

She hesitated, then slowly turned to face him.

Antonia met his gaze with one of her very direct looks. What she saw in his eyes reassured her. "I—" She broke off, frowning, then, lifting her head, swung

to face the gardens. "I find the…sensations of waltzing with you so distracting that I… In short, I cannot
be sure I will not commit some indiscretion."

Tilting his head, Philip studied her face. "While
waltzing?"

Her gaze on the shadows, Antonia nodded.

A slow smile broke across Philip's face. Then he
recalled that he did not always read her aright. "I take
it," he said, carefully composing his features, "that you
would not feel…compelled to indiscretion while waltzing with anyone else?"

Antonia frowned at him. "Of course not." She studied his face. "I had thought I could cope but…" She
gestured vaguely.

Philip caught her hand; he waited until she met his
eyes before raising it to his lips. He paused, studying
her wide eyes, aware of the slim fingers resting in his,
aware of the demon too close to his surface. "Geoffrey
said you had told him he could trust my advice unreservedly." He raised a brow. "Will you, too, place your
trust in me?"

Uncertainty darkened her eyes; Philip allowed his
impatience to show. "I have, as I believe you know,
been waltzing through the *ton*'s ballrooms for rather
many years."

"I know." Antonia felt breathless. They were, she was
perfectly certain, no longer talking about mere waltzing. "But…"

Philip held her gaze; again he lifted her hand, gently
brushing his lips across her fingertips, well aware of the
reaction she struggled to hide. "Believe me." His voice
deepened. "I won't let you falter." He waited, watching her, willing her, then lifted one brow. "Trust me?"

The moment that followed stretched, fragile as spun glass, timeless as eternity. Antonia felt each beat of her heart, felt the shallowness of each breath. "You know I do."

"Then close your eyes. It's time for your next lesson."

Antonia hesitated, then complied.

"Imagine we're in the ballroom at Ruthven House."

She felt Philip's arm slide about her, felt his hold on her fingers shift.

"Geoffrey is supplying the music."

She frowned. "I can hear violins."

"He's brought some friends to help him."

The clipped accents made her lips twitch. Philip raised her hand; his arm tightened about her.

Antonia baulked. "Philip—!"

"Trust me."

A second later she was waltzing.

"Keep your eyes closed. Remember, we're in Ruthven House—there's no one else about."

Antonia knew very well where they were; the cool night air shifted over her bare shoulders, a light breeze played with her skirts. But Philip's arm held her steady; with her eyes closed, she had no alternative but to relax and follow his strong lead. She heard muted chatter and laughter; the musicians were still scraping away. He held her close. As they whirled and twirled, the sensations that had earlier assailed her rose up, heightened by her earlier sensitivity. Detached, distanced from worry, she could not find it in her to fight them; instead, her senses stretched, luxuriating in the moment.

Watching her face, Philip saw her lips lift; his own curved knowingly. He drank in the sight of her face, then said, "Open your eyes."

Antonia did, blinking as her eyes adjusted. She took in Philip's arrogantly satisfied expression, then glanced past his shoulder—and gasped.

They were no longer the only ones waltzing on the terrace. As they revolved, she turned her head this way and that, amazed at the collection of fashionable couples now whirling in the starlight.

"It appears we've started a new trend."

"Indeed."

Seconds later, the music slowed. Philip whirled them to a flourishing halt, touching Antonia's hand to his lips. "Believe me—there's nothing in your behaviour to give you cause to blush."

Antonia met his gaze; a frown slowly gathered in her eyes. "While I concede that your experience might be extensive, I'm not at all certain you're an appropriate judge of such matters."

Philip narrowed his eyes. "Antonia, which of us has been buried in the wilds to the north for the past eight years?"

Antonia's eyes flashed. "And which of us, my lord, has any previous experience of our current relationship?"

Philip held her gaze steadily. "Rest assured, my dear, that should you commit any indiscretion, however minor, I will be the first to bring it to your notice."

Antonia raised a haughty brow. "Unfortunately, it's your definition of 'indiscretion' that I question."

"Indeed? Then you'll undoubtedly be relieved to know that to be a fully-fledged member of the fraternity to which I belong, an exquisitely detailed understanding of indiscretions, in all their varied forms, is mandatory." Philip placed her hand on his sleeve, then calmly raised his brows at her.

Stumped, Antonia cast him a distinctly mulish glance.

With a pointed smile, Philip turned her towards the ballroom. "You may trust me to guide you through the shoals of the *ton,* Antonia."

She glanced at his face, her gaze familiar and open. As they neared the ballroom, she regally inclined her head. "Very well. I will place my reliance on you, my lord."

His satisfaction hidden behind his usual impassive mask, Philip steered her into the throng.

At ELEVEN O'CLOCK the next morning, Philip descended the stairs, very definitely in charity with the world. It was an effort to keep from whistling; he had to keep his mind from dwelling on their interlude in the library the night before in order to keep a smug smile from his face.

Carring appeared from the nether regions; Philip had often wondered if his major-domo possessed some peculiar facility which alerted him to his impending appearance in the hall.

"I'm lunching at Limmer's, then I expect we'll go on to Brooks."

"And then to the Park?"

Philip shot Carring a severe glance. "Possibly." He paused to check his cravat in the hall mirror; a fragment of the past night's activities, when Antonia's fingers had become entangled in the starched folds about his throat, drifted through his mind. "Incidentally, where did the *chaise* that matches the chairs in the library go?"

"If you recall, my lord, we removed it to the back

parlour after you declared that it cluttered up the library to no good purpose."

"Ah, yes." Satisfied with the drape of the linen folds about his neck, Philip resettled his collar. "You may move it back to the library."

"You require more comfortable seating, my lord?"

Philip glanced up and located Carring's face in the mirror. Unless he was grossly mistaken, his major-domo was struggling to hide a grin. Philip narrowed his eyes. "Just move the damned *chaise*, Carring."

"Immediately, my lord."

Philip did not glance back as he went out of his door, positive that if he did, he would see Carring grinning knowingly.

JUST TO PROVE Carring wrong, he returned to Ruthven House later in the afternoon—but only to pick up his phaeton.

Antonia was strolling in the Park with Geoffrey, Catriona and Ambrose, when they heard Geoffrey hailed from the carriageway. Turning, she saw Philip waving from the box-seat of the most elegant high-perch phaeton she had yet set eyes upon. Both Geoffrey and Ambrose needed no urging to cross the lawns to the carriageway.

"I say! What a bang-up set of blood and bone!" Ambrose eyed Philip's greys with fervid admiration.

Geoffrey turned big eyes on his mentor. "I don't suppose there's any chance you'll let me take this rig out, even without the greys?"

Philip, who had been gazing at Antonia, a picture in soft sprigged muslin, her face shaded by the brim of the bonnet he had bought her, shifted his gaze briefly to Geoffrey's face. "None."

Geoffrey grimaced. "That's what I thought."

"Did you want Geoffrey for some reason?" Antonia had spared only a passing glance for Philip's carriage; his horses she knew well.

"Actually," Philip said, his gaze once more on her face, "It was you I came to see. I wondered if you'd care for a turn about the Park?"

Antonia's heart leapt; the subtle challenge in his eyes gave her pause. High-perches were notoriously unstable, safe only in the hands of experienced drivers. She had no concern on that score but gaining the seat, a full six feet above the carriageway, was a different matter.

"What a positively *thrilling* invitation." Standing beside Antonia, Catriona looked glowingly up at Philip, her gaze innocent yet knowing. "You'll be the envy of every lady present."

Antonia looked up at Philip. "I would gladly go with you, my lord. Yet I greatly fear…" She gestured at the high step.

"A problem very easily solved." Philip tied off the reins. "Geoffrey—hold their heads."

Geoffrey hurried to the greys' heads; Ambrose followed. Before Antonia fully grasped his intent, Philip jumped down, drew her forward, then lifted her high.

Antonia bit back a squeal—and frantically clung to the side of the high seat. His expression mild, his eyes laughing, Philip followed her up; Antonia quickly but carefully shuffled along the precariously tilting seat. To her relief, Philip's weight once he sat seemed to stabilise the flimsy contraption.

"Relax." He flicked her a glance as he took up the

reins. "I seem to be advising you to do that rather often these days." He sent her another teasing glance. "I wonder why?"

"Because," Antonia tersely replied, "you are forever giving me cause to panic."

Philip laughed as he set the greys in motion. "Never fear—I give you my word I won't upend you in the middle of the Park. Aside from any other consideration, just think of the damage it would do to my reputation."

"I'm fast coming to think," Antonia returned, holding fast to the railings edging the seat, "that this reputation of yours is all a hum, invented by you as a convenient excuse."

That riposte earned her a distinctly unnerving look.

Before he could think of a comment to go with it, she asked, "Are you sure I'm not breaking any rules in being driven in such a dangerous equipage?"

"Quite sure," Philip replied, his tones distinctly dry. "If anyone is breaking any rules here, 'tis I."

Antonia widened her eyes at him. "You?"

"Indeed. And seeing I have bent my heretofore inviolable rules and taken you up in the Park, I think it's only fair that *you* should entertain *me,* thus leaving me free to devote all my skills to keeping us upright."

Hiding a smile, Antonia put her nose in the air. "I'm not at all sure it's proper for me to run on like some ill-bred gabblemonger."

"Heaven forbid!" Philip dispensed with his town drawl entirely. "Just put my mind at rest and tell me what you four were planning."

Giving up the fight to contain her delight, Antonia smiled dazzlingly, startling a youthful gentleman driving in the opposite direction.

"Cow-handed clunch!" Philip deftly avoided the ensuing melee. "Now cut line. Remember, I've made myself responsible for your brother."

"Very well." Settling more comfortably beside him, shielded from the light wind by his shoulder, Antonia related the latest developments. "Mr Fortescue has not yet shown his face, but as I gather he must come up from Somerset, I don't believe we can hold that against him."

Philip shook his head. "He may be a true knight but he obviously lacks a ghostly steed. Or should that be an errant charger?"

"Mr Fortescue, I gather, is a model of decorum."

"Good lord!" Philip shot her a disbelieving glance. "And Miss Dalling wishes to marry him?"

"Most definitely." Antonia paused, then diffidently added, "Actually, while I originally thought some of Miss Dalling's tales might owe more to her imagination than to fact, the latest involve Ambrose as well and he is undeniably not given to flights of fancy."

"By which you mean he's a slow-top." Philip glanced down at her. "But what are these latest exploits?"

"Not so much exploits as experiences. It seems the Countess of Ticehurst and the Marchioness have taken to engineering interludes when Catriona and Ambrose are left alone."

Philip raised his brows. "I see."

"Catriona and Ambrose are both trying quite desperately to ensure there's nothing improper that can be used to force their consent, but the situation is daily becoming more difficult."

Philip was silent for some minutes, then said, "It's hard to see what they can do, short of Mr Fortescue coming to the rescue. Even then, given Miss Dalling is under age, the situation's likely to be messy."

"Indeed. I raised that very point, but Catriona's convinced all will be well once Mr Fortescue arrives."

Philip raised his brows. "Which event, I suppose, we should all devoutly pray for." He cast a glance at Antonia's pensive face. "Having dispensed with that subject, perhaps we can move to some more interesting topic?"

Antonia opened her eyes wide. "That depends on what you consider *interesting,* my lord."

For one pregnant instant, Philip held her gaze; when she coloured, he smiled and looked ahead. "How about your observations on town life and the Little Season? I dare say I would find those quite fascinating."

"Indeed?" Antonia stifled the urge to fan her face. "Very well." On her mettle, she cast about for inspiration. She found it in a pair of strutting Macaronis, so gaily garbed they resembled walking pansies. "The strongest impression I have of the *ton* is of things being other than they seem. There is, to my mind, a great deal of obfuscation and roundaboutation—a great deal of hiding the truth."

The brief look Philip cast her held a gratifying degree of surprise. Then a curve forced him to give his attention to his greys. Antonia saw his lips firm, then twist in a wry, self-deprecatory smile.

"Remind me, my dear, not to ask such a question of you again."

"Why not?" Tilting her head, she studied his face. "I didn't find it impertinent."

"No—but I'd forgotten your intelligence. Your answers go too deep." Philip shot her a quick glance. "The trick with flirtatious repartee is to keep the tone light."

Antonia blinked. "Flirtatious repartee?"

"Indeed. What else? Now concentrate. Are you intending to grace Lady Gisborne's ballroom tonight?"

"WHAT-HO, MISS MANNERING! Dare I claim this cotillion?"

Antonia turned and, laughing, gave her hand to Hugo Satterly. "Indeed, sir. I had begun to wonder if you had forgotten me."

"Never." Straightening from his bow, Hugo placed a hand over his heart. "After all the trouble I went to to get my name in your card? Fie, my dear—I'm not such a slow-top."

"You are, however, a rattlepate," Philip put in from beside Antonia. "If you don't make a move soon, you'll miss out on the sets."

"Don't mind him." Hugo tucked Antonia's hand into his arm and turned her towards the floor. "He's just jealous."

Antonia responded with an ingenuous look and a confident smile. She felt entirely at ease with Hugo; he was the perfect companion, always charming, never one to take offence or become difficult over some imagined slight. Like all Philip's set, he was an excellent dancer and could be counted on to fill her ears with the latest *on dits*.

As they took their places in the nearest set forming on the floor of Lady Gisborne's ballroom, Hugo winked at her. "Hope you don't mind me trying for a rise out of Ruthven? All innocent fun, y'know."

Antonia smiled and sank into the first curtsy. "I don't mind at all." Rising, she gave Hugo her hand. "I dare say being twitted is good for him."

Hugo grinned back as the dance parted them.

As she dipped and swayed through the measure, Antonia considered his words. He was one of Philip's closest friends; thus far, he was the only one she had encountered who accurately understood Philip's interest in her. Certainly no one would guess it from Philip's behaviour; while he was always by her side, he made no effort to monopolise her company, either in the ballrooms or the supper rooms where, admittedly under his watchful eye, her entire court would adjourn to refresh themselves.

His behaviour, overtly aloof with but the subtlest undercurrent of possessiveness, was, she decided, intended to be instructive. Presumably, this was how she was to comport herself after they were wed. He would be about, but she was not to rely on him for her entertainment nor her male company. Her court, comprised of gentlemen of whom he approved, would provide that.

Discovering her gaze scanning the surrounding crowd, searching for Philip's chestnut locks, Antonia sternly refocused on Hugo, currently on the opposite side of the set. If overtly aloof was the correct image to project, then it was past time she started practising.

"WHAT THE DEVIL'S the matter? Is my cravat askew or what?"

Philip's words, delivered in a growled mutter, succeeded in hauling Antonia's gaze to his face.

Wide-eyed, she blinked up at him, oblivious of the other dancers about them. "What on earth do you mean? Your cravat's perfect—as it always is. The Oriental, isn't it?"

"The Mathematical—and don't try to change the subject."

Astounded, she stared at him. "I wasn't!" She blinked, then added, "I don't even know what the subject is."

Exceedingly irritated, even more so because his rational mind could find no reasonable cause, Philip whirled her into a complex series of turns, supposedly to negotiate the end of Lady Gisborne's ballroom, in reality purely as an excuse to hold her tighter. "The subject is," he said through clenched teeth, "why it is you suddenly seem to find me invisible. You've hardly glanced my way all night. I'm beginning to feel like a ghost."

Antonia felt dizzy and wondered if it was the waltz. He was certainly whirling her around with rather more concerted force than was his custom. "I thought that was what you wanted me to do—that I shouldn't…" To her annoyance, she felt a blush steal into her cheeks.

Philip studied the evidence of her confusion and felt his own grow. "That you shouldn't look at me?"

Antonia flicked him an exasperated glance, then fixed her gaze over his right shoulder. "That I should not display any overt awareness of your presence. As I understand it, such behaviour is construed as wearing one's heart on one's sleeve. I would not wish to embarrass you." She paused, then added, "Your own behaviour is very correct—I naturally took my lead from you."

Philip frowned down at her. "Yes—well." He hesitated, not quite certain which way to step. Then his lips firmed. "Might I suggest that there's a viable path between, on the one hand, clinging to my arm and making sheep's eyes at me, and, on the other, behaving as if I was literally not there?"

Antonia's gaze slid sideways, meeting his. "You know perfectly well I always know you're there."

Looking down into her eyes, Philip felt the dark cloud that had enshrouded him all evening melt away. He held her gaze, then his lips twisted wryly. "A few of your smiles and a few lingering glances wouldn't go astray."

For an instant longer, Antonia studied his eyes—then she smiled up at him. "If you wish it, my lord."

Philip tightened his hold as they went into the turn. "I do."

TWO DAYS LATER, Philip, strolling the broad verges in the Park, happened upon the Ruthven barouche. Languidly coming abreast of it, he discovered Henrietta deep in discussion with two other ladies, *grandes dames* both.

"Ah, Ruthven! *Just* the one we need." Catching sight of him, Henrietta beamed him a smile. "I was just saying to the Countess here, that what we need is a reliable gentleman, one who knows the ropes, to keep an eye on our little party."

"Indeed?" Raising his brows, Philip let his tone convey his utter antipathy to the idea that he might be such a specimen.

"But I don't believe you've met the Countess of Ticehurst?" Blithely oblivious, Henrietta indicated the lady beside her. "And, of course, the Dowager Marchioness of Hammersley."

His expression fashionably distant, Philip bowed gracefully, inwardly conceding that both the Countess, with her sharply angular features and frizzed red curls, and the Dowager Marchioness, heavy and portly with three chins to her credit, bade fair to living up to the varied descriptions he had had of them.

"Indeed, Ruthven, nothing could be more fortunate than your appearance here. The Countess and I haven't seen each other for years—we're keen to have a comfortable coze but her ladyship is uneasy over her niece." Raising her head, Henrietta looked out over the lawns. "She's over there somewhere," she said, waving one plump hand in the general direction of the flower walks. "She's walking with Antonia and Geoffrey. And the Marquess, of course." Apparently realizing that this last needed further clarification, Henrietta exchanged quick glances with the other two ladies, then leaned to the side of the carriage. Lowering her voice, she fixed Philip with a sapient eye. "There's an understanding between the Marquess and Miss Dalling, the Countess's niece, but there seems to be some slight hitch in the works. Nothing serious but you know how these things go." Assured that all was now crystal clear, Henrietta sat back and waved a dismissal. "Sure you'll want to join them."

Philip hesitated, then bowed. "Indeed, ma'am. Ladies." They let him go with thin smiles and magisterial nods. As he strode across the lawns, Philip found himself sympathizing with Miss Dalling and the Marquess.

He discovered Antonia strolling arm in arm with Catriona. The heiress's eyes were alight, her cheeks glowing; it was almost as if Antonia was physically restraining her but from what action Philip could not tell.

Antonia looked up as he approached; she smiled warmly and held out her hand. "Good afternoon, my lord."

Philip took her hand; unable to deny the compulsion, he raised it to his lips, his eyes quizzing her as he said, his voice too deep for even Catriona to hear, "My lady." Antonia blushed delightfully; Philip switched his gaze to Catriona, who bobbed a curtsy then flashed him one of her dazzling smiles. Philip smiled back. "I fear I should warn you that I've been dispatched as an envoy to keep an eye on you all."

Catriona's eyes widened. "How...? Who...?"

"As I understand it," Philip said, smoothly claiming Antonia's arm, thus separating her from Catriona, "my stepmother and your aunt are long-standing bosom-bows. At the moment, they're in Henrietta's barouche, exchanging their recent histories, with Ambrose's fond mama looking on."

"Indeed?" Catriona was hanging on his words. "And they sent you to watch over us?"

"Precisely."

"Behold—the hand of fate!" Hands clasped to her bosom, Catriona pirouetted dramatically. Halting, she fixed glowing eyes on Philip. "*Nothing* could be more fortunate!"

The declaration set Philip's teeth on edge. "I do hope," he said, "that you'll allow me to be the judge of that. Why the transports?"

Noting the absence of his drawl, Antonia quickly explained, "Mr Fortescue has arrived. He's arranged to join us here, but we were worried the Countess would interfere."

Glancing back over the lawns to the distant carriage, Philip humphed. "Not much chance of that at this point." He looked back at Catriona. "But where's this beau of yours?"

He was not about to assist in any havey-cavey affair.

But Henry Fortescue proved to be a great relief. Philip's hackles settled the instant he laid eyes on him, striding along between Geoffrey and Ambrose. Antonia had hurriedly explained their plan—they had sent Ambrose and Geoffrey to fetch Mr Fortescue so as to make it appear he was one of Ambrose's or Geoffrey's acquaintances. Quite what Mr Fortescue had thought of the arrangement Philip found himself dying to know.

Introduced, he shook hands.

In his early twenties, of middle height and powerful build, Henry Fortescue was readily identifiable as a scion of the noble family of that name; he bashfully acknowledged Philip's supposition. "Distant cousin of m'father's."

Catriona, clinging to his arm, declared, "We must be very careful, Henry, or Aunt Ticehurst will descend like the dragon she is and tear us apart."

Henry glanced down at her and frowned. "Nonsense." He took the sting from the comment by patting her hand. "You always were one to overdramatise, Catriona. What on earth do you imagine your aunt will do? It's not as if I'm some caper-merchant with no fortune and less prospects. Given I had your father's permission to address you, it's not as if there was any reason for her to shove in her oar."

"But she will!" Catriona looked horrified. "Ask Ambrose."

Ambrose dutifully nodded. "Terribly set on us marrying, y'know. That's why we sent for you."

"You can't talk to Aunt Ticehurst." Catriona clung to Henry's arm. "She'll banish you. I know she will."

Henry's jaw firmed. "I've no intention of speaking to your aunt—I'll speak to the Earl, as is proper."

Philip held Antonia back, letting the youthful foursome go ahead. Once they were out of earshot, he murmured, "I can't tell you how relieved I am to make Mr Fortescue's acquaintance."

"He does seem very steady." Antonia studied Catriona and her intended. "And he seems to know how to handle Catriona's flights."

"He's just what she needs—an anchor." Ambling in the youthful foursome's wake, Philip idly scanned the lawns. Abruptly, he halted. "Great heavens!"

Antonia followed his riveted gaze to a couple strolling towards them on an intersecting path. The gentleman she recognized immediately; Frederick Amberly was one of Philip's friends. He had not, however, spent much time in her circle, usually drifting into the crowd after the customary exchange of greetings. The young lady presently on his arm, a pretty miss in pink spotted muslin, was unknown to Antonia. From the warm appreciation readily apparent in Mr Amberly's expression, she surmised the lady might well be the cause of Mr Amberly's frequent preoccupation.

"Good afternoon, Amberly."

At the sound of Philip's voice, Frederick Amberly started. "What? Oh—it's you, Ruthven." Consternation showed fleetingly in his eyes. "Didn't expect to meet you here."

"So I perceive." Philip smiled charmingly at the young lady, now clinging wide-eyed to Mr Amberly's arm.

"Beg to make you known to my friends, m'dear." Mr

Amberly patted her hand reassuringly. "Miss Mannering and Lord Ruthven—Miss Hitchin."

Miss Hitchin smiled sweetly and gave Antonia her hand; Antonia returned her smile encouragingly and pressed her fingers. Philip bowed, then looked at Frederick Amberly. "Just strolling?"

"I thought the flowers looked so very pretty," Miss Hitchin volunteered somewhat breathlessly. "Mr Amberly very kindly offered to escort me to see them at closer range."

"They really are very lovely," Antonia agreed.

"I had heard there was a rhododendron walk farther on." Miss Hitchin looked appealingly at Mr Amberly.

"Ah, yes." Mr Amberly smiled down at her. "We'd best get on if we're to see the bushes then get back to your mama's carriage in good time." He nodded to Antonia. "Your servant, Miss Mannering. Ruthven."

Philip watched them hurry away. "Who would have thought it—a miss just out of the schoolroom, barely old enough to put up her hair?" He shook his head. "Poor Amberly."

"Why 'poor'?" Antonia asked as they started to stroll again.

"Because," Philip explained, "being caught strolling in the Park with a young lady on your arm ostensibly viewing the flowers is tantamount to declaring oneself irretrievably smitten."

They strolled on a few steps before Antonia said, her tone carefully neutral, "You're strolling by the flowerbeds with me."

"True—but there's nothing surprising in a man's being smitten with you. But a chit just out of the schoolroom?" Again, Philip shook his head. "Poor Amberly."

CHAPTER ELEVEN

"WELL, MY DEAR? Were you impressed with Hugo's flourishes?" Philip extended his arm as Antonia, cheeks flushed, eyes sparkling, joined him by the side of Lady Darcy-d'Lisle's ballroom.

"Indeed!" Placing her fingertips on his sleeve, Antonia slanted a playful glance at Hugo. "I cannot recall a more *enthusiastic* gavotte in all the past weeks."

Hugo's grin turned to a grimace. "Sssh!" Theatrically, he looked about him. "I declare—you'll give me a bad name. Not a rake in London wants to be known as *enthusiastic*."

His expression had Antonia laughing aloud.

Philip savoured the silvery sound. In the past week, Antonia's confidence had steadily grown; his pride and satisfaction had kept pace, swelling at moments like this, feeding his impatience. Suavely, his expression discreetly restrained, he covered her hand with his. "Come. The ball is ended." Her eyes met his. "It's time to go home."

To his house, his library—and their regular nightcap.

To his delight, she blushed delicately, then lifted her head to look across the room. "It appears we'll have to pry Aunt Henrietta from Lady Ticehurst's side."

"Indeed." Philip followed her gaze to where his stepmother was talking animatedly to the Countess. "I'm not at all certain I approve of the connection."

As they started across the floor, Antonia threw him a puzzled look. Philip saw it. He waited until Hugo had taken leave of them before saying, "To my experienced eye, Henrietta is showing alarming signs of involving herself in your youthful friend's affair."

His supposition proved correct; as they strolled up, the Countess was in full flight, declaiming on the wisdom of young ladies allowing their elders to be their matrimonial guides. "For mark my words, it's substance that counts, as my dear niece will be forced to admit." She capped this grim pronouncement with a severe nod, directing a basilisk stare around the ballroom as if searching for dissenters.

Henrietta dutifully nodded, although her expression suggested her opinion was somewhat less trenchantly set.

Antonia watched as Philip applied his not-inconsiderable charm to disengaging Henrietta from her ladyship's side. That accomplished, they found Geoffrey waiting by the door. With smiles and nods, they took leave of their hosts, then descended to their carriage.

As he handed Antonia in, Philip heard his name called.

Turning, he saw Sally Jersey tripping down to her carriage, a distinctly arch look on her face. He replied with a repressive nod. Her ladyship had not been alone in shooting speculative glances his way. Climbing into the carriage, Philip inwardly shrugged. In a few weeks, possibly less, they'd be back at the Manor; thereafter, the rabid interest of the *ton* would be a matter of no importance, certainly not something he need consider every time he smiled at Antonia. The prospect grew daily more alluring.

Screened by the dark, he settled back against the carriage seat.

Facing him, Antonia sat similarly shrouded by shadows, her thoughts, like Philip's, very much on themselves. Like him, she felt smugly satisfied. She now knew how to act, how to behave as his wife, whilst under the *ton*'s chandeliers. She had paraded before the hostesses' censorious eyes and had not stumbled. No more need she fear to put a foot wrong, to bring opprobrium down on her head through some gauche and unforgivable act—to shame Philip by her lack of sophisticated knowledge.

Under his tutelage, her knowledge, her understanding, had grown in leaps and bounds.

Her eyes sought his face, then scanned his frame, large and impressively elegant in the shadows opposite. Her attention was caught by the diamond pin in his cravat, shimmering in the weak light.

She was now confident she could be his wife—the wife he wanted, the wife he needed, the wife he deserved. His support had been steadfast, underlaid by past affection. In every word and deed, his attitude was evident, a subtle fondness that never overstepped the bounds of propriety.

At least not in public.

Her gaze fixed on his diamond pin, Antonia shifted. His private behaviour had not fitted within her mental framework of a conventional relationship—not until she had admitted the existence of desire. It was not an emotion she had had previous experience of, yet it was there, staring back at her every time they were alone and she looked into his eyes. She had finally accepted that it was an integral part of how he viewed her—she was no longer a girl, after all, but a woman grown.

The thought sent a long shiver slithering down her spine. Abruptly, she straightened and switched her gaze to the passing streetscape.

Despite her sudden breathlessness, despite her leaping heart, she was not foolish enough to confuse desire with love. Philip's comment in the Park three days before, so easy, so open, so very off-hand, had placed the matter firmly in perspective. Not the most ardent of young ladies—not even Catriona—could have mistaken those few words, his roundabout admission he was smitten with her, as a declaration. It had been no more than a simple restating of his fondness for her, an acknowledgement of his clear preference for her company.

That, admittedly, had surprised her. From beneath her lashes, Antonia viewed the still figure opposite. She had imagined, in light of his freely acknowledged reputation, that other women, perhaps even ladies, would feature rather more significantly in his life.

Perhaps he was reforming?

How would it feel to know that she had been responsible for such a transformation?

A yearning rose within her, deep and strong. Swallowing a contemptuous "humph," she straightened her shoulders and ruthlessly quashed it. *That* was no part of the bargain between them; *that* was no part of a conventional marriage. *That* was none of her business.

A part of her mind jeered—Antonia ignored it. She was, she sternly reminded herself, aiming to be a very comfortable wife, one who did not create ructions over matters beyond her jurisdiction.

With that objective firmly in view, she swept into the hall of Ruthven House. Henrietta and Geoffrey were already on the stairs, deep in conversation. With a smile for Carring, Antonia glided into the library.

As she settled in her usual chair, her gaze fell on the *chaise,* set directly opposite the hearth. It had appeared nearly a week before; every night since, Philip had inveigled her onto it—and thence, into his arms. Sternly repressing her memories, she reminded herself there was nothing remarkable in a betrothed couple sharing kisses.

Grey eyes dark with desire swam through her mind. A shiver threatened.

Philip had paused at the door; she heard him speak to Carring, then shut the door. He strolled forward, his gaze meeting hers.

"You seem quite at home in the *ton* these days. I always did think you learned quickly." Gracefully crouching, he built up the fire. The flames transformed his chestnut hair to bronze, each lock burnished bright.

Smiling serenely, Antonia leaned back. "Ah, but I've had an excellent teacher, have I not? I doubt I would have found it half so easy had I had to brave the dragons alone."

Philip straightened, one brow rising. "Flattery, my dear?"

A knock on the door heralded Carring, bearing her glass of milk. Antonia took it with a smile. Carring fetched Philip his brandy then withdrew, leaving them both sipping.

With his usual grace, Philip sank into the chair across the hearth. Silence settled; Antonia relaxed, feeling the warmth of the milk drive the chill from her shoulders. Her lips curved; as peace slowly enfolded her, she lowered her lids.

Cradling his glass in his hands, Philip studied her, his gaze skimming her shoulders, bare above the abbreviated bodice of her evening dress, a confection in pale green silk that had caused any number of ladies to turn greener still. She had not worn her pearls, leaving her throat and the expanse of creamy skin exposed above the low neckline tantalizingly bare. Unadorned, it had drawn more eyes than Lady Darcy-d'Lisle's diamonds. There was an untouched innocence in the gentle swell of her breasts that had halted any number of male conversations.

His eyes on the delicate curves, Philip shifted restlessly.

Antonia blinked. "What's the matter?"

Philip slowly raised a brow. "I was at the point, as it happens, of concluding that women endowed as you are should be forbidden to appear in public without the distraction of jewellery."

As his gaze dropped from hers on the words, Antonia had no difficulty divining his meaning. The warmth that touched her skin owed nothing to the fire. "Indeed?" Determined not to fluster, she sipped her milk.

"Definitely." Abruptly, Philip set aside his glass. Standing, he crossed to his desk; a moment later, he returned, a flat velvet box in his hand.

Placing her glass on a sidetable, Antonia raised wide eyes from the box to his face. "What—?"

"Come—stand before the mirror." Philip caught her hand and drew her to her feet.

Excitement gripping her, Antonia did as he asked.

"No peeking," he said when she tried to glance over her shoulder.

The next instant, he dropped the box on the *chaise* and held his hands high over her head, a strand of sparkling stones strung between them.

Antonia looked up and caught her breath. "The emeralds from Aspreys!" Her words came in a whisper. "I wondered who had bought them."

"'Twas I." Philip lowered the necklace, setting it about her throat. He bent his head to fasten the catch at her nape. "They were obviously made for you—it was only right that you have them."

Her eyes on their reflection, Antonia raised fluttering fingers to the gems. "I...I don't know what to say." She sought Philip's gaze in the mirror; her dazed smile faded. "Philip—I can't wear them. Not yet."

"I know." Grimacing, he placed his hands on her shoulders, squeezing gently. "Keep them until we get back to the Manor. You can wear them at our betrothal ball—my gift to you on the occasion."

For a moment longer, Antonia held his gaze, then she turned. "Thank you." Reaching up, she twined her arms about his neck and, stretching up on tiptoe, set her lips to his.

For a fractional instant, Philip hesitated, then his hands slid around her silk encased form, smoothly gathering her into his arms. For a single minute, he savoured the freshness of her untutored caress, then desire welled; he parted her lips, confident of his welcome, eager for the taste of her sweetness. She responded as she always did, with simple, unrestrained passion, warm and enticing.

Antonia gave herself up to his kiss, swept up, as she

always was, by the warm tide he so effortlessly called forth. When Philip gathered her closer, his head slanting over hers, she tightened her arms about his neck. Her senses drifted; beyond coherent thought, she yielded to the compulsion to press against him.

His hands shifted to her back, tracing the long lines, then dropped to her hips, firming gently, encouragingly. Unable to deny the urging of her senses, she responded, letting her softness sink against his hardness, thrilled, seduced by the unfamiliar excitement that welled within her. The kiss went on; the novel sensation swelled and grew until it filled her entirely.

An indescribable longing swept her.

Philip's hand at her breast felt just right; his gentle fondling eased the odd throbbing ache that had developed there. Then his fingers stroked and her knees went weak; Antonia clung to his shoulders, relieved when his arm tightened about her waist.

Then he was lowering her to the *chaise,* easing her down to the brocaded cushions without breaking their kiss. Unwilling to leave her realm of delight, Antonia clung to the caress, one arm about his neck. Her other hand fluttered along his jaw in pleading supplication.

Philip felt her tentative touch; accurately interpreting it, he devoted one part of his mind to appeasing her innocent hunger with gentle, lingering kisses while his fingers dealt with the tiny buttons of her bodice. As the closures yielded one by one, he tightened his hold on his passions, ruthlessly harnessing them. Step by step, point by slow point, he had been leading her down the road to seduction by the longest route he could devise. He knew precisely how far he would lead her tonight; that far and no further.

It was a point he made very clear to his surging, restless passions before the last button gave and he slid one hand beneath the fine seagreen silk.

Her breast swelled to his touch; her skin, soft as satin, smoother than the silk he brushed aside, burned him. As he gently closed his fingers about one firm mound, he felt her breath catch, felt tension grow then dissolve into desire. Her lips clung to his, urgent, entreating. She shifted beneath him, flagrantly wanton, deliciously divine.

Philip drank from her lips, fulfilling her needs even as his own raged. It was he who eventually drew back, raising his head to catch his breath.

Her skin flushed and aglow, Antonia lay relaxed against the cushions, her lids too heavy to lift, her lips throbbing and tender yet still hungry for his. She floated on a sea of dreams, cocooned by passion, her desire-drenched mind suborned by sensation.

Blissfully content, she sighed.

Philip's hand shifted; long fingers stroked her breast.

Antonia's eyes flew wide. *"Oh!"* Jerked back to reality, her stunned mind registered her position, reclining on the chaise with Philip beside her, one hand cupping her breast. "I…" She faltered to a stop, her dazed wits struggling to recall just what had transpired. What had she said? Done? "Oh, *heavens!*" Sunk in embarrassment, Antonia closed her eyes. Mortification swept her. "I'm so *sorry,* Philip."

Bemused, Philip nuzzled her ear. "Why sorry?" Bending his head, he touched his lips to the pulse beating wildly in her throat. "If anyone should be making apologies, it is I." He looked down to where her breast filled his hand. "But I've no intention of doing so. I wouldn't hold your breath in expectation of the event."

Antonia promptly drew in a deep breath; lips lifting, Philip bent his head.

"Philip!" Antonia's eyes flew open again; this time she was even more shocked. Her indrawn breath was trapped in her chest; her fingers tangled in Philip's hair as he continued his shocking caress. She was suddenly very glad of the *chaise;* if they'd been standing, she was quite sure she would have swooned. As his lips, his tongue, continued their play, her wits whirled. *"Good God."*

Hearing the weakness in her voice, Philip drew back, softly chuckling. "There's no need to be so shocked." He considered the evidence of her agitation, the rapid rise and fall of her bare breasts, with a certain masculine satisfaction. Looking up, he met her befuddled gaze. "We are, after all, going to be married shortly. Thereafter, we'll be doing precisely this rather often."

Antonia's lips formed a silent "Oh."

Philip felt the tremor that rippled through her. Puzzled, he looked into her eyes, only to discover the most peculiar expression—surely it couldn't be anguish?—darkening the hazel depths. He frowned. "What is it?"

She didn't reply. Instead, her eyes glazed as, of their own volition, his fingers caressed the rosy nipple that had been the focus of his attentions thus far. He forced his fingers to stillness but could not bring himself to withdraw his hand from the soft fullness of her breast. Bending his head, he touched his lips to her temple. "You trust me, remember? So tell me."

Her gaze slowly focusing, Antonia blinked up at him. She parted her lips, then had to moisten them before

she could speak. Speech, explanations, were imperative—before events got completely out of hand. "I…
That is…" With an effort, she drew in a deep breath.
"When you kiss me passionately—" She broke off,
blushing vividly.

Philip felt the heat spread through the skin beneath
his fingers; he fought to keep them still.

Antonia swallowed, battling the vice about her chest,
struggling to steady her voice. "When you touch me."
Her hand rose flutteringly to touch his. She looked
down, then abruptly hauled her gaze up and dragged
in a shattering breath. "I can't control how I respond,"
she rushed on. "I feel…" Her eyes darkening, she sought
his; briefly, her tongue touched her lips. "Quite wanton."

Desire surged; Philip fought to shackle it. Before he
could respond, Antonia continued, her eyes locked on
his. "Such unseemly behaviour will give you a disgust
of me." Her gaze fell. "I know it's no way for a lady
to behave."

The agonised sincerity in her eyes, in her voice, slew
any impulse to levity. Philip recognized the dictum to
which she alluded, to which she apparently expected
to be forced to subscribe. He had long ago concluded
that that particular stricture was primarily responsible
for making so many married ladies such easy prey for
rakes—men who encouraged rather than suppressed
their passions. That his wife might, through such reasoning, fall victim to his peers was not a situation he
was prepared to countenance. His lips thinned. "At the
risk of shocking you further, I've a confession to make."

Dazed hazel eyes met his.

Reluctantly, Philip withdrew his hand from its warm

haven and let the halves of her bodice fall shut. "Naturally, I hesitate to make a point of the matter, but I would hardly bear the reputation I do if women's passions—or passionate women—disgusted me." Gazing into her eyes, he added, "Indeed, I can assure you the very opposite is the case."

She continued to look uncertain. His eyes on hers, Philip raised a worldly brow. "It's a well-known fact gentlemen such as I tend to marry late. We wait, hoping to find a lady who responds in the ways we've learned to value—one whose passions are honest and direct, whose delight is natural and unfeigned." He hesitated, then went on, his voice deepening, "You know what I am, what I've been—I see no purpose in any fashionable deceit. Given that background, can you possibly imagine I would be satisfied with mild passions—with the tepid response of a merely complaisant wife—when I know of the fire that flows through your veins?"

His eyes were dark, clouded grey; Antonia struggled to suppress the shudder of awareness his words provoked. Befuddled, uncertain as to whether she should be scandalised or in alt, she shook her head.

Ignoring the tension building within him, Philip continued, "I want you to be wild and wanton, at least in private." His lips twisted into a provocative smile. "I happen to like you that way." Antonia stiffened; he quickly added, his tone tending acerbic, "And I assure you it's perfectly acceptable for a wife to be wild and wanton with her husband."

Antonia threw him a sceptical look.

Philip lifted one hand and tapped her nose with one finger. "I promise I'm not bamming you for my own, nefarious ends." He fought to lighten his tone. "Within the *ton,* there are two sides to any successful marriage— the social and the private. Given the evidence of their Graces of Eversleigh, as well as Jack and Sophie Lester, not to mention Harry and Lucinda—all of whom you have yet to meet but whose marriages I, for one, envy— there's no gainsaying the fact that—" He paused, caught by the tide of his own eloquence. "Marriages based on…" Philip hesitated, then continued, "Deep mutual attraction have a great deal to recommend them."

He looked down and met Antonia's searching gaze.

"I thought you wanted a comfortable wife—one who would not make any…" Antonia blushed again. Irritated, she lifted her chin. "Any demands on your time."

Philip smiled, the gesture strained. "You mean one who would *not* be a constant distraction?" With one tug, he pulled the ribbon from her hair. The heavy mass cascaded down, scattering pins on the cushions. His smile tightened as he plunged one hand into the golden wave. "Who would *not* leave me daydreaming of how she will look, how she will feel, when I have her naked beneath my hands?" His eyes on the golden curls, he spread his fingers, then drew them through the thick mane, laying it across Antonia's shoulder. Then he trapped her gaze in his. "Is that what you thought I wanted?"

Wide-eyed, barely able to breathe, Antonia nodded.

Philip's gaze dropped, fastening on her lips. "Then you were wrong."

His head lowered, his lips found hers. He kissed her and kept kissing her, whirling her back into the mesmerising world of desire and delight, commanding her senses and her responses, murmuring encouragements in gravelly tones whenever her preconceived notions threatened to intrude.

The logs he had earlier placed on the fire were glowing embers when he finally lifted his head. Satisfied with Antonia's regretful sigh, he drew back.

Wits still adrift, her senses swimming, Antonia heard him murmur, "Lady *mine*."

"I HADN'T THOUGHT to see so many here today." One hand on her bonnet, anchoring it against the stiff breeze, Antonia looked ahead to where the usual congestion of carriages constricted the main avenue of the Park.

Beside her on the box-seat of his phaeton, Philip smothered a snort. "Nothing less than a deluge will serve to keep them away. Mere threats—" his glance took in the lowering clouds scudding across the leaden sky "—have no power to intimidate the *grandes dames* of the *ton*."

"Obviously." Sinking her fingers into the swansdown lining of her new muff, Antonia returned the gracious nods of the matrons they passed, her smile serenely confident. Inwardly, she remained amazed at her assurance, at the steady, unruffled beat of her heart.

After last night, and their interlude following Lady Darcy-d'Lisle's ball, she had expected to feel distinctly ruffled when next she set eyes on Philip. Instead, unexpectedly meeting over the breakfast table, they had fallen into their usual friendly banter; there had been nothing in their interaction to unnerve her. Not even the gleam that occasionally lit his eyes, and the understanding she detected behind it, had served to disrupt the deep happiness that had laid hold of her.

Her fingers gently flexed; Antonia glanced down at her muff. Philip's latest present. She eyed it consideringly, then slanted him a glance. "I've noticed, my lord, that any item I admire has a tendency to become mine. Parasols, bonnets, even emeralds."

Engrossed with managing his greys, Philip merely arched a brow.

"Will it work if I admire a high-perch phaeton?"

She had quickly lost her fear of the lightweight carriage, she now revelled in its power and speed.

"No." Philip's answer was unequivocal. Stealing a moment from his cattle, he frowned at Antonia. "I will never consent to letting you risk your neck—don't even *think* it."

Antonia opened her eyes wide.

Philip humphed and turned back to his horses. His tone marginally less severe, he added, "If you behave yourself and don't tease me, you can have a pair of high-steppers for your carriage. I'll speak to Harry when next I see him."

The comment diverted Antonia. "Harry?" He had mentioned a Harry before.

Philip nodded. "Harry Lester—brother of Jack." After a second's pause, he added, "Both good friends of mine."

"Ah." Antonia knew what she was supposed to make of that. "Does this Harry have horses to sell?"

"Possibly." Philip glanced at her, a smile in his eyes. "Harry Lester is the owner of one of the country's foremost studs. That stallion you claimed at the Manor—Raker—is a colt of one of his champions. When it comes to quality horseflesh, you can't go past Harry."

"I see." As they slowed to join the line of carriages waiting to turn and retrace their route along the avenue, Antonia asked, "Is this the same Harry who married a Lucinda?"

Philip nodded. "Lucinda—Mrs Babbacombe that was. They married a few months ago, towards the end of the Season."

"Is there some reason they aren't in London?"

"Knowing Harry," Philip replied, wheeling his horses, "I assume they're too busy amusing themselves at home."

Antonia slanted him a glance. "Amusing themselves?"

Setting his horses to a trot, Philip turned to meet her gaze. "Strange to tell, there's one attraction guaranteed to hold greater allure for rakes than the *ton* in all its glory."

Antonia opened her eyes wide. "What?"

"Their wives in all their glory."

Blushing furiously, she threw him a speaking look, then switched her attention to the approaching carriages.

Hiding a grin, Philip looked to his horses. Antonia blushing was a sight very much to his liking; the response was not one to which she had previously been particularly susceptible. He was becoming adept at making her blush—yet another talent that improved with practice.

He waited until they passed the last of the stationary carriages before glancing her way again. "With the weather turning, the ranks will start to thin soon. There's really only a week more of the Little Season to go."

Antonia met his gaze, her own open and direct. "And then?"

Philip felt a fierce tension close like a fist about his heart. He kept all hint of the compelling force within him from his expression, from his eyes. "If you're agreeable, we'll return to the Manor. And then—" He broke off, quickly glancing at his horses. When he looked back, his expression was mild. "And then, my dear, we'll proceed as planned."

Antonia's gaze remained steady. She searched his eyes, then, her smile serene, inclined her head. "As we agreed, my lord."

Two NIGHTS LATER, Philip stood by the side of Lady Carstairs's ballroom and wondered if there was any way he could make the Little Season end sooner. There were still five full nights of balls and parties to be endured; he wasn't sure his patience was up to it—up to the challenge of toeing the line he had drawn, the line beyond which he would not step. Given they were to wed and wed soon, he was not particularly averse to seducing Antonia. Seducing her while she resided under his roof, essentially under his protection, was another matter entirely, one which impinged on his honour, rather than simply his morals.

Swallowing a disgusted "humph," he resisted the urge to cross his arms and glower at the delightful picture she made, swirling down the room in the Roger de Clovely. Lord Ashby, one of his peers, was her partner; despite that, Philip felt no qualms. The fact gave him pause.

He was, now he thought of it, totally, unshakeably, sure of Antonia—sure of her affection, sure of her loyalty, sure of her wish to marry him. Why, then, was he torturing himself by standing here, watching over her?

None who saw her could doubt her assurance. If she should need any help, Henrietta was there, gossiping avidly with her intimates. Geoffrey, too, was somewhere in the throng, almost certainly with the Marquess, Miss Dalling and Mr Fortescue.

As the music swirled towards its conclusion, Philip cast one last glance about. There was no reason he couldn't do as husbands did and leave the room. Antonia didn't need him; he, however, could use the time to consider an urgent problem—what additional steps he could introduce, what byways they could explore, to lengthen her road to seduction.

Given the unexpected violence of his feelings, and her passionate response, that was an increasingly pertinent requirement.

As she rose from her final curtsy, Antonia laughed gaily at Lord Ashby, then automatically scanned the room. She saw Philip's back as he passed through the main door; smiling, she assumed he had gone to get some air.

Confident, buoyed by content, she chatted with Lord Ashby and the others who gathered around. Ten minutes of artless, on her part distracted, prattle convinced her that her thoughts had gone with Philip. Idly glancing around, she decided there was really no reason she, too, couldn't slip out to get some air. The blustery weather outside had meant the terrace doors were firmly shut; the temperature in the ballroom was steadily rising.

Smiling sweetly, she turned to Lord Ashby. "If you'll excuse me, my lord, I believe I must have a word with my aunt."

Given Henrietta was ensconced in the heart of the Dowager Marchioness of Hammersley's circle, Antonia was not the least surprised when none of the gentlemen present insisted on accompanying her. Slipping through the crowd, initially towards her aunt, she then changed tack and headed for the ballroom door.

In the library, otherwise deserted, Philip paced slowly before the hearth, his mind engrossed with Antonia and the latest unforeseen problem she had managed to present him. He did not hear the door ease open, then quietly close. It was the soft rustle of silk skirts, a very familiar sound, that brought him alert.

He turned, his heart lifting spontaneously, only to find it was not Antonia who stood artfully poised by the end of the *chaise*.

"Good evening, my lord."

Any thought that Lady Ardale had innocently happened upon him was laid to rest by her tone—pure unadulterated adulteress. A stunningly handsome woman, her voluptuous curves were encased in silk so fine it was clear she wore little beneath. Her skirts rustled again, a softly seductive sound, as, her dark gaze on his, she came slowly towards him.

Despite himself, Philip felt a certain fascination— the sort anyone would feel on observing a sight one had heard tell of but had never before encountered. He had certainly heard tell of Lady Ardale. She was one of those he would unhesitatingly label a piranha—in her case, she ate up rakes and spat out their bones. Rumour had it she was impossible to satisfy; attempting that feat had literally brought some of the fraternity to their knees. As Lord Ardale was still strong enough to insist on discretion, her ladyship limited her prey to those already safely wed. Until now, Philip had thought himself safe.

Her ladyship's next words banished the illusion.

"You've been exceedingly clever, Ruthven." Halting

directly before him, Lady Ardale smiled knowingly. Lifting one long-nailed finger, she traced a fold of his cravat. "Finding a friend of the family, a young lady of breeding but no knowledge of the *ton*—a sweet, innocent miss to be your bride." Archly, Lady Ardale lifted one brow. "Very clever indeed."

Almost imperceptibly, Philip stiffened.

"Indeed, my lord, such cleverness fairly begs a reward." Lady Ardale swayed closer. Automatically, Philip put out one arm to steady her; his hand came to rest on one curvaceous hip. Lady Ardale drifted closer still, settling her curves against him. "I expect," she said, her words breathy but definite, "that your plans to marry the chit are well advanced. Might I suggest that, rather than waste the next three weeks at your estate, you join me and my guests at Ardale Place? A convivial little gathering." Lady Ardale's rouged lips curved. Her dark eyes on Philip's face, she caught his free hand and, unblushingly, guided it to her breast, trapping his fingers against the ripe swell. "I can assure you you'll get plenty of opportunity to partake of your just deserts. After all your careful planning, you won't want to deny yourself."

The intensity of the revulsion that swept him, the appallingly strong impulse to fling Lady Ardale from him, forced Philip to pause, to draw a slow, steady breath before declining, with what civility he could muster, her ladyship's salacious invitation. The idea that he would prefer her overripe, tawdry charms to those of Antonia struck him as an insult to his intelligence; her pronouncements on Antonia only raised his hackles further.

Lady Ardale misread his stillness; with a sirenlike smile, she reached up, intending to draw his head to hers.

Philip's expression hardened. The hand at her hip firmed; his other hand, freed, moved to grip her shoulder.

What made him look up he did not know, but he did—and saw Antonia, a wraith in the shadows, standing just inside the door. Philip froze.

Lady Ardale plastered herself to him.

The sob that escaped Antonia broke the web of horror, of utter disbelief, that held her. Philip heard it, a small, broken plaint. She pressed her hand to her lips, suppressing the sound, then whirled and fled the room.

The next thing Lady Ardale knew she lay sprawled upon the *chaise*—in precisely the position she had intended to assume, with one notable correction. Philip was supposed to have been with her, not striding to the door.

"Ruthven!"

Her ladyship's strident outrage brought Philip up short. Swinging about, he transfixed her with his gaze, cold contempt in his eyes. "Madam," he said, biting off the words, "I suggest that in future you exercise greater discretion in selecting your paramours. You are greatly mistaken if you believe that *I* would wish to join their ranks."

With that, he swung on his heel and strode after Antonia.

Entering the ballroom, he paused by the wall and scanned the company. He eventually located his bride-to-be, dancing the cotillion with some youthful sprig. To any casual observer, her carefree expression would have passed unremarked. Philip saw through it, saw the effort she put into every smile, every lighthearted gesture, saw the pain behind her disguise. He fought the overwhelming urge to go to her, to gather her into his arms and tell her the truth of what she had seen, what she had overheard—only his sure knowledge of the *ton*'s reaction to such an act prevented him from committing it.

Tense, impatient, he waited until the cotillion ended, then strolled purposefully across the ballroom to claim his usual place by her side. She did not look up as he did so, but merely inclined her head.

Philip drew in a calming breath—and waited. When a heated discussion of the rival sporting merits of pheasant over grouse claimed the attention of her attendant swains, he leaned closer. "Antonia, we must talk. Come, stroll with me."

She gave a brittle laugh, drawing attention back to them.

"I greatly fear, my lord, that my dance card is full." On pretext of displaying her card, she slipped her right wrist from his hold. "See?" Without looking at him, she held the card up for his perusal, then she beamed upon her court. "Indeed, I couldn't disappoint so many earnest cavaliers."

Her court immediately came to her rescue, decrying his right to take her from them. Gritting his teeth, Philip was forced to acquiesce with a semblance of grace. He had waltzed with her earlier; as usual, she had no further dances free.

With that avenue blocked, he remained by her side, increasingly aware of how tenuous, how flimsy, her blithely gay facade truly was. The knowledge stayed his hand from any further attempt to gain time alone with her; after all her hard work, after all her trepidations, to push her to the brink of some hysterical outburst here, in a *ton* ballroom, would be the act of a cad. The same consideration kept him where he was; if she did stumble and fall, he was one of the few he would trust to catch her.

And, after all, they would shortly be home; the library fire would already be lit.

With that objective in mind, he escorted her smoothly from the ballroom at the close of the evening, shielding her as best he could from any too-observant eyes. Helpfully, Henrietta proved greatly distracted by Miss Dalling's prospects; Geoffrey, drawn into the discussion, filled the gap Antonia left.

She followed Henrietta from the carriage, leaving him to descend in her wake. But Henrietta's slow progress up the steps held her back; coming up beside Antonia, Philip caught her hand and trapped it on his sleeve. She started at his touch, then acquiesced, allowing him to lead her to the door.

Henrietta, still demanding to know more of Miss Dalling, stumped up the stairs on Geoffrey's arm. From the hall, Antonia fast by his side, Philip watched until the pair gained the landing.

"My lord?"

Carring stood waiting to take his evening cloak. Releasing Antonia, Philip untied the loose ribands and shrugged the cloak from his shoulders. Turning back, he discovered Antonia halfway to the stairs.

"I greatly fear, my lord," she said, one hand rising to her brow, "that I have quite the most hideous headache. If you'll excuse me?"

With a swirling bob by way of farewell, she turned and sailed on up the stairs, not once meeting his gaze.

Philip's eyes narrowed as he watched her ascend; his expression hardened with every step she took.

When Antonia had passed from sight, Carring coughed, then murmured, "No nightcaps tonight, my lord?"

His expression like flint, Philip growled, "As you know damned well, I can pour my own brandy. You may lock up."

With that, he strode into the library, shutting the door firmly behind him.

UPSTAIRS, ANTONIA REACHED her chamber only to discover she had to ring for Nell, who had grown used to her interludes in the library. Tense as a bowstring, she waited until Nell appeared, then, resigned, submitted to the maid's ministrations, excusing her departure from the norm with, "I'm merely feeling a bit peaked. A good night's sleep will no doubt see me right."

Busy with her buttons, Nell shot her a searching glance. "Sure you don't want me to mix up a Blue Powder? Or I could fetch you up the jar of Dr Radcliffe's Restorative Pork Jelly. A spoonful of that does strengthen one."

She could certainly use some strength. "No, thank you." Antonia held herself stiffly, restraining her thoughts, her emotions, by main force. "Just help me into my nightgown—I'll do my hair."

Mumbling, grumbling, citing the benefits of Dr Radcliffe's Jelly to the last, Nell eventually took herself off.

Alone, Antonia drew in a deep, difficult breath, then, her brush in her hand, sank onto the stool before her dressing-table. Like one in a dream, she fell to brushing out her thick curls, her gaze fixed on her image in the mirror. The candelabra to her right threw steady light over her face; briefly, she focused on her image, then reached for the snuffer. Only when the candles were doused, leaving the room wreathed in shadows with the only light coming from the single candle by her bed, did she look back at the mirror.

She had no need to see the misery in her eyes to know of the misery in her heart.

For which she had only herself to blame.

She had let her heart rule her head, let love lead her to believe in miracles. Her mother had warned her—she had warned herself—but she hadn't listened. Seduced by love, she'd thought herself safe from its pain. Tonight, she had discovered she was not.

The hold she had maintained over her emotions abruptly shredded; love hit her like a blow, as it had in Lady Carstairs's library, when concealed by shadows, she had watched Philip respond to some sophisticated harlot. As before, the impact left her reeling; pain speared through her, a vice squeezed her heart. A dull ache filled her, a miasma spreading insidiously through her, swallowing all hope.

Dully, Antonia blinked at the mirror, then laid aside her brush. She had always been strong, always able to cope. She would cope with this, too, and she *would not cry*—not even when her mother had sold her mare, the last gift her father had given her, had she given way to tears. Slowly, she straightened her shoulders and determinedly stared at her reflection, all but hidden by the flickering shadows.

Her hurt, her anguish, was entirely her own fault.

Philip had never said he loved her—she had no cause to reproach him. The truth was as it had always been; she had been foolish to imagine otherwise. Her feelings, her unspoken, unacknowledged hopes, were irrelevant. Ruthlessly, she bundled them together, then buried them deep—and spent the next hour sternly repeating all the strictures, the strictures necessary to play the part of Philip's wife, unexpectedly finding strength in the clear-cut, unemotional edicts. Only when she had regained her sense of purpose did she allow herself to think of other things.

The rest of the night went in a fruitless endeavour, a futile attempt to mend her broken heart.

CHAPTER TWELVE

"CAN I FETCH you anything, my lord?"

Seated behind his desk in the library, Philip looked up. Carring stood in the open doorway. Philip frowned. "No. Not at the moment."

Carring bowed and backed out, reaching for the doorknob.

"And you may leave the door open."

Carring bowed again. "Of course, my lord."

Smothering a growl, Philip refocused on the *Gazette*. The weak rays of the midday sun intermittently pierced the clouds, throwing fitful beams across the page.

The weather was not the only thing to have suddenly turned uncertain.

Antonia had given him no chance to explain, no chance to set the record straight. He trusted her implicitly; despite her agreement to do so, she obviously didn't trust him. Admittedly, he carried a certain reputation, one he'd made no effort to hide, but they were friends and had been for years. He had thought that would count for rather more than it had. To his mind, the matter was clear. She should have known better— known him better.

Rather than believe the evidence of her eyes. And her ears.

Philip grimaced. His gaze, fixed unseeing on the page, grew more deeply abstracted.

A faint creak sounded from beyond the library door.

Instantly, he was out of his chair and rounding the desk. By the time Antonia started down the last flight of stairs, he was waiting to greet her.

"Good morning, my dear. I missed you at breakfast."

The rest of his carefully rehearsed speech, his "I trust you slept well?" followed by a pointed request for a moment of her time, went winging from his head the instant he saw her face.

Antonia hesitated, one hand clutching the balustrade, her gaze deliberately unfocused. "I'm afraid..." Dragging in a breath, she lifted her head. "That is, I slept in." She felt chilled to the marrow, very close to shivering, but if she wished to be his comfortable wife, she had to comport herself appropriately, even at moments like this.

Stiffly poised, she continued her descent, concentrating on her carriage. Behind her, Nell's heavier footfalls followed down the stairs. Defiantly, she kept her head high. Nell had ministered with cucumber water and Denmark Lotion; she assumed the worst was disguised. Reaching the last step, she bestowed an unfocused glance on her husband-to-be. "I trust you are well, my lord?"

"Tolerably," came the brief answer. Then, after a fractional hesitation, "I wonder, my dear, whether you can spare me a moment of your time?"

Surprised, not only by the request but by the gentler tone of his voice, Antonia blinked; unintentionally, she focused on Philip's face. The concern in his eyes had her turning her head away; she disguised the movement by flicking out her skirts. "As it happens, my lord, I was on my way to the back parlour to write letters. I regret to confess I've been greatly remiss in my correspondence. There are many ladies in Yorkshire to whom I owe a degree of thanks."

She was determined to make no fuss, but the idea of being alone with him just now was simply too much. Her gaze fixed on his cravat, she continued, "I've put the matter off unconscionably long. I understand that if I complete my letters by two, Carring will be able to post them."

"Carring," Philip said, acutely aware of his major-domo hovering behind him, "may put them on my desk. I'll frank them."

Antonia inclined her head. "Thank you, my lord. If you'll excuse me, I'll begin them immediately." She made to turn away.

"Perhaps we could take the air later—a stroll around the square once your correspondence is dealt with?"

Antonia hesitated. The idea of a walk in the fresh breeze was tempting but the vision her mind supplied— of them, stiff and silent, circumnavigating the square— was more than enough to dissuade her. "Ah—I believe Henrietta and I are due to take tea with Lady Cathie, and then we had thought to look in on Mrs Melcombe's at-home."

The lame excuse hung in the air; Antonia stiffened, her brittle facade tightening. Tension swelled and stretched, holding them all frozen, then Philip bowed with his usual fluid grace.

"In that case, I'll see you this evening, my dear."

UNNERVED BY THE undercurrent she detected in his tone, Antonia cried off from their evening's engagements.

She did not even risk dinner, requesting a tray in her room on the grounds of an incipient headache.

Ensconced in lonely splendour at the head of the dining-table, Philip sat sunk in thought, his gaze fixed on the empty seat beside him. At the table's end, Henrietta and Geoffrey were deep in machinations.

"I have to say that I'm not a great believer in new-fangled notions, yet I cannot see my way clear, in this instance, to agree with Meredith Ticehurst." Henrietta pushed away her soup plate. "There's nothing the least—well, *questionable* about Mr Fortescue, is there?"

"Questionable?" Geoffrey frowned. "Not that I know of. Capital fellow from all I can make out. Drives a neat curricle with a nicely matched pair."

Henrietta returned his frown. "That's not what I meant." Raising her head, she looked up the table. "Do you know anything against Mr Fortescue, Ruthven?"

The sound of his name shook Philip from his thoughts. "Fortescue?"

Henrietta threw him a disgusted look. "Mr Henry Fortescue—Miss Dalling's would-be suitor. I have to tell you, Philip, that I am not at all happy in my mind about the tack Meredith Ticehurst is taking with her niece. No—and not with the Marquess either, although he is, after all, a man and, one would suppose, capable of taking care of himself."

Recalling the Marchioness of Hammersley, Philip considered that last far from certain. "I know nothing against Mr Fortescue—indeed, what I do know would suggest he is an eminently eligible, even desirable, *parti*."

Having delivered himself of that pronouncement, Philip reached for his wineglass. As he sipped, Henrietta's suppositions and concerns and Geoffrey's predictably straightforward views drifted past his ears. Their tacit alliance and their half-formed plans to overturn the Countess's applecart did not even register.

Then the meal was at an end; Philip could not even recall if he had eaten. He did not particularly care; he had lost his appetite, among other things.

But when they gathered in the hall preparatory to quitting the house, destined for Lady Arbuthnot's drum, his gaze sharpened. He glanced at Henrietta, his expression bland. "No doubt you'll wish to check on Antonia before we leave."

"Antonia?" Henrietta looked up in surprise. "Whatever for? She's not seriously ill, y'know."

"I had thought," Philip returned, steel glimmering in his tone, "that you might wish to reassure yourself that her indisposition is indeed merely that, and not something more alarming. She is, after all, in your care."

"Phooh!" Henrietta waved her hand dismissively. "It's doubtless merely an upset brought on by going at it too hard." Slanting him a glance, she added, "Have to remember she's a country girl at heart. She might have adapted well to town life but we've been racketing about in grand style these past weeks. She's entitled to some time to recuperate." Henrietta patted his arm in a motherly way then, beckoning Geoffrey, stumped towards the front door.

His expression stony, Philip hesitated, then reluctantly followed.

They returned from Lady Arbuthnot's drum at midnight; to Philip's relief, Henrietta had shown no interest in attending any other of the parties around town. Heads together, thick as thieves, she and Geoffrey negotiated the stairs; frowning, Philip headed for the library. From the corner of his eye, he caught Carring's expression; he shut the door with a decided click.

He hesitated, then crossed to the sideboard and poured out a large brandy. Cradling the glass, he returned to sink into his chair, the one on the left of the hearth. Slowly, he sipped the fine brandy, his gaze broodingly fixed on the empty chair opposite.

Last night he had paced the hearth rug, glowering, possessed by an impotent and thoroughly uncharacteristic anger. Tonight, the anger was still there but tempered by growing concern.

Antonia was avoiding him; now Carring was regarding him with chilly disapproval.

Philip directed a steely glare at the empty chair. *He* wasn't at fault. Antonia should have been more trusting—ladies were supposed to trust their husbands-to-be. She loved him—

Philip stopped.

For one instant, his world wavered—then he snorted impatiently.

He knew, beyond all doubt, beyond any possibility of error, that Antonia loved him. He had known it for more than eight years. Her love was there in her eyes, a certain wistfully warm expression glowing in the hazel depths. He had not responded to it years ago but he had recognised it nonetheless. It had been there even then.

Philip let the thought warm him. He took a long sip of his brandy then frowned at the smouldering fire.

If she loved him, she should have trusted him. She should have had more confidence in him. She should have had the courage of her convictions.

Again his thoughts faltered and halted; Antonia possessed abundant courage. The courage needed to fearlessly manage high-couraged horses, the courage to face with equanimity eight long years of seclusion and deprivation she had never been raised to expect. Her reservoir of courage could not be questioned; why, then, would she not face him over this? Why had she so readily accepted the obvious and retreated, rather than confronting him and letting him explain?

Why hadn't she had the confidence in him that he had in her?

Philip slowly blinked, then grimaced and took another sip from his glass.

He had told her he was smitten, that they shared a deep mutual attraction—she knew he desired her. Surely it was reasonable to expect a lady of her intelligence to make the appropriate deduction?

His frown deepening, he shifted restlessly.

The clock in the corner ticked relentlessly on; when it struck one, he drained his glass. Grimacing, he stood.

They couldn't go on like this. The pain he had seen in her face that morning was etched in his mind; her misery lay like a lead weight around his heart. If she needed some more formidable declaration, then she would have it.

He would talk to her privately—and sort the matter out.

HE HAD FORGOTTEN what a quick learner she was.

Despite his best endeavours, his next opportunity to speak with Antonia privately occurred the next evening when they took to the floor in the first waltz at Lady Harris's ball. As he drew her into his arms, Philip felt a distinct tremor ripple through her. Drawing her closer still, he deftly swung them into the swirling throng.

"Antonia—"

"Lady Harris's decor is positively inspired, don't you think, my lord? Whoever would have thought of a fairy grotto lined with miniature cannon?"

Philip's lips thinned. "Lord Harris was a naval man—something to do with Ordnance. But I wanted to—"

"Do they fire, do you suppose?" Her features animated, Antonia raised her brows. "I wouldn't think that would be too wise, what with young sprigs like Geoffrey about."

"I doubt anyone else has considered the matter. Antonia—"

"Now there I am sure you are wrong, my lord. I'm perfectly certain the idea of firing one would have occurred to Geoffrey by now."

Philip drew in a slow, steady breath. "Antonia, I want to explain—"

"There is, my lord, absolutely no reason you should." Resolutely, Antonia lifted her chin, her gaze fixed beyond Philip's right shoulder. "There is nothing you have to explain—it is I who should beg your pardon. I assure you such an incident will not occur again. I'm fully conscious of my indiscretion. I assure you there's no reason we need discuss the matter further."

Metaphorically girding her loins, she let her gaze fleetingly touch Philip's face. His expression was hard and distinctly stern.

"Antonia, that's—"

She missed the beat and stumbled.

Philip caught her, steadying her. For an instant, he

wondered if she had stumbled on purpose; the startled, darting glances she sent this way and that assured him she had not. "Nobody saw—it was nothing remarkable." He eased his hold once they were circling freely again. "Now—"

"If it is all the same to you, my lord, I suspect I should concentrate on my steps."

Inwardly, Philip swore. The tremor in her voice was entirely genuine. Reining in his impatience, he guided them on through the couples crowding the floor. When next he spoke, his voice was carefully urbane. "I wish to see you privately, Antonia."

She glanced up fleetingly, then looked away. He could feel the quivering tension that held her.

Antonia took a full minute to gather her defences, to ensure her voice was steady when she said, "I believe, my lord, that it would be wisest for us henceforth to follow the conventional paths. In light of our yet-to-be formalised relationship, I would respectfully suggest we should not meet privately until such meetings are customary."

It took every ounce of Philip's savoir faire to smother his response to that suggestion. To quell the primitive urge that threatened to shatter his social veneer. "Antonia," he said, his voice deadly calm. "If you imagine—"

"Have you seen Lady Hatchcock's new quizzing glass? Hugo said it made her eye big beyond belief."

"I have not the slightest interest in Lady Hatchcock's quizzing glass."

"No?" Antonia opened her eyes wide. "Then perhaps you have heard of the latest *on dit*. It seems…" She babbled on, barely pausing for breath.

Philip heard the brittleness in her voice; he noted her

wide eyes and too-rapid breathing. Frustration mounting, he desisted, only to be forced to listen to her run on without pause until he handed her back into the bosom of her court.

Breathlessly, she thanked him. Philip bestowed upon her a look she should have felt all the way to her bones, then turned on his heel and headed for the cardroom.

HE RAN HER to earth the following afternoon; she had taken refuge in the back parlour, her maid in close attendance.

Antonia looked up as he entered. She was seated at the round table in the centre of the room; thick papers and board, swatches of brocade and silk, ribbons, braids, silk cords and fringes lay scattered across its surface. Her fingers plying a large needle, she was engaged in fastening a circle of brocade over a piece of thick paper.

"Good afternoon, my lord." Blinking in surprise, Antonia succumbed to the temptation to drink in his elegance—then she noticed the gloves he was carrying. "Are you going driving?"

"Indeed." Determinedly languid, Philip halted before the table. "I had wondered, my dear, whether you might care to accompany me? You seem to have been hiding yourself away of late—some fresh air will do you good."

Her gaze fixed safely on his cravat, Antonia blinked again, then looked down. "Unfortunately, my lord, you catch me at an inopportune moment." With a wave of her hand, she indicated the materials spread before her. "I broke my reticule last evening and needs must fashion another to match my gown before Lady Hemminghurst's ball tonight."

"How unfortunate." Philip's polite smile did not waver. "Particularly as I had thought that, perhaps, the day being remarkably calm, I might hand the ribbons to you for a short spell."

Antonia's fingers stilled. Slowly, she raised her head until her eyes met Philip's.

Philip hid his triumph; it was the first time since Lady Ardale's unwelcome intrusion into their lives that she had gifted him with one of her wonderfully direct glances.

Then he saw the reproach in her gaze.

"In your phaeton?" she asked.

Philip hesitated, then nodded.

Antonia sighed and looked down. "I have to confess, my lord, that I'm not feeling quite the thing this afternoon—just a mite queasy—I suspect Lady Harris's salmon patties are to blame. So difficult, these days, to be certain of one's salmon." Laying out a piece of silk fringe, she airily continued, "So I'm afraid I must decline your kind—indeed, your very *tempting* invitation. I really could not trust myself to the rocking of a phaeton." Her face artfully brightening, she glanced upwards, not quite meeting Philip's eyes. "Perhaps if we went in your curricle?"

Philip felt his mask harden, he fought not to narrow his eyes. It was a moment before he replied, his tone determinedly even, "I regret to say I left my curricle at the Manor." A fact he was certain she knew.

Regretfully, Antonia sighed. "In that case, my lord, I fear I must decline your offer." Directing a sweet smile his way, she added, "Do convey my respects to Mr Satterly, should you see him."

Philip looked but she would not meet his eyes again. After a moment's uncomfortable silence, he said, his tone flat, "In that case, my dear, I will bid you a good afternoon." He bowed, the action lacking his customary grace, then swiftly strode from the room.

WHEN, TWO NIGHTS LATER, Philip took refuge in his library, alone yet again, he was ready to freely curse Antonia's quick wits.

Every move he made, she blocked. Every tried and true strategy ever devised for getting a young lady alone, she, an innocent from the wilds of the north, had somehow developed a counter for.

She never went anywhere within the house without her maid; she never went anywhere outside except on social engagements and, while in society, was always either surrounded by her court or anchored by Miss Dalling's side. Short of creating an almighty scene in some *grande dame*'s ballroom, he had to acknowledge himself stymied. And, given Antonia knew he would not create a public fuss, he couldn't even use that as a threat!

He didn't bother with a brandy, but fell to pacing before the hearth.

What could he do? Enact a melodrama in the middle of his hall with Carring and her po-faced maid as audience? The thought made him grind his teeth. He'd be dammed if he'd fall so low. To his knees if need be—but no further.

Overhead, a beam creaked. Pausing, Philip glanced up. His gaze lingered on the ceiling; his irate expression slowly turned considering. Then he frowned and resumed his pacing.

That particular avenue remained open but taking their quarrel—it now figured as such in his mind—to her bedchamber would qualify, he felt sure, as an act of outright lunacy. The potential, not to say likely ramifications, even should she prove willing to listen, were altogether too damning.

However, the alternative—of returning to the Manor, present situation intact and ongoing—was too bleak to contemplate. She had withdrawn from him in a way he could never have foreseen—he'd had no idea that the simple absence of the warmth behind her smiles would affect him so deeply.

Halting, he drew in a breath, battling the now permanent constriction about his chest. Closing his eyes, he focused on his problem. Society had long ago labelled him hedonistic—even now, he knew what he wanted.

He wanted to put the brightness back in Antonia's eyes, wanted to experience again the teasing glances they used to share. He wanted to make her blush again. More than anything else, he wanted her to look at him as she always had before—openly, directly, honestly—with her love shining in her eyes.

Abruptly, Philip opened his eyes. A log settled in the grate—he frowned at it. His lady love was too clever for her own good—and for his—but there was one front on which he had never approached her—in deference to her innocence and some deeply ingrained chivalrous instinct.

The time for chivalry had passed.

Slowly, his expression considering, Philip sank into

his usual chair. As always, his gaze settled on its mate, this time with clear calculation in his eyes.

He had never pursued Antonia.

NEXT MORNING, SEATED beside Henrietta at the breakfast table, Antonia attacked a poached pear with single-minded ruthlessness. The same relentless, dogged destruction she would like to visit upon a certain overblown harlot who made a habit of appearing in public in too-tight silk gowns. Indeed, if Lady Ardale—she had learned the woman's name the very next evening—stood anywhere near a duckpond, the outcome would be beyond doubt.

And the only guilt she would feel was for the startled ducks.

Crunching a mouthful of toast, Antonia mulled on the possibilities of a horse trough.

"No—I'm more than convinced!" Beside Antonia, Henrietta nodded pugnaciously. "My dears, we simply *cannot* let this happen."

"Seems a thoroughly rum set-up," Geoffrey opined, reaching for the marmalade. "The way the gorgon's been talking, if Catriona and Ambrose don't toe the line, they'll be left with no choice. Stuck away in the country with only those two old tartars and a bunch of servants—well, any fool can see how the thing'll be done."

"Hmm." Henrietta frowned. "Such a pity the Earl is so…" She grimaced. "Well—*ineffectual.*"

"According to Henry," Geoffrey said, "the poor old toper's been living under the cat's paw for so long he daren't sneeze without permission."

"Yes, well—he never was a forceful character." Leaning one elbow on the table, Henrietta gestured with her butter knife. "Which is all the more reason we must accept this invitation. If there's any chance of deflecting Ticehurst's intentions, I really feel we owe it to those two poor young things to do our best."

"No doubt about it," Geoffrey concurred. "Got to spike her guns somehow."

"Precisely." Henrietta turned to Antonia. "What say you, my dear?"

"Hmm?" Antonia blinked, then nodded. "Yes, of course."

Her expression resolute, Henrietta turned back to Geoffrey; Antonia turned back to her plate—and her thoughts. On a superficial level, she had remained abreast of the developments in Catriona's drama. The majority of her reflections, however, revolved about her own.

When she had decided how she should respond to what she mentally termed Philip's unfortunate tendency, when she had initially set out to be his comfortable wife, she had been under the impression her emotions would be content to be ruled by her intellect, rather than the other way about.

The reality, consequently, was requiring a degree of adjustment. Indeed, she wasn't sure she would not need to completely rescript her role.

Given the anger that welled within her every time she even thought of Lady Ardale, given the almost overwhelming impulse to march into Philip's library and demand an explanation in a more flagrantly histrionic style than Catriona could even imagine, given that, combined with the determination that had sprung from nowhere, the determination to insist that he was hers and hers alone, the absolute conviction that she could, if she dared, reform even such a rake as he, she was no longer at all sure she was cut out to be a comfortable wife.

She frowned at her plate—then reached for a boiled egg.

The door opened, and Philip entered. In keeping with her recent habit, Antonia allowed her gaze to rise only as far as the diamond pin in his cravat. It was an effort not to scowl at it. The smile she did manage was decidedly tight.

"Ah, good morning, Ruthven. I trust you slept well?"

Philip shifted his gaze from Antonia to Henrietta; his stepmother's fond smile fed the instant suspicion her words had evoked. "Tolerably well, thank you." Taking his seat at the table's head, Philip nodded to Carring, proffering the coffee pot. "I had intended, ma'am, to ask when you intended to remove to the country."

"Indeed—and that's precisely the point I wish to discuss with you, my lord." Henrietta sat back in her chair. "We have all received an invitation to a house party—three or four days in Sussex, just the thing to round off the season."

Philip's hand, carrying his coffee cup, halted in midair. "Sussex?"

"Sussex," Henrietta confirmed. "You're included in the invitation, naturally."

"Naturally?" Philip met his stepmother's eye. "Do I know our hosts, by any chance?"

Slightly flustered, Henrietta fluffed her shawls. "You've met the Countess. The party's at Ticehurst Place." She looked up, prepared to be belligerent, fully expecting to have to do battle to gain her ends.

Philip's slowly raised brows, his unexpectedly considering expression, held her silent.

"Ticehurst Place?" Settling back in his chair, Philip sipped his coffee and cast a quick glance at Antonia's bent head. Her attention appeared wholly focused on a boiled egg, which she was decapitating with military precision. Philip's gaze sharpened. "Three days, I believe you said?"

"Three—possibly four. Starting tomorrow." Henrietta regarded him a trifle warily. "I understand it's to be a smallish gathering."

Philip's gaze flicked her way. "How small?"

Henrietta waved dismissively. "Just the four of us—and the Hammersleys, of course."

"Of course."

When Philip said nothing more, his gaze resting thoughtfully on Antonia, who remained apparently oblivious, Henrietta humphed. "I dare say, if you don't wish to go, we can get along without you."

"On the contrary." Abruptly, Philip sat forward. Setting his cup down, he reached for the platter of ham. "I confess to being somewhat at a loose end. I see no reason I cannot accompany you to Sussex, if you wish it."

Henrietta blinked in amazement; she quickly grabbed the offer. "Indeed—nothing would please me more. I won't conceal from you, my lord, that affairs might become rather touchy—it would be a great relief to me if you were by."

"Consider it settled, then." As he helped himself to three slices of ham, Philip was conscious of Antonia's swift, appraising, distinctly suspicious glance. He resisted the urge to smile wolfishly at her. Time enough for that once he had her at Ticehurst Place—at a house party without the party, in what would doubtless prove to be a huge rambling mansion, mostly empty, with large grounds likewise free of unwanted spectators— all of it glorying in one significant advantage.

None of it would be his.

He had spent half the night and all the morning considering the constraints his honour dictated while Antonia remained under his roof, on his lands.

Ticehurst Place was neither. Not his roof, not his grounds.

Open season.

He slanted a quick glance at Antonia, engrossed in slicing a piece of ham to ribbons. Returning his gaze to his plate, Philip allowed himself a smug smile.

At last, at long last, fate had dealt him an ace.

CHAPTER THIRTEEN

LATE THE NEXT MORNING, Antonia descended the stairs, Henrietta in her wake. Both she and her aunt were ready to depart for Ticehurst Place; they had both elected to breakfast in their bedchambers, Henrietta due to her slow preparations, Antonia due to a sudden conviction that facing Philip over the breakfast table with only Geoffrey for protection was not a sensible undertaking.

There'd been something in his demeanour, a certain intentness in his manner during their previous evening's parade through the ballrooms that had set her senses on edge. She had no real idea what it was she detected—she was not about to hazard a guess.

As they started down the last flight, Antonia keeping a watchful eye on Henrietta's ponderous progress, the front door opened. Geoffrey strode in, his tall form enveloped in a white drab driving coat sporting quite as many capes as Philip's.

Antonia halted on the last step. "Where on earth did you get that?"

Geoffrey grinned. "Philip introduced me to his tailor. Quite a dab hand at his trade, don't you think?" He whirled, setting the capes fluttering.

When he stopped and looked pointedly at her, Antonia nodded. "It's certainly…" She hesitated, then, beguiled by Geoffrey's obvious delight, smiled. "Something like."

Geoffrey glowed with pride. "Philip suggested arriving at Oxford in such togs wouldn't hurt. And, of course, it's the perfect garb for today."

Joining them, Henrietta humphed. "The sun's decided to remember us—you'll be too hot in the carriage in that."

"Indeed."

Antonia quickly turned as Philip strolled into the hall. His gaze met hers fleetingly, then he glanced down, lips firming as he pulled on his driving gloves. "So it's as well he's not travelling in the carriage."

"Oh?" Henrietta asked the question, much to Antonia's relief, allowing her to keep her lips shut and her expression satisfyingly distant.

"I'm taking my phaeton." Philip glanced at Antonia. "Geoffrey may as well come with me."

It was an effort not to meet his gaze. Determinedly cool, Antonia nodded. "An exceedingly good notion." Tilting her chin, she added, "It will leave us more space in which to be comfortable."

For an instant, Philip's gaze rested on her face, then he smiled—a slow, predatory smile. "It would, perhaps, be wise to gain what rest you might. I suspect you'll discover this house party unexpectedly exhausting."

Antonia flicked him a suspicious glance but his expression as he moved forward to help Henrietta down the last steps was bland and uninformative.

The front door bell pealed; Carring came hurrying from the nether regions. He looked out, then set the front door wide. "Your phaeton and the carriage, my lord."

Between them, Philip and Geoffrey helped Henrietta down the front steps. Marshalling his footmen, Carring saw to the stowing of the luggage, assisted by acid comments from both Trant and Nell. Resembling a pair of black crows, the maids between them got Henrietta settled against the padded cushions, protected by a veritable mountain of shawls. Left on the pavement, Antonia glanced about. Geoffrey was already on the box-seat of the phaeton, the reins in his hands as he helped restrain the restive horses.

The sight stiffened her spine. Unbidden, her memory replayed the three separate excuses she had spent the small hours devising, one for every possible tack Philip might have taken to inveigle her into sharing the phaeton's box-seat on the long drive to Ticehurst Place.

Excuses she had not needed.

Suppressing a disaffected sniff, Antonia turned, one hand raising her skirts to climb the carriage steps. Philip's hand appeared before her. For an instant, she regarded it, the long strong fingers and narrow palm. Reminding herself of her role, she lifted her chin and placed her hand in his.

Philip smoothly raised her fingers to his lips, artfully, lingeringly, caressing her fingertips.

Antonia froze, her breathing suspended. She glanced up through her lashes; Philip trapped her gaze in his.

"Enjoy the drive. I'll be waiting at the other end— to greet you."

Eyes widening, Antonia took in the hard planes of his face, the subtle aggression in the line of his jaw— and the clear intent that stared at her from the depths of his grey eyes. A skittering sensation shivered over her skin. Ignoring it, she set one foot on the carriage step. "I dare say there'll be many distractions at Tice-hurst Place."

She'd intended the comment as a dismissal of his avowed intention; she expected it to be the conclusion of their exchange. Instead, as he handed her up, Philip's voice reached her, wickedly low. "You may count on that, my dear."

The promise in his words distracted her all the way to Ticehurst Place.

Although her gaze remained fixed on the scenery, she did not notice the sunshine beaming down from between fluffy clouds, did not feel the soft touch of the unexpectedly mild breeze. Summer's last stand had enveloped the country, a final burst of golden weather that had set the doves to cooing again in the trees along the way.

Lulled by the sound, Antonia found her mind treading a circuitous path, forever leaving her facing one unanswerable question: Just what was her prospective husband about?

She had reached no conclusion when the carriage rocked to a stop on the gravel sweep before Ticehurst Place. As soon as the door was opened and the steps let down, Trant and Nell descended. Two footmen came hurrying down the long flight of steps leading up to the front door; together with the maids, they endeavoured to ease Henrietta from the carriage.

Antonia glanced out of the window—and saw Philip descending the steps, his pace relaxed and leisurely, his expression mild and urbane. Longing to escape the close confines of the carriage, aware of the dull headache its stuffiness had evoked, she gave vent to a disgusted sniff—and struggled to keep her mind from dwelling on how pleasant the drive in his phaeton must have been.

"Heh-me!" Henrietta exclaimed as her feet touched the ground. "My old bones are cramping my style." Grimacing, she leant heavily on the footmen's arms and slowly started up the steps.

Her head haughtily high, Antonia shifted along the seat, then moved to the carriage door.

As he had promised, Philip was there to assist her to the gravel. Alighting, her hand in his, Antonia glanced up—only to see him grimace.

"Much as it goes against the grain, I fear I must plead Miss Dalling's cause. Her situation is more serious than I'd imagined."

Antonia looked her question.

Drawing her hand through his arm, Philip turned her towards the steps. "To use Geoffrey's description, it appears the gorgon has entirely fallen off her perch. On arrival, we were treated to what I can only describe as a supremely distasteful scene in which her ladyship endeavoured to impress upon me that her niece has all but accepted the Marquess."

Outwardly nonchalant, they climbed the broad steps. Philip lifted his gaze to the small knot of people waiting on the porch. "It appears that dramatic flights are a Dalling family trait. The upshot was that Miss Dalling, for whom I must reluctantly concede a certain sympathy, has implored our help in avoiding a marriage by *force majeure*."

"Great heavens!" Antonia followed Philip's lead in schooling her features to the semblance of polite conversation. "Is Catriona in a fury?"

"Worse. She's in a blue funk."

"Catriona?" Antonia looked up at him, her gaze direct. "You're bamming me."

Philip's brows rose. "Not at all—but see for yourself." With a nod, he indicated the reception party now a short way before them.

Antonia followed his gaze. A moment later, they reached the porch—and she discovered he'd spoken no less than the truth. The Catriona who stood mute by her aunt's side was a far cry from the defiantly confident young girl who had first come on the town. Eyes still huge but now filled with die-away despair fastened upon her. As she turned from acknowledging the Countess's somewhat strident greeting, Catriona stepped forward to clasp her hand.

"I'm so glad you've come." Her accents were hushed, fervent. "Come—I'll show you to your room." A quick glance revealed that Henrietta was the focus of the Countess's attention. "I have to unburden myself to someone who understands—I do not know *what* I would have done if you hadn't taken pity and travelled thus, into the lion's den."

Stifling an impulse to suggest that that last should be the "gorgon's den," Antonia allowed herself to be drawn inside. Only to have her nonsensical vision take on real shape. The hall was dark and gloomy; its ceiling was so high it could only be described as cavernous. Panelled in dark wood, the walls were hung with old wooden shields and dark-hued tapestries. A fire smoked and smouldered in a huge stone fireplace; a heavy wooden table stood on the dark flags. The chamber exuded a pervading sense of being the anteroom of some dangerous animal's lair.

Pulling back against Catriona's tug, Antonia halted

in the centre of the room to stare at the huge, ornately carved staircase filling the end of the hall. Its wide treads led upwards into the shadows of what she assumed was a gallery.

"Welcome to the delights of Ticehurst Place."

The deep, softly menacing words, uttered from just behind her ear, made her jump. Antonia threw a frowning glance over her shoulder. Philip had followed them in; he stood close behind her, his gaze roving the shadowed walls.

"It possesses a certain cachet, don't you think?" His eyes lowered to meet hers.

Catriona, apparently inured to the decor, gently tugged Antonia forward. Antonia did not move, anchored by Philip's hand at her waist.

"Don't leave her," he murmured, his eyes holding hers. "Not even when you're dressing."

Fleetingly, Antonia searched his eyes, then nodded and yielded to Catriona's insistent urging. Drawing closer, she tucked her arm in Catriona's. Together, they climbed the stairs, ascending into the shadows.

Philip watched them go, a frown gathering in his eyes.

With no attempt at her usual chatter, Catriona led Antonia to a large chamber, roomy but somehow oppressive. Nell was there, unpacking Antonia's bags. Eyeing the maid warily, Catriona towed Antonia to the window seat, pressing her to sit. "My room's just along the corridor," she said, her voice close to a whisper. Sinking onto the brocaded cushion beside Antonia, she grimaced. "So is Ambrose's."

Antonia blinked. "Ah." That was not, to her understanding, the habit when accommodating young people. "I see."

"I haven't told you the half of it yet." In suitably dramatic style, Catriona proceeded to do so, inevitably embellishing her account.

But no amount of dramatic description could detract from the impact of the basic facts; appraised of the full story of how Ambrose, on arriving late the previous evening, had been shown to Catriona's room, ostensibly by mistake, Antonia had no doubt of the appropriateness of her sympathies.

"If it hadn't been for the fact that I'd asked for more coal and the girl was late bringing it up, Ambrose and I could have been…" Catriona's eyes glazed. "Why—we could have ended sharing a bed." Her voice faded; Antonia did not think her undisguised horror owed much to her histrionic tendencies.

"Luckily," she said, leaning forward to pat Catriona's hand bracingly, "that eventuality was averted. I take it you had not yet gone to sleep and as the girl was there, Ambrose got no further than the threshold?"

Catriona nodded. "But you can see, can't you, how hopeless it all is? Unless Henry can find some way to rescue me from my aunt's talons, I'll be *forced* to the altar."

"Along with Ambrose." Antonia frowned. "What does he say to this?"

Catriona sighed. "He was horrified, of course. But his mother is truly overpowering—she has him well under her thumb. He simply cannot stand up to her, no matter how hard he tries."

"Hmm." Recalling Philip's words, Antonia stood and shook out her skirts. "Come—help me choose what to wear. Once I've changed, we must see what we can do to brighten you up a trifle." When this projected endeavour raised no gleam of response, Antonia added, "I should warn you that Ruthven is something of an authority on the subject of feminine attire. If I were you and wished to retain my standing in his eyes, I would not appear at dinner less than well presented."

Catriona frowned. "He does seem well disposed."

"Indeed. And if anyone can assist you and Henry, it is he." As she sailed across the chamber, Antonia added, somewhat acidly, "I can attest that his experience in arranging clandestine meetings is beyond compare."

As it transpired, that was to be her one and only allusion to what lay between herself and Philip. Absorbed in reinflating Catriona's confidence while simultaneously considering all possible avenues the Countess might attempt to gain her ends, she had no time to dwell on her husband-to-be's unfortunate tendencies.

When she met him in the drawing-room two hours later, she made not the slightest demur when he possessed himself of her hand, kissed it, then settled it on his sleeve. The drawing-room was a cold and sombre chamber, designed on the same grandiose scale as the hall, its walls hung with a dark, heavily embossed paper, the ornately carved furniture upholstered in thick black-brown velvet. A small fire in an enormous grate struggled unsuccessfully to dispel the gloom.

Quelling a shiver, Antonia drew closer to Philip, conscious of the aura of safety emanating from his large, familiar frame. Catriona, who had entered with her, reluctantly responded to an imperious summons; haltingly, she made her way to the Countess's side, to where

Ambrose, looking pale and uncomfortable, stood beside his mama.

Leaning towards Philip, Antonia murmured, "Catriona told me what occurred last night."

Glancing down, Philip frowned. "Last night?"

Antonia blinked, then briefly outlined Catriona's tale. "It's no wonder, after that, that she appears so moped. I believe she feels helpless." Looking up, she saw Philip's jaw firm, his gaze fixed on the unconvincing tableau the Countess had assembled by the *chaise*.

"If I wasn't convinced Miss Dalling deserved our support, I would have you—and Henrietta—out of here within the hour."

His clipped accents left little doubt as to his temper. Antonia studied his stern profile. "What should we do?"

Philip met her gaze, then grimaced. "Stall. Place hurdles in the gorgon's path." He looked again at the group about the *chaise*. "At the moment, that's the only thing we can do. Until we see our way clear, I would suggest the less time Miss Dalling spends in the Marquess's orbit, the better."

Antonia nodded. "Apparently Mr Fortescue remained in town with the intention of making a last push at securing the Earl's support. I understand he believes that it must be the Earl, not the Countess, who is her legal guardian."

"That's very likely." Glancing down, Philip met her gaze. "But from what I know of the Earl, that legal nicety will have precious little practical significance."

"You don't believe he'll consent to come to Catriona's aid?"

"I don't believe he'll stir one step from the safety of his club." Looking again at the Countess, resplendent in bronzed bombazine, a turban of gold cloth perched atop her frizzed curls, her eagle eye cold and openly calculating, Philip grimaced. "Entirely understandable, unfortunately."

The butler, Scalewether, entered on the words. Tall and ungainly, possessed of a distressingly sallow complexion, in his regulation black he resembled an undertaker without the hat. "Dinner is served, m'lady."

At the Countess's urging, Ambrose, all but squirming, led the way, Catriona a martyr on his arm. With suave grace, Philip followed, leading Antonia. He guided her into the echoing dining-room, a chamber so immense the walls remained in shadow.

To Antonia's relief, the table had had most of its leaves removed, leaving space for only twelve. The Countess, sweeping all before her, took her seat at its head; the Marchioness haughtily claimed the foot. Henrietta was graciously waved to a seat beside the Countess. Having claimed Geoffrey's arm from the drawing-room, the Marchioness kept hold of him, placing him to her right—which left Ambrose and Catriona on one side of the table. Antonia felt an undeniable surge of relief when Philip took his seat beside her.

The meal had little to recommend it, the conversation even less. Dominated by the Countess, aided and abetted by the Marchioness, it remained in stultifyingly boring vein. As her hostess droned on, Antonia studied the servitors who, under the direction of the cadaverous Scalewether, silently set the dishes before them.

She had rarely seen such a crew of shifty-eyed, soft-footed men. Crafty, watchful eyes followed every move made by their mistress's guests. As she attacked a custard, unpalatably tough, Antonia told herself she was being fanciful—that their constant surveillance was simply the outward sign of conscientious staff trying to anticipate their masters' needs.

From under her lashes, she watched Scalewether watching Catriona and Ambrose. There was patience and persistence in his unemotional gaze. Antonia felt her skin crawl.

"I must say, Ruthven, that I had thought you would hold a much stricter line in shouldering your new responsibilities." The Countess fixed Philip with a steely eye. "I believe, my lord, that the university term is well advanced."

Languid urbanity to the fore, Philip briefly touched his napkin to his lips, then, sitting back in his chair, regarded the Countess blandly. "Indeed, ma'am. But as the Master of Trinity acknowledged in his most recent communication, we must make allowance for the natural talents of a Mannering." Philip bestowed a swift glance on Geoffrey before turning back to the Countess. "It's my belief the Master thinks to restore the status quo by having Geoffrey start later than most."

Geoffrey grinned.

The Countess humphed discouragingly. "That's all very well, but I cannot say I am at all in favour of letting young people go idle. It's tempting providence and all manner of mischief. While I say nothing to your belief that the boy should gain experience of the *ton,* I profess myself astonished to find him here, amongst us still." Her bosom swelling as she drew in a portentous breath. "Not, of course, that we are not perfectly happy to have him here. But I am nevertheless at a loss to account for your laxity, Ruthven."

Antonia glanced at Philip. He was reclining gracefully in his chair, long fingers stroking the stem of his wineglass. His expression was a mask of polite affability. His gaze was as hard as stone.

"Indeed, ma'am?"

For a defined instant, the soft question hung in the air. The Countess shifted, suddenly wary yet unquenchably belligerent.

Philip smiled. "In that case, it's perhaps as well you won't be called upon to do so."

Antonia held her breath; across the table, she caught Geoffrey's decidedly militant eye. Almost imperceptibly, she shook her head at him.

Stricken silence had engulfed the table; the Countess broke it, setting down her spoon with a decided click. "It's time we ladies retired to the drawing-room." Majestically, her expression haughtily severe, she rose, fixing Philip with a baleful eye. "We will leave you gentlemen to your port." With a regal swish of her skirts, she led the way.

As she rose to follow, Antonia caught Philip's eye. He raised a brow at her. Quelling a smile, Antonia followed in their hostess's wake.

In the drawing-room, Catriona was banished to the pianoforte with instructions to demonstrate her skill. Visibly tired, Henrietta reluctantly summoned Trant; with polite smiles and nods—and one very direct glance for Antonia—she retired. Reduced to the role of unnecessary cypher, Antonia duly sat mum and counted the minutes.

She had lost count and Catriona was flagging before the gentlemen reappeared. They were led by Philip, who strolled into the room as if it was his own. With a glib smile, he appropriated her as if she, too, was his.

Antonia told herself she bore it only because she was all but bored witless. "What now?" she asked sotto voce, watching as, beneath the cool glare of his mother's eye, Ambrose dragged his feet to the piano.

Philip took the scene in one comprehensive glance. "Speculation."

Stunned, Antonia stared. "You can't be serious?"

He was—before her astonished eyes, he overrode all resistance, somehow inducing Scalewether to produce a pack of cards and counters to serve as betting chips. Ambrose, grasping at straws, hurried to set up a small table and chairs. Within ten minutes, the five of them were seated around the table, leaving the two older ladies isolated by the fireplace.

One glance at the Countess was enough for Antonia; thereafter, she studiously avoided their hostess's basilisk stare.

"Five to me."

Philip's demand focused her attention on the game. "Five?" Antonia studied the cards laid on the table, then sniffed. She doled out the required counters, then reached for the pack. She won three back, but her stack of counters was steadily eroded, falling prey to Philip's ruthless machinations. He was, apparently, a past master at this pastime, too.

Reaching for the pack, Antonia cast him a disapproving glance. "I admit I had not thought to find you so expert at this game, my lord."

The smile he turned on her made her toes curl.

"I dare say you'll be amazed, my dear, by just how many games I can play."

Unexpectedly trapped in his gaze, by what she could

read in the grey, Antonia froze, her hand, outstretched, hovering above the pack.

"C'mon, Sis—you going to forfeit your turn?"

Geoffrey's words broke the spell. Glancing around, Antonia drew in a quick breath.

"Not," Geoffrey continued, "something I'd advise—if we don't take care, Ruthven's going to wipe us out. We'll have to use our wits if we're to counter his predatory incursions."

Antonia studied the situation afresh—and discovered he was right. "Nonsense," she declared, straightening and picking up the pack. "We'll come about." She dealt, settled the question of trumps, then turned up her first card; it was the ace of trumps. Smiling, she lifted her chin and glanced Philip's way. "When opponents believe they're invincible, they're sure to be defeated."

She received a very direct, definitely challenging look in reply.

Thereafter, the fight was on. Their attention fully engaged, Antonia and Geoffrey combined to counter Philip's steady accumulation of chips, draining his pile at every opportunity. Philip struck back, catching Geoffrey more frequently than Antonia, who, very much on her mettle, took care to cover her back.

Fifteen minutes later, Ambrose edged his chair from the table and somewhat ruefully declared, "That's my last three counters."

"I've only got one left," Catriona said.

Their comments halted play. Three heads came up; Antonia exchanged a glance with Philip. He grimaced, catching Geoffrey's eye as he pulled out his watch. "Too early," was his verdict.

"Right then." Geoffrey seized the pack and dealt.

During the following fifteen minutes, the three endeavoured to lose as many counters as they had earlier won, amidst a great deal of unexpected hilarity.

"Your pile is still a great deal too high, my lord." Magnanimously, Antonia handed six counters to Catriona. "It's my belief you're not trying hard enough."

Removing the pack from her fingers, his hand closing briefly about hers, Philip caught her eye. "Put it down to my having to fight against deeply ingrained habit."

Antonia opened her eyes wide. "Oh?"

"Indeed." Philip held her gaze. "None of my ilk like to lose."

Antonia's eyes widened even more; with an effort, she directed them to the table, to the cards he negligently dealt. "See?" Righteously, she nodded. "A knave. You will have to do better, my lord."

"Once this present distraction is passed, I will endeavour to do so, my dear."

The promise in those words sent a delicious shiver down Antonia's spine. Determined to ignore it, and the breathlessness it evoked, she fought to keep her attention on the cards, aware that Philip's too-perceptive gaze remained on her face.

Salvation came from an unlikely source; the doors opened and Scalewether rolled in the tea-trolley. Summoned to take their cups, they abandoned their game; by unspoken accord, they all remained together, standing in a loose group as they sipped.

Under the direction of her aunt, Catriona dutifully extolled the attractions to be found within the grounds. "The folly is probably the most interesting," she concluded. "It stands by the lake and is quite pretty when it's sunny."

Her tone suggested Newgate would be more appealing.

Antonia caught Philip's eye. "Actually, I'm rather tired." Delicately, she smothered a yawn.

"Doubtless the effects of the drive down." Smoothly, Philip relieved her of her cup; together with his, he laid it aside. "So enervating," he murmured solicitously as, turning, he met Antonia's gaze. "Travelling in a carriage."

Brows rising haughtily, Antonia turned to Catriona, raising her voice for the benefit of the ladies nearby. "I believe I should retire—perhaps, Miss Dalling, you would care to accompany me?"

"Yes, indeed." Catriona set down her cup.

"Not deserting us yet, are you, miss?" The Countess's gimlet gaze fastened on Catriona's face. "Why, what will the Marquess think of you, leaving him to entertain himself like this?"

"Indeed," the Marchioness of Hammersley opined. "I suspect my son, like any other young gentleman, would be very grateful for your company, Miss Dalling." With a commanding wave, she continued, "The night is quite mild. I dare say a turn on the terrace in the moonlight is just what you young people would like."

"Ah—no. That is…" Aghast, Ambrose goggled at his mother. "Mean to say—"

The Marchioness transfixed him with a penetrating stare. "Yes, Hammersley?" When Ambrose just stared at her, rabbitlike, she enquired, her tone sugar-sweet, "Do you find something objectionable about the notion of strolling her ladyship's terrace?"

"Nothing to say against her ladyship's terrace," Ambrose blurted out. His hand strayed to his neckcloth. "But—"

Philip cut in, his tones dripping with fashionable languor. "Perhaps I should explain, Lady Ticehurst, that Miss Mannering, hailing as she does from Yorkshire, is unaccustomed to finding her way about such..." his graceful gesture encompassed the house about them "...*grand* establishments as your own. I beg you'll allow Miss Dalling to act as her guide. Indeed," he continued, his gaze shifting to Antonia's face, "I must admit the idea of Miss Mannering wandering lost through your corridors quite exercises my imagination. Dare I hope you'll take pity on her poor sense of direction and allow your niece to accompany her?"

Frowning, the countess shifted on the *chaise*. "Well..."

"As for Hammersley," Philip smoothly continued, "there's no need to concern yourself over his entertainment. He and I had thought to adjourn to the billiard-room." Turning, he bestowed an elegantly condescending look on the Marchioness. "I understand that, due to the late Marquess's early demise, Hammersley has lacked the opportunity to polish his talents in such manly arts as billiards. I had thought, perhaps, to be of some use to him while here."

The Marchioness's expression blanked. "Yes, of course. How very kind..." Her frown grew as her words trailed away.

"So—if you'll excuse us?" With a supremely graceful bow, Philip turned from the *chaise*. Avoiding Antonia's eye, he captured her hand and placed it on his sleeve. "Come, Hammersley—let's escort these young ladies to the stairs. Mannering?"

With that, he led the way; in less than a minute, the drawing-room door was shut upon the twin harpies, leaving the rest of them safe in the hall. Pausing at the foot of the stairs to wait for Catriona, Antonia glanced at Philip. "Quite a tour de force, my lord."

Philip met her gaze; he smiled, deliberately, with the full force of his intent. "As I told you, my dear, I'm not one who generally loses." Raising her hand, he kissed each fingertip, his eyes on hers all the while. "I suspect you'll be amazed by what forces I can, when moved, bring to bear."

The ripple of awareness that shivered through Antonia and the soft blush that tinged her cheeks stayed with him long after she retreated up the stairs.

AT EIGHT THE following morning, Antonia slipped from the lowering bulk of Ticehurst Place and headed for the stables. The sun again ruled the sky; as she entered the low-ceilinged stables, she paused, blinking rapidly. As her vision adjusted, she saw a cap bobbing in a nearby loose box. She hurried forward.

"I'd like a horse, please. As quick as you can." Rounding the end of the open box, Antonia cast a swift glance over the bay the stableman was bridling. "This one will do nicely."

The aged retainer blinked owlishly at her. "Beggin' your pardon, miss." He broke off to tug at his cap. "But this one's for the gentleman."

"Gentleman?" On the instant, Antonia felt her senses shiver. She swung around—to find herself breast to chest with her nemesis. She took a step back and hauled in a quick breath. "I didn't see you there, my lord."

"Obviously." Philip studied the tinge of colour highlighting her cheekbones, then let his gaze meet hers. "And where are you headed?"

Inwardly, Antonia cursed. She hesitated, then, recognizing the hint of steel beneath the soft grey of his eyes, capitulated. "I was going for a ride."

Philip's brows rose. "Indeed? Then I'll ride with you." Reaching forward, he took hold of her arm and drew her closer, clear of the bay the stableman was turning. "So much more suitable," he murmured, "than a young lady riding alone."

Suppressing a snort, Antonia swallowed the rebuke with what grace she could muster.

"Here you be, sir." The groom came up, leading the bay. He handed the reins to Philip, then turned to Antonia. "Now, miss. I've a nice steady mare that would suit you. Not one as gets overly frisky, so you won't have to panic."

He turned away on the words, heading for the row of boxes across the stables, leaving Philip as the only witness to Antonia's stunned reaction. Horror and outrage mixed freely in her expression, dazed disbelief filled her eyes. Then her jaw firmed.

Philip swallowed his laughter and called to the stableman. "I fear you mistake Miss Mannering's abilities. She's perfectly capable of managing one of your master's hunters. By the look of them, they could do with the exercise."

Frowning, the stableman shuffled back. "I don't rightly know as how I should, sir. Wondrous powerful, the master's hunters."

"Miss Mannering can handle them." Philip felt his face harden. "She's a dab hand at reining in all manner of untamed beasts." Conscious of Antonia's swift glance, he lifted his head and scanned the hunters shifting restlessly in their boxes. "That one." He pointed to a glossy black, every bit as powerful as the bay he had chosen. "Put a sidesaddle on—I'll take all responsibility."

With a resigned shrug, the stableman headed for the tackroom.

"Come—let's wait in the yard." Taking Antonia's arm, Philip steered her out of the stable, the bay following eagerly.

Antonia glanced about. "I'd thought Geoffrey or Ambrose would be about."

"According to the stableman, they've already gone out. Or should that be 'escaped'?"

Antonia grimaced. "You'll have to admit Ambrose has just cause."

Walking the restive bay, Philip spoke over his shoulder. "You may console yourself with the thought that your brother is doing an excellent job of putting their ladyships' collective noses out of joint."

"Geoffrey?" Antonia frowned. "How?"

"By sticking with Ambrose." When she continued to look bemused, Philip smiled wryly. "I fear Geoffrey is very much the fly in their ladyships' ointment. In case you haven't yet realized, this so-called 'house party' was very carefully designed. We each have specific roles: Henrietta, you and me to lend countenance—imagining, of course, that Henrietta is a like-minded soul who shares their ladyships' proclivities and that you and I will be too involved with each other to notice anything else. Geoffrey's presence, however, has thrown a definite spanner into the works. Although she extended the invitation, the Countess had imagined he'd go up to Oxford after the last of the parties."

Antonia narrowed her eyes. "The Countess is a very manipulative woman."

"Indeed." Philip's tone hardened. "And I do not appreciate being manipulated."

Antonia shot him a glance, then elevated her chin. "Nor do I."

It was Philip's turn to glance suspiciously, but Antonia had turned away to greet the sleek black hunter the stableman led forth. Under her direction, the stableman held the horse by the mounting block. Philip inwardly snorted and swung up to the bay's saddle. The instant Antonia had settled her skirts, he turned the bay's head for the fields.

He held back only long enough to ensure Antonia was secure and in command, then loosened his reins, letting the bay's stride eat the distance to the trees on the first hill. They drew into the shade of the outliers of the wood and Philip drew rein. He waited until Antonia brought the restive black up alongside, then fixed her with a distinctly strait look. "Now—where are you going?"

Inwardly, Antonia grimaced; outwardly, she lifted her chin. "To meet Mr Fortescue—should he be there to meet."

"Fortescue?"

"Catriona arranged to meet him at the end of the ride through the woods. He said he'd come to tell her how he'd got on with the Earl. She was to keep watch every day but at present, she's convinced herself no one can save her from the Countess's machinations."

Annoyance crept into Antonia's voice as she recalled the hours she had spent trying valiantly to raise Catriona's spirits. "From my previous experience of her, I would not have believed she would give up so easily. I've been telling her she must make a push to secure what she wants from life—that if one really wants something, one has to be prepared to fight for it."

The bay jibbed; Philip tightened his reins. His eyes, fixed on Antonia, narrowed. "Indeed." He might have said more had another, more immediate realisation not intruded. "You were on your way to meet a gentleman alone."

Antonia shot him a frowning glance. "Only Mr Fortescue."

"Who happens to be a perfectly personable gentleman some years your senior."

"Who happens to be all but betrothed to a young lady I regard as a good friend." Chin high, Antonia gathered her reins.

Philip held her with his eyes. "I have to inform you, my dear, that meeting personable gentlemen alone is not the behaviour I expect of Lady Ruthven."

Antonia held his gaze, her own eyes slowly narrowing, golden glints appearing in the green. Then she hauled on the reins, pulling the black about. "I am not," she replied, decidedly tart, "Lady Ruthven *yet*."

With that, she touched her heels to the black's sides and took off through the woods.

Philip watched her go, his eyes slitted, his gaze as sharp as honed steel. Suddenly, he recalled he rode much heavier than she—he couldn't let her get too far ahead. With a curse, he set out in pursuit.

Despite his best efforts, Antonia was still in the lead when the end of the ride hove in sight. It led up to a small knoll at the back of the woods; cresting the rise, Antonia saw a single horseman waiting patiently. Recognizing his square frame, she waved; moments later, she drew up alongside Henry Fortescue.

He returned her greeting punctiliously, nodding as Philip joined them, then, somewhat glumly, turned to Antonia. "From your presence, I take it all is lost?"

Antonia blinked at him. "Heavens, no! Catriona is too well watched for it to be safe for her to ride out to meet you—Ruthven and I came in her stead."

Ignoring Philip's glance, she smiled brightly and was rewarded with a smile in return.

"Well, that's a relief." Henry's smile faded. "Not that my news holds out any hope."

Philip brought his bay up beside Antonia. "What did the Earl say?"

Henry grimaced. "Unfortunately, things weren't as we thought. There was no legal guardianship established, so the Earl has no real rights in the matter. The Countess assumed Catriona's guardianship by custom, so there's no gainsaying her. Not, at least, until Catriona comes of age—but that's years from now."

"Oh." Despite her earlier optimism, Antonia felt her spirits sink.

"Not that we wouldn't be prepared to wait," Henry went on. "If that was the only way. But the problem is, the Countess has her own row to hoe. And she's not one to let up."

Antonia grimaced. "Indeed not."

Henry drew a deep breath. "I don't know what Catriona will say—or do—when she hears the truth."

Antonia didn't bother to answer; Henry's gloom was contagious.

"Then before we tell her, I suggest we establish the facts ourselves."

Antonia stared at Philip. "What do you mean?"

"I mean that I suspect we have not yet reached the truth." Hands folded over his pommel, Philip raised a brow at her. "I took refuge in the library last night—a little habit of mine, you might recall."

Antonia narrowed her eyes. "So?"

"So, while idly pacing, not having any other distraction to hand, I noticed a family bible on a lectern in one corner. It's a handsome volume. Out of sheer curiosity, I looked at the flyleaf. It doesn't, as I had imagined, belong to the Earl's family but to the Dallings. Indeed, I imagine it might belong to Catriona as it was certainly her father's before."

Henry frowned. "But what has that to say to oversetting the Countess's schemes?"

"Nothing in itself," Philip acknowledged. "But the information the bible contains bears consideration. Inscribed on the flyleaf are the recent generations of the Dalling family. The history clearly shows the Countess is one of twins—her only sister is her twin. As is often the case with twin females, there's no distinction made between them—no record of who was born first—that fact is stated explicitly in the bible. So, by my reckoning, Catriona's other aunt would have equal right to act as her guardian by custom."

"Lady Copely!" Henry sat his horse as one stunned. "She's always been Catriona's favourite but she couldn't come to Catriona's father's funeral because one of her children came down with whooping cough. Instead, the Countess arrived and swept Catriona up as if she had the right to do so. Naturally, we all assumed she had."

Philip raised a hand in warning. "We do not, at this stage, know if the Countess acted with Lady Copely's assent. Do you know if Lady Copely would be willing to aid Miss Dalling in marrying as she wishes?"

Henry frowned. "I don't know."

"I do." Eyes bright, Antonia looked at Philip. "I saw Lady Copely's daughter and her husband in town. Catriona told me they had married for love." Blushing lightly, she transferred her gaze to Henry. "Indeed, she told me Lady Copely herself had married for affection, rather than status. From all she said, her ladyship sounds the perfect sponsor for yours and Catriona's future."

"If that's so," Henry mused, "then perhaps Catriona could claim her ladyship's protection?"

Philip nodded. "It seems a likely possibility."

"Well, then!" Fired with newfound zeal, Henry straightened in his saddle. "All that remains is to discover her ladyship's direction and I'll apply to her directly." He looked hopefully at Antonia.

Antonia shook her head. "Catriona never mentioned where Lady Copely lives."

Henry grimaced.

"I suggest," Philip said, "that as Catriona may have information on how best to approach Lady Copely, it would be wise for you to meet with Catriona prior to hunting up her ladyship."

Henry nodded. "I confess I would like to do so. But if she's truly kept close, how will we manage it?"

Dismissively, Philip waved one elegant hand. "A little

forethought, a spot of strategic planning and the thing's done. There's a small field, part of an old orchard, at the back of the shrubbery. If you leave your horse in the woods on that side, you should be able to reach it easily. Be there at three this afternoon. The older ladies will be snoozing. I'll arrange for Catriona to be there."

Henry's eagerness was tempered by caution. "But if the Countess keeps watch on her—Catriona said even the servants spy on her—then what hope has she of winning free?"

"You may leave all to me." Philip smiled and gathered his reins. "I assure you the Countess herself will speed her on her way."

Henry managed to look doubtful and grateful simultaneously.

Philip laughed and clapped him on the shoulder. "Three—don't be late."

"I won't be." Henry met Philip's gaze. "And thank you, sir. I can't think why you should put yourself out for us like this, but I'm extremely grateful for your help."

"Not at all." Philip wheeled his mount, collecting Antonia with his gaze. "It's the obvious solution."

With a nod, he clicked his reins; with a wave to Henry, Antonia fell in beside him. Together, they cantered back towards the woods. As they neared the entrance to the ride, Philip slowed and glanced at Antonia's face. She was frowning. "What now?"

From beneath her lashes, she shot him a suspicious glance.

Philip met it and pointedly raised his brows.

Antonia pulled a face at him. "If you must know," she declared, her accents repressive, "I was recalling telling Catriona that you were a past master at arranging clandestine meetings." With that, she tossed her head, setting her curls dancing, then flicked her reins and entered the ride.

Following on her horse's heels, Philip smiled. Wolfishly.

CHAPTER FOURTEEN

OPERATING UNDER STRICT instructions, Antonia said nothing to Catriona regarding her impending salvation. "Her dramatic talents hardly lend themselves to concealment," Philip had drily observed. "The Countess will take one look at her and our goose will be cooked."

Hence, when she took her seat at the luncheon table, Catriona was still in the grip of morose despair. Slipping into the chair beside Philip's, Antonia shot him a reproving glance.

He met it with bland imperturbability, then, turning, addressed the Countess.

The meal passed much as its predecessor, with one notable exception. The previous evening, the conversation had been dominated by the Countess and the Marchioness. Today, Philip set himself to engage, then artfully divert their attention. Applying herself to her meal, Antonia wondered if their ladyships would see the danger therein.

"Indeed." Philip leaned back in his chair, gesturing languidly in response to a comment by the Marchioness on the immaturity of young gentlemen. "It's my contention that until the age of thirty-four, gentlemen understand very little of the real forces extant in the *ton*—the forces, indeed, that will shape their lives."

Antonia choked; glancing up, she caught Henrietta's eye—they both quickly looked elsewhere.

"Quite so." The Countess nodded grimly, her gaze on Ambrose. "Until they have reached the age of wisdom, it behoves them to take all heed of the advice of their elders."

"Indubitably." Across the table, Philip met Henrietta's gaze. He smiled urbanely, a smile his stepmother was unlikely to misconstrue. "So helpful, when others point out the reality of things."

"I can only say I wish more gentlemen had your insight, Ruthven." With that, the Marchioness embarked on a succession of anecdotes illustrating the varied horrors that had befallen young gentlemen lacking such discernment.

By the time the platters were empty, Ambrose was sulking while Catriona had sunk even deeper into gloom. Only Geoffrey, Antonia noticed, appeared oblivious of Philip's defection. She concluded her brother was either too fly to the time of day to believe any such thing, or was already appraised of Philip's plan.

The latter seemed most likely when the Countess leaned forward to demand, "Now—what are your plans for the afternoon?"

"Mr Mannering," Philip replied, "is for his books, I believe?" His gaze rested on Geoffrey, who nodded equably. Philip turned to the Countess. "We discussed the point you made regarding his presence here, rather than at Oxford, and concluded a few hours' study each day would be a sound investment against the time when he goes up."

The Countess glowed. "I'm very glad you saw fit to take my advice."

Philip inclined his head. "As for the rest, Miss Mannering and I are for the gardens. They appear quite extensive—a pity to waste this weather indoors. I wondered if the Marquess and Miss Dalling would like to accompany us?"

"I'm sure they would." The Marchioness nodded approvingly, her compelling gaze fixed on her hapless son.

Ambrose hid a grimace, then glanced at Catriona, mute, beside him. "Perhaps…"

"Of course! *Just* the thing!" The Countess weighed in to stamp her seal on the plan. "Catriona will be thrilled to accompany you."

When everyone looked her way, Catriona nodded dully.

Ten minutes later, they left the house by the morning-room windows and headed into the rose gardens. Strolling on Philip's arm, Antonia studied Catriona and Ambrose, drifting aimlessly ahead, feet trailing, shoulders slumped.

"So—what did you think of my superlative strategy?"

Glancing up, she met Philip's eye. "It was, quite definitely, the most sickeningly cloying exhibition of humbug I have ever witnessed."

Philip looked ahead. "There were a few grains of truth concealed amidst the dross."

Antonia snorted. "Flummery, pure flummery, from start to finish. I'm surprised it didn't stick in your throat."

"I have to admit the whole was rather too sweet for my liking, but their ladyships lapped it up, which was, after all, my purpose."

"Ah, yes—your purpose." Antonia longed to ask,

point-blank, what that was. It was not, after all, Catriona and Ambrose's problem which had brought him here.

The thought focused her mind on what lay, ignored yet unresolved, between them. As they strolled in the sunlight, largely without words, she had ample time to consider the possibilities and the actualities—and whether she could convert the former to the latter.

Beneath her fingers, she could feel the strength in Philip's arm; as their shoulders brushed, awareness of him enveloped her. Like a well-remembered scent laid down in her memories, he was part of her at some deep, uncomprehended level. And just like such a scent, she longed to capture and hold him, his attention, his affection, precisely as laid down in her mind.

"There you are!"

They halted; turning, they saw Geoffrey striding towards them. "You've been with your books barely an hour," Antonia exclaimed.

"Time enough." Grinning, Geoffrey joined them in the middle of the formal garden. "The three *grandes dames* are snoring fit to shake the rafters."

"Good." Philip shifted his gaze to Catriona as she and Ambrose, alerted by Geoffrey's appearance, joined them. "It's time, I believe, that we headed for the shrubbery."

"The shrubbery?" Ambrose frowned. "Why there?"

"So that Miss Dalling can meet with Mr Fortescue and help him with his plan to apply to Lady Copely for aid."

"Henry?" Catriona's eyes blazed. "He's here?" Her die-away dismals dropped from her like a cloak; eyes sparkling, colour flowing into her cheeks, she positively vibrated with suppressed energy. "Where?"

Gesturing towards the shrubbery, Philip raised a cynical brow. "We'll meet him shortly. However, remembering your aunt's servitors—namely the gardener over there—" with a nonchalant wave he indicated a man on a ladder clipping a weeping cherry "—I suggest you restrain your transports until we're in more shielded surrounds."

Catriona, all but dancing with impatience, led the way.

Following more sedately on Philip's arm, Antonia humphed. "You would be hard-pressed to believe that only this morning she was on the brink of a decline."

Entering the shrubbery, screened from prying eyes by the high clipped hedges, Catriona stopped and waited. Philip shooed her on, consenting to halt and explain only when they were well within the protection of the walks.

"The field at the back of the shrubbery," he eventually deigned to inform her. "He'll be there at three." Pulling his watch from his pocket, he consulted it. "Which is now."

With a squeal of delight, Catriona whirled.

"But—" Philip waited until she looked back at him. "Ambrose and Geoffrey will naturally go with you."

That, of course, presented no problem to Catriona. "Come on!" Lifting her skirts, she ran off.

With a laugh, Geoffrey loped in pursuit; dazed, Ambrose hurried after them.

"Just a minute!" Antonia looked at Philip. "Catriona needs a chaperon. She and Ambrose should not be alone at any time—especially now."

Philip took her elbow. "Geoffrey is gooseberry enough. Our appointment lies elsewhere."

"Appointment?" Antonia looked up to see his mask fall away, revealing features hard and uncompromising. His fingers were a steel vice about her elbow. As he guided her inexorably into the maze, she narrowed her eyes. "*This* was what you were planning all along! Not Catriona's meeting, but ours."

Philip shot her a glance. "I'm surprised it took you so long to work that out. While I'm sympathetic enough to Catriona and even Ambrose, though for my money he'd do well to develop a bit more gumption, I have and always have had only *one* purpose in crossing the Countess's benighted threshold."

That declaration and the promise it held—the idea of their impending, very private interview—crystallised Antonia's thoughts and gave strength to her decision—the decision she had only that instant made. They reached the centre of the maze in a suspiciously short space of time. Impelled by a sense of certainty, she barely glanced at the neat lawns of the central square, at the small dolphin gracing the marble fountain at its heart. Determined to have her say—to retain control of the situation long enough to do so—she abruptly halted. Pulling back against Philip's hold, she waited until he turned to face her, brows rising impatiently. Lifting her chin, she declared, "As it happens, I'm very glad of this chance to speak with you alone, for I have to inform you that I've suffered a change of heart."

She looked up—and saw his face drain of all expression. His fingers fell from her elbow. He stilled; she sensed in his immobility the energy of some turbulent force severely restrained.

One of his brows slowly rose. "Indeed?"

Decisively, Antonia nodded. "I would remind you of the agreement we made—"

"I'm relieved you haven't forgotten it."

His flinty accents made her frown. "Of course I haven't. At that time, if you recall, we discussed the role you wished me to fulfil—in essence, the role of a conventional wife."

"A role you agreed to take on."

His voice had deepened; his expression was starkly aggressive. Her lips firming, Antonia stiffly inclined her head. "Precisely. I have also to acknowledge your chivalrous behaviour in allowing me to come to London without formalising or making known our agreement." Gliding towards the fountain, she clasped her hands and turned. Raising her head, she met Philip's gaze, now opaque and impenetrable, squarely. "As it happens, that was likely very wise."

Mute, Philip looked into her wide eyes—and knew what he thought of that earlier decision. He should have kept her at the Manor—acted the tyrant and married her regardless—anything to have avoided this. He could hardly think—he certainly didn't trust himself to speak. He couldn't, in fact, believe what she was saying; his mind refused to take it in. His emotions, however, were already on the rampage.

"Very wise," Antonia affirmed. "For I have to tell you, my lord—"

"Philip."

She hesitated, then stiffly inclined her head. "Philip—that on greater acquaintance with the mores of the *ton,* I have come to the conclusion that I am fundamentally ill-suited to be your wife—at least along the lines we agreed."

That last, thoroughly confusing phrase was, Philip was convinced, the only thing that allowed him to retain any semblance of reason. "What the devil do you mean?" Hands rising to his hips, he glowered at her. "What other lines are there?"

Lifting her chin, Antonia gave him back stare for hard stare. "As I was *about* to explain, I have discovered there are certain…criteria—essential prerequisites, if you will—for carrying off the position of a *ton*nishly comfortable wife. In short, I do not possess them, nor, I have decided, am I willing to develop them. No." Eyes glinting, she defiantly concluded, "Indeed, on the subject of marriage I find I have my *own* criteria—criteria I would require to be fulfilled *absolutely*."

Philip's eyes had not left hers. "Which are?"

Antonia didn't blink. "First," she declared, raising one hand to tick off her points on her fingers. "The gentleman I marry *must* love me—*without reservation*."

Philip blinked. He hesitated, his eyes searching her face, chest swelling as he drew in a slow breath. Then he frowned. "Second?"

Antonia tapped her next finger. "He will *not* have any mistresses."

"Ever?"

She hesitated. "After we are wed," she eventually conceded.

The tension in Philip's shoulders eased. "Third?"

"He cannot waltz with *any other lady*."

Philip's lips twitched; he fought to straighten them. "Not at all?"

"Never." There was no doubt in Antonia's mind on that point. "And last but not least, he should *never* seek to be private with any other lady. *Ever*." Eyes narrowed,

she looked up and met Philip's gaze challengingly, indeed belligerently. "Those are my criteria—if you do not feel you can meet them, then I will, of course, understand." Abruptly, the reality of that alternative struck home. Antonia caught her breath; pain unexpectedly speared through her.

She looked away, disguising her faltering as a gracious nod. Swinging about to gaze at the fountain, she concluded, her voice suddenly tight, "Just as long as you understand that if such is the case, then I cannot marry you."

Philip had never felt so giddy in his life. Relief so strong it left him weak clashed with a possessiveness he had never thought to feel. Emotions rose and fell like surging waves within him, all dwarfed, subsumed, by one steadfast, rocklike reality. The reality that, despite his understanding, still shook him to the core. Recollection of his customary imperturbability, of the unshakeable impassivity that had, until now—until Antonia—been his hallmark, drifted mockingly through his mind.

Drawing in a steadying breath, he studied her half-averted face. "You were going to marry me regardless. What changed your mind?"

She hesitated so long he thought she would not answer. Then she turned her head and met his gaze openly—directly. "You."

Philip felt his lips twist, and recalled his earlier resolution never to ask such questions of her again; she would always floor him with her honesty. He drew in another deep breath—and recalled his purpose—his one and only purpose in engineering this meeting, in coming to Ticehurst Place. "Before I deal with your criteria—your demands of a prospective husband—there's one pertinent point I wish to make crystal clear."

His features hardening, he caught Antonia's gaze. "Lady Ardale's performance was no fault of mine. I did not encourage her in any way, by any look, word or gesture."

A frown slowly formed in her eyes. "She was in your arms."

"No." Philip held her gaze steadily. "She pressed herself against me—I had to take hold of her to set her away."

A slow blush stained Antonia's cheeks. She looked away. "Your hand was on her breast."

Fleetingly, Philip grimaced. "Not by inclination, I assure you."

His tone held sufficient disgust to have her glancing his way again. Her shocked expression tried his control.

"She...?" Confounded, Antonia gestured.

"Indeed." Philip's lips thinned. "Strange to tell, some ladies are exceedingly forward—and not a little predatory. If you'd remained a moment longer, you would have witnessed her comeuppance."

Antonia's eyes widened. "What happened?"

"She landed on the *chaise*."

Philip saw her lips twitch, saw the beguiling glint of laughter in her eyes. The stiffness that had, until then, afflicted him, eased; he held out his hand. "And now, if you'll come here, I'll endeavour to address the criteria you enumerated so clearly."

Antonia studied his face, uncertain of the undertone in his voice. Slowly, she shook her head—and stepped closer to the fountain. "I would much prefer that we discussed this matter in a businesslike way."

Philip opened his eyes at her—and took a strolling step forward. "I intend to be exceedingly businesslike. In this case, by my reckoning, that requires having you in my arms."

"There's no sense in that—I can't think while in your arms, as you very well know!" Frowning as disapprovingly as she could, Antonia circled to put the fountain between them; his intent apparent in every graceful stride, Philip followed. Antonia could not miss the devilish gleam in his eyes. Despite her irritation, she still felt a thrill all the way to her toes. "This is ridiculous," she muttered, feeling her heartbeat accelerate, feeling breathlessness slowly claim her. "Philip—stop!" Imperiously, she halted and held up a hand.

Philip took no notice. In two strides he had rounded the fountain.

Antonia's eyes widened. With a smothered squeal, she grabbed up her skirts and ran.

Unfortunately, she was on the wrong side of the fountain to escape the maze.

And Philip was far too fast. He caught her halfway to the hedge, easily lifting her from her feet. He juggled her in his arms, then carried her, struggling furiously in a froth of muslin, to a weathered stone seat with an ample thyme cushion.

He was grateful for that last when he half sat, half fell onto it, Antonia squirming on his lap. He could hear her muttering a string of curses; he was so gripped by the urge to laugh triumphantly that he didn't dare try to speak. Instead, he caught her chin in one hand and turned her face to his.

Her eyes met his, green spitting golden chips. In that instant, awareness struck—he saw it catch, felt the sudden hitch in her breathing, saw her eyes widen, her lips soften and part. She stilled, her breasts rising and falling, her gaze trapped in his. The same awareness reached for him, effortlessly drawing him under its spell, even while some remnant of sanity frantically fought to remind him where they were, who they were, and how inappropriate was the spectacle they were about to create. As his head slowly lowered, Philip groaned. "God—I must be as besotted as Amberly."

The realization did not stop him from kissing her, from parting her lips and drinking in her sweetness. Like a man parched, he filled his senses with the taste of her, the feel of her, the heady, dizzying scent of her. Experience stopped him from releasing her curls, from running his hands through her hair. But nothing could stop him from laying her breasts bare, from experiencing again the thrill of her reaction as he caressed her.

Trapped in his arms, caught up in the tide, it took all Antonia's remaining strength to complain, "You haven't told me your response to my criteria."

"Do you still need telling?"

His fingers shifted; her mind melted. It was some moments before she could muster enough breath to explain, "I did intend to be a comfortable wife for you but I don't think—" Her breathing suspended wholly; weakly, she rushed on, "That I can manage it."

She arched gently in his arms; Philip groaned again. His lips sought hers, then he drew back enough to murmur against their soft fullness, "I never wanted you as a 'comfortable' wife—that was your idea." The words focused his attention on what he was trying very hard to overlook. "As God is my witness, the word *comfortable* is the very last word I would associate with you.

I've been wretchedly *uncomfortable* ever since I walked into the hall at the Manor and saw you come floating down the stairs, the embodiment of my need, the answer to my prayers."

She was, Antonia decided, adapting to his lovemaking; she could actually think enough to take in his words. "Why uncomfortable?"

Philip gave up groaning; he took her hand and showed her.

"Oh." Antonia considered, then glanced at his face. "Is that really uncomfortable?"

"Yes!" Gritting his teeth, Philip caught her hand. "Now shut up and let me kiss you." He did, delighting in her response, setting aside his rehearsed periods until he had recouped all he had missed through the past week of enforced abstinence.

"I saw them go in—they must be at the centre."

Geoffrey's voice came clearly over the hedges.

Philip raised his head, blinking dazedly. Antonia's eyes opened, then flew wide as she took in her state.

Her *"Great heavens!"* was weak with shock.

Philip wasted no time in curses; with practised speed, he stood, setting Antonia on her feet, steadying her when she swayed. When her hands fluttered over the halves of her open bodice, he swatted them away. "No time—let me. They're only three turns away."

Her head still spinning, Antonia watched in bemused fascination as he did up her buttons with a speed that would have left Nell stunned, then straightened her skirts and settled the lace about her neckline.

Philip barely had time to settle his coat before Catriona rushed into the square, Geoffrey and Ambrose on her heels.

"He was there! Henry told me of your suggestion—Aunt Copely will help, I *know* she will." Eyes gleaming, smile beaming, Catriona was again the stunning beauty of the early weeks of their acquaintance. "It's so wonderful, I could cry!" With that unnerving declaration, she flung her arms about Antonia and hugged her wildly.

"At the risk of appearing a wet blanket, I suggest you restrain your transports, my child." Suavely, Philip settled his cuffs. "If you float into the house at your present elevation, the Countess is likely to puncture your hopes."

"Oh, don't worry." Exuberant, Catriona let go of Antonia to clutch Philip's hand and press it between her own. "I can take care of her—when we go back to the house, I'll be so down in the mouth she'll never suspect we're hatching a plot."

Smiling, pleased to see Catriona so restored, Antonia glanced at Geoffrey, only to discover a quizzical, somewhat speculative look in his eye. As she watched, a slow, oddly knowing smile curved his lips.

To her intense mortification, Antonia felt a blush steal into her cheeks. She shifted her gaze to Catriona. "So, is Mr Fortescue off to plead your case to Lady Copely?"

"Yes!" Catriona beamed delightedly. "And—"

"All's right and tight," Geoffrey remarked. "But we shouldn't discuss anything here—one of the gardeners might overhear. And it's getting on for tea-time. If we don't want to be caught conspiring by one of those odious footmen, we'd better get back to the house."

"Indeed." There was enough frustrated resignation in Philip's tone to draw a glance from both Mannerings. Philip offered Antonia his arm. "I greatly fear your brother is right." As they all turned towards the exit from the maze, Catriona going ahead with Ambrose, practising her die-away airs, Philip murmured for Antonia's ears alone, "We'll continue our interrupted discussion later."

Exchanging glances, neither he nor Antonia noticed Geoffrey hanging back in their shadow, his gaze, shrewdly pensive, on them.

By the time they regained the front hall, Philip had re-evaluated the amenities of Ticehurst Place. While the others continued into the drawing-room where the Countess was regally dispensing tea and cakes, he held Antonia back long enough to whisper, "The library— after they've all settled for the night."

Antonia glanced up at him, meeting his gaze squarely. She read the promise in his eyes. Her heart swelled; letting her lids veil her eyes, she inclined her head. "In the library tonight."

CHAPTER FIFTEEN

NIGHT FELL. IN her chamber, Antonia paced impatiently, waiting for the great house to fall silent, waiting for the last of the servitors to retreat to their quarters and leave the mansion to its ghosts. She felt certain there'd be some lost souls haunting the gorgon's lair; the thought did not trouble her. Philip had yet to reply to her criteria; nothing—not even a ghost—was going to prevent her from hearing his response, from hearing the words she longed to hear.

After their interlude in the shrubbery, she was perfectly confident of the substance of his reply. Confidence, however, was no substitute for direct experience.

Kicking her skirts about, she turned, then paused. A door along the corridor creaked open, then shut. Ears straining, she made out the heavy, measured tread of Trant's footsteps retreating to the servants' stair; Henrietta had, at last, settled for the night. Soon, she could risk going down.

Deciding another ten minutes' wait would be wise, she crossed to the window seat. Catriona's histrionic talents had risen to the challenge of gulling both the Marchioness and the Countess. Neither eagle-eyed lady had batted an eyelid; neither had seen anything in Catriona's drooping stance, in her lacklustre gaze, to alert them.

Crossing her arms on the sill and resting her chin

upon them, Antonia gazed out at the moon-silvered gardens. If Catriona could keep up her charade, then Henry would have time to mobilise Lady Copely. Doubtless, if all was as Catriona had said, Lady Copeley would visit and rescue her from the Countess's talons.

Finding a certain delight in that prospect, Antonia smiled. Catriona's problems would soon be at an end; for herself, resolution was at hand. Love, despite her doubts, would reign triumphant. Her gaze on the shifting shadows, her lips curving gently, she let her mind slide into pleasurable anticipation.

The clip-clop of horses' hooves jerked her back to reality. Straightening, she leaned forward and peered out, just in time to glimpse a gig being driven down the drive at a brisk trot. There were two figures on the seat; as she watched, the smaller, the passenger, a large package clasped in her arms, turned and gazed back at the house. Catriona's heart-shaped face was instantly recognisable.

Stunned, Antonia looked again; the second figure was wearing a white drab driving coat. "*Merciful heavens!* What *are* they up to?"

For five full seconds, she sat transfixed, listening to the hoofbeats grow fainter. Then, with a muttered curse, she grabbed a cloak from the wardrobe, pausing only to swing it about her shoulders before quietly opening her door.

She paid not the slightest attention to the deep shadows, to the gloom that pervaded the darkened house. Not even the suit of armour, shrouded in Stygian shadow on the landing, had the power to make her pause. Hurrying as fast as she dared, she reached the bottom of the stairs; her evening slippers skidded on the polished hall tiles. With a valiantly smothered shriek, Antonia grabbed the newel post just long enough to right herself, then, in a flurry of silk skirts, she dashed down the corridor.

Pacing before the fire in the library dutifully rehearsing his lines, Philip heard the scratch and slide of Antonia's feet on the tiles. The odd sound she made had him heading for the door. He opened it in time to see her pale skirts, visible beneath the hem of her cloak, disappear around a distant corner.

Mystified, he followed.

The turning she had taken led to the garden hall; when he reached it, the door to the gardens stood wide. Frowning, wondering if, by some mischance, she had thought to meet him in the maze, Philip stepped into the night. The gardens were a mass of moonlight and shadow, the gentle breeze creating a fantastical landscape of shifting shapes. Antonia was nowhere to be seen. His frown deepening, Philip strode towards the shrubbery.

He'd reached the centre of the maze when the sound of hoofbeats and the rattle of carriage wheels reached him. For one incredulous instant, he stood stock-still, then he swore.

And ran for the stables.

Skidding to a halt in the stableyard, he caught a glimpse of his greys drawing his phaeton—his *high-perch* phaeton—disappearing at a rattling clip down the drive. Of the identity of the figure holding the reins he had not the slightest doubt.

Cursing fluently, Philip plunged into the dark stables.

By the time he'd saddled the chestnut he'd ridden the previous day, Antonia had a good start on him. Halting at the end of the drive, he scanned the fields—and caught sight of her, tooling his horses at a spanking pace along a straight stretch of lane hugging an already distant ridge. Jaw clenched, his face like stone, Philip set off in pursuit.

Feathering the next corner, Antonia checked the skittish greys. The road ahead was deeply shadowed; she couldn't see if there were potholes. Grimacing, she kept the reins tight as she guided the greys on, inwardly praying the horses, occasionally as devilish as their master, would behave.

Always eager, they had let her pole them up without fuss; luckily, the phaeton was so light she'd been able to manoeuvre it easily. Harnessing had taken longer but she'd forced herself to do it carefully, comforting herself with the reflection that Philip's horses would easily overtake the single beast Geoffrey had put to the gig.

It was only then, as she tightened the final buckles, that she remembered Philip, waiting for her in the library. Focused on protecting Catriona and Geoffrey, used to acting on her own, she had not, until then, considered the possibility of throwing herself on her husband-to-be's chest and demanding he fix things. Grimacing, she hesitated, only to decide she couldn't afford the time to retrace her steps and tell Philip what she'd seen. She couldn't risk Geoffrey getting too far ahead; she was certain Philip had no more idea of what was afoot than she.

Her memory replayed Geoffrey's words in the maze, the odd glance he, Catriona and Ambrose had shared as they'd prepared to retire. She had a strong suspicion her brother had guessed what was in the wind between herself and Philip—and had decided to leave them undisturbed while he and Catriona brought off whatever mad scheme they'd hatched.

Emerging from the shadowed stretch, Antonia set the greys up a long hill. Looking up, she glimpsed the gig, Geoffrey and Catriona in silhouette as they topped the rise ahead. They sank from view; with a muttered curse, Antonia clicked the reins. The gig was more stable than the phaeton; Geoffrey was not having to be as cautious as she. Despite the greys' superiority, the distance between them and the gig had not decreased.

Driving as fast as she dared, she sent the phaeton rushing up the hill. There were lanes aplenty—she had no idea which way they were headed. The thought of the likely outcome if their plans, whatever they might be, went awry, and Geoffrey and Catriona ended spending the night essentially alone, spurred her on, the spectre of the Countess as a relative-by-marriage at her back.

Pushing the greys to the limit of safety, she topped the rise, then rattled on down the slope.

Labouring in her wake, Philip had run through his repertoire of curses. While he presumed his intended had a reason for rushing off into the night, he did not, he had decided, actually care what it was. What he did care about was her safety and the sublime disregard for his tender sensibilities she was presently displaying. Gritting his teeth, he urged the chestnut on. Catching up with his greys was out of the question; all he could hope for was to keep Antonia in sight until she reached her destination.

Once he caught up with her, the rest, he felt sure, would follow naturally.

He quite clearly recalled telling her he would never consent to her risking her neck; he quite clearly recalled warning her not to even *think* of so doing. She had evidently not believed him.

He would make the matter plain—along with a few other points.

"All I want is to tell the damn woman that I love her!"

The wind whipped away the growled words. Gripped by frustration, Philip set the chestnut up the hill.

He pulled up at the top, briefly scanning the valley below. He saw Antonia in his phaeton—and for the first time glimpsed the carriage she was following.

"What the devil...?" Philip frowned. He was too far away to make out the figures in the gig but he could guess who they were. Shaking the reins, he took to the fields, shaving a little off Antonia's lead in the descent from the ridge. But once they gained the flat, not knowing which way they would turn, he was forced to keep to the roads.

Ahead of him, Antonia had managed to draw closer to the gig, but it was still too far distant for her to hail it. Given the state of the country lanes, she'd given up hope of catching Geoffrey this side of a main road. Having assumed his intention was to deliver Catriona to Lady Copely, she was surprised to see him check, then turn the gig under the gateway of what appeared to be an inn.

The small town the inn served lay beyond it, nestled in a hollow, its residents no doubt slumbering soundly. Perched halfway down the slope overlooking the town, the inn looked to be substantial, a solid structure in stone with a good slate roof.

Filled with relief, Antonia whipped up the greys and forged on, drawing rein only to enter the innyard.

A sleepy, middle-aged ostler was leading away the gig. His eyes widened, whether in alarm or understandable surprise Antonia had no time to wonder as she wrestled the greys to a snorting halt.

"Here—take them." She flung the reins at the ostler, grateful when he caught them. Scrambling down from the box-seat with what decorum she could, she added, "And…er…do whatever needs to be done. They're quite valuable."

"Aye, mum." Stupefied, the ostler nodded.

Waiting for no more, Antonia hurried into the inn. The door was unlatched; there was no sign of the host but a lighted candle stood on a wooden table at the back of the hall. Her attention caught by wavering light from above, Antonia glanced up the dark stairwell in time to see shadows, thrown by candlelight, flung up against a wall. The shadows disappeared as their owners continued down one of the upstairs corridors.

Antonia grabbed the candle from the table and followed.

When she gained the head of the stairs, there was no one in sight. Following the corridor she was sure Geoffrey and Catriona had taken, she paused outside each door to place her ear against the panel. She heard nothing more than snores and snorts until she came to the last door, right at the end of the corridor.

Gruff voices rose and fell; others spoke but she could not make out their words. Antonia frowned—then glanced at the door to her right. Ear against the panel, she listened carefully but no sound came from within. Holding her breath, she gently eased the latch free. Pushing the door open, she warily raised her candle.

The room was empty. With a sigh of relief, she whisked herself in and shut the door firmly. Glancing about, she saw another door, set into the wall shared with the last room—the one on which she wished to eavesdrop. Thanking her stars, she set the candle down on a tallboy and gently eased the door open.

Beyond lay a small space, the space between the thick walls, bound by another door. As the voices beyond reached her easily, Antonia surmised this last door opened directly into the room at the end of the corridor.

"I knows as how that was what you asked for, but, like Josh here said, it ain't what you're getting."

The owner of the gruff voice sounded the opposite of refined. He also sounded smugly threatening. Antonia heard Geoffrey answer but her brother's accents were too measured, too controlled, for her to catch what he said. Grimacing, she carefully gripped the knob of the door; breath bated, she turned it until she felt the latch give, then eased the door open the merest fraction.

"Ain't no point arguing no more," came a second, very deep, distinctly menacing voice. "The whelp over there got us here—you've heard our price. T'my way of thinkin', it's take it or leave it."

A whispered conference was the result. Carefully releasing the knob, Antonia leaned as close as she dared to the open door, her senses straining to pick up her brother's and Catriona's words.

A hand came over her shoulder, fastening over her mouth; an arm slid about her waist, hauling her back, locking her against a very large, very hard, definitely masculine body.

Eyes starting from her head, Antonia went rigid.

Then relaxed—and tugged at the hand over her lips.

Philip eased his hold, bending his head to growl directly into her ear, *"What the devil are you doing here?"*

Antonia ignored his tone—and all it promised. Pressing her head back into his shoulder, she managed to catch his eye—she decided to ignore the fury she saw there, too. With her own eyes, she indicated the room beyond the door. "Listen," she mouthed.

"My friend here hired you—you agreed on a sum to take us to London."

Antonia's eyes widened. She tugged again at Philip's hand. "That was Mr Fortescue."

Philip flicked her a warning glance. "Shh."

"Aye, that we did," came in gloating tones. "But that was afore we realized there'd be a young miss making one of your party. The way we figures it, now we knows the score, is that it's got to be worth a great deal more to you to make the trip to Lunnon. What with the pretty young miss an' all."

"Mind," came in the other, even more disturbing voice. "If'n you're pressed for the ready, there's likely other ways we'd agree to take our cut."

Antonia suppressed a shiver.

The suggestion gave rise to a muted discussion centred on the far end of the room.

A long-suffering sigh distracted Antonia. Glancing up and back, she saw Philip close his eyes fleetingly. When he opened them, Antonia saw his jaw firm. Before she could speak, he lifted her bodily and set her back against the narrow side wall of the tiny space they shared.

"Stay there." His eyes boring into hers, Philip put all the dire warning he could into his necessarily muted tones. "Do not move."

"What—?"

"And be *quiet!*"

Suppressing the urge to sniff disdainfully, Antonia did as he said.

Settling his coat with a deft flexing of his shoulders, Philip grasped the door knob and calmly walked into the room.

As he had surmised, the two hulking coachmen had their backs to him; beyond, a quartet of surprised faces stared at him, thoroughly stunned. The door had been well-oiled; no squeak had given him away. The room was furnished with a large square rug, muting the sound of his footsteps. The villainous coachmen had not heard him.

Predictably, Geoffrey was the first to find his wits. Shifting his gaze back to the coachmen, he glibly stated, "Actually, I don't think you've quite taken our measure. We have powerful backers you might not care to cross."

"Ho! That's a good one," the larger of the coachmen jeered. "Very likely, that is, with you three and the young miss making your getaway in the dead of night."

"Indeed, I fear I must agree with our friend here," Philip remarked in his finest Bond Street drawl. "I must admit the point mystifies me—you'll really have to explain to me, Geoffrey, why you saw fit to haul your sister out in the dead of night."

Both coachmen froze—they exchanged sideways glances, then the heavier of the two swung about, huge fists rising. He never saw the clip that caught him on the jaw and laid him out upon the rug. The second coachman came in, arms flailing. Philip ducked, caught his assailant with hip and shoulder and threw him across the room. He landed with a resounding thud against one wall, then slid slowly down to slump on the floor.

Philip waited, but neither villain was in any condition for further argument.

"Great heavens! I never knew you boxed."

Straightening, automatically resettling his coat, Philip glanced over his shoulder; Antonia stood a mere foot behind him, a heavy candlestick in one upraised hand. Lips compressed, he reached out and took the candlestick. "I told you to stay put."

She met his gaze openly. "If you'd told me you boxed, I would have."

"My boxing prowess had not previously figured in my mind as an inducement to wifely obedience," Philip heard himself say—he had to fight an urge to close his eyes and groan.

Catriona arrived to fling herself into Antonia's arms; in the same instant, a furious pounding came on the door.

"Open up in there! This is a respectable inn, I'll have you know."

"The landlord," Geoffrey somewhat unnecessarily remarked.

Philip directed a feeling look at the ceiling. "Why me?" He didn't wait for an answer but strode to the door, indicating with one long finger that Geoffrey and Henry should pick up one comatose coachman.

As they struggled to lift their burden, Philip opened the door. "Good evening. I'm Ruthven. You, I take it, are the landlord?"

With glowing approval, Antonia listened as Philip glibly explained how his wards, never specified, and their friends had decided to return to town rather than remain at a nearby house party and had, for reasons he did not deign to clarify, decided to meet with the coachmen they had hired at the inn, rather than at the residence they had visited, only to be grossly deceived in the character of their hired help.

Under Philip's artful direction, the innkeeper professed all sympathy, agreeing, as they all did, that it was exceedingly fortunate that, responding to the note his wards had sent him, Philip had arrived in the nick of time to rout the villains.

By this time, the villains had been hauled out of the inn and left groaning in the ditch. Catriona, truly rattled, had been soothed.

Having arranged to hire the inn's own coach and the services of a groom and coachman, both of whom needed to be roused from their slumbers at a nearby farm, Philip repaired to the inn's parlour, where, at his suggestion, his party now waited. Shutting the door firmly on the reassured innkeeper, he swept the gathering with a jaundiced eye. "Would one of you care to explain precisely what is going on?"

As intrigued as he, Antonia glanced at the younger members of the party.

Catriona's expression instantly turned mulish. Ambrose squirmed, looking even more gormless than usual. Henry Fortescue reddened, then cleared his throat.

Geoffrey spoke first. "It's straightforward enough—or at least, our plan was. Catriona's sure Lady Copely will take her in and support her in marrying Henry."

"I remembered that Aunt Copely came to visit," Catriona put in. "Quite early on, just after I'd joined Aunt Ticehurst's household. I was banished to my room throughout but I overheard the maids saying that there'd been the most awful row. Aunt Copely must have wanted to see me—if I'd known Aunt Ticehurst didn't have any legal right to insist I stay with her, I'd have gone to Aunt Copely long ago."

"Given that," Geoffrey continued, "there didn't seem much point in going to inform Lady Copely *then* returning to Ticehurst Place to rescue Catriona, particularly if the gorgon was going to keep on trying to marry her to Ambrose."

"We decided that if we four all went up to town together, there'd be no question of impropriety," Henry explained. He glanced at Ambrose. "Hammersley did not wish to remain at Ticehurst Place—particularly not after their ladyships discover Catriona's disappearance. He volunteered to hire the coachmen—unfortunately, they turned out to be less than honest."

Ambrose grimaced. "Didn't want to go to any of the local places—they might have got back to Lady Ticehurst. Found a hedge-tavern—those two were the best I could find."

Philip raised a long-suffering brow.

"Never mind—as it fell out, there was no real harm done." Antonia smiled reassuringly. "Thanks to Ruthven," she added as Philip turned his gaze on her.

"Indeed, my dear—but I have yet to hear *your* reasons for mounting such a dangerous pursuit."

The comment focused all eyes on Antonia; realizing that none other than Philip knew she had taken his horses and phaeton, she kept her expression serenely assured. "I caught sight of Geoffrey and Catriona leaving in the gig. Naturally, not knowing their plan, I hurried after them."

Philip pondered that "naturally." "You didn't, perchance, consider informing me?"

His tone was mild, perfectly polite; Antonia sensed

the steel behind it. "I did consider the matter," she felt forced to admit. "But by the time the thought occurred, the gig was too far ahead to risk further dallying."

"I see." Philip's gaze, narrowing, remained locked on hers.

"I remembered the bible."

Catriona's comment distracted them both. They turned to see her hefting a brown paper-wrapped package from the table. "It *was* Papa's. If it contains the proof of Aunt Copley's right to act as my guardian, I thought I should keep it by me."

Philip nodded approvingly. "A wise move." He hesitated, then grimaced. "Very well—we'll continue with your plan. I agree that if all four of you travel together, there'll be no hint of impropriety. And I can sympathise with Hammersley not wanting to be about when the Countess and his mother discover their applecart has been ditched. Apropos of which, might I ask how you were proposing to convey that news?"

Four blank faces stared at him.

"We hadn't imagined informing them specifically," Geoffrey finally said. He caught Philip's eye. "We thought you'd be there—and you'd guess what was up if we all went missing."

For a long moment, Philip held Geoffrey's gaze, his own distinctly jaundiced, then his expression turned resigned. "Very well—I suppose I can settle that matter, too."

The relief in the parlour was palpable.

Twenty minutes later, Philip watched the four young people climb into the inn's carriage. Geoffrey was the last.

"Here's a note for Carring." Philip handed over a

folded missive. "He'll pay the carriage off and see you to the coaching station. Write once you've settled in—we'll be at the Manor."

"Oh?" Waving a last farewell to Antonia, standing back in the inn porch, Geoffrey looked again at Philip, a question in his eyes.

Philip raised a languid brow. "*And,* given you're the senior male in the Mannering line, I suspect you'd better hold yourself ready to make a dash down—just for a day or two, considering how much of the term you've already missed. I'll send up to the Master."

Geoffrey's grin broke into a huge smile. "Thought so." He clapped Philip on the shoulder, then mounted the steps. Philip shut the carriage door; Geoffrey leaned out of the window to add, insouciantly irreverent to the end, "Don't let her get her hands on your reins."

"Not bloody likely," was Philip's terse reply.

The carriage rumbled out of the yard. Philip turned and strode back to the inn. The innkeeper was waiting just behind Antonia, his keys in his hand.

Taking Antonia's elbow, Philip guided her into the inn. "You may lock up, Fellwell. Her ladyship and I can find our way up."

Antonia's eyes flew wide; Fellwell, yawning as he bowed, did not notice. Steered inexorably up the stairs, she heard the heavy inn door close, heard the bolts shoot home. Her heart started to pound. By the time they reached the door to the inn's main guest chamber, she felt quite giddy.

Opening the door, Philip guided her through, then followed, shutting the door behind him. His face was all hard angles and planes; no hint of his social mask remained.

"Ah...does Mr Fellwell believe we're married?"

"I sincerely hope so." Shifting his grip to her hand, Philip strolled forward, surveying the room. "I told him you were Lady Ruthven." Satisfied with their accommodation, he stopped before the fireplace, turning to meet Antonia's wide gaze. "I couldn't think of any other way to acceptably explain your presence here—alone—with me." He cocked a brow at her. "Can you?"

Antonia was sure she couldn't; breathless, she shook her head.

"If we're agreed on that," Philip said, shifting to stand directly before her, "before anything *else* can happen to distract us, I suggest that I give you my responses to your stipulations on your future husband's behaviour."

Releasing her hand, he raised both of his to frame her face, tilting it up until her eyes locked with his. "Lastly but by no means least, you required that the man you married should not seek to be private with any other lady." He raised a brow. "Why would I wish to be alone with another, if I could, instead, have you by my side?"

Eyes wide, Antonia searched his grey gaze; it was calm, clear, unclouded, as incisive as tempered steel.

"And as for not waltzing with any other lady—if you were there to waltz with me, why would I wish to dance with another?"

Inwardly, Antonia frowned.

"And as for mistresses—" Philip raised a suggestive brow. "If I had you to warm my bed, to satisfy my needs, would I want—or, indeed, have time for—a mistress?"

Disregarding the blush that warmed her cheeks, Antonia raised a brow back. "Your responses are questions, not answers."

Philip's lips twisted. "Imponderable questions, my love. For which the answers lie, all encompassed, in my response to your first criterion."

Antonia felt his strength reach for her, even though his hands remained about her face. His head lowered slightly, his lips hovering tantalisingly above hers. Lifting her gaze from them, she studied his eyes, watched as desire slowly pushed aside the curtain of steel, darkening his gaze. Her "My first criterion?" came on a breathless whisper.

Philip smiled; the gesture did not soften his expression. "I hoped you would know without needing to be told." His eyes held hers; his chest swelled as he drew in a steadying breath. "God—and half the *ton*—know I love you." He searched her eyes, then added, his voice deepening, "Unreservedly, without restraint, far more completely, deeply, *madly* than I suspect is at all wise."

Antonia stared back at him, the words ringing in her ears, in her head, in her heart. Her welling joy showed in her eyes; Philip bent his head and kissed her, the caress direct and deeply intimate.

When he raised his head, she had to fight for breath. "Wise?"

She watched the steel flow back into his eyes, clashing with turbulent desire. He raised one brow slowly, his jaw firming ominously.

"Indeed." His tones were suddenly clipped. "Which brings us to your escapade tonight." His hands fell from Antonia's face, only to slip about her waist.

She blinked. "That was Geoffrey's and Catriona's escapade, not mine."

Philip's eyes narrowed. "No more Mannering logic—I've heard quite enough for one night."

A log crashed in the grate, sending up a shower of sparks; with a muttered curse, Philip reluctantly released Antonia and bent to resettle the logs. Antonia glided a few steps away, out of his immediate reach. He straightened and set aside the firetongs; his eyes narrowed when he saw where she was. "I was referring to your appropriation of my phaeton."

Antonia took due note of the glint in his eye. "You did offer to let me drive it." An armchair stood conveniently before the hearth; she drifted around it.

"I offered to let you take the reins in town, on a Macadamised surface, with me on the box-seat beside you—*not* on a deserted country lane in the dead of night with the road obscured by shadows!" Philip stalked after her; catching her wide gaze, he transfixed her with a distinctly strait look. "See what I mean about wise?" He made the comment through set teeth. "*This* is what loving you does to me. I used to be calm, collected, the embodiment of gentlemanly savoir faire, unruffled, unflappable—*always* in control!"

With one shove, he sent the chair sliding from between them. Eyes flaring wide, Antonia took a step back—Philip caught her by the elbows and pulled her hard against him. "*This* is what loving you does to me."

On the words, he kissed her—parting her lips, possessing her senses, demanding, commanding, letting passion have its say. He felt her sink against him, felt her surrender to the power that held them both, held them fast in its silken web, a web stronger than any man would willingly admit. Drawing back, he spoke against her lips. "Damn it—you could have been *killed*. I would have gone mad."

"Would you?" The words came on a breathy whisper.

Philip groaned. "Completely." He kissed her again, revelling in the feel of her as she pressed against him, soft warm curves fitting snugly against his much harder form, promising all manner of prospective delights. He felt desire, warm and unrestrained, rise strongly within her. Satisfied, he drew back, unable to resist dropping kisses on her eyelids and forehead.

"You're lucky the others were here when I caught up with you." His voice had deepened to a raspy growl. "I spent the last two miles thinking about putting you over my knee and ensuring you wouldn't sit any box-seat for at least the next month."

Adrift on a sea of happiness with no horizon in sight, Antonia sighed happily. "You wouldn't."

"Probably not," Philip temporised. "But it was a comforting thought at the time."

A gentle smile on her lips, Antonia drew his head back to hers and kissed him. "I promise to behave in future. I take leave to remind you this outing wasn't my idea."

"Hmm." Lifting his head, Philip studied her face. "Be that as it may, I plan on using this transgression of yours—your flight into the night—to call an abrupt halt to this peculiar hiatus of ours."

"Oh?"

"Indeed." His lips curved. "I've something of a reputation for extracting the greatest benefit from unexpected situations."

Antonia looked her question.

Philip wondered if she knew how innocent she

looked. His smile twisted then fled; gently taking her face between his hands, he gazed deeply into her gold-green eyes. "I need you, my love. Despite the fact you'll turn me—my life, my emotions—upside down, I want no other." He smiled faintly. "You imagined yourself as my comfortable wife—that was impossible from the outset and I knew it." His lips twisted wryly. "It simply took me a while to acknowledge the inevitable."

His expression sobering, he held her gaze steadily. He spoke slowly, intently, his voice deep and low. "But all that's behind us—our future together starts here, now. We're already married in our hearts—married in all ways bar two. I propose we rectify that situation forthwith. We'll spend the night here—" Philip's hands shook slightly; he willed them still, unaware his gaze had darkened dramatically. The planes of his face hardened as he searched Antonia's eyes. "Don't ask me to let you go tonight. I've waited for weeks to make you mine."

He was confounded by her smile, a bewitching, beguiling, very gentle siren's smile. "I've been waiting—" Antonia declared, her voice soft, serene, her eyes meeting his directly. "I think for years—for you to do just that."

Desire bucked; Philip dragged in a shuddering breath. Very conscious of his limitations, he directed a warning glance at her. "If you could refrain from doing anything *too* encouraging, I'd be grateful."

She shot him a mischievous glance—Philip saw the teasing glint he loved in her eyes. The sight made him groan—just the thought of what it might mean if she brought her usual, questing mind to bear in that arena too, threatened his already overtried control.

Antonia stretched up; shifting his hands to her waist, Philip held her back. "We'll go directly to town tomorrow, given we have my phaeton. We'll stop at Ruthven House so you can change and pick up anything you want, then go straight on to the Manor. We can be married in a few days." He paused to draw breath, then forced himself to add, "Or wait the usual three weeks—whichever you prefer."

Antonia studied his face, his eyes, then raised one brow in open speculation. "I think I'll reserve my decision—until tomorrow." She smiled, and pressed closer. "Tonight, after all, might influence my conclusion."

Philip closed his eyes and groaned. "Is that an invitation or a threat?"

"Both."

Antonia reached up, twining her arms about his neck, stretching up to kiss him, letting her lips, her body, make her promises, purposely inviting, then inciting him to take all she had—all she was.

He did, kissing her until she was breathless, witless, filled with an unnameable longing, before tumbling her into the billows of the bed. Slowly, leisurely, he divested her of her clothes. Passion burned freely within her; she felt neither the chill of the air nor any lingering restraint.

Inevitable, he had termed it; as she lay back against the pillows and waited for him to join her, Antonia felt the rightness, the unquestionable truth, of his words. This had been destined to be. From the first.

Then he returned to her, taking her in his arms, wrapping her in a cocoon of warm desire, sating her senses with delight. The night spun about them, a wild kaleidoscope of stars and suns set spinning by passion's hand.

STEPHANIE LAURENS   337

He held her tight, guiding her through the whirling of their senses, holding her steady, safe in his arms. He conducted her through a landscape she had never known existed, guiding her unerringly through each deepening layer of intimacy until they came together, as it was always meant to be, the ease of old friendship and long-standing love investing each caress with a significance far greater than its physical form.

Later, wrapped in the warm haven of his arms, settled against the heat of him, delicious languor in every limb, she felt his lips at her temple. The words he murmured were so low, she only just caught them.

"Tonight, tomorrow—and forever."

The note of finality in his voice set the seal on her happiness. Buoyed on its swell, Antonia slept.

PHILIP WOKE THE next morning to the distracting sensation of a warm, curvaceous, silk-encased form snuggled into his side. As the silk in question was his wife-to-be's skin, his reaction was instantaneous. He glanced at her—but all he could see was a mass of golden curls fanned out on the pillow. Raising his brows, he considered his next move—and recalled a few loose ends. Carefully, he eased from the bed.

Dressing quickly, he left Antonia slumbering while he went downstairs.

He returned twenty minutes later, having dispatched the Countess's gig along with various missives, some rather longer than others, back to Ticehurst Place, only to discover Antonia still hidden beneath the covers. With a rakish grin, Philip shrugged out of his coat.

He was pulling off his shirt when he heard rustling from the bed. Looking up, he watched as Antonia blinked awake. She saw him; her lips curved in a sleepy, sated, gloriously happy smile.

Philip felt his lips curve in automatic response. Dropping the shirt on a chair, he walked to the side of the bed, his hands at his waistband.

It took a moment for Antonia's mind to clear enough to realise his clothes were coming off, rather than going on. "What are you doing?" With an effort, she tugged her gaze all the way up to his face.

His smile made her toes curl. "I thought," he said, raising a brow in the way only he could, "that I should attend to our unfinished business without delay."

Her mind still dimmed by the aftereffects of the long night, Antonia could not divine what he meant. "I thought," she said, trying to frown as he lifted the covers and slid in beside her, "that we'd concluded things quite satisfactorily." Nagging uncertainty made her add, "Didn't we?"

His laugh was as devilish as his look.

"Indubitably." Philip rolled her into his arms, settling her against him. "However, as we have a little time, I thought it might be wise to grasp the opportunity to…" His lips trailed down her throat. "Get in a little extra persuasion—just to help you make up your mind."

"My mind?" Antonia wasn't sure it was functioning at all. "On what matter?" Her memory tended to stall, fixed on certain memorable moments of the previous evening, all the rest merging into a less interesting background haze.

"On whether we should marry sooner—" Philip bent his head to place a kiss on one pert nipple "—or later." He transferred his attention to its twin, hiding a smug grin when Antonia shifted restlessly against him.

"Ah…" Antonia tried very hard to think. "I don't believe I've yet made up my mind." As his hands fastened on her soft flesh, she was suddenly very sure of her answer. Moistening her lips, she glanced down and found Philip's eyes. "Maybe you'd better persuade me a bit more?"

Philip's eyes gleamed. "That, my love, is precisely my intention."

THEY RETURNED TO Ruthven House late that afternoon. Carring opened the door; Philip smiled, openly smug, when he saw his major-domo blink. A blink from Carring was the equivalent of an openmouthed stare from less controlled mortals.

With a laughing smile, Antonia hurried upstairs, as eager as he to be on their way home—to the Manor, where they both belonged. Her smile hadn't faded all morning—he'd enjoyed every minute of the time he had invested putting it on her face.

His own smile reflected his satisfaction as he stood in his hall and watched her disappear up the stairs.

"And the wedding, my lord—if I might make so bold as to enquire?"

Philip glanced at Carring. "Miss Mannering and I have reached a mutual understanding. We'll be married as soon as can be arranged."

Carring's smile held a reciprocating smugness Philip wasn't at all sure he understood.

"Very good, my lord," Carring intoned. "Might I request to be apprised of the date on which the nuptials will be celebrated?"

Philip fought a frown. "Why?"

"With your permission, my lord, I'd like to close

the house on that day—so the staff can travel to the Manor to be on hand to tender their wishes to you and your lady."

Philip raised his brows. "If they wish it, by all means."

"Rest assured, my lord, we will certainly be there." Magisterially ponderous, Carring headed for the baize door. "Indeed, I have long looked forward to throwing rice at your wedding."

The baize door swung closed before Philip could think of a suitable reply. Eyes narrowed, he glared at the door—and wondered how good Carring's aim might be.

Antonia's breathless return distracted him; he forgot the matter entirely—until the moment, three days hence, when, with Antonia radiant on his arm, he left the safety of the door of the local church to brave a positive hail of rice.

One particular handful hit him on the back of his head; the grains quickly slid down beneath the folds of his cravat.

Philip swore beneath his breath. He wriggled his shoulders to no avail. Glancing back, he searched the crowd—and located Carring, a wide grin on his face.

An answering grin transformed Philip's face. The carriage, bedecked with flowers, stood before them. He pulled Antonia to him; to the cheers of their well-wishers, he kissed her soundly, then lifted her up to the carriage.

Carring, as always, had had the last word; as he followed his wife into the carriage, Philip decided he didn't care in the least.

He glanced at Antonia, gloriously happy as she waved to their friends.

She was the wife he wanted, the wife he needed—not the comfortable wife she had thought to be but one to keep him on his toes.

Smiling proudly, Philip settled back against the squabs, his gaze firmly fixed on his wife.

His thirty-fifth year would be one he'd remember; he was, he discovered, looking forward, not just to the next, but to all the rest of his life.

* * * * *

A LADY BY DAY

CHAPTER ONE

"LA, JOSEPHINE, I'VE heard the most *extraordinary* news!" Honoria's voice rang out in Josephine's dressing room with only two hours left to dress for the evening's ball, and Josephine, Countess of Mareck, knew exactly what fascinating news her friend was about to impart. "Sir *Noah Rutledge* has returned to London—but surely you've heard."

That news. Oh, yes. She'd heard. Instead of continuing to visit aggravation on her from the Mediterranean, Sir Noah had apparently decided to come to London and aggrieve her in person.

Josephine studied the gowns carefully set out on her bed. "Hold up the dark blue again please, Mary." The dark blue had never been a favorite. Perhaps it was finally time to admit the mistake and retire it.

"Josephine, I won't stand for you feigning disinterest." Honoria moved in beside her. "I was just on my way to visit Lady Allen—poor thing turned her ankle this afternoon and can't attend tonight—and I thought surely you would be able to give me some details about Sir Noah's visit with which to entertain the poor soul." She pursed her lips at the gown Mary held. "You aren't finally going to wear *that,* are you?"

"I ought to wear it at least once."

"Oh, fie. Where is that delicious gold taffeta? After

all the trouble you went through with the fitting, I haven't seen you wear it even one time, yet now you're considering *this*. If I wasn't in such a hurry to see Lady Allen, I would *demand* that you find that gold taffeta."

"I'm afraid I can't be of much help about Sir Noah. I knew nothing of his visit until today." A fact that was beyond vexing. He'd given her no warning, no time to plan.

"Mr. Woodbridge said nothing of it?"

"Not a word." Most likely because Josephine had been answering Sir Noah's letters to Elias Woodbridge herself. Well, in a manner of speaking. The signatures all read *Joseph Bentley*.

And now it was a good guess Sir Noah had grown tired of communicating with his cousin Elias by proxy.

"Well, that isn't helpful at all," Honoria fussed. "How is anyone supposed to discuss Sir Noah if those who know the most about him do not share what they know?"

How indeed?

Honoria frowned suddenly at the floor, the chair, the love seat by the window. "Where is darling Bentley?"

"In the girls' rooms. They positively dote on him, and he has abandoned me completely."

"Ha. Only wait until they find husbands, and the poor little turncoat will return to beg your affection once more." Honoria fingered the dark blue gown. "Whatever made you choose a color like this? With your auburn hair?"

Josephine stared at the fabric blankly. Sir Noah, here. In London. And now that he was, she would not be able to keep him and his pernicious business plans away from Elias for very long. It was imperative to thwart him until she could decide exactly how to make sure that his business proposal would fail to pique Elias's interest.

A new shipyard venture in Turkey. At Elias's age. In his condition. With his listless frame of mind.

It was outrageous. Sir Noah hadn't been the one here, in London, looking in on Elias, talking to doctors, watching a decline that seemed impossible to prevent. But Sir Noah certainly did think, according to his letters, that Elias should abandon the London shipyard that represented his life's work and travel to Turkey.

"You aren't even listening," Honoria said, and turned to face her. "Josephine, I'm terribly worried about you."

"Because I might wear the blue?"

"Don't be obtuse. I won't stand for it. Because you aren't trying, when I know very well you could find happiness if you would only put the smallest amount of effort into it. Lord Tidewell will be there tonight."

"Who's to say he doesn't care for blue?"

"Josephine."

"Very well. I shall wear the bronze." She gestured for Mary to set the gown back with the others. "That will be all, Mary. Thank you. I shall be ready to dress in an hour."

"It isn't right that the only male company you keep is with your uncle, dear though Mr. Woodbridge is. It isn't natural. I don't mean you should consider marriage, but for heaven's sake—you had that lover in Paris. I don't know why you couldn't take one now."

"For one thing, we're not in Paris." For another, the brief affair had been nothing more than an attempt to distract herself. It had kept her from hiring a coach and returning to Gibraltar, so in that sense it had been a spectacular success.

"People have affairs in London."

"You are a fount of enlightenment, Honoria. Perhaps, once I have found suitable husbands for both my nieces and a physician who can restore Elias's strength—" and a man of business to take her place working for Elias, as well as a solution that would send Sir Noah back to the Mediterranean alone, and permanently "—I shall turn my attention to romance."

"Of course," Honoria mused, ignoring her completely, "now you'll have Sir Noah's company, as well." Her eyes brightened with possibilities. "Lady Devon said she saw Sir Noah outside Lord Poole's house— she's got a direct view from her window, you know— and she vowed he was the most striking figure of a man she's seen in years. *Years.* Only imagine what that could signify."

"Coming from Lady Devon, I should think it means he has two arms and two legs."

"La, Josephine, you are too contrary! I should think it means a good deal more than that. I'll say this… Sir Noah may only be a knight, but he is rich as Croesus, and he is something new. I daresay he'll offer a bit of exotic spice to our humdrum existence."

Josephine made herself laugh, even as she wondered whether there was anything she could have done differently—or that *Joseph Bentley* could have done differently, rather—to avoid Sir Noah's coming to London in person. "Such high expectations for a mere mortal."

"Is he? Mortal?" Honoria's eyes flashed with mischief. "To hear Lady Devon tell it, I rather think not."

B̲u̲t̲ S̲i̲r̲ N̲o̲a̲h̲ *was* mortal, and two hours later as Josephine and the girls bustled through the entrance hall on their way to the coach, she nearly collided with him on her way out the door.

"Good heavens." She jumped back, looked up, and there was a heartbeat when she couldn't breathe. His eyes were that blue. It didn't matter that she'd never seen him before, that he hadn't introduced himself—she knew immediately who he was.

"Pardon me, madam," he said quickly. "Do forgive me." He offered a bow, and it was all she could do not to stare. He looked as if he'd just disembarked from a ship, which, of course, he very recently had. It was dark outside, but the chandeliers illuminated a face kissed deeply by the Mediterranean sun and cut with lines that creased the corners of his eyes and mouth. His burnished-gold hair was streaked with blond and cropped, yet long enough to testify to his scorn of a wig at sea. He stood with that wide-legged stance that could identify a seaman from a hundred yards.

He was the Mediterranean itself, come wildly to life on her doorstep.

"Sir Noah Rutledge," he said now. Those blue eyes glanced over her, leaving sparks on her skin. "Please pardon my intrusion, but I was told there is a Mr. Joseph Bentley at this address."

She debated the wisdom of letting him think her a complete stranger, but decided it would only make her look foolish when he learned that she wasn't. "How do you do, Sir Noah? What a pleasure to finally make your acquaintance. I am Lady Mareck, Elias Woodbridge's niece by marriage." She glanced over her shoulder. "Lettie, Pauline, do hurry—the carriage is waiting."

And then, "I'm afraid there's nobody by that name here," she said. "There must be a mistake."

There was a small ruckus behind them, followed by an outraged shriek from Lettie. "Auntie Josephine, Bentley just tore a bit of lace from my gown!"

Josephine turned just in time to see Pauline snatch the strip of lace from Bentley's mouth. "Mary, could you bring a pin?" Josephine called. "Quickly, please." Bentley darted toward Josephine in a frenzy of excitement. "Edgar, could you please—" But Sir Noah was already bending down to scoop Bentley into his arms, where Bentley became a wiggly bit of silver fluff with a pink tongue, desperately trying to lick Sir Noah's chin.

"We are just on our way out, as you can see," she told him. "I assume you're in town to see your cousin?"

"Yes." Thick, strong fingers ruffled Bentley's fur and expertly kept that small, furry face at a safe distance from Sir Noah's own very—oh, yes, *very*—handsome one. "It's been a long time—too long," he said. "There's much I'd like to discuss with him." Of course there was. And he would have the opportunity to discuss exactly none of it until she'd had a chance to speak with Elias about his sudden arrival. "Although I understand he's been feeling poorly," he added.

She saw now that the back of his hand had been tattooed with a geometric Ottoman design. She forced herself not to stare.

"I'm afraid Elias *has* been feeling a bit worse than usual these past few days." Which Sir Noah already knew because she'd told him as much in the note she'd sent him earlier today.

Or rather, the letter "Joseph Bentley" had sent him

in response to a note Sir Noah had sent to Elias. It was a miracle she'd been at Elias's house to intercept it.

Edgar reached to take Bentley from Sir Noah. "Pardon me, sir."

"Bentley, you naughty dog!" Lettie scolded from the bottom of the staircase, where Mary was pinning the torn lace, and Josephine felt a twinge of unease. Hopefully, Sir Noah would not make the connection.

When Josephine returned her attention to Sir Noah, she found his unnerving gaze resting somewhere between her chin and her bosom.

"Elias's health is always unpredictable," she told him a bit more sternly than she might have, and his gaze lifted to meet hers once again, which didn't help things because his eyes were a shade of blue she hadn't seen since overlooking the sea at Gibraltar. "It is a very distressing situation." *This* was fast becoming equally distressing. "I can never be certain myself when I might find him asleep—" just to reinforce what she'd said in the note about Elias's sleeping patterns "—but thankfully his staff is adept at having meals ready during any window of opportunity. When he's of a mind to take food, naturally." That might have been a bit of an exaggeration.

"Good God." His lips tightened and he rubbed the back of his neck. "Dare I ask the prognosis?"

"There's no need for that." She hadn't anticipated this level of concern. "His condition is serious—you mustn't misunderstand—but it has been for quite some time. I don't expect any sudden changes. But you may have difficulty catching him awake when you call." Perhaps expectation of failure would keep him away a bit longer.

"Indeed. I ran into exactly that issue this morning,

and again this afternoon." She didn't like the way he was looking at her. "In the meantime, I'd hoped to find his man of business. Joseph… Bentley."

"Of course. Have you inquired at the shipyard?"

"It was the shipyard manager who gave me this address."

Had he. And after being under the strictest instructions not to give the address to anyone under any circumstances.

A sharp bite of anger had her making an effort to keep her lips fixed in a pleasant smile. "A simple mix-up, I'm sure. He must have given it to you by mistake. I do spend a good deal of time with Mr. Woodbridge— perhaps they keep my address in case of an emergency."

"Perhaps they do at that."

"I'm ready, Aunt Josephine," Lettie called.

No, she did not like the way he was looking at her at all.

"I shan't keep you," he said, and bowed again. "A pleasure, Lady Mareck. And a pleasure to meet… Bentley."

The corner of his lip curved a little as he turned away, and her muscles tensed. She had a terrible feeling that her alter ego had just been discovered.

CHAPTER TWO

Josephine, Lady Mareck, had a dog named Bentley.

Joseph Bentley.

It could not be that bloody simple.

It could not *possibly* mean what it implied. *Could* it?

By the time he returned to his lodgings, Noah had decided it could.

An invitation awaited him—a ball, tonight, hosted by the Dowager Lady Wescott.

You shan't be without acquaintance, Lady Wescott wrote. *Josephine, Lady Mareck, whom I expect you know through your mutual relationship with Elias Woodbridge, will be in attendance.*

Then by all means, let him dress at once.

He crumpled the invitation in his fist, made a sudden decision, and headed back out to the street. Twenty-four hours wasn't quite enough to cure his sea legs, and the ground seemed to move beneath his feet. Outside in the cold night drizzle, he ordered another chair.

You may have difficulty catching him awake when you call.

Or perhaps there'd merely been a *mix-up,* and Elias's butler had told him by *mistake* that Elias was asleep.

On Joseph Bentley's orders.

On *Josephine, Lady Mareck's* orders.

The chair clopped along the street toward Elias's

house, and Noah conjured her in his mind's eye: smooth, auburn hair, elaborately coiffed and lightly powdered. Flawless seashell skin. Hazel eyes that gave away nothing. Generous breasts pushed high and round above a shapely waist. Delicate collarbones that had him fisting his hand against the desire to trace them.

Christ. If he could be guaranteed companionship of that caliber, he might welcome the too-fast approach of his own declining years.

He laughed into the empty carriage. Wouldn't that be just his bloody luck? If his cousin was having an affair with the stunning Lady Mareck, convincing Elias to leave London would be next to impossible.

Outside in the darkness, the cold, drizzly, filthy reasons that *anyone* should wish to leave London sat shrouded in all their dreariness. The Mediterranean climate would be so much better for Elias's health. He sat back and rubbed his forehead, considering the possibility that Elias was more ill than he'd believed. That Noah was too late. Had waited too long.

Damn it to hell.

There were other naval architects. He could find someone else to help him revive that old Turkish shipyard. But he couldn't find an architect who was also his cousin. Elias was the only relative Noah had left.

Elias's butler, Mr. Trowe, did not pretend to hide his displeasure at seeing Noah a third time in one day. He wasn't half as displeased as Noah, who stated his business and headed for the staircase.

"Sir, I must insist— Sir, I absolutely forbid you to go upstairs! Quickly—call the footmen!" Noah ignored the footsteps pounding up the stairs behind him. "Sir, you must stop this instant!"

Noah didn't. "You may inform Lady Joseph Bentley that you attempted to stop me from seeing Mr. Woodbridge but were unsuccessful," he said sharply.

Elias's room was easy enough to find—it was the one with the chambermaid standing stubbornly in front of the door. Her resolve fled when she saw him, and she quickly stepped out of the way.

Noah paused and looked at the butler. "Would you care to announce me, or shall I announce myself?"

"This is an outrage. Sir, you do *not* have permission—"

Noah gave a rapid double knock and cracked the door. "Elias? It's Noah Rutledge." Nothing. "Elias?" He opened the door and stepped inside.

The bed was empty. There was nobody in the room.

He turned on the butler. "*Where* is Mr. Woodbridge?" A dozen alarming possibilities tumbled through his mind.

The man observed him, prune-lipped. "He is out for the evening."

"Out for the *evening?* He's a bloody invalid!" Only after the words shot from his lips did it occur that perhaps he wasn't.

Lady Mareck could have been lying about that, too.

"And where," Noah managed to ask through a growing fury, "has he gone?"

Trowe shook his head. "I cannot tell you, sir. I simply do not know."

"You don't know."

"He never tells us what he's about, sir."

Never implied that this was a regular occurrence. "Am I to understand that Mr. Woodbridge is in perfect

health? That there's been no physician here today, as I
was told earlier?"

Trowe's jaw worked a little. "Would that were the
case, sir."

"Then he *is* in ill health."

"Sir, I must ask you to leave."

Oh, he was leaving. Most definitely.

He had a ball to attend.

JOSEPHINE SHOULD HAVE told Pauline she needn't dance
with Mr. Crumley, but it would be impossible for
Pauline to form any real opinion of the man—of *any*
man—if she never spoke to him, or in Pauline's case,
to anyone. The look of betrayal Pauline had cast her as
she'd walked away made her feel like a cruel old auntie, but that was part and parcel of being a proper chap-
erone. Especially when Charlotte already worried that
Josephine hadn't really changed in all these years and
would somehow manage to ruin her daughters during
their first Season instead of finding them husbands.

"I don't know why *I* never think of scalloped lace,"
Josephine was saying to Lady Orville, who was here
with no fewer than three granddaughters. "Your gown
is remarkable. Quite stunning." She tried to spot Pauline through the crowd, but someone else caught her
eye. Her fan stilled.

Sir Noah.

He saw her, and their eyes locked through the crowd
before she pointedly looked away.

"Oh, fie," Lady Orville said. "You are *much* too free
with your compliments, Josephine. I must say, your musical entertainment the other night was splendid. But
then, your entertainments are always exceptional— Oh,

dear. I think he's standing too close. Do you think he's standing too close?"

Josephine followed Lady Orville's line of sight toward her eldest granddaughter, who was talking with the future Baron Lytle.

"I think they turned to avoid the crush, is all," Josephine said, too aware that Sir Noah was systematically making his way toward her.

He stopped to talk with Eleanor, the evening's hostess. Laughed at something she said. His smile sliced across the room, and Josephine's pulse leaped just a little.

"Yes, Josephine." Lady Orville let out a breath of air and fanned herself once more. "Yes, you're right. They are practically besieged. Although I daresay they've talked long enough. I think I should separate them."

"It's only been a minute or two." Sir Noah moved away from Eleanor. He wore a striking jacket unlike anything else in the room, dark green and shimmering with an embroidered pattern of Moorish vines. "You mustn't fret—Davinia is much too attractive to go unsought-after by every eligible possibility. Young Mr. Lytle will not be *able* to monopolize her."

Sir Noah paused to chat with Lord Poole, then Colonel Wenthurst, then Lord Yost, moving ever closer. And closer. And she had an awful feeling she knew why.

Lady Orville squeezed Josephine's arm. "You are too kind, as always. My fears do get the best of me where Davinia is concerned."

"Shall we go see if we can refresh our punch?" Josephine asked.

"Certainly! Oh— Oh, there is Burton. Do forgive

me, Josephine. I *must* go speak with him. I've been so anxious for Davinia to be introduced to his eldest son."

"By all means, go. Oh—there are Honoria and Annabelle."

The hair tingled on the back of Josephine's neck as she moved through the crush toward her friends. The sharp hum of pursuit coursed hot and fast with her pulse.

He knows.

Yet there was a chance he didn't.

Auntie Josephine, Bentley just tore a bit of lace from my gown! A very small breath of a chance.

"La, Josephine! *There* you are."

"Would anyone care to join me in the other room for a glass of fresh punch?" Josephine asked quickly, only to see that Honoria's eyes were already fixed with great interest on something behind her. "Ophelia? Punch?" Josephine tried now "It's so dreadfully warm in here—"

But it was too late, because just then—as if he cared nothing at all for social order—Sir Noah joined them.

"Good evening, Lady Mareck," he said, moving in next to her, so close that the tails of his jacket brushed her skirts.

She turned her head as if only just noticing him. "Sir Noah," she said pleasantly. "What a lovely surprise to see you again so soon."

Amusement creased his eyes, but only just. "The surprise has been mine." He took her hand and brought it to his lips. "Mr. Bentley," he murmured against her skin, looking directly into her eyes.

She withdrew her hand, careful not to react. "Do allow me to introduce Lady Edgethorn—" she gestured to Annabelle "—Lady Nystrom—" Ophelia "—and

Lady Ramsey, whose brother Lord Croston you may be acquainted with, as he captains one of his Majesty's ships in the Mediterranean fleet."

"Ah, yes." Sir Noah smiled at Honoria. "The much-celebrated Captain Warre, and for very good reason. An honor, Lady Ramsey."

"If I'd known you were returning to England," Honoria said, "I would have insisted that you bring him with you. I swear I see my brother so infrequently I hardly recognize him."

"You don't really keep a caged lion aboard your ship, do you, Sir Noah?" Annabelle asked.

He laughed. "If I did, there's no doubt he would also be a seasick lion. That sounds like a good deal more trouble than I'm prepared for. I'm lucky to have room for a dozen chickens."

Ophelia fluttered her fan and perused him openly. "There's been a great deal of speculation whether we might see you riding about London on a camel."

"Perhaps I might at that, if only so I do not disappoint."

"I doubt that would be possible, Sir Noah." Ophelia drew her fan across her neck and swept her gaze across his torso.

Josephine could excuse herself and hope the flattery would keep him there while she made her escape. Or she could remain stubbornly with her friends until sheer awkwardness forced him to remove himself.

"I realize this is hardly the appropriate time or place," he said now, turning to Josephine, "but I hoped I might have a word with you about my cousin." Three pairs of eyes turned on her with simultaneous envy and sympathetic understanding.

Or, she could take a private turn about the room with Sir Noah.

"By all means." Her smile felt brittle on her lips. "I'd been hoping to refresh my punch."

She tucked her hand into his elbow and felt solid muscle ripple beneath brocaded silk.

"What an unpleasant evening," she said as they walked. "I detest when it rains during a ball. One cannot escape outside to catch one's breath."

"The weather has been terrible all afternoon," he said. "Which was all the more aggravating, as I found myself traveling all over town searching for a man who doesn't exist."

"How frustrating that must have been for you."

"Oh, Joseph," he murmured. "You have no idea. But discovering the truth has been worth the trouble, I assure you." He rubbed his jaw, as though he might have had a beard he wasn't quite used to doing without. "Suppose you tell me where Elias is now? Is he here?"

"Here? Heavens, no. And I will warn you, this would not be a good time for a visit. He takes three different medicines before bedtime, all of which contain significant quantities of spirits, and he won't be in his right mind."

"Won't he?" His blue eyes drilled into her, bright with anger and another emotion that was very much anger's opposite. "I might be inclined to believe you, had I not already been to his house and learned he was out for the evening."

He'd returned to Elias's. Naturally. "Sometimes Trowe will say things just so that Elias can enjoy some peace."

"I saw his empty bed with my own eyes."

Trowe had let him upstairs? She tamped down a lick of fury. "I'm afraid I cannot help you, Sir Noah. He could well have been in his anteroom or the library… Who's to say?"

Amusement tugged at his lips. "Trowe, for one. He confessed that Elias had gone out, but could not say where. Or wouldn't say. I have my doubts as to the man's candor."

Elias and his nighttime excursions—what a devil. He'd slept all afternoon, scarcely eaten a thing. Hardly been able to breathe, worse than usual. Taken three spoonfuls of medicine—and *still* he'd gone out despite a hundred discussions about why he should not.

"Thank you for apprising me of the situation," she said, and started to turn away. "I will see that it is resolved, and I pray you will enjoy the rest of your evening."

In the privacy between their bodies, strong fingers curled around her wrist—large, warm fingers callused from years of sailing. "If the situation is to be resolved," he told her under his breath, "we shall resolve it together." Those fingers tightened. "Now."

"Sir Noah, I cannot possibly address the matter now. My nieces are here, and without my supervision there's no contemplating what might befall them. I've left them to their own devices too long already. It *has* been good to see you again, Sir Noah. Do call on Elias again tomorrow, and perhaps he will be well enough to receive you."

"Ah, Joseph." He smiled at her in a way that sent shivers careening across her skin. "Perhaps I haven't made myself clear. Here is what is about to happen. You will beg an emergency, leaving your nieces in the charge of any number of perfectly capable chaperones who will see them safely home. We will order your coach and go to Elias's, where he will either have returned, in which case we will confirm the state of his health once and for all, or he will still be away, in which case we will stay until he returns." Those blue eyes skimmed over her face, flicked to her breasts. Glanced at her hands. "You are making a fist. Could it be you are not as calm as you pretend, Mr. Bentley?"

CHAPTER THREE

INSIDE HER COACH, Josephine kept her hands carefully folded in her lap while she imagined the news of her double identity blazing its way through London, igniting conversation in every drawing room while Charlotte's hopes for Lettie and Pauline went up in the smoke of Josephine's outlandish doings.

"Suppose you tell me why you've seen fit to prevent my business dealings with Elias," Sir Noah said casually, sitting with his arm draped across the back of the opposite seat. A subtle fragrance teased her—spicy and exotic, reminiscent of her girlhood days in Gibraltar.

He was almost painfully handsome. She tried to ignore it, but he sat across from her...*existing*. Watching her with those remarkable eyes. Sitting as if he owned the coach and everything in it, with his legs stretched out in front of him—strong, muscular legs that would be steady and sure even in high seas—as if he hadn't a care in the world.

"I'm not sure what you mean," she said evenly. "Elias has his fingers in many different pies, and managing all of his dealings at any given time can be difficult. It's often a matter of timing. Do accept my apologies for any inconvenience."

All those good intentions of putting an end to this Joseph Bentley business within weeks of the first time

Elias had asked her to write a letter, nearly three years ago… It was too late for that now.

Sir Noah's too-blue eyes glittered in the near darkness. "Inconvenience."

"Certainly you understand that matters must be prioritized according to urgency." His mere presence should not have made it this difficult to breathe.

"Mmm. Yes. And somehow you divined that my business was less than urgent."

"Only on the grounds of its being somewhat unrealistic." In the sense that it absolutely, positively would not come to fruition. "I meant no offense, naturally."

He gave a laugh—straight, white teeth flashing in the shadowy coach. "Naturally. Although by *unrealistic,* I believe you actually mean that you object to my plans on every point and are prepared to go to any length to prevent them."

"Good heavens, you do have an inflated view of the significance others place on your intentions." It wouldn't do to explain that she did, in fact, object to his plans on *every* point—every last self-serving point.

"Your obstructionist tactics have kept me at a standstill for two years," he went on conversationally, but there was no mistaking the edge in his voice. "You will understand if I've had enough."

"I am aware of your discontent, Sir Noah."

"Oh, Joseph, *discontent* doesn't begin to describe it." He leaned toward her and pinned her with his gaze. "Daydreams about what I would do to Joseph Bentley when I finally got my hands on him gave me many a happy hour during the voyage north." The corner of his lips twitched, and a shiver feathered her spine. She would not underestimate him again.

"I understand that a great number of men around the Mediterranean enjoy that variety of indulgence," she said evenly, "so I suppose I oughtn't be surprised. How disappointed you must be."

He smiled at her. "If you order your driver to take a longer route, I'll be happy to show you exactly how disappointed."

Her arm flared to life with the memory of his grip—the press of his fingers into the sensitive flesh on the inside of her wrist. Her fingernails dug into her palm, and she forced them to relax.

"Such a temptation, Sir Noah. But I believe—" she made a show of looking out the window "—yes, I do believe we've almost arrived."

He glanced out the window and looked at her sharply. "This isn't the way to Elias's house." He started for the bell.

"Do not pull it. The driver is following my direction. If you wish to see Elias, I know where you will find him."

The coach slowed to a stop outside a narrow house with brightly lit windows. The sign above the door was barely legible in the dark.

"The Dewy Petal?" he asked incredulously.

"Would you like to go roust him from his entertainments, or shall I?"

There was a heartbeat, and Sir Noah began to laugh. "You surprise me, Lady Mareck."

It took a moment to realize it was because he did not believe her. She reached for the bell and rang it.

"What are you doing?" he demanded.

The door opened. "Please go inside and inquire after Mr. Elias Woodbridge," she told the coachman. "Tell

him there is a matter of great importance—that Sir
Noah Rutledge is here and must see him immediately."

Sir Noah cursed. "That won't be necessary."

"I think it is."

"You have proved your point, Lady Mareck."

"I can't imagine what you mean," she said. "You
wished to see Elias, and I have showed you where he
is likely to be. By all means, go in straightaway and
inform him that he must sell his shipyard, pack up his
household and begin life anew in Turkey."

Sir Noah smiled at her. "I hardly think a *coitus inter-
ruptus* is the way to renew my relationship with Elias,
do you, Joseph?" He ordered the door closed in a ship-
master's tone that brooked no disobedience. The door
slammed, and the carriage lurched forward. "Morning
will be soon enough."

THE DEWY PETAL.

Christ.

Noah stretched out on the bed in his rented lodgings
with a ration of his favorite arak, mixed milky-white
and tasting so strongly of home it was almost painful.

Lady Mareck was Joseph Bentley.

Bloody sodding hell.

There would be no blackening Bentley's eye now,
gratifying though it might be. And there was no doubt
he'd be thinking about those eyes all the way back to
Marmaris. They were hazel, alive with gold and brown
that gave them a fiery glitter, fringed by the prettiest
lashes he'd ever seen. Pity they conveyed as much feeling as a slab of marble.

He thought of her observing him passively from behind her death-mask politesse. She was beautiful, there

was no denying it. If one enjoyed that type of cold, wax-figure elegance.

Well, I've got you now, your enterprising ladyship.

Either way, there could be no doubt that she was doing everything in her power to prevent him discussing his proposal with Elias. Which meant she feared Elias would react favorably.

He splayed his fingers and smiled at the Moresque design scrolled across the back of his hand—one of the more permanent mad whims he and Ahmet had acted on, and they hadn't even been drunk at the time. Lady Mareck's eyes had strayed there more than once during their limited encounters. How *eccentric* she must think him.

He let his hand fall and sipped his drink.

Perhaps Elias really was in poor health, as she claimed. Perhaps not. But he bloody well wasn't on death's door if he actually had been entertaining himself in the—God, Noah couldn't think of it without laughing—the *Dewy Petal*.

Perhaps he should have gone in after all. He might have fancied a look 'round.

In any case, he would discover in the morning whether Lady Mareck's story was true or another of her evasive ploys. He would be able to assess the situation, decide whether it might be prudent to wait before approaching Elias with his proposal.

He closed his eyes and savored the taste of anise on his tongue.

What he wouldn't give to be in Smyrna right now, in that little *meyhane* where the wine was so potent three glasses put him half seas over. Or reclining at Ghalib's villa on Cyprus, smoking a water pipe and enjoying the attentions of a dark-haired beauty. Or even at his own villa on the Turkish Mediterranean, though God knew why he would ever spend time there when there was such fun to be had elsewhere. Damnation, there was always good company at Ghalib's.

But life needed to be more than a collection of half-coherent memories of pleasure-seeking. By now Noah should have had more to show than memories and money. Other men his age had political aspirations, ran commercial enterprises, maintained wives and children and households.

Other men were cogs in the great machine of society. And what was he?

A bit of flotsam, drifting alone on the sea of life.

He had all the evidence he needed in the fact that he'd sailed all the way to London on the hope that if Elias had received his letters, he might have looked favorably on the plan. And on the fantasy that the two of them might work together. Come to know each other. They were each other's only relations, after all.

But the truth was, Elias might very well laugh at him. God knew, more than one of his friends in the Med had done as much. Even Ahmet might have laughed, if he'd still been alive, although the shipyard idea was as much his vagary as Noah's.

But Ahmet wasn't alive—only the memories were. Carousing the ancient seaports, laughing at anything and everything, drinking liquor as fast as the Levant could produce it. Talking about a hundred possible courses of action yet never lifting a finger toward any.

And now here Noah was, finally taking action. Joseph Bentley, Lady Mareck, could step out of the way or go to hell.

CHAPTER FOUR

"IF YOUR DEBAUCHING causes you to live one minute less than you might have, Elias, I shall hunt you down in the afterlife with a pack of rabid hounds." Josephine pulled the curtains back instead of waiting for the maid to do it and faced her late husband's uncle, who squinted at her from his bed like a bat being torn from its cave.

"You shan't be in a position to find me in the afterlife," he said, tugging feebly at the bed drapes, "as you shall reside on a much loftier estate than I. Where has that valet gone?" The question ended in a fit of coughing.

"To get your tea, or have you forgotten already that you asked for it?"

Did Elias look paler than usual, or was she imagining things? Trowe's story of Sir Noah forcing his way upstairs last night had her so furious it was hard to keep her voice calm.

A maid stoked the fire and brought a full pitcher of water. Any minute, Sir Noah would arrive. There would be no keeping him away now, but she'd had time to decide what to do about that. And wouldn't Sir Noah be surprised.

"Good God," Elias groaned. "Feel as if I've been trampled by ten horses."

She leaned forward and kissed the small portion of

his forehead that was visible between his nightcap and the covers. He reeked of perfume. "You've got to stop these nighttime excursions. What if something should happen?" The sight of him was heartbreaking.

"Why would I wish to die in my own bed—" Elias coughed, and the chambermaid quickly pushed a glass of water into his hands "—when I could die in someone else's? If I'm going to go, I'd just as soon do it between a welcoming pair of—"

"You're not going to *go* anywhere." There were times when it would have been preferable if Elias did not feel quite so comfortable in her presence. "I've had a letter from Dr. Waxman in Cheshire. He'll be here by the end of the week. And I expect a reply any day from Dr. Norton."

"Not more of your god-awful doctors." He coughed again, drank more water.

Yes, Elias was given to riotous living. He'd always been that way. But these past two years, it was more than that. He'd lost interest in life. In the shipyard, which for Elias *was* life. There'd been more carousing and whoring, less designing and drafting. He'd hired a young, new naval architect who did most of what Elias had always devoted his life to. Sometimes the changes she'd seen in him these past two years hurt so deeply she wanted to yank him out of that bed and shake him until his teeth rattled. But all she could do was be there for him, the way he'd been there for her. She could be his rock, the way he'd always been hers.

But something was very wrong, and joining Sir Noah in Turkey would only make it worse.

"You'll need to look at those plans before the end

of the week," she told him. "Young Mr. Heckley needs your final approval before they can begin Perry's fleet."

"Already looked at 'em." And from the tone of his voice, not very thoroughly. It was a good thing Mr. Heckley was as talented as he was young.

"He'll be glad to hear it." Josephine glanced toward the doorway. She'd instructed Trowe to let her know when Sir Noah arrived before escorting him upstairs, but there wasn't much time. "Uncle, there is a matter of importance we need to discuss."

"God's sake, Jo, can't business wait for a decent hour?"

"I'm afraid not." Devil take Sir Noah for putting her in this position.

Under ordinary circumstances, she never would have kept something like this from Elias. If Elias had been healthier, she would certainly have told him. If he hadn't made such a steep decline for the worse. If his attitude had showed any sign of improvement.

If you weren't afraid he would go off with Sir Noah and leave you alone.

He might have been her uncle by marriage only, but he was also her truest friend and family in all the world.

Elias groaned. "Whatever it might be, I daresay you are more than capable of seeing to it without my help. Good God." He peeked up at her through one eye. "But if it's got to do with my new wig—"

"It doesn't." She would already lose him to the inevitable soon enough—she would not lose him to a renegade privateer sooner. "Uncle, I have a confession to make."

NOAH KNEW THE effects of a night of hard drinking when he saw them. He was familiar with the effects of old age, too, and when he walked—finally—into Elias's bedchamber, it was difficult to tell where one ended and the other began.

"Noah, my boy!" Elias broke off in a fit of coughing as he struggled to sit up in a sea of pillows and coverings. "By *damn* you're a welcome sight. Been a long time. A very long time indeed! Josephine, help me sit— bloody *hell,* my head hurts."

Noah moved in to help, but a chambermaid beat him to it. He watched the maid and Lady Mareck stuff a pair of pillows behind Elias's back. When Lady Mareck stepped back, she offered him a pleasant smile. "Good morning, Sir Noah."

"Lady Mareck." The state Elias was in put Noah in no mood for Lady Mareck's games, so he bowed to her and reached for his old cousin's hand. "Overjoyed, Elias," he said past a sudden thickening in his throat. "Truly." He inhaled deeply past the unexpected attack of emotion and stepped back.

"A very great joy, indeed," Elias breathed on a long exhale. "*Very* great." His eyes shifted to the bottle Noah carried. "What have you there?"

"Just a small token." And one that Elias would clearly do better to avoid, but Noah held out the bottle of arak anyway.

"Some of that devilish Levantine stuff," Elias declared, taking the bottle appreciatively. "Customs must have charged you a pretty penny."

"Show me a trader who doesn't slip through the odd bottle or two," Noah said, and winked at Lady Mareck just because he knew it would irritate her.

She regarded him as if he were the dullest bore in existence.

The tawdry reek of perfume told him Lady Mareck hadn't been staging theatrics last night. Elias had been out—if not at the Dewy Petal then somewhere similar. Which made two things very clear: there was no reason whatsoever why his cousin could not come to Turkey with him, and this was not the Elias he remembered.

"See now, Josephine," Elias said, coughing again, "here's someone who understands what a man needs in the morning."

Noah laughed. "Well, now, I wouldn't say—"

"None of that stuff," Elias told a maid arriving with coffee service. "Bring us three glasses."

"You'll kill me before I've got my land legs," Noah said, though in any other situation he would have happily indulged. "I'll have the coffee."

"Good God, not you, as well."

Josephine cast a quick look at Noah before brushing a wisp of Elias's hair from his forehead and smoothly divesting him of the bottle at the same time. "You know how sorry you'll be if we drink this all now and you don't have any for tonight." She gave his nightcap a gentle tug and touched his whiskered cheek. Elias reached up and squeezed her fingers, and she moved away to instruct the maid that the coffee service could stay.

And then, as though that was all he could manage, Elias sank into the pillows with a groan. "Aach. Not what I used to be, my boy. Devil of a thing, old age."

Old age, Noah wondered, or hard living? Noah's gut knotted with the fear that he was too late. It was barely three years ago Elias had sent Noah a letter in which he'd blisteringly vented his frustration with the London shipyard—the accounts, the employees, pressures from the East India Company. This man, who had always lived and breathed shipbuilding, who Noah remembered from childhood days talking of nothing but ships, had been enraged by the changes of time.

The Turkish shipyard, Noah had thought—had hoped, if he were honest—might present the perfect answer to Elias's discontent, while giving him and Noah a chance to get to know each other, like a real family.

All he could do was wait and see how much of this was the wild night talking. "What does the physician say?"

"Which one? Josephine's subjected me to so many. They all try to force some foul-smelling tar down my throat and tell me it's past time I gave up my evening entertainments, but good God—a man's got to have his fun." He coughed some more. "All this endless pulse-taking and bloodletting. Christ. A fortnight's sleep and some decent port would do the trick, mark my words." And then, "Berwick! Where is that wig?"

"I've sent young Thomas to find out any news of it, sir," his valet said from the doorway to the anteroom.

Elias grumbled something that sounded like "Excellent" and closed his eyes. "My dear niece has just been confessing her sins against you," he said on a sigh.

Noah looked sharply at Lady Mareck. "Has she?"

"I felt it only right, under the circumstances," she said pleasantly.

"Resurrecting an old Turkish shipyard," Elias breathed, and Noah realized exactly what she'd confessed. "Good God, my boy. I can barely manage a shipyard in London. If only a thief would take it from me in the night. Let alone—good *God*—a new enterprise in some godforsaken Moorish outpost, though heaven knows Josephine here would go in a heartbeat."

Noah clenched his jaw. She'd *told* Elias about the shipyard idea. Two bloody years of obstructions and excuses and intercepting his efforts to involve Elias in the venture, and *now* she'd told him.

Because she'd known exactly how Elias would react.

And because she was a smug, presumptuous interferer who thought the world ended at the Thames and was probably a damned hypochondriac herself, hence all the doctors, and probably only cared about Elias out of an artificial sense of charity. She wasn't even related to Elias by blood.

"It sounds as if there's been a bit of a misunderstanding," he said. "I am indeed considering the possibility of a venture in Turkey—more than considering, in fact. I'm planning on it, and I've secured the approval of the local governor. And nothing would please me more than to have your expertise and even your partnership, but the idea that you would abandon your own shipyard to help me start mine..." Noah offered what he hoped sounded like a self-deprecating laugh. "Well, that would be damned ballsy of me."

Noah looked at Lady Mareck—directly into those cool, hazel eyes—and smiled.

"The whole idea *is* rather ambitious," Noah added, just to see how Elias would respond.

Elias made a noise. "Not for a man in his prime."

But Noah was quickly hurtling past his prime, without a single meaningful, lasting legacy to show for the years he'd lived. "No limit to what a man can imagine while adrift on a calm summer sea." Or while huddled over endless pieces of paper, drafting plans and calculations and correspondences, but Elias—and especially Lady Mareck—didn't need to know all that. "I can't claim to be a naval architect, so I'd hoped to benefit from your expertise while I'm in London."

"Nothing like I used to be, my boy. Hardly keep my eyes open these days. 'Course, getting to bed before five might help." He looked at Josephine.

The valet cleared his throat from the doorway of the anteroom. "Mr. Woodbridge, I've received news that the wig—"

"Ah, sod the bloody wig." Elias sighed. "Just…" He waved his hand and let it drop back to the covers. "Put it with the others when it arrives."

"Very good, sir."

"Perhaps you ought to take a look at things while you're here," Elias muttered to Noah, shifting against his pillow. "The accountings, the records, the entire shipyard. Learn the working of things. In fact—" He looked up at Noah. "I've a good mind to sign it all over to you now and be done with it."

A moment's alarm lit Lady Mareck's eyes before she managed to hide it. "I cannot imagine that Sir Noah wants a shipyard in London," she said.

"So let him sell it. Take Archibald to Turkey. Devil of an architect, Archibald."

Noah didn't want some architect named Archibald. He wanted Elias. His cousin. But he couldn't— God. He couldn't simply say as much.

So he said, "There's no need for anything so drastic. I'll be in London for a while—perhaps I can help sort out whatever trouble you're having with the shipyard. You could direct me to your man of business—" no reaction, none at all, from either of them "—and perhaps I can be of some assistance."

"No, no, no." Elias waved the idea away. "There's no telling how much longer I'll be around—"

"Elias, hush," Lady Mareck said.

"If those doctors of yours have their way with me, it may well be sooner rather than later. Better you have it all now, my boy. Josephine will make sure you have all the records. Everything you need. She'll make sure you have every last scrap."

Devil take it. He didn't *want* every last scrap. Something had to be done.

CHAPTER FIVE

"I SUPPOSE THIS means you'll be *my* man of business now, Joseph," Sir Noah said outside Elias's rooms when they left him to dress, and Josephine smiled, because she knew that would irritate him more than anything.

"You *will* need a London man of business now that your plans have taken such an unexpected turn," she told him. "How fortuitous that you may receive a shipyard after all, and under much less ambitious terms than you originally contemplated. I expect once you reaccustom yourself to London once again, you will be reminded of its many benefits and you will hardly miss your Mediterranean life."

"You say that as if you plan to simply stand by while Elias signs the shipyard over to me."

"It has nothing to do with me. Elias is master of his own affairs." But there would be no signing of the shipyard over to Sir Noah.

"It seemed to me he is master of little more than a whore's quim and several bottles of port. Tell me, is that the reason for your employment, Mr. Bentley?"

He was furious. It was there in his blue eyes, cold as the Arctic now and brimming with aggravation.

"I do hope the state of Elias's health has impressed itself upon you," she said as she started down the stairs, "and that you can understand now that involving Elias in a Mediterranean venture would be impossible. I do regret how disappointed you must be."

"This has nothing to do with any bloody shipyard venture, in Turkey or London or anywhere else. The last time I saw Elias—and granted, it's been nearly twenty years—he lived and breathed that shipyard. Even the last letters I received before you began intercepting them gave no hint of this. Frustration? Aggravation? Yes. But never apathy."

She paused on the landing, listening to Sir Noah's memories and concerns. They mirrored hers so perfectly. But if Sir Noah's presence in London had less to do with the shipyard venture than with Elias himself, it changed everything—for the worse, because it would make him all the more tenacious.

"Perhaps, as Elias has aged, he has begun to see that things like shipyards and construction contracts are not what our Maker will ultimately be concerned with," she said.

"If that were his line of thinking, I doubt very much he would suppose his Maker would prefer a list of brothel triumphs. Let us cut to the chase, Joseph. Elias may be suffering some effects of age, but that's hardly the entire story."

"I never meant to pretend that it is."

"It's as if he's lost his interest in life. As if carousing has become his only interest. And—good God—*wigs.*"

"I won't deny it." Trying to deny it further would only make her look foolish.

"Then it appears we are both in agreement that something needs to be done."

"We are. And I am in the process of addressing the situation." Her voice came out a bit too sharply. His shipyard plans she could combat—Elias himself had no interest in that kind of effort. But if Sir Noah got it in mind to help Elias, that would be another matter entirely.

"You are?" he asked skeptically. "How?"

"I've identified a house in the country that is for sale. I have an appointment to view it this week. I'm told it's lovely—very quiet."

"Oh, yes." His words dripped with sarcasm. "A fine solution indeed."

"Mays Abbey presents the exact kind of calm and peaceful setting which will best promote Elias's health and soundness of mind, and where he may repose himself with a minimum of distraction."

"Does it?" He laughed, closing the gap between them. "Perhaps you haven't considered that there are any number of savory Covent Garden ladies who would happily settle into this *Mays Abbey* permanently. Elias Woodbridge, host of the never-ending house party." It was far too easy to imagine. "On the other hand," Sir Noah went on, "he could fare very well under my supervision in Turkey."

And there it was: Sir Noah's true intentions revealed.

She allowed her lips to curve, as if she found the idea amusing. "An excellent idea, Sir Noah. Nothing could suit Elias's condition more perfectly than the exotic indulgences of life in the land of the Moors."

His lips curved. "You could always come with us. To ensure his safety and well-being."

The idea unfurled like a sail being hoisted to catch the wind. For one vivid moment she saw herself during the voyage from Gibraltar to England all those years ago, standing on the deck with the wind in her hair and a fine, salty spray in her face. Watching the seabirds, the porpoises…the impossibly handsome first mate, Ahmet, who had let her look through his little telescope.

Mama and Charlotte and even Father had spent nearly the entire time below. But the sea—and Ahmet—had called to Josephine like the Sirens themselves.

"To ensure his early demise aboard an uncomfortable ship bound for the Mediterranean," she countered.

"Ah, Joseph. I could make Elias every bit as comfortable aboard my ship as he is in his own bed. If you doubt it, perhaps you would care to join me for an evening in my cabin."

His words settled over her like a touch, and intimate places on her body flared suddenly to life.

"Such a tempting offer, Sir Noah. But I shall take your word for it. Anyhow, Elias's hypothetical comfort aboard a ship is irrelevant, as he has already declared himself uninterested in going anywhere." She did not want to see how deeply Elias's situation troubled Sir Noah. Did not want to remember the emotion in his voice when he had first clasped Elias's hand. "Country air and quiet will do him a world of good," she added.

"While his mind atrophies and he quietly goes insane. Or supplies himself with every kind of ribald entertainment available to a man with a large house in the country."

She thought of the way he had insisted on having that coffee, so smoothly that anyone would have imagined he *wanted* to open the bottle but feared the result. If not for Elias, perhaps he would have gladly indulged.

"But I would hazard a guess that your influence could change his mind about my Turkish shipyard," he said.

He thought she would try to change Elias's mind? She couldn't help it—she laughed. "My goodness, Sir Noah, you *have* spent too much time away from civilization. I shall see that the necessary papers are delivered to you as soon as possible. Of course, it will take time to compile everything in a manner that promotes ease of viewing."

"Oh, I would hate for you to go to any trouble, Joseph. I'm sure I can decipher the papers myself. I propose we begin with the account books. Those shouldn't require any preparation on your part. Shall we say this afternoon?"

"I'm afraid that won't be possible. I must take my nieces visiting this afternoon."

"This evening, then."

"This evening I must return to see Elias, and then I am to accompany my nieces to a private musical entertainment. Quite frankly, Sir Noah, I can't imagine I shall have time to produce any records before next week. I must return home to see to my nieces—*do* have a lovely afternoon."

IF SIR NOAH thought she was simply going to hand over all of the shipyard business and allow him to use it to his own advantage, he was very wrong. Elias *needed* that shipyard. What little work he still did was the only thing preventing him from sinking into complete oblivion.

He would find interest in it again once he was away from the baser distractions of London.

"Do forgive my tardiness, dears," she said, sweeping into the upstairs drawing room having just arrived home. At the writing table by the window, Pauline flipped her sketchbook shut and turned abruptly in her chair. "My visit with Mr. Woodbridge took longer than expected. I must change into a different gown, and then I shall be ready for our afternoon."

"Do you think we shall see Captain Ryson, Auntie Jo?" Lettie asked, sitting in a chair with Bentley on her lap. "And do you think Papa would approve of him?"

Pauline pushed at her spectacles and peered over her shoulder.

"Darling, everyone approves of Captain Ryson," Josephine said. And it seemed he was developing a keen interest in Lettie. Hope for a quick understanding welled up from a deep place that wanted desperately to fulfill her promise to Charlotte, to prove to her sister that there was no more reason to worry. She was no longer the young, reckless Josephine who listened to her heart instead of to reason. She would use her station to see that the girls made excellent marriages, and Charlotte could put her mind at ease. If Lettie became engaged to Captain Ryson, there would just be the matter of Pauline.

Josephine looked at Pauline now, and her heart squeezed. She might have been the elder, but she wasn't ready for marriage. Josephine knew it, Charlotte knew it—the only one who refused to consider the obvious was Charlotte's husband. For heaven's sake, at eighteen Pauline looked twelve. Small bones, delicate features, huge childlike eyes… With her auburn hair swept up and her intricately embroidered sacque gown, she looked more doll than woman.

Josephine rubbed her temple against a small, throbbing headache.

Lettie set Bentley aside and stood gracefully. "Aunt Josephine, are you feeling quite well?"

"Just a small headache. Nothing a cup of tea won't soon banish."

"Don't fret about us," Lettie said, touching Josephine's hand. Her dark hair and eyes were exactly like Charlotte's—if her somewhat flighty personality was not. "We have plenty to occupy ourselves, *don't* we, Pauline?" She turned her head and pointedly arched a brow at her sister.

"Indeed." Pauline put a small drip of sarcasm into her timid voice. "I would be perfectly amenable to staying indoors this afternoon."

"No doubt you would, so that you may continue drawing your ships." Lettie turned back to Josephine. "Mother doesn't like her to draw ships. She says they represent a coarse and wild existence that should not occupy a young lady's imagination."

A bark of male laughter came from the doorway. "A true representation indeed!"

Josephine turned abruptly, just as Edgar announced their visitor and Bentley jumped off the chair and ran to the doorway in a frenzy of wagging and wiggling.

"Sir Noah Rutledge, your ladyship," Edgar said.

Sir Noah picked up Bentley and strode into the drawing room as if it was a ship and he was its master, showing off his coarse and wild manners by appearing not half an hour since she'd left him with Elias. What the devil did he think he was doing?

"Sir Noah," Josephine managed to say calmly. "What a happy surprise."

"How gratifying that you think so." His blue eyes sparkled with calculations that told her this visit was part of some kind of strategy. He rubbed Bentley's neck and looked at Pauline with interest. "Someone is dreaming of the sea?" He spoke as if they'd all been closely acquainted for a lifetime.

"These are my nieces, Miss Pauline Eckert and Miss Leticia Eckert." Lettie dipped a graceful curtsy. Pauline pushed herself out of her chair and managed a small bob.

"Pauline is forever drawing ships and turbulent seas and pirate coves," Lettie informed him. "Other young women draw flowers and fruit. Pauline draws cannonballs and barrels of rum."

"Vastly more interesting subjects," Sir Noah agreed.

Pauline—quiet, sensible Pauline—moved her arm over her sketchbook as though it contained nudes. "I draw flowers and fruit," she protested.

"Passiflora and coconuts," Lettie scoffed. "I daresay she came to London with the singular hope of hearing Auntie Josephine tell stories about Corsair Kate."

"I did not."

"Corsair Kate." Sir Noah's brows edged upward. "I had no idea your ladyship kept such company." His mouth said *your ladyship,* but his eyes roamed over her with anything but respect, lingering near the base of her throat.

"Katherine Kinloch was a childhood friend," Josephine explained evenly. "I haven't seen her since we were girls—" since before Katherine's ship was tragically captured by Barbary pirates en route to Gibraltar "—so I have no stories to tell, as Lettie well knows." She gave Lettie a scolding look. "Now. Do forgive us, Sir Noah, but we are expected elsewhere within the hour."

"I'm nothing if not forgiving," he said, handing

Bentley into Lettie's waiting arms and following Josephine out.

Outside the room, she faced him. "I'm sure I remember telling you I could not possibly have any papers ready this quickly," she said evenly.

"Oh, certainly not." His tone said he didn't expect her to ever have them ready. "I thought perhaps, since you plan to be out for the afternoon, I might be permitted to view some of the shipyard records while you're away. Since you won't be working on them, it seemed the perfect time."

"They're in a terrible state of disorganization, I'm afraid. It would avail you nothing to see them now."

"Wouldn't it."

"But I will let you know the moment I've been able to put something in order."

"I'm sure you will. In the meantime, I would be just as happy to merely *discuss* the situation with the shipyard."

"As would I, and I certainly would make the time to discuss it with you now, except that my nieces are waiting, and I am not dressed for visiting. So I'm afraid our discussion will have to wait."

"On the contrary." He smiled wickedly. "I'm happy to discuss it while you prepare for your afternoon."

Irritation reared up, but she laughed. "Sir Noah, I am not one of those ladies who make a habit of inviting men into her dressing room. You may see yourself out."

"Very well. Perhaps another time."

Josephine turned her back and went to her dressing room, where Mary already had her afternoon gown set out. She was nearly down to her shift and stays when Mary let out a small cry. "Your ladyship!"

Josephine turned to find Sir Noah lounging in the doorway, watching her. "Have I done something out of turn? Do forgive me. There are so many rules of behavior in London that I've forgotten over the years."

The devil he had. But if he thought she was going to scream and cower, he was destined for disappointment. "Please continue, Mary."

After a moment's hesitation Mary unpinned the right side of Josephine's stomacher. "What information about the shipyard do you find such a pressing need to discover, Sir Noah?"

More pins, and Mary lifted the stomacher away.

Sir Noah's eyes roamed over Josephine's shift and stays. "I suppose we could start with the number of ships currently under contract," he suggested.

"Seventeen."

"*Seventeen.* I saw only four in the shipyard yesterday."

Off came the morning's jupe, billowing over her shoulders and head before Mary whisked it away and left her in petticoats. "Shipbuilding is a robust business—or were you not aware of that when you arrived at the idea to start your own shipyard?"

He smiled a little. "Truth be told, I wasn't aware of much. Bit foxed at the time, I'm afraid." He rubbed his chin, and her eye followed the Ottoman design tattooed on the back of his hand.

"Do you always develop ideas for grand business ventures when you're intoxicated, Sir Noah?"

"Mmm," he said noncommittally. Those blue eyes wandered over her lazily while Mary cinched a new petticoat. "Sometimes I develop other ideas."

A sensation like a warm wind feathered her skin.

"But this *particular* time," she pressed, ignoring all that, "you decided that your life would not be complete until you'd uprooted your elderly cousin and built a ship-yard of your own."

His eyes flew sharply to hers, but as usual, he smiled. "The flight of fancy of a pair of drunken sailors," he said. "Turned out not to seem so fanciful by the light of day."

"You have a partner in this undertaking?"

"Not unless Elias changes his mind."

"You said *pair* of sailors."

"A friend." Sir Noah pushed away from the doorjamb and idly crossed the dressing room, pausing to study a statuette while Mary briskly added the afternoon's jupe and pinned on a gray stomacher with blue lace.

"One who apparently did not find the idea quite so unfanciful," she said.

"My friend is dead." He walked to the connecting door and looked into her bedchamber.

"I'm sorry." She watched him cast his eye about her bedchamber—the walls, the furnishings.

The bed.

Something captured his attention and he took a few steps into the room where he had absolutely no right and no business being, to look at—devil *take* it—the painting of Gibraltar over her fireplace.

Already her mind raced for an explanation, reached for a cool tone that would betray nothing of what the painting meant to her.

"This is quite a magnificent rendition of the Rock at sunset," he called.

Sunset, not sunrise—he knew it that intimately, her beloved Rock.

Mary finished pinning the robe into place and finally—*finally*—Josephine was dressed for the afternoon. "Please tell Lettie and Pauline that I shall be with them shortly," Josephine said to Mary. And then to Sir Noah, "When I saw how the colors in the painting matched the room, there was no question I had to have it." He did not need to know that the painting had come first and the room decor second.

He emerged from her bedchamber, and she finally drew breath. "And here I thought perhaps you had a secret fondness for the Mediterranean," he said.

She wanted to ask if he'd been ashore at Gibraltar recently, and if it had changed, and what he thought of the Rock when it was shrouded in mist.

Instead, she laughed. "The Mediterranean is *your* province, Sir Noah."

He stopped in front of her. "And London is yours." He fingered a lock of hair falling at her neck The corners of his blue eyes creased with amusement. "Joseph."

CHAPTER SIX

"YOU WANT TO TURN the screws on Lady *Mareck?*" In the crowded coffeehouse, Nicholas Warre leaned back casually in his chair, shook his head and laughed. "Let me put this in terms you'll understand, Rutledge. You're firing a blunderbuss at a twenty-gun brigadoon."

It was not what Noah wanted to hear, but he smiled. "Perhaps I ought to consider a full broadside."

Nick only shook his head. "I know a dozen men who've been hoping to give her a full broadside for years." The Earl of Croston's youngest son had the kind of perfect face that would have ladies trampling each other to attract his attention, but the dark circles beneath his piercing green eyes were something new. "She'll turn a man's proposition over her knee and give it a good thumping, and he'll walk away feeling as if he's been given a macaroon and a pat on the head." The corner of Nick's mouth curved. "She's impenetrable."

"Is she, now?" Noah laughed, even as his hand tightened around his coffee. He remembered how she'd looked, standing there in nothing but her underclothes. Watching her maid undress her had turned the screws on *him.* It was easy to imagine what she would look like with all of it stripped away—panniers, stays, shift, all of it.

And not too big a leap to imagine spreading her

across that perfectly furnished bed, proving just how penetrable she really was.

God. He imagined how outraged she must have been when he'd followed her into her rooms, and smiled.

"Certainly she and Woodbridge are close," Nick said, "even if their only relation was through Mareck. But she can't have much influence over his business decisions."

"This is about more than just business," Noah replied. "And my impression is that her influence over him runs deep." He thought of the way she'd touched Elias, the way Elias's eyes had warmed when he'd looked at her even as he complained about everything under the sun.

"I wouldn't doubt she resents the hell out of you over this shipyard business," Nick said, "though who's to say what stirs inside that pretty head." Pretty? Lady Mareck had to be one of the most stunning women in London. "Why not join Woodbridge here in London? No, never mind—anyone can see you've practically become a Moor yourself." Only Nick could say that in a way that made it sound like a compliment. "I doubt Lady Mareck shares your affinity for the Mediterranean. Could be part of the trouble you're running up against. Spent a year or two in Gibraltar, from what I understand—"

"Gibraltar."

"Yes, and I doubt she remembers it with much fondness. Trapped in some godforsaken outpost while other girls her age were preparing for their first Season."

"When?"

"Just before the war, I believe. Her father was lieutenant-general with the engineers there."

His mind did the math, came up with a year. Lady

Mareck. *Josephine*. Gibraltar. An old story of Ahmet's whispered through his mind, suggesting an impossible connection.

He thought of that painting in her bedchamber. In every other respect, Lady Mareck's private rooms were a perfect reflection of the lady herself. Elegant. Fashionable. Luxurious yet restrained. But then there was that painting. The Rock of Gibraltar. It took up practically the entire space above her fireplace. Dominated the room. It would be the first thing she saw when she awoke in the morning and the last thing she saw before closing her eyes to sleep—and the thing she would look at while doing anything else that might happen in that bed... But that was a dangerous line of thinking.

"And since we're on the subject of the Mediterranean," Nick added, "what can you tell me about Katherine Kinloch that I haven't already read in the papers?"

"I suppose that depends on what you've read. I haven't met her, if that's what you mean, though a friend of mind did once." Ahmet's wistful, grinning face exploded into his memory.

"Is she a pirate?" Nick asked.

"Not in the traditional sense."

"Explain the atraditional sense."

"I would describe Katherine Kinloch as a merchant trader with a penchant for making prizes of vessels of questionable activity," Noah told him.

But it wasn't Katherine Kinloch that Ahmet had usually spoken of. It was a young woman he'd met on a voyage to England.

Her family passed the voyage below, sick as dogs. But my sweet little Josephine, she loved the waves.

Lady Mareck—Josephine—had lived in Gibraltar at exactly the right time.

It didn't necessarily mean anything. There could have been any number of young English girls of military families with fathers stationed in Gibraltar. Josephine wasn't such an uncommon name.

"What do you want with Katherine Kinloch?" he asked absently.

Nick's lips tightened grimly. "Every bloody thing she's got." Nick began talking about a bill of attainder he was sponsoring in the House of Lords, but Noah was hearing Ahmet's drunken reverie, telling the tale of the young lover he would never forget—an English girl on a ship bound from Gibraltar to London, on which Ahmet had merely been a lineman. It was surprising that Ahmet could remember a lover at all, he'd taken so many. But this one, this young Josephine, had been special.

It just wasn't possible that Lady Mareck could be the Josephine of Ahmet's reveries.

Was it?

THAT NIGHT AT the Bylar musicale, it became clear that as long as Sir Noah was in London, there would be no escaping him. There he was, talking with Lord Bylar himself, casting Josephine a knowing glance that made it clear he was remembering that afternoon.

Oh, Sir Noah. After inviting yourself into my bed-chamber, you can hardly imagine I could be moved by your presence at a musicale.

No. The sudden tension in her spine was entirely due to the fact that Pauline was conversing with Mr. Crumley, and Josephine's complete inability to determine whether the man had sparked even the slightest bit of Pauline's interest.

It had nothing to do with the memory of Sir Noah's eyes roaming over her half-clad body, or the fact that it was impossible not to be aware of him at every moment. She knew exactly where he was, exactly when he was looking at her and when he wasn't.

Already the company had begun to be seated. Josephine moved toward Pauline, intending to help things along in any way possible, but Sir Noah intercepted her before she'd gone ten steps.

Her fists curled. She made a studied effort to relax them.

Sir Noah's eyes creased with amusement, as though he could read her every thought and was enjoying himself tremendously at her expense. "Have you consulted a doctor about your nervous condition?" he murmured. "You seem a bit tense."

"As a matter of fact, I have. He recommended solitude."

"Then by all means, let us seek it out."

"The music is about to begin, Sir Noah." A quick glance told her Lettie and Captain Ryson were already comfortably seated together, and Pauline—heaven be praised—was seating herself next to Mr. Crumley.

"Then let us be seated. Do, allow me." He showed her to a seat near the back of the artfully arranged chairs, where few eyes would watch them during the performance. She started to object, but the other seats that caught her eye were suddenly filled.

She arranged herself on the chair Sir Noah found for her. He took the liberty of pulling the adjacent chair a little closer to hers before seating himself.

"I find it difficult to believe," he said under his breath, "that there isn't a soul in London who has suspected your double life."

"By the time you leave, will there be a soul who isn't fully informed?"

"I have no desire to disrupt your life the way you have disrupted mine, Lady Mareck."

"Then by all means, do let me know if there is any way I can assist with reprovisioning your ship for the return south."

His eyes had a way of lingering where they didn't belong—on her lips, the base of her throat, the tops of her breasts.

The music began and conversations quieted.

Josephine fixed her attention on the quartet. Sir Noah's arm rested close enough to touch her skirts at the slightest motion. From the corner of her eye she saw him flex his right hand. His fingers were long. Thick.

She inhaled deeply. Silently.

Exhaled slowly.

A tiny itch irritated her right shoulder.

Ignore it.

The itch grew. She lifted her left hand and rubbed her fingers over it. Saw Sir Noah turn his head to watch. She didn't need to look to know his gaze had shifted to her breasts.

Her skin flushed, and she tried to remain perfectly still. Inside her stays, the tips of her breasts grew firm.

She returned her hand to her lap. Realized she hadn't drawn breath in half a minute.

Sir Noah shifted in his seat. His knee nudged her skirts. It was a strong, solid knee, joining a muscular limb made steady by years of fighting for balance atop the waves. His stockings hugged every contour, disappearing inside large, buckled shoes.

One of Honoria's favorite proverbs about the size of a man's feet lodged itself in her thoughts.

Suddenly, Sir Noah leaned close—so close she could feel his breath against her ear when he spoke. "Truth be known, they're bloody uncomfortable," he murmured.

She frowned and slanted her eyes toward him.

"My shoes." He extended his leg a little.

Devil take the man.

She fixed her attention firmly on the cellist. From the corner of her eye, she saw Sir Noah smile.

The quartet transitioned from a lilting, rhythmic piece to a slow and stately one, then picked up the tempo once more. Quiet conversations whispered here and there among the audience. It didn't take long for Sir Noah to murmur in her ear again.

"When we were discussing your painting, you failed to mention you actually *lived* in Gibraltar."

Every nerve went on alert. "That is hardly remarkable."

"Some might argue that point." And a few moments later, "Being a girl on the verge of womanhood, no doubt you begged every day to return to London." His whisper feathered her jaw just below her ear, and she shivered.

"Yes. Every day."

"Not many interesting gentlemen in such a coarse and ugly garrison."

"Gibraltar is not—" *Coarse and ugly.* "Few indeed."

In her mind she saw Gibraltar—colorful baskets of flowers adorning tile-roofed houses, the sun sparkling on the sea, groups of children playing on the beach.

Sails unfurling on ships leaving the harbor for exotic destinations farther east.

Her heart squeezed. Hard. So hard it constricted her lungs.

"Officers, merchants," Sir Noah mused under his breath. "Perhaps a wealthy Spaniard or two."

"Please, Sir Noah. I would like to enjoy the entertainment."

"By all means." But a few moments later... "No interesting naval officers on the return to London? Or perhaps you were too struck by *mal de mer* to notice."

"We traveled by merchant ship." She looked directly at him to make her next point more clear. "Sir Noah, the music."

He smiled. "Of course."

He did not disturb her again.

WHATEVER HAD CAUSED Sir Noah's sudden interest in her time at Gibraltar, it could not continue.

At the card table during her weekly game at Annabelle's, Josephine divided her attention between her annoying hand of cards and the even more annoying fact of Sir Noah's busybody tendencies.

Why should he care whether she'd ever lived in Gibraltar? Or even *been* there? Let alone whether she'd found any matrimonial prospects—either there *or* on the return voyage to England.

Someone had told him about her father's post in Gibraltar. Elias? No. He knew how cautiously she guarded that time of her life. Which meant Sir Noah had been talking about her to others.

The idea set a small nerve aflutter in her belly, which she ignored as she stared at her hand of cards.

And now, armed with what he imagined was special knowledge of her, he was toying with her. Trying to keep her perturbed, as if that could possibly gain him anything but her displeasure.

And she reacted to him like butter on warm bread.

It was unacceptable.

He was only a man—just another of Elias's business acquaintances, albeit a much closer one, given that he was Elias's heir. But still, only a man. Who happened to reside in the Mediterranean. On a ship.

She selected a card from her hand.

A *man*. Not a ship, or the sea or a small outpost at the gates to an exotic world. There was no reason to react to him as though he embodied all of those things.

"I've heard he keeps monkeys loose on his ship," Annabelle reported with a wicked light in her eye.

Oh, for heaven's sake. Was there no refuge to be had from Sir Noah anywhere in London?

She bit her tongue to keep from pointing out how ridiculous and impractical loose monkeys would be. It would never do to be seen as defending him—especially during Thursday afternoon whist, from whence Annabelle, Ophelia and Honoria could carry all manner of speculation at lightning speed into the world.

"Monkey *skins* is what I've heard," Ophelia said, sipping her tea. A painted-on mole sat delicately above one corner of her curved lips. "I'm told he serves refreshments from their shriveled hands."

"Disgusting!" Annabelle declared. "What a dreadful rumor."

Josephine tried for a change of subject. "I saw Lady Abbingale's new gown last night. It was everything everyone said it would be. Such lovely lacework on the stomacher."

But that hadn't been the Bylar musicale's main distraction.

"I do hope Sir Noah decides to host something," Honoria said, as if Josephine hadn't mentioned Lady Abbingale at all. "He is *such* a fascination. I daresay he could become the catch of the Season. Do you not agree, Josephine?"

She gave a laugh that came out a little too aghast. "I doubt the men of London will be forming a queue to send their daughters off with him to live among the Ottomans. But as for anyone else, there's certainly no accounting for the vagaries of opinion."

"So true," Ophelia said. "Do you remember last year, when half of London was chasing after Curry? Good heavens. I don't know when I've ever seen such a pasty complexion."

Annabelle made a noise. "I seem to recall you being one of those attempting to *curry* favor—or favor Curry, rather."

"This is outrageous. Josephine, tell her to stop."

"It isn't kind to air a person's past failings, Annabelle," Josephine scolded.

"Oh!" Ophelia slapped a card onto the table. "Outrageous."

"Do you suppose Sir Noah dresses in Moorish clothes when he's not in London?" Annabelle asked. Her eyes swept down and she plucked a card from her hand. "No doubt he speaks the language, as well."

No, there was to be no reprieve. As if Sir Noah himself wasn't vexing enough, he'd attracted the interest of every woman in London practically overnight.

She played a card. Every woman except her, of course.

"If he spends his time among the Moors," Josephine said reasonably, "no doubt he does speak the language and dress the part. He could hardly get along otherwise."

"It just makes him so...*fascinating,*" Annabelle insisted. "What do you think it could mean for his performance in bed?"

"I daresay a Moor makes love the same as any other man," Ophelia scoffed. "Clumsily and without much to recommend."

"Oh, I do hope not." Honoria laughed. "How inconceivably disappointing that would be."

Vivid images of stolen moments from years ago came alive—moments aboard the ship from Gibraltar. Whispered words in that foreign, Moorish tongue. Sweet, lingering kisses that were anything but clumsy.

"If Philomena were here," Honoria said, "I have no doubt she could tell us. Oh, I do miss her. And I am nearly blind with envy. Imagine, being rescued by Katherine Kinloch and then joining her pirate crew."

"*Merchant* crew," Josephine corrected.

"Yes, well, be that as it may," Annabelle complained, "it doesn't change the fact that Philomena has *all* the excitement."

"How she does love to take things to the extreme." Ophelia sighed.

"But we've been blessed with a glimmer of excitement, too—haven't we, Josephine?" Honoria's too innocent green eyes turned in Josephine's direction. "What do *you* think? Would making love with Sir Noah be the same as taking any other man to bed?"

"Not if he's a eunuch." The words shot off Josephine's tongue, and Ophelia nearly spewed her tea.

"La, Josephine— A eunuch!" Honoria's eyes went wide.

Josephine wished the words back with a vengeance. "It's common enough in Moorish countries, is it not? But I can't imagine *that* rumor is true."

"A eunuch," Annabelle said thoughtfully, sipping her tea. She set her cup down and slid her pondering gaze to Honoria. "Only imagine what a creative lover he would have to be."

The fact that Josephine found the idea even *remotely* arousing only infuriated her more. "I doubt a eunuch has the desire to be anyone's lover," she said, even as a deep, intimate nerve pulsed to life. "Creative or otherwise."

"Hmm," Honoria said doubtfully. "He seems excessively virile for someone whose masculinity has been compromised."

"There certainly didn't *seem* to be anything missing," Ophelia said.

Honoria raised a curious brow. "Is that based on careful observation?"

Josephine selected a card and set it down. "I can only imagine that if I were in that condition, I would make an effort to…*augment* my appearance. To avoid anyone remarking anything amiss, naturally." She glanced at Ophelia. "Or missing, I should say."

"Josephine." Ophelia set down her cards and fanned herself vigorously, while Honoria and Annabelle laughed.

"La, Josephine." Honoria laughed. "You've given the subject a good deal of thought, haven't you?"

CHAPTER SEVEN

SHE KNEW BETTER than to give a man like Sir Noah a good deal of thought.

The next morning Josephine could hardly keep her eyes open at breakfast, even though she'd slept a few minutes longer than she should have. If it weren't for the girls, she would have taken breakfast in her room. It had been a long night of reading correspondence and drafting responses, making lists of urgent matters to discuss with Elias—if he would consent to discuss any matters at all—and generally doing anything but sleep.

Something needed to change. She could not sustain this for the entire Season. Not and do what she needed to for the girls.

The girls were her first priority. As a maid poured more coffee, Josephine decided it was finally time to seek a replacement for Joseph Bentley. It wouldn't be easy. It would have to be someone trustworthy, discreet.

Charlotte would be mortified if she ever learned Josephine had been transacting business for Elias, and under a male pseudonym. Josephine should be mortified herself. *Would* be, of course, if the need to help Elias weren't so urgent. She thought of Charlotte—always a little unwell, always a little afraid, always the one to cling to Mother. All the way home from Gibraltar, Charlotte had worried how they would be received, while Josephine had feared she would never see the Mediterranean again.

Josephine remembered how Charlotte had withdrawn in fear after Josephine's mistake with Matthew and quickly thrown together marriage. The invitations Josephine had sent to Charlotte's family after the wedding, and the always kindly worded refusals. Until the girls had come of age, and Josephine had begun to receive worried letters from Charlotte, full of fears about the girls' futures.

She'd come so close to ruining Charlotte's life with her carelessness all those years ago. She would not allow her unusual work for Elias to put her nieces at risk.

Nor your feelings for Sir Noah.

"Captain Ryson's aunt is coming to London," Lettie was saying. "He says he can't wait to introduce me. She's like a mother to him, you know. I think it's a good sign. Do you not agree, Auntie Josephine?"

"A very good sign," Josephine said, then she looked at Pauline optimistically. "You seemed to be enjoying Mr. Crumley's company last night."

"I daresay it was the other way around," Pauline said, stirring sugar into her tea.

"I daresay it was," Lettie said, "since Pauline isn't interested in Mr. Crumley at all."

It was hardly news, but the confirmation was disheartening. "I can't imagine why. Mr. Crumley is very amiable. I suggest you talk with Lady Ramsey about him this afternoon. She is very well acquainted with the family and is no doubt privy to any number if interesting tidbits about him." The girls would be visiting with Honoria that afternoon while Josephine made a trip to view Mays Abbey and determine its suitability for Elias.

It had been a foolish mistake to mention her plans to Elias, who had in turn mentioned them to Sir Noah, who promptly suggested that he impose his company for the outing. He would arrive within the hour.

"I doubt there *are* any interesting tidbits about Mr. Crumley," Pauline said.

"There are interesting things to know about everyone, dearest, if one only takes the time to listen."

Just then, Edgar came in. "Forgive me, your ladyship. The painting has been taken to the attic, but there are three paintings of the countryside in storage and we cannot determine which one you wanted."

I want you to put the original back. "The one I'm thinking of has a flock of sheep."

"There are two that fit that description, your ladyship. One has a cottage in the background."

"Yes, that one. Thank you."

It served nothing to be reminded of Gibraltar at all hours—nothing except to fuel her imagination with every kind of impractical, nonsensical daydream. She was not returning to Gibraltar. What did she imagine she would possibly do there if she did? She wouldn't know a soul. Her title would give her entrée, but to what? A society of military up-and-comers? She would hardly fit into any of the other communities there.

Damn Gibraltar, anyway. She'd tormented herself with those memories long enough.

"You shouldn't have that one over your fireplace taken down, Auntie Josephine," Pauline said with dismay. "I love that painting."

"Of course you do," Lettie told her. "It has ships in it. And speaking of ships, you may be interested to know,

Auntie, that Pauline may be deaf to Mr. Crumley's merits, but she *does* have her eye on *some*one."

"I do *not* have my eye on *any*one."

Lettie made a noise. "You do, and I know who it is."

Pauline's cheeks were red and her gaze was fixed on her plate—all the hallmarks of a girl with a *tendresse* for a man. "Lettie," Josephine admonished gently, "it isn't kind to force secrets if Pauline isn't ready." But if not Mr. Crumley, then who? Josephine bit back the urge to prod her for information.

"I do hope Captain Ryson will be there this evening," Lettie said. "Oh, Auntie Josephine, he is absolutely the handsomest man I've ever seen." She glanced at Pauline. "Infinitely more handsome than a certain *other* someone."

"Lettie, hush!" Pauline stabbed a piece of egg that promptly slipped back to the plate.

"Pauline, you could catch the attention of any number of men if you wanted to," Lettie pushed on. "But I daresay you'll turn a blind eye to them all in favor of a *certain newcomer,* and you know as well as I that Mother won't be pleased."

Josephine looked at Pauline. "Newcomer."

"You speak beyond your knowledge, Lettie," Pauline said, but her cheeks pinkened.

"I am only trying to help. Auntie's acquaintance with him ought to put you at an advantage, don't you think?"

And suddenly Josephine knew exactly who this *certain newcomer* was: Sir Noah.

Good God—Josephine looked at Pauline and knew the worst was true. Pauline fancied herself in love with Sir Noah.

"Remarkable," the certain newcomer said sarcastically a few hours later as they emerged from the carriage at Mays Abbey, despite Josephine's insistence that she hadn't required his company in the first place.

They stood in the drive before a rectangular gray-stone house with neat rows of small windows marching across three levels. Misshapen hulks of unattended shrubbery blocked some of the windows on the ground level. She could see some buildings toward the back—a stables and an outbuilding. The closest stand of trees was some distance away, leaving the house itself jutting from the ground like an ancient stone rising from a meadow.

"An open mind is a testament to an enlightened soul, Sir Noah."

He laughed. "If enlightened souls live in places like this, a lowly estate will do for me."

A light drizzle began to fall, and they hurried for the door. "I'm told a man in the village has been hired to take care of the place until it's sold," Josephine told Sir Noah as they went inside. There were fully furnished rooms to the right and left of the entrance hall. Some pieces of furniture were draped with sheets. Some weren't. A light dust covered everything.

"The furnishings will come with the house," she added, watching him lift the edge of a sheet to peer at the table beneath.

"Debtors?"

"So I'm told."

Josephine looked into a salon, a dining room, a library only half stocked with books. Next she climbed the stairs, acutely aware of him a few steps behind, even more aware that except for the coachmen outside, they were alone. A step creaked beneath her feet, then his.

Sir Noah. No matter how hard she tried, her senses filled with him.

Apparently she and Pauline had more in common than their looks—and *that* was a disaster in the making. Of course Mr. Crumley appeared uninteresting to Pauline. Every man would when compared with Sir Noah. And if Sir Noah was the kind of man who caught Pauline's interest, it would be impossible for Josephine to fulfill her promise to Charlotte.

Had there been some hint that Pauline was developing an interest in him? Josephine should at least have noticed something.

Upstairs, she peered into one bedchamber after the next.

"Plenty of accommodations for the ladies," Sir Noah remarked. "Or guests, rather. I do believe I meant to say guests." A little smile played at the corner of his lips.

It was only too easy to imagine what Charlotte would think if she knew this man had caught her daughter's interest. Josephine saw her sister's ever-worried face in her mind. Imagined Charlotte's delicate hands wringing the way they always did, as if worry was her natural state.

But she'd promised Charlotte no ill would come of the girls' visit, that Charlotte's instincts were right to let Josephine introduce them into society. And that was exactly the way it would be.

"Elias will not be keeping any ladies here," she said firmly, though she wasn't entirely sure how she would stop him if he decided to try.

They finally entered what was clearly the master

bedroom. A great bed sat in one corner, an armoire stood against the wall, and a collection of other furnishings dotted the rest of the room: bedside table, writing desk, several chairs, sooty fireplace screen decorated with a needlework foxhound scene.

She imagined Elias here, spending too much time in that bed, confining himself to these rooms because there was little else to do.

"It will require some work," she said, "but I think it could be made very comfortable." She went to the bed and fingered the horrid brown draperies. They would need to be changed.

"No doubt there will be a good deal of activity taking place in this bed," Sir Noah said, coming up behind her. "I could be persuaded, as an act of kindness and generosity, to help you test it for comfort. Prove your theory, so to speak."

His words feathered her skin, making her suddenly much too aware of her own body. Of *his* body, standing right behind her. "If only the art of persuasion were among my skills," she said and went to look in the dressing room.

His laughter as he followed was a complete contrast to the room's gloomy sobriety. "I assure you, I could be persuaded with no skill whatsoever."

The rich tone of his voice made it impossible not to imagine herself in his arms on that bed, doing exactly what he was suggesting.

For a moment she could hardly breathe.

"It isn't kind to present one with such a powerful temptation, Sir Noah. Shame on you."

She forced her attention to the details of the room.

There were no sheets up here—only an abundance of solid, simple furnishings covered with a layer of dust.

"I can't believe you honestly think a place like this would do Elias good," he said.

"It certainly would. It needs a good cleaning, to be sure, but only see how peaceful it is."

A little gust of rain pattered the windows. She went to them to see the view. Sir Noah joined her, standing much too close.

There were no gardens at the back. Just the stables and a vast meadow. The grove of trees she'd spotted earlier stood off to the right. "Look," she said. "It has a folly." The faux ruins sat at the edge of the grove, a few columns lying as if they'd fallen millennia ago next to a small stone archway.

"Folly indeed," Sir Noah said.

"It adds a bit of interest."

"You can see very well there's nothing the least bit interesting about this place. If it's ruins you think he wants, let him come live at my villa. I unearthed a Roman temple while building the east wing. Columns aplenty—and real ones."

An image came to life in her mind: olive trees and broken ground like an open grave, with the bones of an ancient world jutting from dry soil.

Suddenly she wanted to hear about his villa almost more than she wanted to breathe.

"Improvements can be made," she said. "It won't take long."

"It will take longer than a voyage to Turkey, and to what end? This place is misery in a stone box. Mays Mausoleum."

She watched him stare out the window while dirty

beads of water slid endlessly down the glass. His face was set, but emotions churned inside—a muscle worked in his jaw, his throat moved when he swallowed, his chest rose and fell with deep breaths.

"Not everyone dislikes England as you do, Sir Noah."

"Not everyone has something to compare it to."

"And if they did, you imagine there would be a mass exodus to foreign lands?"

He smiled. "Only to warm and sunny ones."

She looked out the window at the gray, wet day. "The rain only makes the landscape more green," she said. "It's beautiful here." It was. It really was.

She couldn't afford to admit that her heart cried out for the same thing his did.

"Forgive me if I prefer a different sort of beauty," he said.

"And, naturally, you only do that which you prefer."

"If that were true, I would not be in England now."

The declaration condemned her, because neither would she.

"Perhaps. Although if you truly cared about Elias, the obvious way to show it would be to stay in London and run the shipyard here. But it's clear enough that you won't do that."

His expression hardened. "No, I won't."

"Why not?"

He turned on her suddenly. "Because I don't want to *be* here. I don't *belong* here. I want to be where the sun shines hot on my skin and the water is so clear and blue you can see every pebble on the sea floor as if looking through stained glass. *That* is my home," he said violently. "Not this."

"Then why are you here?"

"Why are *you* standing in this god-awful house even though you can see as well as I that it's miserable?" He stared down at her, eyes ablaze with churning emotions. For a moment his nonchalance slipped away and it was as if she could see directly into him—his hopes, his fears, his dreams. It was so easy to imagine what he described, and she wanted it as much as he did. Perhaps more.

But she understood responsibility.

Duty.

The safety that came with meeting others' expectations.

The only part of herself she ever dared give to the Mediterranean was the part she'd bestowed on Ahmet years ago, somewhere off the foggy coast of France, as they'd closed in on England and all that was left of the region she loved was the language on the tongues of the ship's crew.

"What I can see—" she managed, looking up at him even though the very fact of standing this close to him made her feel practically on fire "—is its potential."

Its potential to drive Elias to an early grave, she could almost hear him thinking.

"You question my motives, but you would do well to look in the glass on that point. Here—here's one that will do the job." And then he was touching her—pressing his hand against the small of her back and steering her to the dressing table. His touch was a shock, burning through layers of fabric as though she wore nothing at all. He pushed her in front of the looking glass, and she saw herself with him standing behind her, standing a head taller, observing her closely. "What do you see, Lady Mareck?"

The sight of herself standing so intimately with Sir Noah left her momentarily speechless.

"Shall I tell you what I see?" he pressed, holding her gaze in the glass.

If she moved, they would touch. If she walked away, he would win. She reached deep and found her voice. "There's no need for that, Sir Noah. You've already made it clear what you see—a bored lady amusing herself by dabbling in business."

"You forgot high-handed." Even in the dusty glass, he was so handsome she could spend a lifetime staring at him. "A woman whose experience ends at the edge of London, but who purports to know what's best for others." He filled every breath with a scent that spoke of ancient trade routes and warm desert nights.

"Some might frame my actions as helpful."

"Or haughty." He spoke so close that the rumble of his voice hummed against her ear.

"That covers *H*. Shall we move on to *I?*"

As if she were a spectator watching two other people, she stared as he raised his hand and traced a finger along the side of her neck. "Interfering," he said.

Her skin came alive with a trail of fire. She needed to step away—*now*—but her feet were planted to the floor.

"Oh, yes." Her voice was a strangled whisper, pushed from lungs that refused to work. "I pride myself on interfering."

"Impenetrable." His tone dropped. Roughened.

Her voice failed entirely. As she watched in the glass, he bent his head toward the curve where her neck met her shoulder. She felt his breath against her skin. Knew he was about to kiss her there, and that if he did, she would lean into him and be lost.

She forced herself to move away a hairbreadth before his lips met her skin.

"Sir Noah." She bumped into the dressing table but managed to move out of arm's reach. Her breath came too fast, and her skin felt much, much too alive. The spot he'd been aiming for on her neck keened with the need for his touch. "I shall not attempt to prove you wrong on that point."

"What a shame." He watched her with eyes that burned with desire.

She walked briskly to the door. "I've seen everything I need to. I shall return to the front and order the carriage around." In truth she hadn't seen nearly enough, but remaining alone in this house with Sir Noah a moment longer was out of the question. "Whatever my shortcomings, I have done nothing but act in service to Elias. Perhaps you should consider doing the same."

CHAPTER EIGHT

HE WAS LOSING his mind.

Whatever this was that drove him to provoke Lady Mareck, it was going to end with him going mad—and not because it wasn't working. No. Quite the opposite.

Yesterday, at Mays Abbey, he'd cracked her facade. He had seen it in her eyes. In the involuntary parting of her lips, the tension in her body when he'd touched her.

Touched her.

In that single moment, what had started as a powerful desire exploded into a raging need. He needed more—her skin laid bare, her breasts in his hands, her legs wrapped around his hips.

Except that wasn't what he needed at all. What he *needed* was to pique Elias's interest in the Turkish shipyard and snuff out Lady Mareck's resistance to the idea and be done with all this.

With *her*.

As if on cue, Trowe appeared in the doorway of Elias's sitting room and announced Lady Mareck—exactly as Noah had expected.

He wasn't going to let up now. Not even if it killed him.

"Ah, Josephine!" Elias said, gesturing to her from where he and Noah sat at the table by the window. The exclamation made him cough. "Come and see Noah's magnificent house."

Noah stood, watching her approach, and that need snaked through him. She walked beautifully, as if floating on air. But she wasn't an ethereal figment. She was real, flesh and blood, and yesterday he'd been playing with fire.

Ahmet's Josephine. It was all but certain.

It should have repulsed him. Instead, it inflamed his curiosity. It made him imagine a woman very different from the one presented by Lady Mareck. A reckless, passionate woman. A woman open to a world of unknowns—who might appreciate the sparkle of sunlight on the waves and the haunting call of prayer from a mosque.

A woman who existed only in his imagination.

"This must be the villa you mentioned," she said pleasantly, glancing over the large sheets spread across the table.

"It is." Her soft, flowery perfume floated around him as he offered her his chair.

"How lovely." She kissed Elias's cheek. "I'm so pleased to see you up and about. How are you feeling?"

"Old," he grumbled, and then, "Berwick! Have you brushed my new coat?"

"I have, sir," Berwick said, lingering in the side doorway.

Elias grunted, and Lady Mareck seated herself, glancing up at Noah. She met his eyes briefly, directly, giving no sign that she was thinking of yesterday at all.

But he was bloody well thinking of it. Had thought of it half the night, in fact, as he'd lain awake wanting a damned sight more than a soft touch on her neck. His eyes went to the curve of her shoulder—to that spot he'd nearly kissed. He very definitely wanted more than that. He wanted hours and hours of hard and fast, punctuating several long nights of slow and deep.

"The architect drew these while the house was being built," he told her, inhaling sharply, and took the chair opposite. "They've turned out to be an excellent likeness of the finished product."

"Never seen anything like it," Elias grunted.

"Yes, well… As soon as I saw the site, I knew it had…potential." He met Lady Mareck's eyes briefly across the table. "This is the main entrance." He pointed to the pair of ornately carved wooden doors he'd designed himself.

Elias coughed and drank some water. "Excellent craftsmanship."

Noah watched Lady Mareck survey the colored sketches of his sprawling, tile-roofed house with its stucco walls. The orange trees he'd insisted on everywhere there was space. The pomegranate shrubs and bright pink and orange flowering vines.

Oh, yes—his home was peaceful and comfortable and even beautiful. He looked at the drawing and wished suddenly, fiercely, that he could be there now, even though he hadn't visited for nearly a year before he set sail for England.

He worried suddenly whether the caretaker he'd hired was doing his job, and whether the trees and bushes might have died and the place gone to ruin.

"The window sashes have the same design as the doors," Lady Mareck commented.

His attention snapped from the drawing to her face.

They did, but it was a detail that wasn't immediately noticeable. "I decided to continue the theme."

"Is it olive wood?"

"Yes." He watched her more closely now.

"Excellent choice," Elias said. "Strong, durable. Heavy, but hard. The ancients used it for joint work on their ships."

"Lovely grain, as well," Lady Mareck said. "The doors must be stunning."

It took him a moment to realize there was no pretense in her voice. "They are, rather." He watched her across the table, daring her to look him in the eye and say she preferred Mays Abbey to this.

"There's a courtyard through here with a fountain where the four wings of the house are joined." He turned the first drawing aside and revealed the next. There was his courtyard like something come to life out of antiquity, dotted with statuary and great urns from which spilled exotic plants. "These are some of the columns I told you about," he told Lady Mareck. "The ones we unearthed during construction."

"You incorporated them into the house," she exclaimed, taking him by surprise.

He'd expected a reaction more along the lines of, *Mmm. Interesting.*

"The discs had come apart, but we were able to fit them back together and build the columns into this east wall. The stone wall was built from the rubble, and the old foundation has become part of the floor inside the great room." He turned the page to show her.

"Their floor has become yours."

"Yes."

His mind suddenly transported her there, and he saw

her sitting by his fountain draped in exotic, flowing silks instead of the stiff casements of London. For one heart-stopping moment he could see her laughing and free, completing his villa with something he never expected it would have.

No. Bloody *devil* no. He hadn't come to London seeking that kind of complication.

He took the conversation in a safer direction. "I had great plans to turn the north wing into a harem, but a stable of concubines sounds like a good deal more trouble than…" He gave Lady Mareck a calculated grin. "Well, I won't say *than it's worth.*"

"A harem!" Elias leaned forward, looking at the drawing more closely. "Berwick, pack my bags!" And then, reaching for his glass, "Apologies, Josephine. Good God, no need to look so alarmed. Noah was just having a bit of fun." He chuckled. "Certainly does know what a man wants to hear."

He didn't suppose Elias wanted to hear that a man's harem normally included, among others, his daughters, wives and even his mother. But there was no sense offering unsolicited facts if they didn't work to his advantage.

He leaned back in his chair and raised a brow at Lady Mareck across the table. "A harem," he mused. "It would require some *work—*" he paused to let her recall their conversation at Mays Abbey "—but I daresay it would make the guest quarters very…*comfortable.*"

She smiled, unmoved. "And here you allowed me to believe you disapproved of folly, Sir Noah."

"Oh, I don't know. I've been told it can be rather interesting." He glanced at Elias, found the man watching them a little too closely. "But for now, it is simply the guest wing." He reached to slide another drawing from the stack. "Here," he said to Elias, "let me show you."

He flipped through the drawings, yearning to see his home again more and more with each page. No, not only to see it. To *live* there. After it had been built, there had been little reason to move in. His life was at sea. He would have rattled around his giant villa alone.

But the more he spoke about it now, the more he began to imagine Elias there. To imagine finally, perhaps, calling the villa home.

And the more he glanced across the table, the more he wondered what it might be like to have a woman share that home with him.

Thoughts of Noah's enchanting villa haunted Josephine that evening when she took the girls to the theater, and the following day during morning and afternoon visits. The villa haunted her this evening at yet another ball with the girls, where Sir Noah—as usual—just happened to be.

And it was haunting her now, after the rest of the household had gone to bed and she sat alone in the library signing Joseph Bentley's name to a letter, an invoice, a bank draft.

It was too easy to imagine Sir Noah at home at his magnificent villa. To imagine *herself* there, dipping her fingertips into the fountain's cool water or sitting on one of the stone benches beneath an orange tree in the courtyard.

Or lying in his bed, feeling his languorous touch on her skin.

She shivered, remembering the way he'd touched her at Mays Abbey. The way he'd looked at her while

she'd studied those drawings. The way he'd spoken to
her tonight at the ball. Oh, they had shared the usual
conversation—"Lovely to see you again. Elias appears
in slightly improved spirits... I don't suppose I could
have a look at Joseph Bentley's papers tomorrow?"—
but the tone of his voice had communicated an entirely
different message.

*You do realize I was controlling myself at Mays
Abbey, don't you, Lady Mareck? And I am controlling
myself now. Do you see me staring at your lips? It's because I'm contemplating kissing you. Right now. Perhaps even right here, in front of everyone, because
propriety bores me.* She could practically hear him saying it.

He had proposed an outing to the shipyard tomorrow and requested her company, and she had started to
decline before deciding it might be a useful exercise.
They had discussed whether to try to pique Elias's interest in the outing, as well. And the whole time, Sir
Noah's eyes had burned with far more intimate ideas.

*I haven't forgotten that I watched you undress, Lady
Mareck. In fact, I remember it every time I see you. I'm
thinking of it right now.* Oh, yes. There was no doubt
he'd been thinking of it. *Can you tell I'm not satisfied?
I want to strip that gown away and see you entirely
nude. I want to put my hands on you and make love to
you, and I'd lay money that you would enjoy it, Lady
Mareck, because I've a sneaking suspicion you're not
what you seem to be.*

All that and more had been plainly readable in the
way his eyes had wandered over her body, in the little
half smile that played at the corners of his mouth, in

the way he'd stood closer than he should have while they'd spoken.

The control she'd held with an iron grip then was nowhere to be found now, while she sat alone in the darkened library in her nightgown and wrapper, thinking of him. Imagining what would happen if he *did* kiss her. Touch her.

Make love to her.

Good God.

She dipped her pen and scribbled a few furious words in a ledger, but it was no use. Sensations came alive everywhere. She wanted to feel his touch again. Breathe his scent. Make a reality out of all of it.

It was a desire that had to be conquered. She had far, far too much to lose to abandon herself with him now the way she'd naively done with Matthew all those years ago.

If you have an affair with Sir Noah, all of London will know it, she scolded herself, and dipped her pen once more.

Eyebrows will rise. People like Lady Orville will cut you in the street. She scratched a few figures in the book.

Was not once enough to teach you the isolation of scandal? It was enough. If she marred her carefully built reputation now, there wasn't a soul who would forget. And she might have been fortunate enough to have found an unexpected friend in Elias back then, when she'd been a young bride in a family that despised her, but she had so much more to lose now.

A thought whispered that nearly all of London was having affairs, and she was a widow, and taking a lover was practically de rigueur.

Oh, indeed—if she took a lover such as Lord What-ley or Camden or Osburton. But if she took Sir Noah Rutledge as a lover—

"Auntie Josephine?"

The soft words caught her by surprise and she stood abruptly, scooting from behind the desk. "Pauline. Is something the matter?"

"I didn't mean to startle you."

"Of course not." Her cheeks felt hot, as if Pauline could read her mind and knew what she'd been thinking.

"I couldn't sleep. Or, I confess, I was up reading. I've been reading old accounts of the late war in the Mediterranean."

"Have you?" And dreaming, no doubt, of Sir Noah's privateering exploits during that war.

Pauline gestured a little timidly to the chair opposite Josephine. "May I— Do you mind if I sit?"

She should suggest that they order tea and sit to-gether on the settee by the fireplace, but suddenly Josephine wanted the safety of the desk between them, as if somehow it could shield her wicked thoughts from being discovered by her innocent niece.

"Of course," she said. Already her mind raced for the perfect words, the exact right things to say that would steer Pauline in a different direction.

The direction of one Mr. Crumley, for example, who had begun to show a keen interest in Pauline.

Pauline seated herself and immediately looked at her hands. With her braid falling over her shoulder and her small, heart-shaped face set off by a froth of lace around the neckline of her nightgown, she reminded Josephine of herself so many years ago.

"Aunt Josephine, I don't know what to do. I read of

these exotic places and all their wonders, and I can see them in my mind as if I'm really there, and I want to be there so badly it's as if I'm being strangled. Lettie says I'm being ridiculous. But you don't think so, do you? You've *been* to exotic places."

Her description was so terribly accurate that for a moment Josephine could hardly breathe herself. "The lure of faraway lands can be very...bewitching," she allowed. "But surely there are other things that interest you just as much. Drawing, for example." As if a simple pastime could ever cure a lust for adventure.

But Pauline had to be cured. The alternative was unacceptable.

Josephine imagined herself explaining to Charlotte that she'd failed at finding a match for Pauline, or that Pauline fancied herself in love with Sir Noah Rutledge and refused all others. There would be no cries of outrage, no accusations. Only those little, fretful gears turning behind Charlotte's soft, brown eyes as she contemplated the worst.

Pauline wrung her hands. "The only reason I draw is to do something with all these imaginations in my head. Auntie Josephine—" Pauline scooted to the edge of her seat "—I was thinking, since you are acquainted with Katherine Kinloch, perhaps...perhaps you could write to her and ask if I might have a place aboard her ship. Lady India Sinclair is there," she rushed on, "so there must be *something* acceptable in it."

"There isn't." Good God. Pauline had thought of the one thing that was actually *worse* than a fancy for Sir Noah. "Your mother would break down in a nervous condition if she knew you were even thinking of it."

"I know." Pauline sighed and sat back, clearly not

surprised by Josephine's reaction. "Mother wants me to marry a quiet, dutiful man who will provide me a home and children and— I know I *should* want that. I *should.* But I don't think I could stand it. I want to marry someone like Sir Noah. He is *so* handsome. So exciting. Sometimes when I close my eyes I can practically see him aboard his ship, sailing amid the Greek isles with billowing sails above and pots from ancient shipwrecks beckoning from the clear water below."

Josephine could see it, too, and her heart ached.

"Life aboard a ship can be very confining," Josephine pointed out.

"Oh, but only think of the liberating waves and the porpoises and the endless sights to be seen!"

"And the worms in the flour and the water gone stale in the kegs."

"I wouldn't care about any of that." Pauline dropped her gaze to her lap and picked at a fingernail.

Josephine remembered how, when her family had returned from Gibraltar, the social Season had met her like a full-frontal assault of worries and musts and don'ts. Compared to Ahmet, all the men seemed feminine and pasty and boring. They'd buzzed around her like flies, and she'd hated all of them, cried tears at night that she could not have married Ahmet and spent her life at sea.

"I'm dreaming in the clouds anyhow, aren't I?" Pauline said. "Sir Noah—" For a moment she almost looked in pain. "He could have any woman he wanted. And I'm not stupid, Auntie Josephine. I'm hardly pretty enough to attract his attention."

"You're beautiful enough to attract any man's attention, Pauline."

"Do you really think so?"

"You mustn't doubt it for a minute. Only see how much you've drawn Mr. Crumley's interest. He is a very handsome young man, and very desirable."

Pauline looked at her as if she'd grown horns. "Mr. *Crumley* has never been on a ship, not even once in his entire life."

Josephine might have laughed, but Pauline's measure of a man was too alarming. "There are many other redeeming qualities to be found in a man," she said reasonably.

And yet it was so easy to be fooled, as she'd been that day at the assembly where she'd first seen Matthew. For the first time since leaving Gibraltar, something had stirred inside her—something very small, very tentative. There'd been something a little wild about him. He had a quick, dashing smile like Ahmet. He hadn't changed the subject when she'd spoken of Gibraltar. He'd *wanted* to hear about it—or so he'd said. He'd encouraged her to talk about her dreams, her secret desires.

She'd found out too late that he'd only been trying to seduce her, that he was clever enough to know the easiest way was to feign solidarity with her deepest longings.

Their secret tryst had quickly been exposed. Angry words and then money had been exchanged. There was the cold stripping away of her fantasy that she'd found a man in England who understood her. Grief that she'd given him what she'd given Ahmet and it was too late to take it back. And then the horrible, lonely months after the wedding but before Matthew's father had died and he'd inherited the Mareck title.

"The important thing is to find a *good* man," she said now, squeezing Pauline's hand. "One who will care for you the way he ought to."

Pauline's gaze slid to her lap. "Auntie Josephine...I know I was being fanciful about Katherine Kinloch's ship. But you are well acquainted with Sir Noah because of Mr. Woodbridge, and I truly was wondering... Do you think you could arrange for us to be...thrown together?"

"Oh, Pauline..." What could she possibly say to that? "Your mother would never approve Sir Noah."

"She would if you approved."

"Not even then." Because Charlotte had not forgotten that tragic misjudgment of years ago that had nearly cost them both their reputations. If Father hadn't been a friend of the elder Lord Mareck, things would have turned out very differently. Even now, if not for Josephine's status in society, Charlotte never would have entrusted the girls into Josephine's care in the first place. "And I don't think Sir Noah is looking for a wife," she added. "I daresay he is quite happy with his carefree life."

"But nobody is truly immune to cupid's arrow, are they?"

Heaven help her, Josephine hoped so—for her own sake. "You mustn't be carried away by romantic notions. Being struck by cupid's arrow doesn't always lead to marriage. Sometimes it leads to—"

"Ruination. Yes, I know. But Sir Noah is much too honorable to even think about ruining anyone. I know he is."

Josephine held her breath. Surely Pauline could see that Sir Noah was more than twice her age. Surely she could sense his potent virility, could feel a small frisson of fear that it might come unleashed, and that she would be ill-equipped to contend with it if it did.

"And as for Mother, Sir Noah is a knight, which makes him a good deal more impressive than Lettie's Captain Ryson, and he is wealthy. Neither Mother nor Father could possibly object."

"They could object to your living aboard a ship in the Mediterranean." She didn't dare mention Sir Noah's villa. Good God.

"If we married, certainly he would buy a proper house." Pauline blushed and looked at her lap, as if only realizing how forward she sounded.

"Pauline," Josephine said softly, "has Sir Noah given you any indication of his interest?"

"No. Except that he is very kind when he visits here."

"You wouldn't expect him to be rude when he visits, would you?"

"No." The disappointment in Pauline's voice made Josephine feel very cruel. But then Pauline looked up. "Aunt Josephine," she said with complete gravity, "what can I do to make Sir Noah notice me?"

CHAPTER NINE

THE SHIPYARD MAY not have been as private as Mays Abbey, but it could present as many opportunities, and Noah fully intended to take advantage of them. He contemplated his strategy now, standing in front of the windows in Lady Mareck's drawing room waiting for her to be ready for their planned outing, staring absently at the street below.

Letting his imagination wander up Lady Mareck's undoubtedly creamy thighs, to a passage that would lead to pure satisfaction.

It was a channel he fully intended to navigate. He would slice through her deceptively calm waters, skillfully use her strong currents to his advantage. And when her tempest came up, he would ride it out until the last ripple died, and he would glory in his triumph.

Like a notoriously treacherous sea, it was the challenge of her that kept him so enthralled. Once conquered, she would lose her mystery. He hoped.

And the sooner the better.

There was no real need for her to accompany him to the shipyard today. He could go alone, speak to the manager, tour the yard. He still hadn't had a look at those papers, but he could address that situation later. It would be the intelligent course of action. The wise thing to do. The safe thing.

But he was in no mood for anything safe, wise or intelligent. He wanted Lady Mareck lying prone on the desk in Elias's upstairs office with her skirts pushed past her hips and her legs spread wide, begging him to—

"Sir Noah?"

He spun abruptly from the window. "Miss Eckert." He offered her a hasty bow, careful to keep his hands clasped in front of him to hide his embarrassment, which—thank God—instantly began to subside.

"How do you do, Sir Noah?" Miss Pauline Eckert came into the room clutching a small frame.

"Very well. Thank you." Thank God, she couldn't read his mind. Could she? No. Of course not.

She was small, delicate, childlike, with Lady Mareck's auburn hair but none of the cool detachment that cloaked Lady Mareck's expression. He felt like a lecherous old goat.

"I have something for you," she said in a small voice. "Forgive me if I'm being too forward—" she came toward him now "—but I thought… Well, I thought you might like it, is all." Dark eyes and lashes swept downward, and a blush pinkened her cheeks as she held out the frame, and a hole opened up in Noah's gut.

Surely the girl didn't— No, surely not. *Definitely* not.

Good God, he was in rare form this morning. Sir Noah Rutledge, catch of the Season? Fantasy of London's young maidens? *Very* definitely not.

"I'm honored, Miss Eckert," he said, seeing now that he held one of her drawings. Inside the frame, an exquisitely detailed pirate ship battled gale forces alongside what could only be an island in the West Indies. Palm trees leaned furiously in the wind, waves crashed over the side of the ship, and the Jolly Roger was on the verge of being torn from its mast. "What an uncommon talent you have for capturing the whims of the sea. This is excellently done. Masterful, in fact."

She beamed at him. "Do you really think so?"

"I already count it among my most prized possessions. I've a place in my great-cabin that will be perfectly suited for it." He bowed and kissed her hand. "Thank you, Miss Eckert. You do me too much honor."

She blushed again. "Aunt Josephine says you and she are to visit Mr. Woodbridge's shipyard today."

"Yes." He forced himself not to think of desks. Or hips. Or legs.

"How fascinating it must be. I should dearly love to see it."

He laughed. "You won't find any pirate ships there, I'm afraid."

"I don't suppose one can know for certain what the future holds, can one?"

"Good God. No, I suppose not." For a girl so small, so prone to avoiding looking one directly in the eye, she had a rather bloodthirsty outlook. "But one can hope for the best."

"Hope for the best about what?" queried Lady Mareck's voice from the doorway. "Pauline, *there* you are."

Faced with Lady Mareck, hoping for the best took on an entirely new meaning. His mind leaped ahead, rehearsing the seduction that would finally break her control. She was perfectly put together now: the elegant drapery of a finely tailored gown, the artful upsweep of carefully coiffed hair. Passive lips. Pale, porcelain skin.

He wanted that skin flushed with desire. Those lips

dewy and swollen from his kiss. That hair tumbling down. He wanted—

"Sir Noah was waiting by himself, Aunt Josephine. I thought I would keep him company."

Noah inhaled silently. Deeply.

"Your lovely niece has just honored me with the most amazing present," he said. "It's got me wanting to batten down the hatches and ready the cannons all at once." He bowed to Pauline. "Thank you, Miss Eckert."

"One of your drawings? How thoughtful of you, Pauline. But you'd best come now—you're needed upstairs. Lettie is asking for you." Lady Mareck held out her hand, beckoning Pauline, and Noah imagined taking that hand himself and leading Lady Mareck upstairs to her bedchamber, where he would make short work of that gown.

"We were just speaking of the shipyard, Aunt Josephine."

If he took over Elias's shipyard instead of rebuilding the one in Turkey, there would be no need for the mystery of Lady Mareck to end so quickly. If he played his cards right, he could become her lover and then—

Bloody hell.

"I was telling Sir Noah how very much I would like to see the shipyard," Miss Eckert was saying. "Perhaps—perhaps I could accompany you."

Had he really just contemplated *staying* in *London*? He needed to stop fantasizing about Lady Mareck's thighs and put some distance between them. Immediately. Flirtation and fantasy was one thing. The future was entirely another.

"Oh, Pauline, I don't think—"

"An excellent idea," Noah said abruptly. "I should

very much enjoy the opportunity to show Miss Eckert the shipyard."

They both looked at him.

"Lettie isn't feeling well this morning," Lady Mareck said evenly. "Perhaps it would be best for Pauline to stay and keep her company."

"Lettie always sleeps when she's feeling poorly," Pauline was quick to respond. "She won't want me disturbing her."

"Then it's settled," Noah said, and offered Pauline his arm. "Shall we?"

FROM THE SAFETY of a Vauxhall dinner box, Josephine tried to pretend she wasn't watching Sir Noah as she contemplated what to do about the day's disaster at the shipyard.

"Confess," Honoria said, leaning close and not the least bit fooled. "You find him attractive."

Josephine watched him through the crowd as he stood laughing with a group of men. He was quicker to smile than most, had a more infectious laugh. His teeth shone brilliant white. Mesmerizing lines cut deep around his mouth. As she watched, he slapped both hands together—the back of one inside the palm of the other—emphasizing a point that was impossible to hear from this distance.

"Pauline has a tendresse for him," she told Honoria.

"*Pauline.* La, Josephine, that won't do. It won't do at all. Are you absolutely certain?"

"Positively."

"What a terribly awkward position that puts you in."

"It isn't an *awkward* position. It's an unfortunate one."

"Well, yes, that, too."

"Because he isn't an appropriate match for her," Josephine said.

"No, I daresay not. Not for her."

"She will end up with her heart broken when she learns that he doesn't share her inclinations." Which would come as an even more painful blow after today's outing to the shipyard, where Sir Noah had regaled her the entire time with talk of his sailing adventures and colorful Mediterranean port cities and the countless antiquities to be seen.

And all the while, every time his gaze collided with Josephine's, she'd felt a small explosion of desire deep in her belly, and she'd been grateful—*grateful*—that Pauline was with them.

She was the most irresponsible aunt in all of England.

"You must tell her in no uncertain terms that Sir Noah is not for her," Honoria said.

"I've tried that."

"Then you have no choice but to tell her that you have feelings for him yourself. Better for her to hear it from you now than to find out some other way after her own feelings have deepened."

"I'm not going to tell her I have feelings for Sir Noah when I don't."

"Nonsense. But you may tell yourself whatever you like, of course. Only, think of this… What is she going to do when she discovers that Sir Noah's interest lies with you?"

At that moment Pauline hurried into the dinner box, glancing over her shoulder. "Auntie Josephine, Mr. Crumley is suggesting a walk. *Please* say I can't go."

"Mr. Thomas Crumley?" Honoria asked Pauline, though she knew precisely who they were talking about.

"Yes—oh, here he comes. Auntie Josephine, *please*."

"Why, Mr. Crumley is the son of a dear friend," Honoria declared. "A lovely young man—and handsome, too. Why would you not wish to walk with him?"

Pauline looked utterly dismayed.

"The young man is smitten with you, Pauline," Honoria said. "At least do him the kindness of a short turn about the gardens."

"But, Aunt Josephine, look. *Sir Noah* is coming this way."

And so he was, heading directly for them with a small group of people. They converged on the dinner box at the exact same time as Mr. Crumley. There was a moment of chaos as a trio of women began talking to Honoria and a pair of men stood talking on the threshold and Pauline's window of opportunity to decry Mr. Crumley slammed shut. Mr. Crumley led her unhappily away just as Sir Noah slid into the chair next to Josephine.

"Enjoying the evening?" he asked, leaning closer than she might have preferred.

"Very much," she told him, even as butterflies in her stomach went all aflutter. "I always enjoy nights in the gardens."

"Mmm." If it were possible, he leaned even closer. "It's come to my attention that there is a rumor afoot," he said. "And since you are so well acquainted with London society, perhaps you might help me figure out how to set it right."

She felt his nearness as though he had taken her in his arms. "Sir Noah, London is flooded with rumors.

You must simply learn to ignore them. London requires a very thick skin."

"Mmm." His eyes roamed over her face. Flicked to her breasts. "I daresay this one has to do with skin, in a matter of speaking. And in a rather delicate way."

"Do tell."

He lowered his voice, leaned close to her ear. "It concerns a vital part of my anatomy."

His breath against her ear sent a shock of sensation shooting down the side of her neck. Honoria's group of ladies erupted into laughter, and the two men at the entrance seemed oblivious to everything but their own discussion.

"Sir Noah," Josephine said, "if everyone listened to other people's opinions of their intelligence, nobody would ever emerge from their apartments. People are forever calling others hare-brained, mutton-headed, feather-brained... You must simply learn to ignore it."

His lips curved.

She shivered.

"While I confess my brain is indeed a vital part of my anatomy," he allowed, "these rumors concern what might be deemed an equally...*serviceable* organ." He glanced around. Lowered his voice even further. "Forgive me if I shock you, but it's being said I've been castrated."

"Shocking indeed."

"I thought perhaps if I prove to you that I am intact, your reputation being what it is, you could assist me by actively countering the rumor. I feel certain you would be believed."

"I rather think you'd have a more immediate result by exposing yourself publicly, would you not?"

He laughed out loud, even as one of the men called to him. "No doubt it would." And then, murmuring in her ear as he got up, "But somehow, my dear Joseph, I feel a need to demonstrate myself to you personally. Perhaps you will indulge me one day soon."

CHAPTER TEN

ONE THING WAS certain: There would be no indulging Sir Noah.

Late at night after they'd returned from Vauxhall, the library was cold. Only the faintest glow of embers still burned in the fireplace, and Josephine's skin prickled. Her candle flame flickered in the darkness as she searched through Elias's papers for the correspondence he'd asked her to answer.

It was past time to find Elias a real man of business. If she hired a replacement, she would be free to…to sew. Perhaps learn a new piece on the harpsichord. Attend a lecture.

A lecture would be very edifying.

An affair with Sir Noah would be more edifying.

There was no ridding her mind of Sir Noah. It was as if he had taken up residence there. She set down her pen and rubbed her arms, but her skin was alive with the memory of him, sensitive to the whisper of her nightgown as though it was his touch.

Upstairs, Lettie and Pauline lay trustingly in their beds knowing that Aunt Josephine would smooth their way into society. Miles away in Suffolk, poor Charlotte probably lay awake worrying that sending the girls into Josephine's care was a mistake.

All across London, people believed she was so sensible. How many times had she been told "Josephine, I only wish I had your composure in these situations" or "If only I had your restraint of temper, Josephine"? Oh, yes. Restraint indeed.

Sir Noah would make a mockery of her restraint if he could, and it would be so easy to let him.

Just then, Edgar appeared in the doorway in his nightclothes, wig askew, holding a candle. "Sir Noah Rutledge answering your summons, your ladyship."

Sir Noah? Now? "But I didn't—"

It was too late. Sir Noah walked into the library.

"Will you require any refreshment, your ladyship?" Edgar asked.

"No, thank you. You may return to bed." She tightened her shawl around her shoulders, too conscious that she wore her own nightclothes. "What's happened?" she asked Sir Noah. "Is Elias all right?"

"As far as I know, though I didn't follow him to Covent Garden to find out." His eyes roamed over her and dropped to the papers on the desk. "I admit to having wanted to see Elias's paperwork for myself, but I didn't expect to do so at this hour."

"And you shan't," she said, coming out from behind the desk. "What are you doing here?"

"Don't play coy with me, Joseph. Your note was clear enough."

"I sent no note."

"'I so enjoyed our day together,' it said." He came forward, closing in on her. His eyes drank her in as if she were his favorite liquor. "'I only wish we could enjoy a private meeting.'"

A private meeting? "Sir Noah, I didn't—"

"Is this private enough for you, Joseph?" He ran a

finger along the neckline of her nightgown, and her mouth went dry. "I confess I didn't expect you to indulge me this soon, but it would seem we've been of the same mind."

Yes. No. No, they hadn't. "You misunderstand," she said, but his touch left a trail of heat along her collarbone and made it very, very difficult to think.

"Do I? Because finding you here in your nightclothes after sending that note, I feel I have a firm grasp on the situation. Or at least—" he slipped his hand behind her head and slid his other arm around her, pulling her against him "—I do now."

I sent no note, Sir Noah. You must leave. Now. That was what she needed to say. Instead, she stood perfectly still as he dipped his head, slanted a little and touched his mouth to hers. Her blood raced, and every nerve came alive. She forced herself to breathe. His scent inflamed her senses.

"I've been wondering whether you take your hair down at night," he murmured against her lips. She felt his hands in her hair, working the simple tie that held it back from her face after Mary had brushed it out. "It's a good thing I didn't lay any wagers on the question. Ah, God— You have no idea how I've wanted to touch you like this, Joseph."

His lips moved on hers—calculated, controlled, while she fought for sanity. She fisted her hands to keep from touching him.

He meant nothing to her. It was only a kiss and not even a very—

God in heaven. He traced her lower lip with his tongue, and secret places ignited that had long lain dormant and cool. He urged her to open to him, and she did. He was poison, but she couldn't say no. He felt too good.

She met his tongue, and the careful control of his kiss began to slip.

His lips were fire. Demanding. Pure, carnal danger, and they tasted divine. She drank him in, aware she was returning his kisses and hating herself for it. Her tongue met his, and her body turned to pure fire. His grip on her tightened. She clutched his lapels, splayed her hands against his chest.

Knew it was imperative to back away, but couldn't quite make herself do it. Teetering on the edge of control. Wanting to touch him. To tear his shirt from his breeches and push her hands beneath the linen to touch bare skin.

Push him away.

Her fingers curled into his shirt.

Break the kiss.

She met his tongue more deeply.

His hands came around her waist and he lifted her onto the desk. Skimmed her nightgown up her legs. Urged her thighs into a vee. He stood between them, and she clung to him while he played his hands over her skin higher, higher—

She gasped when he found her. Melted when he stroked her. Moaned into his mouth when he pushed a finger inside her—Noah Rutledge, *inside* her—and sought her breasts with his other hand. He found a nipple easily through the fabric and closed his fingers around it.

Exquisite pleasure ripped through her. She was pure need in his hands, tumbling toward fulfillment. Somewhere through the fog of desire, an image: Sir Noah with a secret smile in his eyes, knowing he had made her climax.

Climax.

God in heaven. No—

But he rolled her nipple into a tight, aching slave to his touch. Pushed his fingers rhythmically in, out, in. Out. Stroked the slick point of her pleasure, skillfully circling before plunging deep again.

She couldn't let it happen.

But her thighs had become his servants, and they strained apart while he stood fully clothed, making no move even to unbutton his breeches. He kissed her cheek, her jaw, her neck, nipping her flesh while his breath labored heavy in her ear.

This was costing him.

And then it was too late to stop. A great wave rose inside her, pushing, throbbing, tossing her into climax. His mouth crushed down on hers and she gasped into it while her body pulsed and pulsed around his fingers, slaking itself on him, squeezing every last shudder of fulfillment while she clung to him, helpless in the aftermath.

"I think we should finish this in your bed," he said, kissing her deeply, madly, leaving no doubt of exactly what he meant.

No. No, they shouldn't. But he slipped his fingers out, and raw, empty need keened through her, and all she wanted was to feel him inside her again. *All* of him. "The girls…"

"Will never be the wiser." Pulling down her nightgown, he lifted her into his arms, turning away from the desk, kissing her again.

There was a creak and a small cry, and Josephine's attention snapped to the doorway.

Pauline!

Noah stopped.

"Aunt Josephine, I—I—Oh!" On that ragged cry, Pauline turned and fled.

"Pauline, it isn't—" But it was, even as Noah quickly set Josephine onto legs still shaky from the intensity of release. "Pauline, wait." But it was too late.

Josephine started after her, but Noah held her back. "Don't go. You can only make it worse."

Worse? This was the worst moment she'd lived in nearly ten years. And then, on a sudden realization, "*Pauline* wrote that note."

"That's impossible. Why would she possibly—" Except even as he spoke, she could see him answering his own question. "Good God. I had no idea she'd…"

And still she was standing here with his hands on her, as if they were…

Lovers.

She pulled away and went to the desk, even as her skin still tingled madly where he'd touched her. "Young girls are capable of all kinds of fanciful notions." She snatched up her shawl from where she'd let it fall from her shoulders only minutes ago, when she and Sir Noah had— "I really must go up and speak with Pauline. I hope you won't find it an affront to let yourself out."

"Not at all," he said, watching her through eyes that had seen far, far more of her than she ever should have allowed. A moment ago she'd been about to go upstairs with *him*. To her bed.

"I shall have some papers delivered tomorrow for

your review," she said without looking at him. She pulled the shawl around her. Tight. "Good evening, Sir Noah."

UPSTAIRS, JOSEPHINE LEANED against the wall outside Pauline's door, breathing deep to cleanse away the effects of Sir Noah's touch, but they gripped her too deeply to be banished so easily. Her knees still trembled, and her most intimate flesh still pulsed and tingled. Sir Noah's taste still lingered on her lips.

She could hear Lettie's muffled voice inside the room, talking to Pauline.

Disaster. That's what this was. It was inevitable that Charlotte would hear of it. And Charlotte would be shocked, but not surprised.

What on earth could she tell Pauline? That she'd made a mistake?

Yes. That was exactly what she would tell her, because that was exactly what happened. A mistake, and all because of a misunderstanding thanks to Pauline's foolish note.

Was it a misunderstanding when you were going to let him carry you to your bed?

The very idea made her breath catch, and she struggled to steer her thoughts away. She could not let her passions get the best of her now, when her nieces' futures depended on her being everything that was proper and reliable and laudable. She knew how to keep her passions under control. How to identify folly and stamp it out before making the mistake of acting on it. It was a skill she'd worked very hard to acquire.

For heaven's sake, she hadn't run off to Gibraltar, had she? No. Because she'd known exactly how that would set tongues wagging. How it might reflect on Charlotte and the girls to have an aunt who was known for indulging eccentric whims.

Josephine's passions had very nearly ruined Charlotte's hopes once before. They would not do so now.

She made herself knock on the door. It cracked open a moment later, and Lettie's angry face glared out at her. "She doesn't wish to talk right now, Aunt Josephine."

"I'm afraid we must. Pauline?" she called. "I need to speak with you. Open the door, Lettie."

Inside, she found Pauline madly scratching away at a letter, dashing tears from her face with Bentley sitting worriedly at her feet.

"You've been telling her she shouldn't fancy Sir Noah," Lettie accused, "and now we know why."

"Do not speak where you are not informed, Lettie," Josephine said sternly.

Pauline did not look up from her letter.

"Now Pauline is going home, and Mother is going to be beside herself because Pauline was *supposed*—" she looked meaningfully at the back of Pauline's head "—to meet an appropriate young man and form an attachment."

"Nothing about this situation warrants going home." Josephine moved to the side of the writing desk so Pauline could not ignore her. Pauline's face was damp and blotchy, her handwriting shaky. "Pauline," Josephine said gently, "it was you that sent Sir Noah the note, wasn't it?"

"You sent the *note?*" Lettie exclaimed. "Pauline— Aunt Jo, I *told* her not to send it."

Pauline's cheeks turned hot red. "You send notes

to Captain Ryson," she said, scratching angrily with her pen.

"Not to meet me in the middle of the night! What would Mother think?"

"Your mother isn't going to think anything, because there's no reason to tell her," Josephine said firmly. "Pauline, you have my deepest, most painful apologies. I know you fancy Sir Noah, and I would never, ever betray your heart on purpose. I think both of you are old enough to understand that men and women sometimes do things they didn't set out to do."

"You and Sir Noah are going to marry, aren't you," Lettie said.

"*Marry.* No, we most certainly are not."

"No?" Pauline finally looked up. "But you love him."

"Let me make one thing very clear. An embrace doesn't always signify love. Sometimes it signifies a mistake. Let my mistake be a lesson to both of you about the dangers of meeting a man alone at odd hours."

"That's right, Pauline," Lettie scolded. "It could have been *you* in Sir Noah's arms, and *then* what would you have done?"

"Lettie, if you don't mind, I should like to speak with Pauline alone."

"I can tell her exactly what I write in my notes to Captain Ryson if you like, Auntie Josephine."

"Thank you, Lettie, but that won't be necessary."

Lettie pursed her lips in disappointment. "Very well. Good night."

As soon as she was gone, Josephine pulled a chair next to the writing desk and sat down. "I can't blame you for being drawn to Sir Noah, Pauline. He is a very attractive man, for a great many reasons."

"I'm so embarrassed," Pauline said, staring at her letter. "I never would have… If I'd known that you and he…"

"Sir Noah is no more right for me than he is for you, Pauline. And he *isn't* right for you—you know that."

"When he invited me to the shipyard, I thought…" Her cheeks flushed again. "I'm such a fool. He must be having quite a laugh over me."

"Sir Noah isn't the type to laugh at something like that." Which only made him more attractive. "He had no idea you felt so deeply until tonight. And you're not a fool." Josephine reached out and brushed a lock of hair from Pauline's face. "Please forgive me."

"I never should have written that note."

"If it helps, I can assure you Sir Noah is not in London looking for a wife. But even if he was, your mother would have my head if I allowed you to make an understanding with him. He is everything a young woman trying to carve her place in society should shun."

"Which is precisely what makes him so fascinating," Pauline said, blinking back tears. "I haven't set my eye on a single man but someone has told me he is unsuitable. But the ones that are suitable are horrid."

And didn't that just sum things up perfectly.

It was a perfect disaster, and he had only his cock to blame.

Noah sat slouched in a chair in the common room at his lodgings, nursing a drink.

Pauline— Good God. The note had come from *her*. How could he have ignored the obvious signs of her affection? The drawing. Her rapt attention at the shipyard. The innocent blushes, the averted eyes.

The answer was simple. His entire focus had been on Josephine. On *not touching* Josephine, to be precise, and the fact that the very idea of touching her had made him think the unthinkable.

Staying in London.

He may as well consider lopping off his own head. London was like death. A few happy hours in Lady Mareck's bed wouldn't change that. But, Christ, it might almost be worth it.

He wanted to touch her—*all* of her. Every depth, every peak. And he had, but it wasn't enough. He wanted to make love to her. Strip off that bloody mountain of fabric and put his hands on her flesh. Part those silken-soft thighs and put his mouth where his hands had been. Bury his cock where his fingers had delved.

Ah, God. He wanted to drive her mad. He wanted to hear her scream with mindless pleasure while he drove into her.

He wanted to make her lose control.

If Pauline hadn't interrupted when she had, he would be in Lady Mareck's bed right now. *Josephine.* In Josephine's bed. She hadn't been going to stop him from carrying her up there.

And then Pauline—

Christ.

The look on the girl's face had been pure horror. Utter betrayal.

He was definitely, absolutely, going to hell.

He should have thought, before he'd touched Josephine. Should have realized that someone might—

Oh, indeed. But that was precisely the point. He *hadn't* thought. He'd seized an opportunity. And he may have been adept at impromptu strategizing on the high seas, but strategizing while he had Josephine's tongue in his mouth was impossible.

And now he knew firsthand what he hadn't wanted to contemplate: beneath Josephine's cool Lady Mareck mask was a living, breathing woman who melted beneath his hands. And now every time he saw her, he would remember those whimpers of pleasure tumbling into his mouth, those nipples pebbling tightly through her nightgown, those intimate muscles clenching fiercely around his fingers.

He stared blankly into the fire. No, he would not stay in London. Not under any circumstances. But now he imagined making love to Josephine in a different bed—his own. At his villa. Smooth skin against silk. A warm night breeze heady with orange blossoms, wafting through the window with a spill of moonlight while she opened to him completely. He could bury his face in her hair, fill his hands with her breasts, sink himself between her soft, soft thighs.

Lose himself there.

Every night.

For the rest of his life.

For a long moment his mind emptied of everything except the image of it. And then, slowly, he realized what he'd been thinking.

Josephine. For the rest of his *life*.

Bloody hell. He pushed from the chair and stalked across the room, but there was nowhere to go. Two other patrons stared at him as if he'd lost his mind, so he set his glass on a table and went upstairs.

This had gone too far. Tonight, that note… He never should have acted on it, but he had, and now he was imagining… What? Marriage?

The only thing he wanted—all he'd thought of for two years—was a shipyard. A *shipyard.* Not a wife, not even a lover, at least not one who would have expectations.

No. He had come here with a plan, and it was time he moved forward with it.

CHAPTER ELEVEN

THE NEXT MORNING, Noah sat at Elias's breakfast table and watched the man poke at a boiled egg and a roll piled with jam. "Nothing tastes right anymore," Elias was complaining. "Bah. I've no appetite in the mornings these days." He pushed his plate away and reached for his coffee, adding a spoonful of sugar.

"The shipyard appears to be running with extreme efficiency," Noah said, sipping a cup of tea. He'd eaten his own breakfast hours ago.

"Good."

"Your manager seems competent enough."

"He does what needs doing."

"About the shipyard itself, and my part in it—"

"Good God, boy." Elias erupted into a fit of coughing into his napkin. "I'm not going to foist the bloody thing on you. I'd never expect you to leave that villa and come to London. I may be old, but I've still got a measure of sense."

It was as good an opening as any. "Then come with me." Although that wasn't exactly how he'd planned to say it. But now that he had, more words tumbled out. "It's the reason I'm here, the entire reason I'd been trying to correspond with you before. You'll have an entire wing of the villa to yourself. I won't ask you to do any of the labor, naturally—except to tell *me* what to do."

Noah laughed, but it felt tight in his chest, and his gut clenched with the near certainty that Elias would refuse. "There's little doubt the climate would be a boon to your health."

"Good God. Staying away from the Strand would be a boon to my health."

"You would be far away from it there—not, of course, that you would lack entertainment."

Elias grunted. "Might be half inclined to do it." Noah's attention snapped from the table to Elias's face. "But I couldn't leave Josephine."

It was exactly what he'd expected, yet still disappointment knifed through him, stronger than he was prepared for.

He watched Elias scoop some jam off his roll and eat it—the jam, not the roll. Was this really what Josephine wanted for him? A listless existence picking at unwanted breakfasts? A stab of anger had him opening his mouth again and letting more words come out.

"It appears to me that Lady Mareck is a grown woman with a well-established life of her own. I realize the two of you are close. Hell. I know about the work 'Joseph Bentley' has been doing for you."

"You know about that?" Elias's hand stilled, spoon in midair with a blob of jam sitting inside. "Good God—"

"I'm not going to *tell* anyone."

"Bloody well better not." He brought the spoon to his lips and ate the jam. "You think Josephine ought to be able to fare well on her own, and I ought to do what I damn well please."

"In a word… Yes."

Elias narrowed an eye at Noah across the table and

put the spoon on his plate. "And here I'd been thinking you might be falling in love with her."

Love. He recoiled on the inside as if he'd been struck by a pistol shot.

"For God's sake, Elias. No. I'm not."

"A husband," Elias declared, picking up the spoon once more and gesturing with it. "That's what she needs, and not one like that bloody bastard Mareck."

Noah didn't even want to know what Mareck had done to deserve that description. He started to get up. "I'm sure she can manage to—"

"Thought he was going to seduce her and leave her to be someone else's baggage," Elias went on. "Don't know who took the harsher punishment—him or Josephine for having to marry him. Mareck didn't care one whit for her. Never seen anyone so terrified as that girl at her first family dinner."

Noah sat back down.

"All the family despised her. Not good enough for their precious Mareck. I'll tell you this... Mareck was never good enough for her. And that sister of hers. Wouldn't have a thing to do with her till Mareck took the title, then suddenly there they were—father, mother, sister. All of 'em. Never seen more obsequious folk in all my life. And now this business with her nieces. That sister of hers will use Josephine as an entrée for her daughters and that will be the end of it—mark my words."

Noah cleared his throat and told himself everyone had unpleasantness in their families. In their pasts. But it was impossible not to think of Josephine—serene, well-behaved Josephine—privately desperate to atone a mistake and finding no forgiveness. To think of her as a young girl thrust into London society fresh from Gibraltar, falling prey to the future Lord Mareck's tricks.

It lit a fury inside him. Made him feel things he didn't want to feel.

"I promised Josephine years ago that I'd stand by her as long as I draw breath," Elias finished. "I won't abandon her now. I'll do whatever I can to help you, though. You have only to name it. Young architect down at the shipyard—Archibald Heckley. Wager he'd go with you in a heartbeat. Devil of an architect, too. Hell. I'll send as many men with you as you like."

But there was only one man whose presence mattered, and Noah was looking at him right now. None of those men was related to him. None was family. And once Noah left England, he would likely never see Elias again.

He shifted in his chair. Tried to tell himself this was what he'd anticipated all along. That it was for the best.

Besides, it would take time before he'd be ready to return. And if this Archibald Heckley agreed to go with him, it could take even longer. The man would have business to take care of first. A household to settle.

There was plenty of time yet to spend with Elias.

And then, when everything was ready, Noah would return to his Turkish seaside town with a handful of Elias's men, and by this time next year his new shipyard would very likely be building its first ships.

A DAY. TWO DAYS. Three. In that time, Josephine went from seeing Sir Noah every day and practically everywhere to seeing him… Never.

The night in the library had changed everything, and clearly not just for her.

It was a relief, she thought as her coach carried her to the shipyard on a fresh matter of important business. Really, it was.

And now a new development would simplify things even further: she'd found a man to replace Joseph Bentley. She'd interviewed him yesterday and immediately known he would be perfect. Quiet, discreet—not that he would ever know anything but that Joseph Bentley had abruptly left Elias's service, and a replacement was needed immediately. He was experienced. Good with figures, good with letters. She could hand over the entire business to him and he would soon have it figured out.

Joseph Bentley would disappear without a trace. She'd already spoken to Elias about it, and he agreed that it would be wise, if they were to sell the shipyard.

Josephine's coach pulled to a stop in front of the shipyard building, where she would meet the new man—Mr. Lind—and show him Joseph Bentley's office. Which was why she'd arrived early, with a satchel full of papers.

A coachman helped her out and held the door to the shipyard offices. Inside, there was a scramble of bowing and "your ladyship-ing," complete with papers falling to the floor and even a chair being knocked over.

"A man has been hired to replace Joseph Bentley," she informed the shipyard manager. "I should like to put these papers in Mr. Bentley's office for him, and then I shall meet with him upstairs in Mr. Woodbridge's office."

"Of course, your ladyship. Of course. But—ah—Mr. Woodbridge's office is, um, occupied at the moment. By Sir Noah Rutledge, your ladyship."

Her breath caught, but she recovered quickly. "Is it? Very well, I shall simply meet with Mr. Lind in Mr. Bentley's office."

She went into the small office and busied herself, too aware that Sir Noah was just upstairs and that he would certainly seek her out when he learned she was there. She tensed at every set of footsteps passing outside the door, relaxed when nobody entered.

Until, after about ten minutes, someone did.

"I'm told you wanted to use Elias's office to meet with a replacement for Mr. Bentley," Sir Noah said from the doorway.

She stood, facing him for the first time since that night in the library, and tried uselessly not to remember the feel of his hands on her body. "We shall be perfectly fine here."

"The office upstairs is available. I've just finished my business."

"Very well." The tiny office seemed even tinier with him in it. Sensual memories crowded in with them, and her palms grew damp. "May I ask what business?"

"Elias didn't tell you?"

"No."

He glanced over his shoulder. "I would prefer to discuss it upstairs."

Moments later they walked into Elias's office, where a bank of windows faced the dry docks where the ships were under construction. Sir Noah looked out and shook his head.

"God, they're magnificent," he said.

They were. So magnificent she felt it like a swelling inside her chest, a deep yearning for something more. What she wouldn't give to climb up into the half-constructed hull, run her hands along the new railings and plant her feet on the fresh deck. She imagined the ship oiled and painted, in full sail on the ocean with the wind billowing in fresh, white canvas and seabirds calling out, gliding and diving on currents of wind and water.

She didn't realize she'd wandered closer to the windows until she caught herself staring—staring at the ships, while Sir Noah stared at her. She looked at him, and all she could think of was what Sir Noah would look like on the deck of his ship in nothing but a linen shirt and breeches, with his sleeves rolled up and his hands gripping the deck railing as he fixed those eyes on the sea.

For a moment she could feel the water's swell and plunge beneath her own feet.

"You do realize not even your influence is enough to persuade Elias to retire to Mays Abbey," Sir Noah said.

"He will change his mind once he has seen it." She hoped. "About this business of yours…?"

They stood near the desk, and she became acutely aware of what had happened the last time they were together in a room with a desk. She shifted a few steps away, but there was no escaping the sensations humming madly through her blood.

"I shall be returning to Turkey without Elias," he said.

Emotion—relief?—slammed into her. For a moment she thought she might be sick. "You've changed your mind?"

"About the new shipyard, no. I've spoken with Elias, and he would prefer to stay here. But he's offered to send a group of men to help me get started, provided they're

willing to accompany me, naturally. I've just spoken
with the architect Elias recommends—Mr. Heckley—
who says he can be ready almost immediately. I expect
to set sail within the week."

Elias had refused. Because of her. She told herself it
was for the best, that such a dramatic change at his age,
in his condition, could only be disastrous.

"I wish you the best of luck," she said.

"Thank you. I suppose I shall need it." He looked at
her, and she could swear she saw memories of the other
night playing out behind his eyes. "How is Pauline?"

"Very well. A young man has showed a great deal of
interest in her. A Mr. Crumley. I believe she is finally
starting to return his interest."

"Excellent." He rubbed his jaw, shifted some papers
on the desk. "Well. There are a few others downstairs
I ought to speak with. I shall leave you to prepare for
Mr. Lind's arrival."

NOAH STARTED TO turn, but there was something else
he needed to tell her, and he couldn't make himself go
without saying it, so he stopped. "There's something
you should know."

She stood silently, waiting, so beautiful with the half-
built ships in the distance behind her that he could almost imagine her aboard his ship. But that would never
happen.

"I believe you were once acquainted with an Alex-
andrian by the name of Ahmet," he said.

The smallest intake of breath, barely audible, confirmed it.

"A sailor by trade," Sir Noah clarified, just to be sure
there was no mistake.

"I do remember someone by that name," she said evenly. "He was aboard the ship that brought my family from Gibraltar to London."

"He certainly remembered you."

Noah might have thought her completely unmoved if she hadn't reached for the back of a nearby chair.

"You knew him?" she asked.

"He was my first mate for seven years, and a good friend." No, she was not indifferent. He pressed on. "He was more than that to you."

She paled. "Is there a reason why you are dredging up past indiscretions?"

"Is that what he was to you? An indiscretion?"

She started toward the door. "I must go meet Mr. Lind."

"Josephine... Ahmet is dead."

She froze, and the callousness of his words condemned him. The emotion he'd been looking for was there in the stricken look she was valiantly fighting. "How?"

"Fever." And he was sorry, now, that he'd told her, because the fact that Ahmet was more than an indiscretion—much more—was written all over her face. "My ship's surgeon did everything possible—" Noah swallowed past a lump in his throat. Damnation. "*I* did everything possible. Until there was nothing more to be done."

"Why are you telling me this?"

"That day at Mays Abbey, you asked me why I'm here. Do you remember?"

"Yes."

"The shipyard in Turkey—it was a flight of fancy Ahmet and I conjured up one night while we—" He managed a laugh. "Were drinking ourselves into oblivion on a calm sea in summertime. Ahmet always spoke of the things he thought of doing, but he never did them. He spoke of his family, but never saw them. And now he's gone, and there is nothing to keep him from being forgotten." His throat was so tight he could barely speak. "And that, Lady Mareck, is why I am here."

CHAPTER TWELVE

SIR NOAH WAS WRONG. She would never forget Ahmet. But even more than that, she would never forget Noah.

"La, Josephine, you haven't heard a word I've said," Honoria complained as she peered through a glass case at a collection of tiny jeweled boxes. "Whatever is the matter? But never mind—I daresay I already know what's the matter. Sir Noah is leaving." Honoria looked up, took Josephine's hands and lowered her voice. "I know I've done little else but joke you about him, but it's only too plain that you have real feelings for him. Please, Josephine, don't deny it. I can see in your eyes that you're hurting. I don't know when I've seen you so drawn."

Josephine felt drawn. Her chest ached with the feeling that her last chance at true happiness would disappear the day Sir Noah sailed out of the Thames.

But that was ridiculous. It had to be.

"Has Sir Noah not considered staying?" Honoria pressed on. "Has he given no hint that he might be interested in buying Mr. Woodbridge's shipyard for himself?"

"I *adore* London." The words ripped from Josephine as if she'd been holding them on her tongue for ages.

Honoria's delicate dark brows dove quizzically. "That's never been in doubt. Has it?"

Oh, yes. Yes, it had—from the moment that ship had arrived from Gibraltar all those years ago. From the moment she'd been forced to marry Mareck and make her home with him, knowing that he was busying himself between the legs of any number of women about town.

"It has." Honoria realized this aloud, and moved Josephine away from the glass cases and the too-curious gaze of the shopkeeper. Now she gripped Josephine's hands all the more firmly. "Listen to me, Josephine. If you love Sir Noah, you cannot allow him to simply sail away."

Josephine stared at her, and for a terrifying moment the truth sat on her tongue: *I want to go with him.* Abandon everything, turn her back on Lettie and Pauline, disregard the effect her actions would have on them and on Charlotte.

"I don't love him," she said, pulling away.

"Oh, for heaven's sake!" Honoria whispered fiercely. "One has only to look at you to see the truth."

"A fanciful infatuation. Nothing more."

"And he shares your feelings. It is only too obvious."

"I have no idea. That is to say, I have no feelings to be shared."

"La, Josephine, you are the worst liar in London. You must find out."

For a wild, reckless moment the entire story filled her mouth, demanding to be told. Her girlhood love for Ahmet. Her secret yearning for Gibraltar. The feelings for Sir Noah that had grown to eclipse both of those, and her fierce desire to sail away with him. To watch the sun set over the Mediterranean. To make a place for herself in his villa.

"Only imagine what everyone would say if they

thought I was having an affair with Sir Noah." The words were barely audible. Over by the glass cases, a man and two ladies occupied the shopkeeper's attention.

"*Are* you having an affair with him?"

"Certainly not." One encounter—one *mistake*—did not add up to an affair.

"I daresay they would have a great deal to say about it, as they do about everything. But you can't conduct yourself according to that, for heaven's sake."

"Can't I?"

"Josephine! Is that all that's keeping you from him? The raised brows of the ton? *You?*"

"*Wisdom* is what's keeping me from him."

"La! Wisdom!"

"A virtue, or so I've always understood."

"And therein lies the trouble with virtue," Honoria said firmly. "It does not account for happiness."

"I *am* happy."

"Are you? I've only just begun to wonder."

Josephine tensed. "Honestly, Honoria, it won't do to imagine things."

"Only look at you—always a pillar of perfection, never a flaw to be seen. Always just the right words on your lips. Flawless entertainments. A perfect hostess. Always kindness toward others, even when they aren't there to hear what you say. Even after Mareck's accident, you were the picture of poise. No one in the world could find fault with you."

"I'm not perfect," Josephine whispered suddenly. Harshly.

"No?"

The truth came pouring out. There was no holding it back. "If I could, I would leave London tomorrow. I would sail to Gibraltar. I would buy myself a small cottage on a hill, surrounded by olive trees and lemon trees and flowering vines, overlooking the sea, where I could watch the ships come and go." Honoria would know everything now—almost everything—and there would be no taking it back. "I would take a lover—someone exotic and exciting who would worship me like a goddess. I would spend my afternoons wearing flowing gowns from the Orient and sipping mint tea and gazing out at the turquoise blueness of the sea."

Honoria's green eyes glistened with tears. "Oh, Josephine."

Disappointment, naturally. It was all she could expect now. But it hurt—oh, how it hurt, even though she'd always known what would happen if any of her friends knew the truth. "You needn't stay," she said. "But if you would keep my confidence, I would be forever grateful."

Honoria moved in next to her. "How can you have held this in? It's the most heartbreaking thing I've ever heard."

"Not so heartbreaking as what would happen to Lettie and Pauline if my errant desires were made known."

"Nonsense!"

"I won't have their reputations tainted, not in any way."

"Tainted? Because their widowed aunt has decided to *travel?*"

But what Josephine longed for was more than mere travel. "As soon as Sir Noah is gone, it will be as if he was never here. I'm sure I shall hardly think of him at all."

EXCEPT THAT THE thought of Sir Noah leaving occupied her thoughts incessantly.

The reality of it throbbed with a small headache in Josephine's temple during the evening's entertainment at the theater, at which Captain Ryson and Mr. Crumley joined them in their box—and at which Sir Noah was nowhere to be seen.

It clutched at her heart later that night, when Josephine summoned Pauline to her dressing room to tell her the news.

"I thought you would want to know that Sir Noah will be leaving England within the week," Josephine told her, reaching for Pauline's hand as they sat on the settee in their nightgowns. Bentley jumped up with them and curled up in Pauline's lap. "He and Mr. Woodbridge have come to an understanding about Sir Noah's shipyard in Turkey, and Sir Noah will be returning home to see the project under way."

Home. To that beautiful villa on the Turkish seaside with its fountain and its orange trees and its private, sunny courtyards.

"I see," Pauline said, and sighed a little. "I hope he will be very successful."

"I have no doubt that he will."

Pauline smiled a little and stroked Bentley's wavy, silver fur. "Only imagine how triumphant he will feel to see his first ship set sail on the Mediterranean."

It was too easy to imagine the satisfaction that would settle into his blue eyes. The way he would shout with triumph and raise his fist into the air at the sight. The flash of his teeth as he grinned, victorious.

"Only imagine the sails, clean and white and new against the blue sky and sea," Pauline said, pulling her hand from Josephine's, resting her elbow on her knee and her chin in her palm. "Think of the waves splashing the hull for the first time. The spotless cannons at the ready."

Josephine tucked a wisp of hair behind Pauline's ear. "Why do I suspect it was Sir Noah's ships, and not his qualities, that caught your interest?"

Pauline leaned back and sighed. "It won't matter now, because I shan't have either." She toyed a little with Bentley's ears. "Mr. Crumley wishes to ask Papa for my hand. And I already know Papa will approve."

Josephine tried to be happy at the news. "Mr. Crumley is...very amiable."

"*Very* amiable."

"He will make an excellent husband."

"Yes." Pauline was very quiet. And then, "I know it isn't right for a girl to think of ships and faraway lands."

Josephine opened her mouth to say very firmly that there wasn't anything wrong with it at all, except the effect of that could be disastrous, and Charlotte would never forgive her. "You're hardly the only one who thinks so, or there wouldn't be so many sensational tales of pirates."

"Mother says you had the same flights of fancy when you were my age, and that it has caused you a great many regrets. Please forgive me if I've distressed you with my behavior."

"You haven't distressed me, Pauline." Regrets? It wasn't difficult to imagine what Charlotte had been telling them. "And you don't have to marry Mr. Crumley just because he's showed an interest. There will be others. There is still time."

"Mother won't be happy if she learns I turned down Mr. Crumley."

No, Charlotte would not be happy. "We wouldn't have to tell her."

Pauline smiled up at her, but sadly. "Thank you, Auntie Josephine. That means a great deal to me, really it does, but we can't be sure there *would* be anyone else, or that if there was, that he wouldn't be dreadful. I can't imagine anyone less objectionable than Mr. Crumley. But I've told him he must speak to you before he makes any declarations to me."

"Pauline, are you certain?"

"Yes, Auntie Josephine. Although I am sorry that Sir Noah is leaving. For your sake."

"Dearest, there's no reason to be sorry." There wasn't. Because Pauline was courageous enough to do the right thing.

Recklessly following one's heart regardless of the consequences—that hardly required any courage at all.

JOSEPHINE ENTERED ELIAS'S dressing room to find him seated by the window with a book.

"What are you reading?"

He grunted. "Nothing of importance." He fumbled the book closed and set it aside. "Impossible to find a skilled periwig-maker these days. Berwick! Bring my powdering gown."

Josephine helped him out of his chair, glanced at the book's spine. *A History of Turkey and the Ottomans.*

Guilt tore through her. "I have news," she said brightly. "I've hired Mr. Lind. He started this afternoon at the shipyard."

"Glad to hear it," Elias grumbled, searching the

pockets of his dressing gown and finally coming up with a handkerchief.

"He had excellent references."

"I don't doubt it." Elias dabbed his nose, tucked the handkerchief away and pushed himself out of his chair when Berwick arrived with the gown and powder. "By the way, I've offered Sir Noah any assistance he requires with his new shipyard. I believe he'll set sail in a matter of days." He sat in his favorite powdering chair while Berwick settled a new wig on Elias's head. Soon a cloud of powder filled the air around him.

Readying for another debauch at the Dewy Petal, or perhaps he'd tired of that one by now.

She thought of Sir Noah's villa, of the obvious regard Sir Noah had for Elias, of the warm, dry Mediterranean climate.

"Yes, he told me," she said. "I saw him at the shipyard."

Elias wanted to go with Sir Noah. As if that book wasn't evidence enough, she'd seen it in the animated way he spoke when Sir Noah visited. The questions he'd asked, the interest he'd showed in Sir Noah's shipyard plans. These days, even food barely interested him.

Berwick finished, and the air around Elias began to clear. "Rather ride a horse backward to Bath than sail from here to Turkey," he grumbled.

It was a lie. She should tell him she knew it, and she should tell him he was free to do as he pleased.

But if she did, Elias would go with Sir Noah to the Mediterranean and she would stay behind, because she was too afraid to go herself. And she would be completely, entirely alone because he was the only person in the world who truly knew her.

Berwick removed the powdering gown, and Elias stood. "Perhaps I ought to send *you* along to make sure he doesn't mistreat my men."

"Uncle—"

"A joke, Josephine. Merely a joke. Stop looking so terrified."

"I'm not *terrified*." She stood abruptly.

"You don't fool me, Josephine." Elias reached out and touched her cheek, and she stood perfectly still while her heart swelled into her throat and made each breath a struggle. "I'm not going to leave you," he said. "If you won't go, then neither will I. We're family, Josephine."

"You and Noah are family, too."

"Yes. But Noah knows his way around the world. He'll do fine."

She wanted to say that she would do fine, too, if Elias went with Sir Noah. That she knew her way. That she loved Elias too much to keep him in London when he was so clearly intrigued by other possibilities— possibilities that put a fresh spark in his eyes when for so long that spark had been gone.

But old fears bubbled up like hot tar, smothering and suffocating her and sucking her under. She imagined a shipwreck, a heart attack, an accident. The horror of receiving a letter from Sir Noah bearing the dreadful news.

"Yes," she said, and kissed Elias's cheek. Her stomach tightened, and she felt a bit ill. "I daresay Sir Noah will do fine."

CHAPTER THIRTEEN

JOSEPHINE LAY IN bed that night, trying not to think of Noah leaving, wanting him so desperately the very sheets were a torment against her skin. Was it only days ago she'd nearly let him carry her here and make love to her?

She rolled to her side, plumped the pillow beneath her head. Her breasts grazed the inside of her nightgown, sending white heat searing to a dozen intimate places.

After tomorrow, the possibility of ever making love with Noah would be gone.

She reached out and caressed the pillow next to her, as though she caressed *him*. Firelight flickered over her skin, and she imagined the way it might flicker over his if he were here. What he would look like lying next to her. Moving over her.

Inside her.

God in heaven. The flesh between her legs pulsed hard, as though he were already there. She shifted, and her thighs brushed together.

You could go to him.

It would be a mistake. Oh, it would. To open herself to him that way... To watch his face as he moved inside her body and feel him there, deep inside her... She would be lost.

But she wanted him there more than she'd ever wanted anything in her life. Needed him there, as if there was a place deep inside that would never be fulfilled unless he touched it.

She shifted restlessly beneath the linens, wanting. Needing. She turned onto her stomach and felt it even more keenly with her breasts pressed into the mattress beneath her. She parted her legs slightly and remembered something Mareck had used to want, something she hadn't cared for. But perhaps…

The idea burst to life and now she imagined Sir Noah behind her, moving powerfully between her thighs, urging her up—

God in heaven, yes. *Yes.*

It would be perfect. There would be no looking at his face, no gazing into his eyes when he filled her. There would only be Noah, inside her, giving her the one part of him she might dare to take.

She could take that memory, just the way she'd dared to take the memory of Ahmet. And just as her memories of Ahmet had carried her through her awful marriage, her memories of Noah would carry her through the quiet, lonely years ahead.

HALF OF AN afternoon and all of an evening was plenty of time to move his ship from its moorage at the shipyard to the London docks to begin reprovisioning. It was not enough time to come to terms with the fact that he would be leaving London without what he'd come for.

It was an hour till midnight, and Noah stalked the decks of his ship like a restless specter, checking lines and sheets and guns and anything else that could easily wait for morning, but he felt a pressing need to look at now. In the dark. When the only light came from the lantern he carried and the taverns along the river.

I'll make sure you have everything you need, Elias had said.

That was impossible. He needed not to return home alone.

You need Josephine.

No. He didn't *need* Josephine. He *wanted* Josephine. There was a difference.

But God, he wanted her as he'd never wanted anything. The hot depth of her body around his fingers nearly killed him every time he remembered it.

He splayed his hand in the near darkness and looked at those fingers now. They'd been inside her, as deep as he could push them. She'd climaxed around those fingers.

God.

He dropped his hand and shook it as if it had caught fire. Inside his breeches, his cock swelled.

Perhaps he did need Josephine. He needed to make love to her before he left London. Finish what they'd begun in that library—but without losing any more of his control than he already had.

And there were ways to make it less personal. An image ignited in his mind—Josephine with her back to him. Smooth, satin skin, round inviting buttocks. Bending over the edge of the bed, giving him perfect access to her body without the risk of having to look in her eyes—

His breath came hard. Labored. He gripped the starboard railing, digging his fingers into the wood.

Yes. He could do it. *Would* do it.

He would have Josephine tonight, and he would leave London with at least one thing he wanted.

He turned abruptly from the railing and started across the deck. Stopped. Someone was coming up the gangplank—a cloaked figure he would recognize anywhere.

THIS WAS NO time for rational thought, and Josephine was determined not to have a single one as she walked up the gangplank. Clouds churned in a teasing hide-and-seek with the moon, and there was Sir Noah: blond hair in the moonlight, white shirt fluttering in the breeze, miles of lines crisscrossing the yards above him.

A mad tangle of nerves quivered in her belly at the sight of him, knowing why she was here and what she planned to do.

But she wasn't going to turn back now. She could have this one thing. She *would* have it. And after he was gone, she would treasure it like a secret jewel.

She walked the rest of the way up the gangplank. Sir Noah caught her by the hand and helped her aboard.

"I was just going to come find you," he said.

"You were?"

The words scarcely left her lips before he kissed her—a deep, intense moving of his mouth over hers, demanding the reason she'd come, telling her exactly what he planned to do about it.

"I can't leave London without making love to you, Josephine," he said roughly against her lips, and her breath caught in her throat. "I won't."

Somehow she managed to laugh, but it came out low. Breathy. "That's not your choice to make."

"No." He looked down at their joined hands and

toyed his thumb across her knuckles. Looked up. "It isn't."

The wind kicked up with a fierce gust that pulled at her careful coiffure and flipped back one side of her overskirt. His light grip on her fingers lured her like a silken snare.

This was not going to turn out the way she'd planned—she knew it now the way she knew her own heartbeat. Giving herself to Sir Noah, and then returning to her town house and her London life... It was going to be the most painful thing she'd ever done.

More painful than the last sliver of Gibraltar disappearing in the distance.

More painful than that last glimpse of Ahmet out the carriage window as her family had ridden away from the docks.

More painful, even, than those desolate months of loneliness after the wedding when it seemed there was nobody in the world who cared for her except Elias.

Noah put a hand on her face and brushed her cheek with his thumb. "You shine on me like the sun in Tangiers, Josephine."

She closed her eyes, feeling his heat like the very rays of the sun he spoke of.

He pressed his cheek to hers, brushed his lips over the sensitive skin by her ear. "Allow me inside you tonight, and I could die a happy man without ever touching another woman as long as I live."

The words were ridiculous. Exaggerated. And they shot straight to an intimate nerve that pulsed hotly, urgently, in precisely the place he wanted to touch.

Waves whipped by the wind lapped against the hull. Ships all around them creaked and lolled. Somewhere a bell rang, and another, fading into the distant shouts of revelry in the night. They were not alone. But the wall supporting the upper deck gave them privacy from the riverside.

Beneath her cloak, she wore a simple gown not meant to be seen outside her dressing room—but one that would be very little obstacle. Under it she wore only her shift, and her breasts hung heavy and yearning beneath the fabric. She parted the cloak and let him see her state of undress. His eyes dropped instantly to her body, and a sudden, hot impulse had her bringing her hands up to pull the fabric aside and expose her breasts. Immediately, the sharp wind kissed her nipples into hard nubs.

"Is this what you wanted to touch?" she asked, scarcely recognizing her own voice.

Hunger flared in his eyes, and then he was touching her, kissing her, with her exposed breasts crushed against his coat and his hands gripping her waist and his tongue battling fiercely with hers. He tasted of anise liquor and forbidden pleasure, smelled of distant, sensuous lands.

The wind whipped around them and he closed his hands over her breasts, moving his thumbs hungrily over her nipples, biting at her lower lip, devouring her.

"Your hair," he said against her mouth. "I want to see it."

"Good God," she breathed, "you have no idea—"

But he was already tugging, pulling, tossing pins aside, plundering her hair until it came tumbling free. He lifted it up and shook it in the wind until it was completely liberated—a wild, tangled mess falling around her shoulders and teasing her flesh.

"You are," he said roughly, pulling her close, touching her lips with his fingers, drawing them across her chest to brush the hair from her breasts, "the most beautiful woman in all of creation."

She dug her fingers into his hair and pulled him down, urging, gasping when he took a nipple in his mouth. The sweet pull seared every nerve. Her most secret places pulsed with hot need.

She reached for him, for his breeches, and closed her hand over his shaft. He groaned, freed himself with one hand, and her fingers met hot flesh.

He sank to his knees and pushed her skirts up and then—

Oh, God. He pressed his face between her thighs and his seeking tongue thrust into her folds, finding its treasure. Thick, strong fingers found her passage and pushed inside, stroking into the wetness of it.

She clung to his shoulders, dug her fingers through his hair, gasped uncontrollably until... Until...

A ragged cry tore from her throat, and she pulsed, pulsed, pulsed. And then he was standing. Pushing his breeches farther past his hips with the fiercest, most feral expression she'd ever seen. She was desperate to reach for him, but somehow through the fog of pleasure she remembered what she'd planned. She started to turn, only to have him hurry her on, turning her to face the side of the staircase that led to the upper deck. She braced herself against the wood. Felt him lift her skirts. Grip her hips.

Her passage throbbed, slick and hot and ready. His phallus brushed her buttocks on its way to what it sought: entrance.

The tip of him found her. She felt him groan—he was

pressed that closely against her. She widened her stance,
bent forward just a little. Felt him penetrate. Stretch.

Enter.

Thrust.

The wind caught her ragged cry and carried it away
as he plunged inside her deep, deep, deep.

And then he was pulling her back, flush against him,
pressing fierce, hot kisses against the side of her neck.
She felt him slip from her body. Felt him turning her,
shoving her skirts up again, lifting her, carrying her
three steps to the wall that enclosed the cabins, urging her legs around him even as he pinned her against
the wood.

And then he was inside her again, face-to-face, kissing her and gripping her buttocks and oh, oh, *oh.* She
dug her fingers into his hair, kissing him as if she could
swallow him whole. His erection thrust deep inside her
yet all she wanted was to be closer. *Closer.*

"Noah."

All restraint fled. He speared inside her and she was
completely, utterly open. She gasped against his mouth.
Opened her eyes and looked at him—at that face she
could stare at for a lifetime—and took all of him inside
her, feeling herself shudder and climax again, and even
then she wasn't close enough to him.

She wanted more. She wanted him forever.

By the time Josephine left Noah's ship, the night was
nearly over and her entire plan was in tatters.

They'd made love again on the bed in his cabin—
slowly, sweetly, with long, deep kisses that mimicked
the stroke of his body inside hers. With murmured en-
dearments. She'd watched his face as he moved inside

her. As he'd climaxed in her body, finally spending himself completely.

There wasn't an inch of him she hadn't touched. Tasted.

There wasn't a single place on her body he hadn't explored, and that didn't pulse and ache even now as she sneaked into her own home a disheveled mess.

The moment she came in the door, Edgar met her with a note. His eyes widened a little at the sight of her, but beneath her cape he couldn't see the half of it.

"The wind is fierce tonight," she said, unable to quite look at him.

"Indeed, your ladyship," he replied with complete lack of inflection.

The note was from Trowe.

Mr. Woodbridge badly injured. Please come immediately.

She looked up, her heart racing, the evening's activities suddenly forgotten. "The coach. Immediately. And send a footman to the docks to tell Sir Noah he must come to Mr. Woodbridge's house at once."

Moments later she was clattering down the streets still in her cloak and disheveled undress, desperately trying to wind her tumbling hair into some sort of order but having no pins, praying Elias was all right.

CHAPTER FOURTEEN

AT HIS HOUSE, she raced up the stairs to Elias's bedroom, no longer caring who saw her cloak and nightclothes. Nobody would know where she'd been anyhow.

"What's happened?" she asked, rushing into the room.

Elias's physician was already there. Elias lay in the bed, his face a ghastly red and purple against the linens.

"A gang of street toughs," the physician said gravely. "A kind soul found Mr. Woodbridge lying in an alley on the Strand and brought him home."

Elias writhed in the bed and groaned something unintelligible. Josephine grasped his hand and pressed her lips to his forehead. "I'm here, Elias. I'm here." Her throat felt so thick it was difficult to speak.

"The damage is mostly to his head and torso," the physician told her. "I would be lying if I told you his prognosis was hopeful."

The news took the strength from her knees and she sagged against the edge of the bed. She clutched his hand for long, heartrending moments, offering up silent prayers.

Finally, the physician murmured at her side, "Forgive me, but I must finish tending to him."

"Of course." She made herself let go of Elias's hand and step out of the way, but still each breath was an effort—until Noah finally strode into the room, and she saw the fear on his face, and suddenly she felt less alone.

One look at Elias and Noah cursed violently. "I'll kill whoever did this."

Josephine watched through eyes that swam with tears while the physician gave Noah the details and showed him the worst of the injuries. And then Noah turned to Josephine. Their eyes held, and then she was in his arms, weeping on his shoulder. She felt his lips against her hair, his heartbeat beneath her ear, his hand moving in slow circles across her back.

He was so strong, so sure. So real.

And he was leaving. The truth of it ripped her nearly as raggedly as her fear for Elias.

Finally, the physician turned to them and said he'd done all he could. "Summon me if things take a turn for the worse," he said, and left them alone with Elias.

"I must send a note to the girls to let them know what's happened," Josephine said after they'd stood watching Elias for what seemed like an eternity—still in each other's arms, as if it was the most natural place in the world at a time such as this.

"There's no reason to wake them," he murmured into her hair. "You can send a note in the morning."

He was right. Waking them now would only frighten them.

Noah's arms tightened around her, strong and safe, holding her as if he would never let her go. The taste of their lovemaking still lingered on her tongue. Her body felt steeped in the fullness of his touch. And her heart—

God help her, her heart ached for everything it couldn't have, because being in Noah's arms *was* the most natural place in the world. Because she loved him.

She *loved* him.

As if her own thoughts mocked her, Noah chose that moment to release her. "Here," he said, guiding her to a chair near Elias's bed. "There's no reason for you to stand."

No reason, except the only place she wanted to be was in his arms. But she sat, hardly daring to look at him. "Thank you."

"Do you need anything?" he asked gravely.

You. I need you.

She reached for Elias's still hand. "Tea would be nice."

"Of course. I'll call for some now."

WAITING BY ELIAS'S bedside gave Noah far too much time to think.

About that Turkish shipyard. About Elias. About London, and all the reasons he'd come. The reasons why, if Elias hadn't been beaten, he would have been two days gone.

About Josephine, and the way she'd felt in his arms, and the fact that even if he could sink himself into her every day for the rest of his life, it wouldn't be enough.

By the third day, Elias's breathing had steadied. His slumber grew more peaceful. That morning, the physician announced he was all but certain Elias would live.

Elias would live.

Noah exhaled sharply and left the room. Across the hall, in the room he'd been occupying for a few odd naps the past three days, Noah leaned against the wall and let the full weight of what that meant sink in. He stood there for long minutes before Josephine's voice came from the doorway.

"Noah?"

He hadn't bothered to close the door, and now Josephine came in. She stopped when she saw him leaning there. Just the sight of her turned his blood to fire.

"The physician says a nurse should be hired," she told him.

They could discuss nurses later. Now, after three days of hell, he needed release. "Come here," he said roughly.

For a moment he didn't think she would. But then she came toward him, and a heartbeat later he had her in his arms and he was kissing her and kicking the door shut behind them.

The kiss turned wild in an instant, like a squall that blew up out of nowhere. He touched her everywhere— her breasts, her waist, her hips—or as much of any of them as he could fill his hands with given the devilish barrier of stays and panniers and petticoats. He needed *her*. Josephine. And not the guarded, cautious Josephine—the one who lived inside all that, who lit up when she saw his villa and had dared to seek him out on his ship.

Her touch drove him mad. She clutched his shoulders, ran her hands down his back, gripped his buttocks. Ah, God— He picked her up and carried her to the bed. Pushed her skirts awkwardly to her waist while he invaded her mouth—damnation, she tasted like heaven—and worked the placket on his breeches. And then—

Yes. *Yes.*

He was pushing into her as far as he could go, needing to go even deeper. Be even closer. He pulled back and thrust again, again, again, but God—*God*—this was as close as they could be. It wasn't enough. It hadn't been enough the other night, and it wouldn't be enough now. It couldn't be. He wanted all of her, wanted to melt into her. He felt her clutching him, clinging to him, heard her whimpers and soft cries, and knew she was nearing release.

And *dam...na...tion* he let himself fire like a cannon into her.

And then he lay on top of her, gasping for air, while the last pulses of her release shuddered around him. He looked down at her, into those hazel eyes he never wanted to look away from. At those lips he would never in ten lifetimes grow tired of kissing. And he knew, right then and there, that he was in love.

With Josephine, Countess of Mareck.

With Joseph Bentley, thwarter of plans.

It should have made his next words easier. "I've decided to stay in London," he told her.

She touched her fingertips to his lips. "Until Elias has recovered. Of course."

"No." The words should not have been this difficult to say. "Permanently."

He felt her tense beneath him. "Noah, no."

It wasn't the reaction he'd expected. "No?"

Now she was struggling to sit up, alarm in her eyes. "You can't. You *mustn't*."

He rolled off of her. "I realize you fear my influence on Elias—"

"But you *despise* London." She sat up in a pile of skirts and petticoats.

"There are more important things to consider, under the circumstances." He got up and fastened his breeches.

His decision, now that he'd spoken it aloud, squeezed his chest so hard it felt as though he was suffocating.

"But your villa—"

"Has had caretakers these past five years. It can have caretakers for five more. Or ten." He couldn't let himself think about that, so he reached for his jacket. "By then I'll have experience running the shipyard here."

"But will your opportunity still be there?"

"There will be other opportunities. Elias, on the other hand… There's no telling how much more opportunity I shall have with him. I can go back to the Med after—" After Elias was gone. "Later." He reached for his greatcoat. "I must go. I'd like to return before dark."

"Go where?"

"To make an offer on Mays Abbey."

"Mays Abbey!" She took a step forward. "For heaven's sake, Noah, there's no need for that. Elias is better off here for now, and once he's recovered we can talk with him about where he'll be most comfortable."

"As you pointed out, Mays Abbey can be made quite comfortable. At least it will give him an option other than London."

"No. No, this isn't right. You can't simply walk away from everything you—"

"Enough." The word came out more sharply than he'd intended, but he couldn't take another minute of this. "I'm staying in London, and that's the end of it."

JOSEPHINE WATCHED HIM shrug into his greatcoat. He could not do this. He didn't belong here. His heart, his passion—they were in Turkey. At his villa, in the shipyard he dreamed of.

She'd made a mistake. Such a fearful, dreadful mistake, and somehow she had to fix it before he sacrificed everything he loved because she hadn't had the courage to let go of Elias.

To embrace herself.

A wild idea formed in her mind and before she had time to think better of it she said, "Then give me leave to make use of your villa myself."

He froze with his hands gripping his lapels. "What?"

Her heart beat so hard she was certain he would see her shaking. "I should very much like to live there."

"*Live* there."

Recklessly she added, "With Pauline."

"Pauline?"

"And Elias, as soon as he's able to travel." She drew in a breath, steadied herself. Smoothed her hands down the front of her dress, even as her body still throbbed and ached from the love they'd just made on the bed behind her. "In fact, perhaps you would be so good as to allow the three of us the use of your ship. I shall hire a master to sail us to Turkey and return the ship to you here."

"The hell you will." He yanked his greatcoat into place and came toward her.

She held his gaze and raised her chin. "I do hope you will forgive me for not accompanying you to Mays Abbey. There are a hundred arrangements to be made if I am to leave London. And *do* keep me apprised of any developments—it would seem you will be purchasing Mays Abbey for yourself, and I wish you every happiness and comfort there."

His eyes were blue fire now as he closed in on her with determined steps. "What the devil are you saying, Josephine?"

The last step brought him so close she could see the full battle of emotions raging in his eyes—anger, resignation, hope. Close enough to feel the tension coming off him in waves.

"I think I've made myself clear."

"Oh, yes," he drawled. "Immensely." Close enough she could feel the whisper of his words against her lips.

"You are free to do as you wish," she managed. "I shan't stand in your way again."

Her heart broke, looking into his eyes, imagining him living in London, huddled in his greatcoat against the drizzly rain he hated so much, ferrying about in chairs and coaches instead of sailing gloriously free on the sunny deck of his ship.

She wouldn't stand in his way, never again. Tears pricked her eyes. She loved Noah Rutledge too much to watch him deny himself.

"And if what I wish is to stay here?" he asked sharply.

"Then you are a fool."

"And if my wish is to return to Turkey?"

Do you love him enough to go with him yourself? Everything inside her seemed to slow, until her thoughts became still and the only thing in the world was Noah, standing in front of her with raw hope in his eyes.

"In that case, it is my understanding—" she could scarcely breathe the words "—that there is an appalling lack of concubines at your villa."

He stared at her. "Indeed there is." His voice was barely above a whisper. "Am I to understand that you fancy a stay in the Mediterranean playing mistress to me?"

No. She wanted—she *needed*—a Mediterranean life with him as her husband. But he hadn't so much as hinted at anything like that, so she said, "It might be an amusing diversion."

His eyes flashed. "Let me make one thing perfectly clear, Joseph. If you come with me, it will be as my wife, and you won't be sleeping in any bloody harem. You will be in my bed. With me."

"That would also be acceptable."

He stared. "It would?"

Her pulse thundered in her ears. "Are you asking me to marry you?"

"Yes. Yes, I am." God in heaven. He was. "Are you accepting?"

She stared at him, hardly daring to believe this was happening.

"Yes," she breathed, and he closed her fiercely in his embrace. She put her arms around him and spoke against his lips. "Yes, Noah. I'm accepting with all my heart. And I can't wait for the entire world to hear about it."

EPILOGUE

JOSEPHINE STOOD AT the edge of the courtyard in the dappled evening sun, beneath a canopy of ancient olive trees overlooking the terraces that led to the turquoise sea below. She gripped the stone railing and tipped her head back, letting the warm wind caress her face and the railing press against her gently rounding belly.

"Pauline." The deep voice came from the direction of the villa behind her. "If you keep giving Bentley bits of that sweet cake, he's going to be ill."

"I can't help it, Uncle Noah. He makes such an adorable face when he eats the sticky part. But don't worry—I only gave him a few tiny pieces. Come here, Bentley. Let us read what Lettie has to say."

Josephine heard footsteps behind her, felt a pair of strong hands settle at her waist. Noah brushed his lips across her temple and let his face linger against hers as they looked out at the water—a deep, blue harbor edged by a ribbon of pale soil that disappeared beneath a carpet of green. "Aniqa is finally asleep," he said. "I can't seem to tear myself away when she keeps calling 'Papa.'"

"Especially when she's got your shirt in her fists," Josephine teased, and turned to watch the breeze toy with his hair. "She doesn't want to be separated from you any more than I do."

Noah smiled into her eyes, and the thoughts playing in his wicked gaze were meant for her alone. Then he looked past her to the water. "No sign of it yet," he said.

"It will be here."

"Lettie's letter says Mr. Crumley has finally married," Pauline reported from the bench where she sat with Bentley. "A Miss Davinia Wentley. Auntie Josephine, do you know her?"

"Davinia? Why, yes—she's Lady Orville's granddaughter."

Noah leaned a hip against the railing and looked over at Pauline, even as he drew lazy designs on the back of Josphine's hand with his finger. "No regrets on that score, I trust?" he called to Pauline.

Josephine glanced over her shoulder in time to see Pauline look up from the letter and give him a look of mock severity. "None at all. I can scarcely recall what he looks like. Marriage is not for everyone, you know."

Noah laughed, deep and rich, and just then Elias came out of the villa. "What's so damned amusing out here?"

"I do believe our Pauline has taken a vow of spinsterhood," Noah said.

Josephine swatted his arm. "Hush."

"I'm too young to be a spinster," Pauline informed him. "But if I wish to be a spinster, then I shall be, and no one will stop me."

"Mark my words," Elias said, making his way to the railing, "if Noah wants you to marry, he'll find you a husband and that will be the end of it."

Pauline gasped at Noah. "You wouldn't do that! Would you?"

Josephine saw Elias hide a smile as Noah scratched

his chin, pondering the question. "I suppose that depends on whether your demand for sweet cakes becomes more than my purse can bear."

Pauline rolled her eyes at him and pointedly returned her attention to the letter.

"Any sign of her yet?" Elias asked, joining them at the edge of the terrace a few feet away.

"Not yet," Noah said, and plucked a spray of jasmine from the vine that twined around the railing nearby. "I'm beginning to think it will be tomorrow." He tucked the flowers into Josephine's hair. "I could look at you forever," he murmured. "I wish I had a portrait of you standing here exactly like this."

She raised a brow. "If you'd rather have a portrait of me than the actual me..."

"*Very* amusing." He took her face in his hands. "There is nothing on *earth* I would rather have than the actual you."

"Uncle Noah, that is the most romantic thing I've ever heard," Pauline exclaimed.

He grinned over at her. "Perhaps there's hope that you might spurn spinsterhood, after all."

"Auntie Josephine, Lettie says to tell you she and Captain Ryson saw Mother and Papa last week, and Mother says to tell you she hopes you're content."

Content.

Noah put his arm around her shoulders, and she nestled against him in the warm evening air, with the smell of jasmine wafting around them. Oh, yes. She was more than content. She was—

"Look," she said suddenly, pointing. "There it is."

A beautiful ship slipped into view from around the point, white sails billowing against the sea and sky, new wood gleaming in the setting sun. It was the first of Noah and Elias's new ships, fully christened and sold to a local trader, returning from its first merchant voyage to Alexandria.

Noah straightened, staring for a long moment. *"Sadiqi,"* he murmured. *My Friend.* It was the name they'd chosen together to honor the man who had meant so much to both of them, for such very different reasons.

She squeezed Noah's hand. "She's beautiful."

Watching the ship cut through the water, Noah leaned close to her ear. "You make this moment alive for me, Josephine," he whispered. "I love you."

She turned and brushed her lips across his cheek. "You make the whole *world* alive for me. I love you, Noah. Always."

She stood in the arms of the man she loved, with Pauline blossoming into more confidence every day and Elias in better spirits than she could ever remember and her husband's triumph sailing into port, with her baby daughter asleep inside their magnificent villa and a new life growing in her belly.

Content?

Oh, yes. She was much, *much* more than content.

* * * * *

JEANNIE LIN

THE LOTUS PALACE

It is a time of celebration in the Pingkang li, where imperial scholars and bureaucrats mingle with beautiful courtesans. At the center is the Lotus Palace, home of the most exquisite courtesans in China....

Maidservant Yue-ying is not one of those beauties. Street-smart and practical, she's content to live in the shadow of her infamous mistress—until she meets the aristocratic playboy Bai Huang.

Bai Huang lives in a privileged world Yue-ying can barely imagine, but as they are thrown together in an attempt to solve a deadly mystery, they both start to dream of a different life. But can Yue-ying sacrifice her pride to follow her heart?

Available wherever books are sold!

Be sure to connect with us at:

Harlequin.com/Newsletters
Facebook.com/HarlequinBooks
Twitter.com/HarlequinBooks

From *USA TODAY* bestselling author

NICOLA CORNICK

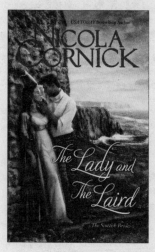

Lady Lucy MacMorlan may have forsworn men and marriage, but that doesn't mean she won't agree to profit from writing love letters for her brother's friends—letters that become increasingly racy as her fame grows. That is, until she inadvertently ruins the betrothal of a notorious laird…and a tempting suitor from her past.

Robert, the dashing Marquis of Methven, is onto Lucy's secret. And he certainly doesn't intend to let her have the last word, especially when her letters suggest she is considerably more experienced than he realized….

PHNC741

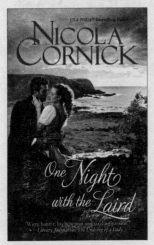

REQUEST YOUR FREE BOOKS!

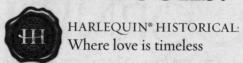

HARLEQUIN® HISTORICAL:
Where love is timeless

2 FREE NOVELS PLUS 2 FREE GIFTS!

YES! Please send me 2 FREE Harlequin® Historical novels and my 2 FREE gifts (gifts are worth about $10). After receiving them, if I don't wish to receive any more books, I can return the shipping statement marked "cancel." If I don't cancel, I will receive 6 brand-new novels every month and be billed just $5.44 per book in the U.S. or $5.74 per book in Canada. That's a savings of at least 16% off the cover price! It's quite a bargain! Shipping and handling is just 50¢ per book in the U.S. and 75¢ per book in Canada.* I understand that accepting the 2 free books and gifts places me under no obligation to buy anything. I can always return a shipment and cancel at any time. Even if I never buy another book, the two free books and gifts are mine to keep forever.

246/349 HDN F4ZY

Name _____ (PLEASE PRINT) _____

Address _____ Apt. # _____

City _____ State/Prov. _____ Zip/Postal Code _____

Signature (if under 18, a parent or guardian must sign) _____

Mail to the **Harlequin® Reader Service:**
IN U.S.A.: P.O. Box 1867, Buffalo, NY 14240-1867
IN CANADA: P.O. Box 609, Fort Erie, Ontario L2A 5X3

Want to try two free books from another line?
Call 1-800-873-8635 or visit www.ReaderService.com.

* Terms and prices subject to change without notice. Prices do not include applicable taxes. Sales tax applicable in N.Y. Canadian residents will be charged applicable taxes. Offer not valid in Quebec. This offer is limited to one order per household. Not valid for current subscribers to Harlequin Historical books. All orders subject to credit approval. Credit or debit balances in a customer's account(s) may be offset by any other outstanding balance owed by or to the customer. Please allow 4 to 6 weeks for delivery. Offer available while quantities last.

Your Privacy—The Harlequin® Reader Service is committed to protecting your privacy. Our Privacy Policy is available online at www.ReaderService.com or upon request from the Harlequin Reader Service.

We make a portion of our mailing list available to reputable third parties that offer products we believe may interest you. If you prefer that we not exchange your name with third parties, or if you wish to clarify or modify your communication preferences, please visit us at www.ReaderService.com/consumerschoice or write to us at Harlequin Reader Service Preference Service, P.O. Box 9062, Buffalo, NY 14269. Include your complete name and address.

HHI3R